SEVENTH RETRIBUTION

Torrents of flame poured through rents in the ceiling, or burst in geysers from the floors below. Madmen gibbered prophecies even as they burned. Those who could move gouged at their eyes or tore out their entrails. Those who could not were broken and misshapen by straining against the spiked chains that transfixed them in place.

Lysander had seen such scenes before. They were always different, for Chaos could not do its work in the same way twice. But they were always made of madness, the expression of the fools and maniacs who had given in to the warp's promises. It was human madness, not yet the full insanity of the warp. It was human evil, and Lysander had fought his way through human evils for centuries.

'Brothers!' yelled Lysander as he drew his thunder hammer, the Fist of Dorn, from its scabbard on the back of his Terminator armour. 'Here the Enemy lurks, ignorant of his death! Let us educate him! Let the Emperor's cold wrath extinguish this pyre!'

A WARHAMMER 40,000 NOVEL

SEVENTH RETRIBUTION

Ben Counter

BLACK LIBRARY

A BLACK LIBRARY PUBLICATION

First published in Great Britain in 2013 by
Black Library,
Games Workshop Ltd.,
Willow Road, Nottingham,
NG7 2WS, UK.

10 9 8 7 6 5 4 3 2 1

Cover illustration by Hardy Fowler.

A CIP record for this book is available from the British Library.

UK ISBN13: 978 1 84970 477 9
US ISBN13: 978 1 84970 478 6

See Black Library on the internet at

www.blacklibrary.com

Find out more about Games Workshop
and the world of Warhammer 40,000 at

www.games-workshop.com

Printed and bound by CPI Group (UK) Ltd, Croydon, CR0 4YY

It is the 41st millennium. For more than a hundred centuries the Emperor has sat immobile on the Golden Throne of Earth. He is the master of mankind by the will of the gods, and master of a million worlds by the might of his inexhaustible armies. He is a rotting carcass writhing invisibly with power from the Dark Age of Technology. He is the Carrion Lord of the Imperium for whom a thousand souls are sacrificed every day, so that he may never truly die.

Yet even in his deathless state, the Emperor continues his eternal vigilance. Mighty battlefleets cross the daemon-infested miasma of the warp, the only route between distant stars, their way lit by the Astronomican, the psychic manifestation of the Emperor's will. Vast armies give battle in His name on uncounted worlds. Greatest amongst his soldiers are the Adeptus Astartes, the Space Marines, bio-engineered super-warriors. Their comrades in arms are legion: the Imperial Guard and countless Planetary Defence Forces, the ever-vigilant Inquisition and the tech-priests of the Adeptus Mechanicus to name only a few. But for all their multitudes, they are barely enough to hold off the ever-present threat from aliens, heretics, mutants - and worse.

To be a man in such times is to be one amongst untold billions. It is to live in the cruellest and most bloody regime imaginable. These are the tales of those times. Forget the power of technology and science, for so much has been forgotten, never to be re-learned. Forget the promise of progress and understanding, for in the grim dark future there is only war. There is no peace amongst the stars, only an eternity of carnage and slaughter, and the laughter of thirsting gods.

PROLOGUE

K-Day −550 Days
The Kekropian Persecution

Upon the first day, it was traditional for the peasantry of Opis to take upon themselves the sins of their betters, and so absolve the planet's aristocracy of their wrongdoings. This would make the nobles of the Aristeia fit to hold the great feasts and festivals to come.

The first day of the festival season, then, was a day of great pain and bloodletting, for the sins of the Aristeia were many. The Aristeia traced their bloodlines back to the signatories of the charter that decreed Opis a vassal of the Imperium, an event that went back almost ten thousand years. That was plenty of time for the countless bloodlines of the Aristeia to spawn murderers, heretics, madmen and tyrants, and all those sins had to be cleansed every year before thanks could be given to the Emperor and those appointed to rule in His stead. Every single peasant had to do penance. Some opened last year's scars with scourges or bleeding-irons. Others had already fasted for many days. The infirm and elderly were permitted simply to donate a portion of their blood.

In the planet's second city, the vast and many-layered sprawl of Makoshaam, this penance was traditionally performed on one of the thoroughfares that were reserved on all other days for members of the Aristeia. The younger daughters of the aristocracy went among the penitents here, binding wounds with silken bandages or administering pain-relieving draughts from silver ewers carried by their servants. Even so, many of the more extreme penitents, who let life-threatening amounts of blood or severed body parts, were crippled or killed by their exertions.

This scene, which mingled celebration and suffering, was repeated throughout Makoshaam. It was particularly obvious along the Manticore Gate Processional, the route from the city outskirts to the Basilica of the Thousand Wounds, a wide avenue paved with slabs of polished decorative stone and lined with sculpted reliefs. A small army of household menials had been despatched to mop up the penitents' blood almost as soon as it was spilt, and the younger daughters moved among the penitent throng wearing heavy white gowns and veils treated with germicide. One member of a peasant household might be nailed to a wall by his wife and children, while another might be tied to a post and whipped by a sibling, who wept every time the lash landed home. Some of the Aristeia emerged from their fortified manors to watch, but most did not, for it did not do to encourage the self-importance of the peasantry by acknowledging their devotions.

The sounds were a dismal mixture of the groans of the pained and the thuds of cudgels and whips on flesh. The smell was of blood and sweat mixed with the everyday spice and aromas of Makoshaam.

Into this scene came a strange band of newcomers. The penitents paused in their self-mutilation and the younger daughters of their betters shied away, seeking the comfort and safety of the household servants who accompanied and guarded them. The strangers were not only from beyond the city – they did not wear the long, white garments of the Aristeia or the grey overalls of the peasants, or the dyed trains that denoted rank. They were like nothing that had been seen on Opis itself since the last time the Emperor's tithe-takers had descended thirty years before. And where the tithing mission had been grim and monastic, dressed in black habits and carrying golden icons of the Imperial creed, these strangers were a colourful and fearsome band without uniform or badge of allegiance. Most of them were armed to the teeth, with an armoured monster as a leader.

This man – for there was presumably a man inside the crimson armour, beneath the torches burning on his shoulder guards and collar – did not acknowledge even the patriarchs of the Aristeia who emerged from their manors to demand to know his business. Anyone who tried to bar his way was pushed aside by those who accompanied the armoured giant, with shields or the points of chainswords. He strode all the way to the Basilica of the Thousand Wounds, and when he passed into the shadow of the gilded minarets a crowd had gathered around the basilica gate just to see the man who so flouted every convention of Opis's society.

The armoured man stood at the gates, with their silver sculptures of the many Imperial saints venerated within. He slammed an armoured fist into the doors three times. The doors were hauled open a crack by some unfortunate lackey.

'I will speak with the Aristeia,' said the armoured giant. 'Their representative in this place will receive me. I command this by the authority of the Holy Ordos of the Emperor's Inquisition.'

The doors were closed in his face as those inside, who numbered the most senior patriarchs and matriarchs of Makoshaam, dithered about what was to be done and which one of them would step forth to speak for them. The armoured giant, who had claimed the authority of the Emperor's Inquisition, became impatient and barked a few orders to the band who accompanied him. One of them, who wore medals and honours from many Imperial Guard campaigns, stepped forward and took a plasma gun from the soldier's pack on his back. With no ceremony, he blew the hinges off the doors. They toppled forward with a terrific sound which scattered many of the crowd who had crept up to get a closer look at these strange people.

The armoured man walked into the Basilica of the Thousand Wounds, taking barely a moment to genuflect at the threshold in honour of the Imperial saints whose martyrdoms had given the place its name.

'I am Lord Inquisitor Kekrops, and I bring with me the authority of the Emperor Himself as devolved upon the Ordos of His

Inquisition.' Kekrops stood in the debating chamber of the basilica, his warband gathered behind him. Before him were rather more than two hundred members of Opis's aristocracy, dressed in flowing floor-length silks with turbans and veils of every colour. 'It matters little to me which one of you speaks for your city, but one of you will.'

Silence met him. Eyes passed from the inquisitor to the warband assembled behind him. The inquisitor alone was an impressive enough sight. His armour was polished red inlaid with gold filigree, and it seemed impossible that anyone could walk encased in such a splendid, but surely vastly heavy, personal fortress. The torches mounted on it burned with gas fed from bottles mounted on his back, where also was held in a scabbard a sword rather longer than most men were tall. The inquisitor's face was that of an old man, but somehow seemed no weaker for all its age. It was as if the deep lines and grey hair suggested the things he had done just to survive this long.

His warband were no less exotic. One of them was a tall and slender woman with plaited hair down to her waist, wearing a sleeveless, backless gown of emerald green that would have created a scandal in the salons of the Aristeia. She carried an enormous book with brass covers chained shut, and around her hovered a pair of skulls with lenses fixed over the eye sockets. Several of the warband, including the man carrying the still-smouldering plasma gun, were from the Imperial Guard, but the similarity between them ended there for they each wore the uniform of a different regiment (in many cases, pieces taken from several regiments). One of them carried a banner pole with a standard, presumably the colours of Inquisitor Kekrops, furled around it. Another of the inquisitor's acolytes was a skeleton of a man whose black hooded habit could not hide his lack of substance, or the band of embroidered cloth around his eyes.

One of the Aristeia, after much searching for another speaker among the faces of his fellow aristocrats, raised a hand.

'The masters of this world,' he said, 'reside in Khezal.' He was younger than most of the dignitaries, and he wore fat, uncut gemstones on a silver chain around his neck. 'They carry the greatest authority among us. I have no doubt that–'

'I am not in Khezal,' replied Kekrops shortly. 'I shall visit every city of this world, and I shall reach the capital in good time, but this day I am in Makoshaam. I hold this city to account for its wrongs, and you to account as those who claim to rule it.'

'Then I shall speak,' said the nobleman. He swallowed and drew himself up a little, as if about to deliver a speech. Kekrops did not look impressed. 'I am Eshrahem Wrathful Mountain, Third Lord of the Amethyst Court. I have as much right as any to speak in this chamber for the interests of my city.'

Inquisitor Kekrops snapped his fingers and one of his troopers, who wore a fanciful brocade dress jacket over a pair of threadbare camouflage trousers, handed him a roll of parchment. Kekrops unrolled it in his huge metal paws and read from it.

'The planetary government of Opis,' he said, 'stands accused of permitting the manifold depravities of worshippers of enemies of mankind, the practice of warpcraft and the festering of organisations devoted to the Dark Gods and the destruction of the Imperium of Man. The Holy Ordos have assembled a great many accusations based upon intelligence gathered by our agents and those of the Imperium at large, and they present such a body of woe that I have taken upon myself the task of purging this world's wickedness and bringing those responsible to account.'

'Now... now, let's not say anything that might be inflammatory,' said another of the Aristeia, a woman of such advanced age it seemed she was held upright only by the great volume of silks in which she was swaddled. 'One may not simply–'

'One may do as the Emperor demands!' retorted Kekrops, 'if it so pleases the Emperor and confounds His foes! Opis is a sick world. A diseased world. And yours is a diseased city! Among its people are cults of the powers of the warp, whose names are not fit for the lips or ears of those not trained to resist their lures. Among you, its nobility, are doubtless members of those very cults, and many more who through their dereliction of duty permit them to exist! And should I be denied any resource or answer I demand, as I purge Opis of this disease, then I shall bring all the wrath of the Imperium down to do with the gun and the sword what you will not! For I am the Emperor on this world, with every power the Emperor would claim were He to rise upon this benighted planet. For all practical purposes, I am a god, with the power of a god, such is the authority I carry with me.'

One of the soldiers behind Kekrops hurried to the inquisitor's side. In his hands was a device with a screen that was flashing with red icons.

'Intruders,' said the soldier, who wore khaki fatigues with dozens of holsters, each one carrying a well-used pistol. 'There are weapon signatures all over the auspex.'

Kekrops drew his sword. Its blade thrummed and glowed blue. 'Explain yourselves!' he shouted at the Aristeia members. 'Do you dare take up arms against me?'

'They are no troops of ours!' replied Eshrahem Wrathful Mountain. 'No soldiers are permitted within the basilica!'

'If you lie,' said Kekrops, 'you shall burn at the stake!'

'They are no soldiers of this world,' said the acolyte with the hooded robe and the bound eyes.

'Lysshe, how can you tell?' said Kekrops.

'Because only off-worlders would possess the camouflage fields needed to get that shot on Beskrin.'

A moment later, a las-bolt spat from the darkness of the dome overhead, fizzing through the skull of one of the Imperial Guard, temple to temple.

'He aims at you next,' said Lysshe.

Inquisitor Kekrops brought up a huge gauntlet to shield his face as a second shot from the same direction streaked towards him, cracking against the gauntlet instead of hitting him in the head.

'You will pay!' yelled Kekrops at the assembled Aristeia, who were only just starting to look for cover among the hardwood partitions and upholstered benches of the basilica. 'You will all pay for this betrayal!'

'We didn't know!' cried Eshrahem Wrathful Mountain. 'This is–'

His words were cut off as the fire fell among the Aristeia.

The silenced shots sounded more like snapping wood or sharp footsteps, but they blew wet, ragged holes through silk-wrapped bodies all the same. Eshrahem Wrathful Mountain's arm was blown off entirely and he keeled over to the side. A head burst in a shower of shredded silk and blood.

'Keep close and fall back!' yelled Kekrops.

His warband returned fire. A heavy bolter, clutched in the hands of a man whose musculature rendered him almost as big as Kekrops himself, thundered a chain of fire into the painted dome. The images of Imperial saints disappeared in bursts of shrapnel. Las-fire and plasma bolts shrieked into the balcony running around the dome and a shadowy shape fell, his camouflage malfunctioning and rendering him fully visible just as he hit the floor. He wore a black bodyglove wrapped around with webbing, and a rubberised cowl over his face with lenses for eyes.

A missile or grenade exploded, blowing two veterans off their feet. Kekrops led the way towards the doors, grimacing as hot shards of stone and wood rained down from the explosion.

He emerged from the doorway into the open, feet booming on the fallen door. Immediately, the gunfire started.

Half of it fell against the basilica, aiming for Kekrops. Kekrops ran to one side as las-bolts thudded and fizzed against his armour. The other half was aimed into the crowds of penitents. It seemed barely a second before bedlam broke out. Hundreds of people were screaming or running in every direction, or stood staring insensible at the people who were shot dead in the first volley.

The woman with the book ran out into the open behind Kekrops. She opened the book to one of the many markers held between its pages, and yelled a sentence in a language that bore no resemblance to any tongue of Opis. A hemisphere of blue-white light appeared around her, and the las-bolts aimed at her burst against it like fireworks. Veterans dived from the doorway into the area bounded by the light, for they had been well drilled to recognise the psychic shield and make the most of it while it lasted.

The shooters were everywhere. Not all of them wore the camouflage that had let them get so close to the warband in the basilica, and they could be seen crouching among the rooftops and balconies of the buildings along the Manticore Gate Processional. One fired a missile launcher into the penitents, and broken bodies were flung everywhere. The younger daughters, who a few moments ago had been tending to wounds, ran about screaming in terror or fell over the household servants trying to bundle them to safety. Everywhere, people were dying.

The Guardsman with the mismatched medals ran to Kekrops's side. 'Down!' he barked, standing out in the open as he took aim with his plasma gun. Kekrops dropped to one knee, giving the Guardsman a clear shot at the trooper on the roof of the basilica overlooking them. The plasma gun fired and the trooper's leg disappeared in a burst of liquid fire. The trooper fell and crunched to the ground beside Kekrops.

Kekrops grabbed the fallen man by the arm and slung him over one shoulder as he strode out of cover and down the processional. Members of the crowd were running in every direction, many towards the crushes already developing around the alleyways leading away from the open ground of the processional. Kekrops batted a few out of his way with the flat of his sword even as more shots fell around him. He held up his free hand in a fist and the knuckles of the gauntlet opened up to reveal miniaturised gun barrels. They fired a burst of crackling fire and the tiny bolter rounds they ejected hit two attackers sheltering in a window. Another volley shot one off a rooftop. The Guardsmen were firing, too, all manner of weapons being unleashed in every direction.

Kekrops ran through the fire, his armour now pocked and smoking. Ahead was the relative cover of a roofed structure built for the use of the penitents. It was closed on three walls, and from its wooden ceiling hung hooks which penitents had used to suspend themselves from their backs or chests. A couple had already made it down and were helping the others extricate the hooks from their skin. Kekrops ran into the building, followed by the be-medalled Guardsman. The Guardsman slid to the ground, skidding in the blood that had fallen from the penitents' wounds – a smoking hole between his shoulder blades suggested a las-shot had burned right through his spine.

Kekrops threw the wounded trooper to the ground. The psyker, still surrounded by her dome of light, ran into the building surrounded by half a dozen Guardsmen and the second psyker, Lysshe.

'What is he?' said Kekrops to Lysshe. 'Hurry!'

Lysshe knelt beside the wounded trooper and pulled the cowl off his face. Aside from his covered eyes he had a completely normal face, with bland features and cropped brown hair. His throat had two implants that hooked to tubes running to a rebreather unit at his waist.

'Serrick,' said Kekrops. 'How much longer can you shield us?'

The female psyker shook her head. 'There is much pain and misery surrounding us. It… it drains me. These men picked their time to attack us. I can barely see through the anguish.'

'Can you get us to the shuttle?'

'No. Forgive me, inquisitor, but I cannot.'

'Then it must come to us. Vel!'

'Sir!' replied one of the warband. He did not look like a man of the Imperial Guard, or if he was he had abandoned any uniform long ago. He was dressed in patchwork leathers and carried a shotgun that looked like he had cobbled it together from junk.

'Signal the shuttle. Tell them to expect incoming fire.'

'Yes, sir!' Vel produced a handset and began barking orders into it in a shortened war-cant.

'Lysshe?' said Kekrops. 'Who are we fighting? Is it the Aristeia?'

Lysshe seemed untroubled by the sound of gunfire slamming against the penitents' building, or the return fire of the Guardsmen crouched around its entrance. He ran a hand along the wounded trooper's face, and froze.

'Speak to me,' said Kekrops.

'I… I cannot…'

Kekrops grabbed Lysshe's shoulder and pulled the frail man away from the trooper. 'Lysshe! I said speak!'

'He does not know,' said Lysshe. For the first time he looked shaken. 'He does not know who he is. It has been… torn away from him. I can feel scars in his mind, like the stump of an amputated limb. And someone has taught him how to be a soldier. But there is nothing else. Even insanity would be something, lord inquisitor, but instead there is… there is but a void.'

Kekrops grabbed Lysshe's arm, pulling his hand away from the wounded trooper. 'That's not possible.'

'It is what it is, lord inquisitor. I can say no different.'

'They have nothing like this,' said another of Kekrops's Guardsmen. 'This world's top military is Guard-spec at most.'

'Then they're not from this world,' said Kekrops.

The low growl of twin rotors rumbled underneath the gun-fire. Kekrops knelt down by the edge of the wall and glanced out of cover. A craft was approaching, weaving between the piping and raised roadways that crossed over the Manticore Gate Processional. It had a cylindrical body and cockpit with a bulging windscreen that resembled the eyes of a giant insect. Two rotors, one on either side, supported it, with a smaller one on the tail giving it the manoeuvrability to make good speed towards Kekrops's position. A cannon, mounted under the nose, spat bursts of fire across the upper floors of the buildings along the road, sending the hooded troops diving for cover.

'Stay close and move!' yelled Kekrops. 'If you fall behind, we leave you!'

The Guardsmen gathered around Serrick, who leafed through the book she carried until she reached a page that suddenly glowed with power as it was turned. She held her hand over the writing and grimaced as it scorched the skin of her palm.

'Ready?' said Kekrops.

Serrick nodded.

'Move!' shouted the inquisitor. A globe of shimmering light appeared around Serrick and the Guardsmen broke cover, Kekrops running with them.

Lysshe was the first to fall. He could not keep up, and a las-round sliced through his thigh. His severed leg skidded along the pavement and he flopped to the ground. No one turned to help him. He was not the first psyker to fall in the service of Lord Inquisitor Kekrops.

A missile streaked in from a rooftop and detonated against the psychic shield. The blast sent shrapnel carving through two more men, and others fell. Serrick stumbled, and Kekrops grabbed her arm in his huge armoured paw to drag her along behind him. The shuttlecraft was now directly overhead, banking around as it descended and brought its tail towards the warband. A rear ramp opened up into the passenger compart-ment, and a pair of crew stood ready to help the warband embark.

Serrick's eyes rolled back and the book dropped from her hand. Kekrops picked her up but the shield faltered, flickering out of existence. The Guardsmen knelt by the ramp, which only had another couple of metres to descend before it touched the ground, and they fired up almost at random into the rooftops and windows around them. More fire stuttered back and more men fell.

Kekrops threw Serrick into the back of the shuttle.

'Get her stable!' he yelled to one of the shuttle crew, who wore the colours of an Imperial Guard medic. The medic barely had time to nod before the craft slewed sideways, gouging sparks out of the Manticore Gate Processional. Kekrops jumped back to keep from being ground into the paving beneath the hull.

One of the rotors had blown up. Its housing was torn open and the rotor had been stripped of its blades. Thick black smoke began spurting from the severed fuel lines.

'Serrick!' yelled Kekrops. 'Get her... Get her safe! Get to the buildings and–'

A single round thumped into Kekrops's skull, right between his eyes.

Kekrops seemed to take a moment to realise he was dead. He stared straight ahead, as if trying to remember a lost train of thought.

Then he fell to his knees, the sound of his armour ringing out like a bell, and toppled to one side.

The shuttlecraft, unable to gain height or control itself, skidded across the road and crunched into one of the buildings. The front of the building collapsed, four storeys pancaking onto the body of the shuttle.

Lysshe lived for a while, able only to writhe and let out a low moaning. By the time a gaggle of household servants emerged from hiding to search for the wounded, however, he had died from blood loss and shock. While most tried to tend to the wounded and the dying, several gathered around the huge armoured corpse of Inquisitor Kekrops, and wondered who this man could be to have been the epicentre of such destruction.

Those who knew about such things recognised the emblems

of the Imperium on Kekrops's armour and the wargear of the soldiers who had died beside him. The Imperium, that over-lord who left the people of Opis alone provided they paid their tithes and obeyed the Imperial law. And provided they did not harbour the enemies of the Imperium.

Those who knew about such things also knew that this was not over.

The outskirts of Khezal hurtled past, too fast to make out any detail among the sandstone walls and verdigris tiles, the ornamental waterways and flagstoned streets. The city sprawled in every direction, a shining jewel set into the rocky equator of Opis, the picturesque spread of the city punctuated by great stone spires and pyramids in which tens of thousands were housed, or the city's greatest had their palaces and pleasure gardens.

'Too beautiful,' said Brother Ucalegon, 'to be a battleground.'

Ucalegon, as befitted the Emperor's Champion, would be first out of the Thunderhawk gunship, first to jump down from the ramp even now opening and providing a view of Khezal streaking underneath. His golden armour had been overpainted in black, and in his hands he carried a sword with a blade of gleaming obsidian.

23

His fellow Imperial Fists craned their necks to get the first sight of the city they were to fight over. One of them, in huge Terminator armour, had to stoop even though the gunship's passenger compartment had been built to accommodate the exaggerated frame of a Space Marine. He carried a shield and an enormous thunder hammer, and his face bore a mix of pride and weary wisdom that only a lifetime of war could bring.

'We care nothing for beauty,' he said.

'What ugliness we bring is the fault of our enemies, captain,' replied Ucalegon. 'The scars we shall leave on this world were etched by their hands. It is one more sin upon their shoulders.'

'Then punish them for it,' said the captain, clapping a huge gauntlet on Ucalegon's shoulder. 'You are the Emperor's hand on this world. Punish them.'

Ucalegon bowed his head in deference to these words for they were uttered by Captain Lysander, the First Captain of the Imperial Fists Chapter, and a man who had earned greater respect in war than all but a handful of men that lived.

The Thunderhawk banked and the engines screamed. The ten Space Marines on the Thunderhawk could see the fortified surface of the Chalcedony Throne, the massive pyramid encased in precious-stone battlements that was their target. For many hours they had pored over its floorplans and the details of its defences, in the full knowledge that what they found inside might bear no relation to the intelligence they had gathered.

'Ten seconds!' came the voice of the gunship's pilot up ahead. The passenger compartment was bathed in red light and the roar of the air outside was joined by the howl of the gunship's engines as they fired to arrest the craft's descent. Ucalegon pressed the stone blade of his sword to his forehead and let the words of a familiar battle-prayer run through his mind, blessing the blade and his soul with words Rogal Dorn had written down ten thousand years before. Then he fastened his helmet on his head, squad icons lighting up against the helmet's eyepieces.

He was the Emperor's Champion. He had been anointed as such just a few days ago. The Emperor was watching.

A break in the decorative stonework yawned suddenly below, a gun port with the muzzle of a huge artillery piece ready to defend the Chalcedony Throne from assault. But the history of Khezal had seen no enemy assault its palaces and bastions for hundreds of years. Not until that very day, when the first shots of the war for Opis were being fired all across the planetary capital.

'Go!' yelled Captain Lysander, and the gunship pivoted. Ucalegon grabbed the edge of the ramp and braced himself, ready to jump, as his grav-restraints detached and left him free to move. He powered forwards, the nerve-fibre bundles of his armour adding to his own strength, and he was falling, the darkness of the Chalcedony Throne's interior rushing up to swallow him.

His auto-senses adjusted instantly. The barrel and machinery of the artillery piece had coalesced from the darkness before the next Space Marine landed beside him, followed by Captain Lysander. In a few seconds the whole force had disembarked.

Even the filters built into his armour could not conceal the smell. It was familiar from a hundred battlefields. Not just rotting flesh, although that was the greater part of it, but everything that accompanied it – old blood, stale sweat, smoke, hot metal.

Beneath Ucalegon's feet was sandstone, cut into decorative tiles. Behind him was a square of Opis's sky, bright and clear. Above him was the barrel of the gun, polished and unused for a century.

And in front of him was hell. There was no other way to put it. He was in hell.

But he was an Imperial Fist. He had been in hell before. And this time, he was the champion of the Emperor.

The stone blade seemed light in his hands as he yelled and charged into the madness.

The battle had come swiftly to Khezal.

The inhabitants had known that it was coming. The people of Khezal had been raised to believe the words of the Aristeia, to accept that these great and wealthy people had the right to speak for them and decide what the truth really was. But even so, the reassurances of the Aristeia's highest echelons, who deigned on occasion to address them from the balconies of their palaces and temple complexes, had not satisfied them completely. Some said the massacre in Makoshaam was the elimination of malcontents among the peasantry, the beginning of a purge. They had happened before, leaving shadows and lacunas in the history of Opis. Others maintained that the Aristeia were fighting among themselves, and that soon armies of peasants would be trained up to join them. That had happened before, too, and whole generations were missing from the family trees as a result.

But some said it was even worse. Some said that Opis was under the threat of something that it had not been troubled with since the dawn of the Age of Imperium. Something from outside. Something from off-world.

The first sight of that threat dropped into the Cemetery district of Khezal on columns of burning exhaust, in the form of cargo landers fitted with armour and disembarkation ramps. They crashed into the tangled, ancient streets of the district, one of the historical hearts of the city where the criminal guilds and secret societies ruled the alleyways, and disgorged the heavy infantry of the Mhosis Karn Avengers. The Imperial Guardsmen wore body armour of such weight that only men from a high-gravity world like theirs could wear it and fight at the same time, perfect for the cramped streets.

They met Aristeia's troops there, in the shape of two household regiments carrying the banners of their patron aristocrats. The Aristeia were on high alert, ready for both civil unrest and open warfare, but the Imperial Guard specialised in the close-quarters butchery with bayonets and lascarbines that ensued.

The docks of Khezal, with the expanses of industrial yards where generations of warships had been assembled from the steel flowing from their glowing forges, were the next to feel the footfall of an outsider. The men of the Gathalamor 912th Light Infantry jumped from fast Valkyrie gunships, and rushed between the forges and dry docks to capture the anti-aircraft guns that had barely been able to respond to the suddenness of the assault. The Gathalamorans cut prayers into the chests of the Aristeia soldiers defending the guns, and even before the guns were spiked and blown up they had built a heap of bodies to burn as their offering to the God-Emperor.

The Subiaco 27th, fabled killers drawn from prison worlds and made useful with mental surgery and combat drugs, landed in the waters off the picturesque Pearl Dragon Coast. Many were killed by the impact of their low-firing grav-chutes against the water, or were knocked out and drowned. A good three-quarters of them survived to attack a huge villa complex, one of dozens along the coast where many Aristeia spent their days when not attending to matters of household governance or planetary politics. The Subiacans threw the bodies of the few defenders out into the ornamental ponds and off the cliffs into the sea.

The picture was repeated on a dozen battlefields scattered across the city. Most took down defences, like radar towers or anti-aircraft installations, and in doing so unlocked the door that would let the main Imperial force land for the major assault on Khezal. But others were looking for something. They had been briefed by the intelligence officers of Commander Tchepikov's staff, and their own officers led them in the knowledge that they were hunting moral threats in the streets of Khezal.

The armed forces of Khezal were huge, numbering hundreds of thousands the Aristeia could put under arms along with their own standing household forces, but defeating them would be only half the battle. There were worse things in Khezal than men with guns.

The Imperial Fists were among those sworn to find them.

The raw stuff of the stars poured down the walls, liquid fire like multicoloured lava spewing from the molten emotions of the warp. Bodies writhed in the fire, naked and contorted. Hands reached blindly. Disintegrating human forms rose like ash above a fire, screaming as they merged with the flames rippling along the ceiling. The walls of fire seemed to be held in place with chains, the iron glowing red in the heat. The floor was a mass of charred bones and red scorched bodies, the living writhing through the ashes of the dead. Serpentine creatures, with boneless limbs that whipped and coiled, lashed the figures immolated in the walls and columns of fire, leaping in a frantic dance from victim to victim.

Torrents of flame poured through rents in the ceiling, or burst in geysers from the floors below. Madmen gibbered prophecies even as they burned. Those who could move gouged at their eyes or tore out their entrails. Those who could not were broken and misshapen by straining against the spiked chains that transfixed them in place.

Lysander had seen such scenes before. They were always different, for Chaos could not do its work in the same way twice. But they were always made of madness, the expression of the fools and maniacs who had given in to the warp's promises. It was human madness, not yet the full insanity of the warp. It was human evil, and Lysander had fought his way through human evils for centuries.

'Brothers!' yelled Lysander as he drew his thunder hammer,

the Fist of Dorn, from its scabbard on the back of his Terminator armour. 'Here the Enemy lurks, ignorant of his death! Let us educate him! Let the Emperor's cold wrath extinguish this pyre!'

Lysander's squad, along with Emperor's Champion Ucalegon, forged through the fire in Lysander's footsteps. It was indeed like fighting through a funeral pyre. Lysander's armour heated up, the joints scorching. Bolter fire snapped at the daemons who danced through the flames – whip-fast, like sea creatures disturbed by a predator, they flitted into hiding.

'Who will face the Hand of the Emperor?' yelled Ucalegon above the screaming of the damned. 'Is there a champion of your gods who will test himself against this blade, or does the warp vomit forth only cowards?'

The answer came in the form of burning hands that tore out from the cataracts of flame. They belonged to serpentine daemons that slithered through the fire. They had a dozen eyes each, smouldering deep-crimson scales, and they drooled sizzling venom from mouths full of asymmetrical fangs.

'Fast drill!' yelled Lysander. 'Volley fire and advance!'

Almost before the first trigger finger was down, the daemons were among the Imperial Fists. They tried to wrap their snake-like bodies around the Space Marines to crush and burn them. Bolter fire shredded many, but others slipped through the gunfire as if they barely existed in real space at all.

A daemon whipped through the flames towards Lysander, fast and straight as an arrow. Lysander crunched the Fist of Dorn into its ribs, its own momentum driving the head of the hammer into its body. Lysander slammed his storm shield into the daemon and drove it into the floor with enough force to flatten its body.

'Forward!' yelled Lysander. 'Forward!'

'Pierce the heart!' echoed Ucalegon, who was already kicking free of a daemon's coils and pushing on through the walls of flame. The black sword reflected the fires so it glowed orange in his hands, like a shard of the sun.

Lysander and the Imperial Fists followed him deeper into the inferno. The Space Marines who fought with him were veterans of the First Company, the company of which Lysander was the captain. He had picked them from those who excelled in boarding actions or siegebreaking assaults, in the short-range combats sure to be plentiful in the opening gambits of the war for Opis. Brother Beros decapitated one of the slithering daemons with a slash of his lightning claw, shattering what was left with a rattle of fire from his bolt pistol. Sergeant Kirav was dragged down into the fires, and was pulled free by Apollonios and Stentor.

Between the columns of flame rose a chamber of black stone, its sides rising to a point overhead. Surrounded by heaps of gilded statues and grave goods had once reared a seated statue of a past king of Opis, carved from ivory and jade. Its upper half had been shattered and dozens of corpses heaped up on it, creating a throne of butchered meat. Upon that throne sat a creature with the head of a fly, segmented eyes rolling in a head covered in bristly black hair.

'Only the strongest disease can suffer the flame and not be cleansed,' it said. Its voice was a cloying, seductive sound, as different to its foul appearance as could be. Its hands, folded across its bulging, writhing belly, reached beside the throne and picked up one of the grave goods buried alongside the king – a jewelled scimitar with a blade of rose gold. 'But you do not belong here.'

The flame daemons slithered among the heaps of treasure and sarcophagi. Lysander dropped to one knee and raised his shield as one of the daemons hammered into it, the impact almost throwing him onto his back. He ripped the hammer down through its head and crushed it flat onto the stone floor. Another coiled up over him, pinning his hammer-arm with the coils of its body. Lysander jammed the upper edge of his shield up under the daemon's drooling jaw, holding it off as its teeth snapped wetly shut in front of his face.

Lysander could see Ucalegon vaulting a sarcophagus, sword in hand. In response, the fly-thing rose from its throne, and its abdomen unfolded from beneath it, a rubbery black mass that made up its lower body held up on six segmented legs. Fat white worms shuddered from the folds of its body. The emerald robes it wore could not cover up the abomination. Spindly wings fluttered from its back. Nests of black tendrils burst from the floor as the sticky pads of its feet touched the stone.

The challenge was unspoken. Ucalegon and the fly-thing were both champions: Ucalegon of the Emperor, the fly-thing of its dark god. Face death in single combat, each said without words, or die a coward.

A blue-white burst of energy flashed in front of Lysander's eyes and the weight of the daemon was off him. Sergeant Kirav had punched the daemon off Lysander with his power fist, the power field discharging and throwing the daemon against the wall of the pyramidal chamber.

'Close in!' ordered Lysander. 'Back to back, my brethren! Hold them off! Ucalegon, take the head!'

The Imperial Fists drove through the wreckage of the burial chamber and formed up like a firing squad. Bolters chattered and a plasma gun hissed. The daemons did not have to die now, not every one of them. They just had to be kept at a distance while the real fight was decided.

Ucalegon had reached the champion of Chaos. The fly-thing moved far too quickly for its corpulent bulk and the scimitar met Ucalegon's blade in a shower of sparks. Snake-daemons converged on the two but the Imperial Fists shot them down or intercepted them with blade and fist.

The fly-thing gibbered a stream of madness, syllables ripped from the warp, and the floor liquefied underfoot. Ucalegon dragged his feet from the sucking bog, and jumped up onto a sarcophagus to keep him clear of the quagmire. Fat white eggs burst to the surface and split, and buzzing insects the size of a fist uncoiled in their thousands. The air turned dark with them and Lysander could barely make out Ucalegon through the haze of bodies and wings.

'Apollonios!' shouted Lysander. 'Bring the flame!'

Brother Apollonios slung his bolter and took from his back the flamer, which had been useless in the cathedral of fire he had just fought through. Now, though, the spray of fire cut through the mass of flies billowing over the Imperial Fists. Hundreds of burning bodies fell.

The lids of the sarcophagi shattered and the foul things

inside reared up, their flesh liquefying and yet still clinging to their bones. Rubbery black tentacles unfolded from their innards. Lysander smashed one aside with the Fist of Dorn and another fell, shredded with bolter fire. Tendrils snagged the Imperial Fists as they tried to fight on.

And still, Ucalegon and the champion of Chaos fought. Ucalegon had been selected as the Emperor's Champion because of his skill with the sword, but he was young for his role – when the previous Champion had fallen three months before, Ucalegon had surprised many by duelling for the honour with the Chapter's finest warriors. But as the fly-headed thing slashed at the Imperial Fist with the scimitar, and Ucalegon parried every blow into a rapid thrust or slash of his own, Lysander realised the Chapter had made the right choice.

The walls of the pyramidal chamber were melting away now, the black stone suddenly transformed into corpse liquor that ran down to reveal heaving structures of bone and rancid muscle. Lysander forged his way through the gore and filth gathering around his feet to rip the head off one of the ancient corpses with a swipe of his shield. It fought on, yanking the shield from his hands with a bundle of animated entrails, so he plunged his fist into its chest and tore out the nest of mummified organs inside.

Time. They needed time. Just a few moments. Ucalegon would win or die, but either way, he needed just a few moments more.

The champion of Chaos shattered its scimitar against Ucalegon's shoulder guard. In response it heaved its bulk into the air to slam down on top of Ucalegon, its many legs wriggling as if eager to burrow through armour and tear at the meat inside. It crashed down on top of the Emperor's Champion, and Ucalegon disappeared from Lysander's sight as he fell.

Lysander tried to extricate himself from the mass of muscle and filth that was bubbling up from the sarcophagus underneath him. Mouths were opening in the structure above now, yawing down as they forced the chamber out of shape in their hunger. Lysander fought to get closer to Ucalegon, but the fat flies descended thicker and all but blinded him. Spears of bone slammed down from overhead, like the bars of a cage cutting Lysander off from where Ucalegon might be lying dead, or might be fighting on. He shattered them with a swipe of his hammer but more fell, like a rain of bony spikes.

'Ucalegon!' yelled Lysander. 'My brother! Feel the strength of Dorn! Shine in the light of the Emperor!'

Sergeant Kirav was beside Lysander, ripping a bundle of tentacles away from him.

'Apollonios is down,' he shouted over the din of gunfire and buzzing wings. 'We hold!'

From up ahead reared a dark form, visible through a break in the cloud of flies. It was the champion of Chaos, hands held high as if delivering a sermon.

Beneath it was Ucalegon, sword held close to his chest, the point of the blade jutting upwards and impaling the champion through the abdomen.

Ucalegon twisted the blade, and the wound opened. Entrails, black and filthy, spilled out, the slithering brine of its blood flooding over Ucalegon. Ucalegon drew the blade down the champion's abdomen, ripping it open. Pulsing hearts and stomachs tumbled out.

Almost split in two by the sword, the champion of Chaos flopped backwards, draping wetly over the pile of corpses on its throne. Ucalegon pulled the blade free and swung a final overhead blow into the champion's head, bisecting it between two of its segmented eyes.

The walls were screaming. The daemons were writhing, tying their long wriggling bodies in knots. The grip on Lysander slackened and he was free.

Lysander ran up to Ucalegon. Ucalegon's armour was slick with slime that hissed as its acid ate through the black paint, showing patches of gold beneath. The smell was awful. Even the filters of Lysander's armour couldn't mask it.

'We are done here, Champion of Dorn,' said Lysander.

'This must burn,' said Ucalegon. 'All of it.'

'It will,' said Lysander. 'Let the Imperial Guard see to it.'

A foul sucking sound alerted Lysander before he saw the movement. The limbs of the Chaos champion were moving, with more purpose and coordination than a post-mortem spasm. The ruined head lolled up, the eyes glittering as their many facets tried to focus.

'It lives!' said Ucalegon.

'It will wish it did not,' replied Lysander. He raised a massive booted foot, and slammed it down on the Chaos champion's face. The thing fell still again.

'Kirav!' yelled Lysander. 'How do we stand?'

'Apollonios is dead,' said Kirav. As the flies dissipated, Lysander could see where Apollonios lay, with two of the squad standing over him reading his lifesigns off his armour. They rolled him over, revealing that Apollonios's left side was almost completely melted away.

'He will be avenged over again,' said Lysander, looking down at the unconscious champion of Chaos. 'We must leave this place. And bring the prisoner with us.'

'Captain!' called Brother Beros. He shoved a sarcophagus lid aside with his boot, lightning claw held up ready to impale whatever emerged. 'This one is alive!'

Inside the sarcophagus was a woman. Filthy hair clung to her face. She wore scraps of a green dress so ragged she covered her modesty with the funeral shroud of the body she had lain beside in the stone coffin. Her skin was streaked with grime.

'I am not an enemy,' she said. Her voice had a tremor to it – but considering where she had been held and the violence that had finished moments ago, she should have been insensible or incoherent. 'That thing held me here. I do not know why.'

'Who are you?' demanded Lysander.

'Serrick,' the woman replied. 'My name is Serrick. In service to Lord Inquisitor Kekrops of the Ordo Hereticus. Please, take me with you. I don't care where. I know things that must be passed on.'

'I am sure you do,' said Lysander. 'Imperial Fists, take up our fallen brother and move out! We have two prisoners to deliver.'

K-Day −10 hours
Intelligence acquisition and collation prior to Operation Requiem

Lord Commander Tchepikov believed in leading from as close to the front as was sensible for a man of his rank. The first assaults on Khezal had been accompanied by the dropping from orbit of the *Merciless*, an ocean-going command vessel from which Tchepikov could command the battle's opening stages beyond the range of Khezal's defences. The *Merciless* was one of the most advanced vessels of its kind in the segmentum, being festooned with sensor-baffling and defensive systems, and a comms and tactical cogitator suite that allowed Tchepikov's staff to coordinate the whole assault. At that moment it knifed through the ocean's swell, surrounded by a buzzing halo of scout aircraft scouring the surface for threats.

Inside, the controlled atmosphere was kept calm and chill. Everywhere was dark, pools of light around cogitator screens and map tables serving to focus attention where it was needed.

The labyrinth of corridors and sub-decks concealed the ship's most sensitive areas, such as the brig where a single prisoner squatted in the middle of its cell.

Six cells made up this block of the brig. Each cell was devoid of doors or windows, with the only way in or out a trapdoor built into the transparent ceiling. A walkway crossed above the cells, and it was on this that Lord Commander Tchepikov of the Imperial Guard stood to get a look at the first high-value captive of the war for Opis.

Three officers of the Battlefleet Obscurus Naval Intelligence Regiment accompanied Tchepikov, in their almost featureless dark-blue uniforms. Tchepikov had once been one of them in a long-distant career, and still entrusted to them the intelligence functions of his command.

'It calls itself Janeak Filthammer,' said one of the officers.

'Is that all we know?' said Tchepikov. He was a tall man who had once been well built, but who had lost the muscle of his youth. The aged fatigues of his old Naval regiment hung on him, as did the black greatcoat he wore over them. Countless medals were attached to his chest, or to the lapels of his coat, a jumble of colours and shapes from many ships and campaigns. Later medals were honorary, awarded for service and victories as a commander over whole Imperial armies. Over his long, lined face was the peaked cap of a Naval officer.

'We have not conducted a thorough interrogation,' came the reply from another officer. 'It was not thought sensible to question a moral threat such as this without your authorisation. Such courses of action have unpredictable consequences.'

'Very well,' said Tchepikov. 'You have my permission. It

is time to see what gift the Imperial Fists have brought us. Ensure the first stages are handled by someone who will not be gravely missed. Extracting intelligence from such a thing is rarely without casualties.'

'Yes, commander.'

The thing in the cell looked up at Tchepikov as if it could hear him, though the cell was soundproofed. It was half-man, half-fly, with several extra limbs, a fat pendulous abdomen and segmented eyes. A hastily sutured wound split its face in two, with another running from its sternum down the whole underside of its body. A cursory medical examination had shown it had suffered injuries too severe to survive, but it was kept alive by something more malevolent than the integrity of its body. It was chained to the floor with links of gold and silver, inscribed with anti-psychic wards that dampened whatever mental powers Janeak Filthammer might still possess. Even so, the polished steel of its cell was discoloured and rusted around it, the thing's aura of decay bleeding through the psychic defences built into the brig of the *Merciless*.

Mandibles flickered from between its torn lips. Its mouth opened, revealing a long, parched tunnel of a throat. Whatever the Chaos creature ate, it was being starved of it in the brig.

Heavy footsteps caught Tchepikov's attention. Into the brig had walked a man who was not a man. He was enormous, his head brushing the ceiling of the brig more than two and a half metres above the floor. His armour was polished blue, with the yellow shoulder pads emblazoned with the symbol of the clenched fist. The intelligence officers looked at the newcomer with apprehension but Tchepikov did not flinch.

'Commander,' said the Space Marine. 'I have come to see that the moral threat you hold here is properly contained and interrogated. I am Deiphobus, Librarian of the Imperial Fists, and I am here under the orders of First Captain Lysander.'

Deiphobus emerged into the better light that shone down into the cells. His smooth, dark skin was interrupted by the band of silver around his brow, with circuits and interfaces leading off from it. The collar of his armour rose up into a hood, arching over his head with the inner surface studded with purple crystals. He carried a long staff of gnarled wood, topped with the gilded, horned skull that was the symbol of a Librarian's office.

'My officers have the means to extract whatever this creature has to tell us,' said Tchepikov. 'I thank you for you offer, Librarian, but Filthammer is to be dealt with under my orders.'

'I doubt very much, commander,' replied Deiphobus, 'that you have on your staff a psyker as powerful as I, much less one who has dealt with such moral threats many times in the past. Furthermore, the Imperial Fists are under no orders from you, and are here to fulfil their honourable duty to the Throne of Earth. It is an act of goodwill that saw Janeak Filthammer delivered to you at all. This war is in far too early a stage to begin taking that goodwill lightly.'

Lord Commander Tchepikov considered this for a moment. Then he looked down at the thing in the cell and held his arms wide. 'All yours,' he said. 'Good luck.'

A ladder was reeled down from above, down through the trapdoor in the transparent ceiling, and Deiphobus descended into the presence of Janeak Filthammer.

Previously, Filthammer had been a horror. His full height was greater than that of a Space Marine and his sorcerous powers had given him an aura of terror that had cowed lesser minds that approached him. The sheer implications of his shape were bad enough – he must have entered into some awful pacts with the powers he served to grant him the aspects of a disease-bloated fly, or perhaps he was the result of some cross-breeding project pursued by the cultists hidden in Opis's society. Nothing about him was natural, and in any other situation everything about him would have been horrific.

But he was chained and imprisoned. His wounds were barely dressed and they wept yellowish gore down the matted bristles that covered his hide. He was bent and constrained, unable to reach his full height or unfurl his many limbs. His head was forced down by a chain around his neck so he could barely lift his faceted eyes to look at the Space Marine who now stood before him.

'My kind are legion,' Janeak Filthammer lisped through his torn mouthparts. 'We will–'

'Your kind will be rounded up, shot and incinerated. The ashes will be mixed with psyk-nulling acid and fired into the nearest star,' replied Deiphobus. 'Do not waste my time, or your rapidly shortening life, with threats. I have been threatened by far more dangerous creatures than you and none of them have yet outlived me.'

Filthammer did not reply. His mandibles chittered and lapped, as if he were trying to think up a reply. Perhaps, without his mind dulled by the psychic wards built into the brig, he would have come up with something.

'How came you to be on Opis?' said Deiphobus.

'The warp willed me into being,' said Filthammer. 'I was born from the mud of the ocean floor.'

'You were a man,' retorted Deiphobus.

'I hatched from the belly of a virgin maid.'

'You were a man. Nothing more. How came you to Opis?'

'The ordure of this city flowed into the lowest clogged pits of its sewers and there I emerged, congealed from their leavings as worms in meat–'

'You are boring me, whelp!' snapped Deiphobus. 'Why always the same charade?' The Librarian unclasped the gauntlet from his left hand and pulled it away. He placed his bare hand on the bristly forehead of Janeak Filthammer. The one-time champion of Chaos tried to recoil, but his chains gave him no range of movement to avoid Deiphobus's hand.

Flesh smoked. The most appalling smell of burning filth filled the cell. Filthammer's mandibles yawned open and he let out a rattling, gargling sound, perhaps the closest his physiology could make to a scream. Deiphobus's fingers sank into the flesh of his forehead, the corrupted skin blistering and peeling away.

Deiphobus's teeth gritted. The metal walls of the cell buckled and warped.

'What you will not tell me,' he grimaced, 'I will tear from your mind.'

Deiphobus's mind was a carefully prepared place, a battlefield built to give the advantage to his own consciousness when arrayed against an enemy. That enemy was the mind of Janeak Filthammer, and in the psychic concept that Deiphobus had prepared, Filthammer appeared as a great seething horde, a crawling darkness. Isolated memories stood like banner bearers or generals, with cavalry darting and writhing on the flanks and masses of barely-formed infantry flowing into the enormous banks of dark filth that heaved in the centre.

Deiphobus had spent endless sessions of meditation preparing his own mental army, visualising every component. Rogal Dorn himself stood at their head. A legion of shining, gilded Imperial Fists marched alongside him. Deiphobus had memorised the faces of the Chapter's long-dead, resurrecting them in his mind to give his mental defences and psychic probing a concrete form.

Rogal Dorn motioned for the charge. The gilded legion stormed into the mass of Filthammer's corrupted mind, silver blades cutting through the darkness. With every pace, Deiphobus cut deeper into Filthammer, peeling back the layers of defences and laying bare the secrets he now fought to preserve.

In another part of Deiphobus's mind, carefully separated from the conflict by a great battlement modelled after the defences of Terra which Dorn himself had designed, Filthammer's memory fragments played out as if projected onto a bank of pict-screens. Deiphobus discarded those which were irrelevant – insane revels, mad rantings, dark rituals to reanimate dead followers or mutate living ones. They had little more value than to illustrate what the Imperial force on Opis already suspected – Chaos demagogues and champions had been here for some time, marshalling the resources to operate in safety for perhaps decades.

Several fragments were assembled by Deiphobus's mind into a sequence showing Filthammer's arrival. A derelict ship, its crew dead by plague, drifted as if by accident (but most definitely by design) into Opis's orbit. A salvage crew had brought a strange, biomechanical container to the surface, hoping it was some piece of valuable archeotech. It was, in fact, the cocoon Filthammer had extruded around himself. He had promised to teach the crew of this Chartist craft the secrets of immortality, as he had demonstrated to them by surviving extremes of vacuum and supposedly mortal wounds. Instead, he had repaid them for passage on their ship by seeding it with fatal diseases and setting the ship to drift to Opis. The space lanes of the Imperium were full of such tales.

More interesting was why. Filthammer had not chosen Opis by accident. He had been called. Deiphobus strove to find out just why he had come, out of all the millions of planets in the Imperium, to this one.

The army of his mind was tearing through Filthammer. The champion's mind was a foul place, crammed with memories and instincts, beliefs and perversions, which gave birth to a legion of ill-formed horrors. Deiphobus joined his warriors on the battlefield, drifting like an astral projection through the carnage until he found a place in Filthammer's mind that did not fight – hardened, calloused, a rigid caul of gnarled emotion thick enough to withstand the rest of the champion's soul tearing at it.

Deiphobus sorted through the mental constructs he had created for just this task. He rejected a sword and a boltgun, crafted from gold, that he imaged hovering in the air in front of him. From his mind's armoury he selected an axe and, like a lumberjack, set about hacking his way through Filthammer's defences.

The fragments poured thick and jumbled from the wounds. The other part of Deiphobus calmly reviewed and rejected them. Half-remembered fragments of a childhood and early adulthood on some teeming industrial mass of a hive world. Filthammer, whoever he had once been, had been brought up in squalor and brutality. Probably he had used that as an excuse in the early stages of his corruption. Deiphobus discarded all this. The monster's childhood did not have any bearing on the war for Opis.

Piece by piece, a figure was revealed. Naked and filthy, crouched in a grime-streaked oubliette. It was a man, with sandy-coloured hair, a body worked to wiry strength by manual labour and the scarred hands that told of a lifetime in the manufactorum or at the mine face. The figure was scared and alone, starved, and confused.

It was Filthammer. Or rather, it was the man he had once been, buried and cut off and surrounded by a prison of hatred and determination, where he could not bother Filthammer with the conscience and abhorrence of a normal human mind.

The man looked up at Deiphobus. His eyes were deep, as if sunk back into his skull, and tears ran from those dark hollows.

'Tell me,' said Deiphobus. 'Everything. All that you know, about why you are here and who brought you to this world.'

The man who had become Janeak Filthammer shook his head in confusion.

The prison shook.

Deiphobus turned his mind back to the surface of Filthammer's mind, where the monster fought off the Librarian's psychic assault. The legions of darkness were turning on themselves, limbs and tendrils tearing at malleable bodies. Deiphobus's legion wallowed through a swamp of black gore as the enemy dissolved in a frenzy of self-mutilation.

'I have no time!' demanded Deiphobus. 'Tell me! Everything!'

The man stared open-mouthed. The cell around him was coming apart. The walls were flaking away, revealing the layers of petrified muscle and bone in which Filthammer had hidden this place.

The world was falling apart. Deiphobus could not maintain the integrity of the battlefield. He rolled back his consciousness and his legion withdrew, leaving in their wake a gaping black void which grew as Filthammer tore his own mind apart. Oblivion, like a freezing ocean, welled up in its place, destroying everything in the Chaos champion's memory.

The ocean flooded into the oubliette. The walls dissolved and the man was hanging in a void, his own shape barely coherent among the chaos.

'Legienstrasse,' the man said.

'What does that mean?' yelled Deiphobus. 'Is it a name? Who is it? Who brought you here?'

Then everything that Janeak Filthammer was, and had been,

was swallowed up by oblivion, and Deiphobus was plunged into the freezing abyss of an annihilated mind.

Deiphobus pulled his hand away from Filthammer's skull. Filthammer sagged in his chains, his head hanging and mouth lolling open. The flesh of his forehead smouldered around the charred imprint of Deiphobus's hand. The eyes were dull.

'Life signs nil,' came the voice of one of the intelligence officers, observing from the walkway overhead.

'Did he know anything, Librarian?' asked Tchepikov.

Deiphobus regarded his hand with some distaste. Filthammer's rancid flesh stuck to his palm. 'No,' he replied. 'Aside from that he did not come from this world. But that is hardly a surprise. A planet like Opis can only breed so many like this on its own, no matter how deep its corruption.'

'A shame,' said Tchepikov. 'But it is surely too much to ask for the key to Opis's liberation to be delivered to us in the first exchanges, is it not?'

Deiphobus looked up at the lord commander. It was impossible to read Tchepikov's expression or voice.

'There will be others,' said Deiphobus. 'Kekrops's findings suggested several moral threats on Opis. Filthammer will not be the last nor the most senior we encounter.'

'And as fellow servants of the Emperor's will, we shall all reap the benefits when they are brought low,' said Tchepikov. 'If Filthammer has taught us all he can, you will forgive me if I join my regimental advisors. In light of the day's actions there are many decisions to be made regarding the principal landings.'

'Of course,' said Deiphobus. He indicated the sorry remains of the champion of Chaos lying at his feet. 'Destroy the body. Leave not even ashes.'

K-Day −8 Hours
Rear echelon interdiction prior to Operation Requiem

Though Scout-Sergeant Orfos's mind was set in the grim, serious path of warfare, though the weight of his duty and his orders held his soul down, still he could not help but feel exhilaration at the sheer speed.

The engine of his bike shrieked as Orfos gunned it to its maximum, a great plume of dust shredded up into the air behind it as it streaked across the plain. Some distance to the east rose the outskirts of Khezal, the glittering spires already marred by a few columns of smoke. It was on this plain that Khezal had been forged in Opis's ages past, in a series of battles that had seen the Aristeia win the lordship of the planet they had held ever since. Mass war graves and abandoned siege engines had been preserved as memorials and triumphs, breaking up the dusty plain between the city and the wooded foothills to the west. This was a place denuded of life by the battles that had been fought here, as if the war dead beneath the surface were too jealous of life to let anything else live where they had died.

Squad Orfos tore in a wide arc around a triumphal arch, hammered into shape from the armour-plates of war machines captured centuries before. Ahead of them another spray of dirt marked the location of a convoy that from this distance Orfos could see was composed of four vehicles. They were fast and rugged, each with eight wheels riding over the uneven terrain, and gun turrets mounted on the tops of their hulls.

'Evade and close in!' shouted Orfos into his vox-link. He ripped the handlebars to one side and the bike slid around, almost sideways, as the convoy's first fire fell among them.

His squad burst into different directions, five bikes executing an approach pattern they had practised so many times they no longer needed to think. Within a few moments the distance had closed, so that the opening salvoes of heavy stubber fire ripped into the earth well behind them.

Scouts Privar and Geryius opened to full throttle and shrieked towards the front of the convoy, turning as they overtook it to approach it head on. Orfos led Vonretz and Enriaan to approach from the rear, sliding through twin arcs of stubber fire.

Orfos squeezed the firing stud beneath his thumb and the twin bolters of his Scout bike scattered explosive fire across the back of the rearmost vehicle. It was an armoured personnel carrier, painted in the bright livery of a house of the Aristeia. Armour-plates buckled and sparked. The rear ramp swung down and Orfos could see men moving inside, black-clad with featureless visors, hellgun carbines levelled to fire.

Orfos swerved to one side as the troops opened up. Vonretz took a handful of shots on the front fairing of his bike and he fought to keep control, falling behind the convoy as the bike wriggled underneath him as if trying to escape. Orfos passed behind the APC, firing his fairing-mounted guns as he went, and bodies fell from the back as bolter fire thunked into flesh.

Enriaan was alongside the rearmost vehicle. He had a melta bomb in his hand, a disc-shaped magnetic charge.

'Do it!' shouted Orfos into the vox.

Enriaan threw the charge against the side of the vehicle, the magnetic surface clamping on to it just above the wheel arch. The melta bomb detonated in a burst of cherry-red, throwing clots of molten steel into the air. The front wheels came clean off and the APC ploughed into the ground, burying its nose in the dirt and flipping end over end.

A moment later Privar and Geryius roared past in the opposite direction. In their wake the first vehicle in the convoy rolled over and over, the wheels on one side blasted off, components flung clear as the structure disintegrated.

The second vehicle collided with the first, slamming into it heavily enough to spin it right round. The remaining APC braked, turrets trying to get a bead on Orfos's squad as they circled the wreckage of the convoy.

The troops were jumping from the vehicles. Many had survived the crashes, and Orfos could see their uniforms did not match the bright livery of the vehicles. They wore black, without the rank flashes, brocade or household banners common to the soldiers fielded by the Aristeia. One among them was different – instead of functional body armour he wore a suit of plate-steel inlaid with gold, and he carried what looked like a crossbow with a magazine of bolts allowing it to be fired rapidly without reloading. Streamers of crimson and emerald silk fluttered from the crest of his helm – the faceplate was open and he had a face lined with the arrogance of the Aristeia, locked into a permanent sneer.

'That's their package!' shouted Orfos. 'Two passes and close! Vonretz, are you with us?'

'At your side, brother-sergeant!' replied Vonretz.

Las-fire buzzed through the air as Orfos led the squad in. Orfos drew his combat knife as he closed in, firing as he weaved between volleys of las-shots. The enemy, whoever they were, had decent training. Most men would break and run, to be chased down by the bikers. These stood and fired, side by side.

Some fell to the bolter fire. Orfos streaked past them and lashed out with his blade. A head came away from its body, the impact running up Orfos's arm.

The squad roared around for a second pass, leaving half a dozen dead in their wake. More fell as they approached and Orfos aimed for the knot of troops forming up around the armoured aristocrat. This time he cut down low and sliced a man halfway through at the waist, the blade carving down and through the leg of a second before Orfos was past. As he wheeled back around he saw Geryius's bike losing control and sliding out from under him, the Scout vanishing as he skidded into the cloud of dirt and wreckage.

Orfos braked and slid in, leaping from the bike. He drew

his bolt pistol and fired even as he ran behind the overturned rear vehicle, snapping off shots at the troops. Las-fire hissed against the hull of the wrecked APC and a pair of grenades sailed towards him.

Orfos ran out of cover, firing as he did so, falling to one knee. The grenades cooked off and showered him with earth and debris. He kept his footing and rattled off another volley, black-clad figures falling. Enriaan skidded right into them, his combat knife in one hand and pistol in another, and in a few seconds he had killed two men and was setting about the others.

The enemy were better shots than they were fighters up close. The Imperial Fists Scouts had all the fury of their fully armoured battle-brothers, and Enriaan was as fine a close combatant as Orfos had led in his short career as Scout-sergeant. He jabbed his blade up under the chin of one enemy as he stamped down on the leg of another, shattering the enemy's femur and crushing him down to the ground. A moment later Privar's bike ran through the fallen man, flipping his broken body into the air as the bike skidded to a halt.

The remaining vehicle ground through the wreckage, its turret tracking. Orfos ducked back into cover to deny it a target, just as Brother Geryius emerged, on foot, from the swirling dust in Privar's wake. He had unhooked his plasma gun from the holster on his back and, firing as he walked, spitted the turret of the APC on a lance of liquid flame. Glowing molten holes opened up in the turret and ammunition detonated inside. The rear doors sprang open and smoke billowed out, followed by the troops who had been sheltering inside.

The Scouts were all dismounted and fighting now. The troops they faced were disciplined and seemingly fearless, but Enriaan and Privar were among them, the monomolecular edges of their combat knives slicing through flesh and body armour. The troops were unable to pick out the Scouts amidst the swirling dust from the bikes and the smoke from the wrecks, but the Scouts had the senses of a Space Marine and battle-instinct served them almost as keenly as their enhanced sight. Orfos vaulted from cover and ran through the dust, leaping into the troops still tumbling from the back of the APC.

His knife found the first at waist-height, impaling him through the stomach. Orfos spun and lunged again. He aimed high, avoiding the hellgun the next trooper brought up to parry the stroke. The blade punched through the featureless visor and the man fell limp, dead before he slid off the knife into the dirt.

The dust was clearing. Between them the Scouts had killed all but a handful of the troops. The nobleman knelt surrounded by the corpses who had been shot down around him, clutching the ruin of his arm to his chest. The wounded arm still had its steel gauntlet and bracer, but hung by a taut strip of tendon from just below the shoulder. His face was pale with growing shock beneath his open visor.

Enriaan killed the wounded where they lay, before they could find a gun lying in the dust and try to exact revenge. Bolter shots rang out, isolated now instead of rattling volleys, as Brother Vonretz shot the handful who were still on their feet, trying to find cover in the wreckage.

Orfos levelled his pistol at the aristocrat's head. Up close he could see the man was perhaps fifty years old, with the military bearing of someone who had stayed ready to lead from the front at the age when most would have considered the battlefield a place for younger men. A tight, black moustache clung beneath his long nose, and were it not for his pallor and sweat he would have seemed an intense, intimidating man, perfectly suited for screaming orders on a parade ground.

'Who are you?' Orfos said.

'I might… I might ask the same,' said the nobleman, but any defiance in his words was nothing compared to the shaking of his voice.

'Your city will fall. It will happen soon. You were ready to flee it as soon as the first attacks came. What makes you too valuable to leave in Khezal?'

'You have no idea,' said the nobleman. 'No idea what we are.'

'So talk,' replied Orfos. The barrel of his bolt pistol never wavered, aimed right between the nobleman's eyes.

'We're the same as you,' the nobleman said. 'We are but pawns.'

Orfos saw the man's good hand wasn't just holding his ruined arm. The fingers were working at his belt. The grenade's pin pinged off just as Orfos realised what he was doing, and began to move.

Orfos leapt clear and the grenade in the nobleman's hand went off. The man disappeared in a burst of shrapnel and dust. Clods of earth and pieces of armour pattered down over Orfos as the detonation died down in his ears.

'Filth and damnation,' hissed Vonretz. 'We would have broken him.'

'And he probably guessed the same,' replied Orfos.

'He won't tell us anything more,' said Geryius, 'but these have a few things to say.' He was kneeling over one of the troopers, tilting the dead man's visored head. 'They're not Aristeia troops.'

'Are you hurt, brother?' said Orfos.

'My pride is mortally wounded,' replied Geryius. 'The rest of me has no complaints.'

'Then what do you think?'

'I think,' said Geryius, 'that our exploding friend might not have had much choice about his escort or where he was going. They weren't his household soldiers, that's for sure.' Geryius pulled the helmet off the dead man's head. The cropped hair and cranial scars underneath did not seem to suggest the grandly uniformed men of the Aristeia. Geryius picked photoactive lenses from the corpse's eyes. Quite possibly, the soldier had not removed his visor for a very long time.

'No rank or regiment symbols,' said Orfos. 'And these are the scars from cortical grafting. Opis does not have such technology freely available, certainly not for anyone not of noble blood. I do not think this man is a native of Opis.'

'On Malacios Tertius,' said Geryius, 'our Chapter fought with the Third Menandrian Crusade. The Inquisition sent their own troops. An inquisitor's personal regiment. They had been mind-wiped so often they weren't men any more. They didn't have names or memories. They were programmed as soldiers and nothing more. This man reminds me of them.'

'It was the Inquisition that brought this crusade down upon Opis,' said Orfos, 'after Kekrops's death. For their troops to be fighting alongside the Aristeia makes no sense.'

'You speak as if there is but one Inquisition, and its members are all of one mind,' said Vonretz. 'I may not be long a battle-brother, but even I know that is not the case.'

'Bag up a corpse and bring it with us,' said Orfos. 'Geryius, you take to the air so readily I think you can do with the extra weight. Sling it over the back of your bike.'

'Yes, sergeant,' said Geryius.

'More rats will be fleeing this decaying craft,' continued Orfos. 'They will bring with them whatever they cannot bear to be captured. That is reason enough to capture it. Saddle up, brethren. The eyes of our Chapter must never close.'

Scout Squad Orfos jumped back onto their bikes, checking their fuel loads and refreshing the ammo belts for their front-mounted bolters. Then, as the sun began to dip behind the smoking skyline of Khezal, five plumes of dust streaked across the Battle Plains again.

K-Day, K-Hour
Operation Requiem: Invasion of Khezal

Khezal had always held firm against invasions from the ground and the sea. Enormous armies of siege engines and cavalry, condemned prisoners loaded with explosives and tamed warbeasts, had pounded at the walls and were repulsed.

Huge siege-fleets, spraying naphtha fire and volleys of rockets, had sailed into its harbour and been sunk by cannon or snagged on underwater defences to be boarded and scuttled. A few hulks still lay in the harbour, slowly decaying, as a reminder of how Khezal had endured. But those attacks had been few and always disastrous – attempts by despots, sick of seeing their armies hurled back from the walls and buried in their thousands on the Battle Plains. Three times such attacks had come from the one-time Naval superpower of the Dvolian Coil, whose Navarchs had lost army after army trying to reduce Khezal by land; with the failure of each a new dynasty had taken over the lordship of the Coil. Another attack came from the mad traitor Locasis, who had led a cabal of rogue geniuses whose masterful weapons nevertheless foundered against the rocks flanking the harbour, or crumbled under fire from the dockyard batteries. In these modern times, when Khezal's ruling caste had expanded to rule the whole planet as the Aristeia, there was never any danger of anything coming from the sea.

The defences were there, but they were still designed with a view to dissuading a renegade city-state or the treacherous forces in a civil war. Any significant military invasion, anything from off-world, would be by land, with a force assembling among the foothills and then advancing across the Battle Plains.

And so, with a few well-led strikes against the coastal guns and sensorium arrays, the seaward defences of Khezal were all but paralysed. Imperial Guard storm troopers blew up missile silos and radar stations. A gunship assault from the Imperial Fists toppled a sensorium tower whose vast dish took in readings from across the seaboard, blinding the gun batteries that flanked the entrance to the harbour.

In the confusion of the multiple assaults on the city, few of the Aristeia paid much attention to the explosions coming from offshore. They were, in fact, the result of operations by sapper platoons of the Hektaon Lowlanders, planting demolition charges among the rocks of the jagged spurs forming the walls of the city's natural harbour. The narrow entrance was the biggest hindrance to a fleet trying to enter the harbour by force, but the sappers blew channels in the spits of rock wide enough for smaller troop ships to force their way through. A natural defence of the city was suddenly rendered completely porous, and the few who realised it struggled to make their voices heard as the defence guns fell silent.

K-Hour arrived. Transport craft loomed down from orbit a few kilometres out to sea, flying low enough to drop the ocean-going Imperial Guard craft they carried. Three large ships, the size of the *Merciless*, bristling with guns to serve as floating gun batteries. The sections to assemble two enormous floating docks for repair and resupply. Fuel tankers. A hospital ship. And hundreds of troop transports.

The men of the 91st, 120th and 309th Deucalian Lancers. The Lord Sorteliger's Own Regiment of Foot. The Gathalamor 912th Light Infantry and the Kirgallan Heavy Grenadiers. The remnants of the Hektaon Lowlanders, the 122nd Storm Troopers Division and the Luthermak Deathworlders, joining their fellow troops already fighting in the city. Almost fifty thousand men, and seventy-five tanks of the 4th Plaudis Shock Army. An army of the Imperial Guard the equal of any force the Aristeia of Opis could muster. The hammer of the Emperor, wielded with overkill force to shatter Khezal so completely that for light years around no world would question the authority of the Imperium for centuries.

The ships advanced towards the harbour. The few guns still operating around the harbour and along the coast opened up, fat whistling shells falling into the waves. The darkness was just starting to lift, with a grey dawn emerging from beyond the highlands to the west of the city, and the light found the sloping front ramps of the troop ships and the support gunboats weaving between them.

The *Penitent's Due* and the *Glorious* headed straight for the harbour entrance. Their guns fired a few ranging shots, tracers that cast a harsh red glow over the quays and shipyards, the enormous dry docks and the industrial piles that made up the dockside quarter of Khezal. Then the fire began, the guns booming curtains of fire down onto the docks.

The din was appalling. The Imperial Guardsmen gritted their teeth as the reports buffeted their craft. Almost half of them aimed for the channels blown in the harbour walls, and the rocks scraped against their hulls as they navigated the newly made narrows. Some foundered, and were dragged clear or pushed through, or clogged up their channel completely, stranding thousands of men. The first made it through to be greeted by the sight of the dockyards' burning buildings collapsing into the sea, in scarcely better repair than the rotting hulks of ancient shipwrecks.

Thousands of men forced a beachhead onto the ruins of Khezal's docks. The Plaudian tanks were floated onto the quays and the guns of the *Glorious* and the *Penitent's Due* now sighted on the residential districts just inland from the docks, dropping shells to topple buildings and clog the roads inwards with rubble. The Aristeia's troops would be kept from retaliating and throwing the Imperial Guard back into the sea.

The refugees numbered in the millions. They streamed out of the city, all vehicles soon abandoned in huge pile-ups as the people left them and headed westwards on foot. Panic spread faster than the fires dotting the eastern cityscape.

They had to get out. Not just because of the guns and

bayonets of the Imperial Guard, the cannon of their tanks or the shells falling down from the battleships at sea. They knew what would happen to them if they stayed. Even if they could not give it a name, or describe exactly what form it would take, they knew. They had known for a long time.

The lords of Khezal, those who cowed the Aristeia in fear and majesty, emerged from their cabals and lairs, from the ancestral tombs they had infested and the regal spires given to them in tribute. They demanded an army. Those who did not kneel and take up arms would be changed into whatever the lords of Khezal needed. The people of Khezal fled in such numbers that streets were crammed with them, clambering over one another to get away from a fate they feared to imagine.

'I have the square sighted,' said Brother Gorgythion. Through the viewscreen of the gunship he could make out, through the plumes of black smoke and the palls of dust, a city square bounded on all sides by the ravaged buildings of Khezal. A couple of hours ago it had been one of the more upmarket places to live, separated from the fleshpots near the docks by a canal that acted like a moat against the city's poverty. Grand columned frontages looked down on a square of elegant tiled mosaics, watched over by dozens of equestrian statues of Aristeia generals and rulers. One magnificent spire rose at the south-west corner of the square, almost twice as high as anything else nearby, crowned with leonine heads and flying the flag of several lesser houses of the Aristeia.

The artillery barrage had not been kind to the place. Several statues lay toppled from their plinths, only the broken bronze feet of their horses remaining in place. Craters had been blown in the square and many of the buildings around it had been blasted open, spilling the rubble and twisted metalwork of their entrails over the mosaics. Many more were on fire, belching black smoke from their windows.

'No contacts,' said Gorgythion. Beside him his co-pilot, Kebriones, rapidly switched through readouts on the cogitator console in front of him. The chatter from several vox-channels chittered tinnily from the cockpit vox-casters, rising and falling as Kebriones sifted through the controlled bedlam of battle in the city below.

'Guard to the south-east,' said Kebriones. 'Should be in visual soon.'

Gorgythion banked the gunship, circling the square.

'Still nothing,' said Gorgythion, peering among the rubble and the scorched facades of the gutted buildings.

'They are there,' said Kebriones. 'Everything we know says Khezal will fight.'

Gorgythion focused on a retinal icon and brought up the weapons status, projected onto the inside of the viewscreen. In the cramped cockpit, everything was edged with the pale green and winking red of the weapons readouts.

The Shadowhawk had started out its life as a Thunderhawk gunship, used to transport the Space Marines of the Imperial Fists and provide them with air support once they were on the ground. But the Chapter armoury had transformed it into something very different – the Shadowhawk, based on some of the oldest Standard Template Construct fragments ever recovered by the tech-priests of Mars, was a dedicated weapons platform, its passenger compartment sacrificed to house the craft's missile batteries and ammunition stores. The readout confirmed a full missile load, targeting array and autocannon on-line, countermeasures loaded and ready to deploy.

The Chapter had christened her the *Sanctifier*.

'There they are,' said Kebriones. In the south-east corner of the square could be seen a trio of tanks advancing, wearing the blue and gold colours of the 4th Plaudis Shock Army. They were equipped with dozer blades that forced through the rubble, all the artillery barrage had left of the streets east of the square. Alongside them walked a couple of hundred men of the Imperial Guard, their grey camo body armour marking them out as Kirgallan Heavy Grenadiers. At this height Gorgythion could make out the heavy weapons teams hauling wheeled heavy bolters and lascannon, as the grenadier units swept the empty windows and doorways around them with their lasguns.

'*Sanctifier* here, we see you,' said Kebriones.

<<Axefall Squadron, 4th Shock,>> came the vox reply. <<Good to have you, *Sanctifier*.>>

<<Kirgallan welcomes you, *Sanctifier*,>> came another voice, that of the Guardsmen's vox-operator in the streets below.

'Still clear,' voxed Gorgythion. 'Report contacts.'

'Getting reports on both flanks,' said Kebriones. The pictscreens were cycling through vox-frequencies, the voices of the various Guard vox-operators appearing as juddering, jagged crimson lines on the screens. 'Doesn't seem organised. Militia and household troops. They're running or being mown down.'

Down below, the Kirgallans were walking across the square, into the open. They clung to the cover provided by fallen masonry and statues, their old soldier's instincts automatically steering them away from the open. The lead tank rode up over a fallen statue, treads grinding down through the torso of a bronze horse.

'Wait,' said Gorgythion. Almost without registering on his mind, movement had scuttled across the corner of his vision. Even a Space Marine, whose peripheral vision was among the many senses augmented by his transformation into a battle-brother, could easily have missed it. Gorgythion had been a pilot, attached to the Chapter's armoury and Techmarines, since he had been recruited by the Imperial Fists. He saw everything on the ground. He had the eyes of a bird of prey.

Gorgythion looked closer at the buildings along the square's north edge. He was certain he had seen something – someone – moving there, perhaps in a window or a doorway.

A body lay, surrounded by crimson spattered across the paving slabs, at the foot of one of the buildings. Many had died in the first bombardments, and many had no doubt been blown from the windows or chosen to jump to escape the fires still smouldering in many of the buildings.

But this body was still bleeding. Crimson was spreading behind it.

'Be advised on the ground,' voxed Gorgythion, 'I see possible contacts to your north.'

<<We see nothing,>> replied the Guardsman on the vox. <<We're staying on mission.>>

Gorgythion saw the body fall this time. From an upper window it tumbled, thrown some distance as if thrown from the window. Or as if it had jumped.

Because it was not dead. It – she, Gorgythion saw, a woman going by the long hair that streamed out behind her – wind-milled her arms and kicked her legs as she fell. She wore a forge worker's uniform, dirty dark-green coveralls with a sash in the colour of whatever noble house owned the rights to her labour. She hit the ground hard enough to force her body out of shape, landing feet-first, her lower body forced up into her torso.

And another. A clerk, in the white toga of the underlings who kept the ledgers in Aristeia counting-houses. Then more forge and factorium workers. Beggars in rags. A periwigged legal scholar, robed academics from one of Khezal's competing universities. Men and women. Old and young. Rich and poor.

<<We see that,>> said the vox-operator. <<Is anyone to our north?>>

'No Imperial forces there,' said Kebriones.

'Then they're not running from us,' said Gorgythion.

Twenty had fallen. Thirty. Forty. The building was a high-end residential block, its view of the square and lavish style putting it well out of reach for commoners with anything but the highest status in Khezal. Far beyond the forge workers and street people leaping now from its windows.

A hundred. More. Two hundred, piling up beneath the

windows. Blood thickened, spreading across the northern edge of the square as corpses thumped wetly onto corpses.

Gorgythion brought the *Sanctifier* down low, targeting oculi playing across the buildings along the northern edge. The *Sanctifier's* instruments could see in the thermal spectrum, which in other circumstances could pick out the body heat of enemies lying in wait – but the smouldering fires blinded it, creating just blooms of incoherent light.

'Throne knows what these heathens were told about us,' said Kebriones, 'if this is what they choose instead of submitting to their Imperium.'

'I don't think that is why they are dying,' replied Gorgythion.

The last few bodies fell. The blood was thick and wet, mingling with the masonry dust in the square into a sluggish purple-black mass.

'What do you mean?' said Kebriones.

'I think it's a sacrifice,' replied Gorgythion. He opened the vox-channel to the ground. '*Sanctifier* here. Potential moral threat. Moral threat to your north.'

<<What is it?>> asked the Kirgallan vox-operator.

'Something that needs blood,' replied Gorgythion.

The tall building at the north-west corner shuddered, as if explosives had been detonated around its foundations. The front of it fell away and dark purplish light blazed out, as if the building was the false front of a deep cave lined with glowing amethyst. The light filled the cockpit of the *Sanctifier*, obliterating the viewscreen readout.

The sound of orders and yelled curses came from the vox-link to the ground. The pict-screens in front of Kebriones flickered and went dark. The *Sanctifier* yawed as a shockwave hit it, the air pushed outwards as something forced its way into reality.

Rubble slewed across the square from the flayed tower. A shape, like a vast bird with long, coiling feathers of multi-coloured fire, swept out of the purple blaze.

At its centre was a humanoid shape. A woman. At first glance she was beautiful. Her perfect body was pale and flawless as a sculptor's marble. But her arms and legs ended in sprays of feathers and her eyes were not eyes at all, but black hollows that bored through her face and gave a glimpse of a void contained within her. What seemed at first to be her hair were strips of skin, extruded from her scalp in a fleshy mass that fell halfway to the ground.

She had wings, too, a huge spread of burning feathers that unfolded from behind her.

She held up an arm, and the feathers unfurled and coiled like the fronds of an underwater plant. With a gesture, she cast a long line of pink fire across the square, rushing out from a point beneath her feet.

The flames rushed through the lead tank. The tank was engulfed by them, disappearing in the luminescence that flowed over it like liquid. The Kirgallans caught in it disappeared, burst into showers of burning ash.

<<What the hells is that thing?>> came the vox-operator's voice, forgetting his voice was being transmitted.

'*Sanctifier* is engaging!' voxed Gorgythion, and fired the vertical engines to force the Shadowhawk higher over the battlefield.

Las-fire streaked up at the abomination. A missile spiralled towards her and detonated a short distance away, as if it had struck an invisible sphere surrounding her body.

No, not her body. *Its* body.

Gorgythion told himself it was not a woman. It would have to be human to be a woman, and it had shed whatever humanity it possessed a long time ago. He aimed the nose of the *Sanctifier* at the centre of the blaze surrounding it, and the targeting runes lit up. The archeotech targeting systems, using technology from before the Imperium's founding, seemed eager to launch everything it had at the moral threat. It seemed to know. Quite possibly, given the antiquity of the cogitators which housed its machine-spirit, it did.

The six missile pods, whose bulk replaced the passenger compartment in the Thunderhawk chassis, rumbled angrily as a salvo was chambered and the rockets primed. The cogitators shuddered, throwing incandescent launch paths across the viewscreen in front of Gorgythion.

Piloting the *Sanctifier* was more than just a question of aiming the craft's weapons. Gorgythion had learned to hold it back, too, until the time was perfect.

The Shadowhawk arrowed downwards, plunging steeply towards the target. A wave of pink fire scythed towards it, scouring along the top of the fuselage, just off-target. The abomination's eyes turned towards the *Sanctifier* and Gorgythion was sure those windows into the void were focused right on him.

A ring of runes lit up around her inhuman face. Targeting solutions rattled past. Gorgythion slammed a fist onto the firing stud on the instrument panel.

The cogitator seemed to roar in delight, the sound mingling with the shriek of the missile exhausts igniting. A salvo of six missiles, each tipped with a Harbinger warhead, lanced towards the abomination. Each one split into a dozen bomblets, and every bomblet burst in a shower of silver flame and shrapnel.

Gorgythion yanked the controls to one side and the *Sanctifier* shuddered in the shockwave from the exploding missiles. The gunship rose on the wave of superheated air, carrying it over the head of the abomination and through the fan of flame that adorned its wings.

Arrows of fire spat up at the gunship. The craft flipped, one wing struck, and Gorgythion shut down the main engines and gunned the landing jets.

The craft fell for a second and a half, the spinning tiles of the square sprinting up towards it. The jets, fired independently as Gorgythion's gauntlets danced across the instruments, forced it level again and arrested the plunge.

The abomination, thrown back by the volley of explosions, slammed into the front of one of the square's northern buildings. The void bled from her eyes, liquid blackness running down her face like dark tears. She shrieked, perhaps less at the pain and more at the indignity of being thrown out of the air and sprawled like a discarded toy.

'Terra's hearth,' said Kebriones. 'It bleeds, at least.'

'Damage?' said Gorgythion.

'Left wing is holed,' came the reply. 'Left bow jet burned out.'

'Good,' said Gorgythion. 'We can still fly and shoot.' He swung the gunship back around, just a few metres above the ground, nose panning across the square.

'Wait,' said Kebriones. 'The north side. More of them.'

Gorgythion could see them. They were not sacrifices. They were armed – they were soldiers.

Most of them were drawn, by the looks of it, from the forces of the Aristeia. Their bright uniforms, however, were unkempt and ragged, and they were a mismatch of household colours. Mixed in with them were the same random assortment of Khezal's social castes who had thrown themselves from the buildings above. They carried lasguns and autoguns, a few heavy stubbers, swords and knives. Several hundred of them were emerging from the shadows around the buildings, advancing over the bodies of those who had died a few minutes earlier.

And there was something appallingly wrong with them. It might have been the pallor of their skin, either dusty white or the lifeless grey-brown of asphalt. The way they shambled as much as walked, snapping shots less in the hope of hitting anything and more because some old instinct told them that was what soldiers did. But mostly, it was their faces. The same void that filled the abomination glimmered behind their eyes, too.

'Contacts, north!' voxed Kebriones. 'Kirgallan, 4th Plaudis Shock, you have enemy militia approaching in strength from the north!'

Gorgythion could see the Kirgallans responding. Already in disarray from the multicoloured flame raining down among

them, they now scattered and leapt into the cover afforded
by the collapsed buildings of the square. The two remaining
tanks took aim and hammered battle cannon shots into the
approaching enemy, throwing bodies into the air.

The enemy did not stop. They sped up, breaking into loping
runs. They barely seemed to notice the lasgun fire from the
Kirgallans that mowed them down in tens and twenties. Their
own fire did barely anything to the armoured, disciplined
Guardsmen.

Gorgythion aimed the *Sanctifier* into the enemy ranks and
sprayed assault cannon fire into them, and the kill was huge.
Fifty militia must have died as the Shadowhawk gunship
yawed sideways, the cogitators hungrily rattling through
ammo belts to tally the kill.

Gorgythion could see the enemy up close now. Their
humanity had been shorn from them as surely as from the
abomination now spreading its burning wings again. They
charged into the Kirgallans even as the Guardsmen's guns
mowed down another hundred of them, the bodies sent
sprawling, spraying gore, across the square.

The enemy tore open their uniform jackets and overalls.
Beneath them, they had long, straight slits running from
collarbone to waist, like lipless vertical mouths. The mouths
opened, revealing the shuddering masses of polyps that clung
to the wet redness inside.

The polyps burst. A greyish haze flowed over the Guardsmen. Every biological weapon alert in the cockpit of the
Sanctifier lit up at once.

'Kirgallans, bioweapon alert!' voxed Gorgythion.

There was no reply, just the scratchy echo of las-fire and screaming over the open vox-link.

'Kirgallan, come in!'

<<This is… I can see it! I can see the Hells! Right… right to the centre of the world…>> came the vox-operator's voice.

'Kirgallan, please acknowledge, bioweapon alert!'

<<It is the end! I can see the end of it all! Whole worlds… whole worlds boiling down there. These are all my brothers! I belong here! Here! With my family!>>

Beneath the *Sanctifier*, Gorgythion could see Guardsmen collapsing under the cloud of spores emanating from the enemy troops, or shooting one another, or weeping, or dancing. The enemy were cutting the throats of the helpless ones, while the few Guardsmen who retained their senses were falling back out of the square, rifling through their packs for their rebreather masks.

One of the remaining Plaudis tanks exploded, throwing its turret high on a burning cloud of detonating ammunition.

'It's a general retreat,' said Kebriones, monitoring the command vox-channels linking the various Imperial Guard units. 'Abandon open ground and dig in.'

Gorgythion tried to cover the Kirgallans' retreat, but there was little he could do. The enemy were many and he could only kill so many of them. The Kirgallans dug in on the lower floors of the buildings south of the square, and once inside they were on their own. The enemy were wheeling missile launchers and autocannon on limbers across the square, even a couple of lascannon from the armouries of the Aristeia. Gorgythion pulled the *Sanctifier* up and back, out of the range of the heavy weapons.

From here he could see the fires of battle added to the blazes begun by the Naval bombardment. Buildings were alight with gunfire from their windows, and narrow streets were choked with the living and the dead as they fled or tried to advance. Everywhere the Imperial Guard were falling back, when every strategy of the Guard colonels had assumed they would advance unopposed into the heart of Khezal in a couple of hours.

Gorgythion flew back towards the Imperial lines around the docks to refuel and rearm. He would fly out again soon, he was sure, but not to harry the defeated enemy everyone assumed would flee before the Guard. Instead, Khezal had proven it could fight back.

Lord Speaker Kallistan vel Sephronaas cut much the same figure as the ancestors whose portraits hung around the auditorium of House Sephronaas. On a smaller man his gut would have made him obese, but on him, it somehow made him even more kingly than the bottle-green velvet and ermine trim in which he was enrobed. Even the wig he wore, powdered curls with strings of gemstones embroidered into the locks that tumbled over his shoulders, seemed on him the garb of a monarch rather than an affectation. The Aristeia's defenders often claimed that the various household blood-lines were maintained to create men and women with the genes required for leadership and majesty, and Lord Speaker Kallistan vel Sephronaas was the man they pointed to when asked for proof.

The auditorium, somewhere in the vast, mostly underground House Sephronaas estate, was designed to amplify the Lord Speaker's majesty. Gilded ribs divided the dome into slices of fresco, with past luminaries of the house enthroned on clouds like saints. The Lord Speaker was alone, save for his translator, but still he seemed to fill the place. Even via pict-broadcast, the effect was total.

He snapped his fingers. The translator, a small woman with short blonde hair seemingly selected for her plainness, scurried forwards and knelt by her master's feet.

'I shall stoop,' he said via the translator, 'to addressing you in the tongue of the common Imperium, though its sounds shall not sully my mouth.' The Lord Speaker's own words were in the breathy, booming language of the Aristeia, an old tongue that was still illegal for commoners to use, extinct outside the most senior of Opis's aristocracy.

'As the Lord Speaker of our people, the one to whom the responsibility for Opis's place in the galaxy falls, I am to be considered the greatest authority on this world as far as the emissaries of the Imperium understand it. Therefore, the whole of Opis is bound to my word.

'In the last three hours the determination of Opis to resist the Imperial tyranny has been demonstrated. My world will not kneel and beg for forgiveness. Our only crime was the execution of a malefactor who sought to denigrate the name of the Aristeia with his accusations. Lord Inquisitor Kekrops was justly slain by the ancient laws of Opis. The Imperium's invasion of my world is, similarly, a crime, and like any crime, punishment will be exacted.

'Every man and woman you send to Opis, Lords of the Imperium, will die in the streets of Khezal, and anywhere else you care to fight over. We are not alone in our fight, and our allies will fight just as fiercely as we do. Our whole population is at our disposal, and if their lives must all be spent to throw your verminous kind back into the void then spend them we will. Not the Imperial Guard, nor the Imperial Navy, nor the Adeptus Astartes themselves will sway us from our course of freedom and independence.

'Leave Opis, and you will suffer nothing but the humiliation of your loss. Stay, and you will all die. This I swear, by the swords of my ancestors and the very stones of Opis.'

Lord Speaker Kallistan vel Sephronaas snapped his fingers once more and the translator crawled backwards behind him, out of pict-shot. He said a final sentence, again in the language of the Aristeia, but even without translation the look on his jowly, furious face gave little doubt that it was the most venomous insult in the long history of Aristeia politics. Then, the broadcast ended.

'Technically, he is the planetary governor,' said the intelligence officer, indicating the frozen image of vel Sephronaas on the pict-screen. 'Since it is to him that the tithing and legal responsibilities fall.'

'Have we dealt with him before?' said Lord Commander Tchepikov, who sat at the head of the briefing table in the map room aboard the *Merciless*. Beside him were liaison officers from Imperial Guard regiments currently embattled in Khezal, many of whom were now among the few survivors of their regiments. The form of Librarian Deiphobus loomed, standing, for none of the map table's thrones were large enough for his armoured size.

'Only the Administratum,' replied the officer, referring to a pile of parchments in front of him. 'He was always high-handed, but nothing that cultural differences could not explain. The last tithing mission thought him to be a reliable link between the Imperium and the Aristeia. Never any problems.'

'There are problems now,' said Tchepikov. 'Would you not agree?'

'Yes, Lord Commander,' said the officer.

'Get that jackal off my screen,' ordered Tchepikov, and the image of Lord Speaker Kallistan vel Sephronaas vanished.

'He blusters like a prizefighter who knows he is outclassed,' said Colonel Hartz of the Lord Sorteliger's Own, a hereditary officer who had nevertheless earned every medal he wore on his chest along with the duelling scars on his face. 'He seeks to intimidate. These are the words of desperation.'

'But the allies of which he speaks are real enough,' replied Colonel DuKrastimir of the Luthermak Deathworlders. 'I have bodybags to fill with the evidence of that.' DuKrastimir pointed with a meaty finger to illustrate his point. He was as huge as a shaven bear, his physical presence somehow enhanced by the fact that both his legs and his left arm had been lost in combat and replaced with oily, functional bionics. 'This is a message for his own people. They have been conditioned to obey everything the damned Aristeia say. There are only so many moral threats on this world for him to call on. He needs the people of Opis to believe they can beat us, too.'

'And what news of these allies have we collated?' said Tchepikov. 'They have shown their hand, in Khezal at least. Lieutenant Mace, what are we dealing with?'

One of the intelligence officers cleared her throat and stood up. She had a greyish, drained look to her, with a tight, lean face and black hair drawn up in a severe bun. 'Kekrops had compiled the likely identities of some moral threats he believed were hiding on Opis. Some of those in turn have appeared to defend Khezal. Karnikhal Six-Finger is the warrior witnessed by the 120th Deucalians. He is believed to be a renegade Adeptus Astartes, probably in a military command role. Hektaon sappers infiltrating the underground transportation system encountered a witch who can be identified with Dravin Stahl, a long-time Inquisition target. And the creature engaged by the Kirgallans was probably a possessee and witch named by Kekrops as Antiocha Wyraxx.'

'One of yours,' said Tchepikov to Deiphobus.

'My brother Imperial Fists brought Wyraxx to battle,' said Deiphobus. 'The heretic was engaged by our support craft. I have offered all intelligence gained in this to your staff.'

'Where did they come from?' said Tchepikov. 'Kekrops was so close to finding out when he was killed. What secrets the Aristeia must have been keeping, to have executed an inquisitor and brought the Imperium's vengeance on their world.'

'And why?' said Deiphobus. 'What prize is Opis to such a gallery of traitors and witches? This is a populous world, it is certain, and the Imperium would suffer much from its loss.

But the same could be said of any one of a million worlds. These threats are not home-grown; they are not native to this world. Something brought them here. If we knew what it was, we might understand much more about who is really in control of the enemy here.'

'Then it is not vel Sephronaas?' said Colonel Hartz.

'Indeed, it is not,' replied Deiphobus. 'Many times have the Imperial Fists taken to war against the slaves of the Dark Gods. And every one of those traitors has believed that he is in charge of his own destiny. They are never in charge of anything. They are puppets of a greater power, a power which must be hunted down and destroyed as the true enemy. Vel Sephronaas probably believes that he is the leader of Opis's resistance to the Imperium, but in truth, he is being controlled by something far worse than a renegade governor.' Deiphobus paused, holding out a hand as if weighing something. 'But don't let that dissuade you from killing him.'

'He will be added to the target list,' said Tchepikov. 'It is getting rapidly longer. On which note, gentlemen, the defence of Khezal has forced us to alter our plan for Opis. The moral threats of the city are utilising its population in numbers we did not expect. This is unfortunate but not without precedent and has been planned for. We will not behead the resistance on Opis by storming and capturing Khezal rapidly. A secondary plan to surround, invade and reduce other key cities of Opis will be instituted immediately. Naval and Guard reinforcements have been demanded and the reserves currently in orbit, which were to be used in refounding and subjugation duties, will be committed on the ground. This has gone from a battle to a war, but we were prepared for war and it will be won.'

Librarian Deiphobus listened to the intricacies of the plan that Tchepikov had drafted. It was thorough and detailed, completely within the dictates of the *Tactica Imperium* with which all officers of the Imperial military were trained. Opis's key cities – Makoshaam, Diretz, Rekaba – would be encircled and besieged if necessary; cutting off movement of fuel, supplies and manpower from one another until they collapsed and all the moral threats and Aristeia members inside were hunted down and executed. It would be a long, cruel process, and the people of Opis would suffer much even if they avoided the forced recruitment into the Aristeia forces which was happening across Khezal. But Tchepikov was right – the Imperium would win.

If Kekrops had not underestimated the number of witches and arch-heretics on Opis. If the enemy was only able to use Opis's citizens as suicide troops and militia. If killing off the Aristeia would actually make any difference to the true leadership on Opis.

Deiphobus looked through the files the intelligence staff had collected on the moral threats so far encountered. Deiphobus had already seen the reports from Gorgythion, the Shadowhawk pilot, on the appearance of Antiocha Wyraxx and what she had done to the citizens under her command. He noted that she had been seen before, and committed a string of heresies on worlds along the galactic eastern rim – half a galaxy away from Opis. Karnikhal Six-Finger had last been seen trying to break through Naval cordons around the

Eye of Terror. What were any of them doing on Opis? Who, or what, had the power to bring them here? And what was it on Opis that they were trying to achieve, at the expense of being brought to battle by the full might of the Imperial military?

Answers would be found in the battles to come, as more and more of Opis was prised open to uncover the corruption within. And Deiphobus knew it would be the Imperial Fists who would find themselves in the toughest of the fighting – that the Space Marines would have to cut all those answers from the flesh of the enemy.

Lysander had set up the Imperial Fists camp on the Battle Plains where the Chapter's Scout bikers had conducted their interception missions just a few hours before. Bunkers had been dropped from orbit to half-bury themselves in the parched ground. Between them, tanks and aircraft were parked between the structures and sentry guns tracked across the plains. The Imperial Fists force consisted of around a half-company strength, a little more than fifty Space Marines, along with the same number again of unaugmented Chapter maintenance crews and other menials. Many of the Chapter's crewmen were working on the *Sanctifier*, repairing the wounds it had suffered at the hands of Wyraxx and her sorcery, and the mobile forge belched smoke as its artificers repaired and adapted weaponry and vehicle parts to suit the battles now being laid out by Commander Tchepikov. Squadron Sthenelus's Vindicator self-propelled siege weapons were being loaded and fuelled to join the advance into Khezal. From this stronghold, codenamed Sigismund Point, the Imperial Fists readied themselves for the missions sure to be needed in Khezal over the next few days. As moral threats revealed themselves, the Imperial Fists would have to be the ones to intercept them.

One of Sigismund Point's bunkers was not a barracks or an armoury, but a mobile prison block with half a dozen cells. A pair of Imperial Fists stood guard outside the windowless block and inside, in the cool, dry recycled air and gloomy half-light, the only prisoner so far locked up inside sat in the corner of her cell.

Captain Lysander hauled the doorway open. The woman looked up at him, squinting in the relatively bright light from outside the cell. She was dishevelled and dirty, as she had been when Lysander brought her here, but she was alive and healthy.

'You cannot leave,' said Lysander. 'Not yet.'

'I know,' replied Serrick. 'Moral quarantine.'

Lysander motioned to a table outside the cell. On the table was a meal of water and ration blocks. Serrick sat down and began eating with as much speed as dignity would allow. She had not eaten for a long time.

'Lord Commander Tchepikov does not know you exist,' said Lysander. 'He would expect us to hand you over to his intelligence staff. But the Adeptus Astartes keeps its own counsel in such matters.'

'And,' said Serrick between mouthfuls, 'there is something happening on this planet that goes a damn long way beyond a madman deciding he doesn't want to cough up his tithes any more. You don't know who to trust except yourselves. So here I am.'

'We have contacts with Tchepikov's staff,' continued Lysander. 'We know that you are Lukrezzia Mosherham Serrick-Vaas.'

Serrick laughed a little, snorting water from her glass. 'Lukrezzia is my given name. It comes from a grandmother on my father's side who was supposed to have been a very poisonous woman. Mosherham was the manufactorum who owned my father, and Vaas was my mother's caste. So I just go by Serrick. It was the town where I was born. It seemed the least offensive of all my names.'

'You are a psyker,' said Lysander.

'On my good days. I am a telekine.'

'And you were part of Kekrops's mission to Opis.'

'I was there when he died.'

Lysander sat down opposite Serrick. 'What happened?'

'It was an ambush. Whoever hit us knew where we were going to be and how to hit us. And they were off-worlders, too. Not anyone from Opis.'

'Could they have been mercenaries?'

'They were mind-wiped,' said Serrick. 'So no, I don't think so. They weren't corrupted, either. Whoever sent them it wasn't one of the moral threats Kekrops was after. Not without a couple of layers between them and us, at least.'

'And then?'

'I hid out,' said Serrick. 'In Makoshaam. But the Aristeia were after me. I think it was them, anyway. I got out of Makoshaam and made it to Rekaba. There was a safehouse there Kekrops had set up. When I reached it, it was full of Aristeia troops. The next thing I know, I'm in the pyramid. In the coffin. They asked me the same sort of things as you are. I think they wanted to know how much Kekrops had found out.'

'They? Janeak and his cult?'

'Throne of Terra, yes. I saw him. Believe me, seeing him was enough. Something like that, just being in the same room as it… it pollutes your soul. I think they were keeping me intact, for whatever reason. We have… we have exercises they teach us. Mental exercises. I didn't let myself think of what they were going to do with me. I've seen men go mad in places like that. I didn't let myself become one of them. I think that is the difference between people who can do the kind of things we do, and everyone else. We're not stronger or smarter or anything like that. It's not being psychic or three metres tall or whatever we do that counts. We can see the worst of what there is, and we can carry on. That's the difference. We can be trusted with knowing things that make everyone else go crazy.'

'Who is Legienstrasse?'

Serrick shrugged. 'Janeak asked me that, too. I got the impression he knew the answer. Again, he just wanted to know if we knew. And as an agent of the Throne, I swear I do not know. I have never heard the name, or whatever it is, before. But there is something that he didn't get out of me. Something I knew that he didn't.'

Lysander looked at this woman. She was wasted from malnutrition, but her eyes were still bright. The Inquisition had done well in picking an agent who could go through the hell the Holy Ordos required of her. The real question was, whether she could be trusted at all.

'Then tell me,' said Lysander.

Serrick shook her head. 'Get me off this world, back to the Inquisition where I can carry on my work. And do not let me go through Tchepikov's people. You make this happen yourself.'

'And in return for this great generosity?'

'I'll give you the location of the thing I hid in Rekaba before I was captured. It's proof of what you are really dealing with on Opis. You will know what it signifies when you see it.'

Lysander sat back. 'I am not one given to negotiations.'

'But I am, captain. Believe me, I have something you want and you can give me what I want. It is not much I ask.'

'We could tear what you know from your mind,' said Lysander.

'I know,' replied Serrick. 'But that is a resource better used on the enemies here on Opis, is it not? And besides, we are both servants of the same Emperor. We both seek vengeance for the death of Kekrops and the destruction of the heretics on this planet. Such treatment of an ally would hardly become the honour of the Imperial Fists, now, would it?'

'No, it would not,' conceded Lysander. 'But you will not go beyond our sight. If you do not deliver, you will be back in our custody. Or handed over to Tchepikov, a situation you seem to fear greatly. Understood?'

'Of course,' replied Serrick.

'Then I shall have a pilot to deliver you to the *Wings of Dorn* in orbit.'

Serrick took another mouthful of rations. She paused, and

looked up. 'I have yet to thank you for saving me.'

'As you say,' replied Lysander, 'we are on the same side.'

K-Day +2 Days
Internment of refugees from Khezal
Interception and elimination of Aristeia members fleeing Operation
Requiem

Scout-Sergeant Orfos could barely see where the refugee camp
ended, the mass of prefabricated hab-blocks and handmade
shanties almost merging with the dusty horizon. The Imperial force had brought a great many buildings to construct the
camp but they were not nearly enough, and the people fleeing Khezal had done their best to make up the shortfall with
whatever material they could scavenge from the Battle Plains.
Their shacks were built from rusted armour-plates and tank
wheels dug from the dirt.

Orfos watched the people as the Chimera APC drove
through the camp. The top hatches were open and from this
vantage point he could see citizens hurrying through the
dusty streets and herding their families out of sight, for the
Imperial army – especially the Space Marines – were icons of
fear. Orfos had brought only Geryius along from his squad,

knowing that a full unit of Space Marines would be enough to spark a panic riot.

'Have they named this place yet?' asked Scout Geryius.

'The Emperor's Embrace,' said Orfos. 'But I doubt many of these people are calling it that.'

'They're saying we'll have four hundred thousand here before it's all done,' said the Chimera driver, an Imperial Guardsman of the 309th Deucalian Lancers. 'Good money says every fifth one of 'em will be a heretic.'

Orfos watched as another Chimera, this one with its passenger compartment replaced with a flatbed, trundled through the cramped alleyways collecting bodies. Many of the people trickling out of Khezal were wounded or diseased, and the dead mounted up in spite of the efforts of the Sisters Hospitaller who had set up a medicae post in one of the hab-blocks. And some people who came in healthy were turning up dead to violence. It was impossible to see what happened below the surface of the Emperor's Embrace. No one here trusted the forces of the Imperium. The only thing they feared more than the Imperial Guard and the Space Marines were the powers of Khezal from whom they had fled.

'This place could blow up any second,' said Geryius. 'All it needs is a few heretics to stir up revolt and Tchepikov will have the whole camp bombed into ash.'

'These are the people for whom we fight,' said Orfos. 'We must never forget that.'

'These people would stab us in our beds given the chance,' said the driver. 'That's what I won't forget.'

The Chimera pulled up to one of the hab-blocks. Already,

the inhabitants had boarded up its windows with armour-plating and a slab of rusting steel stood in front of the doorway. Orfos jumped out. 'Stay here,' he said to Geryius.

Orfos hauled the slab away from the doorway. It was dark inside, and fearful eyes watched him from the shadows. He walked in, letting the slab fall into place behind him.

The hab-block was a dismal single-storey building, shoddily prefabricated and already home to what looked like dozens of people huddling in the bunks hanging from the walls. At the far end was a makeshift partition of rags. A few citizens, rather bolder than the rest, stood in front of it as if on guard.

Orfos approached. The men stood aside for Orfos, and he pulled the curtain back.

A man lay among rag-stuffed cushions, the most comfort the people here had been able to fashion for him. He was in late middle age, Orfos guessed, although it was difficult to tell given the strange greenish-grey tinge of his skin and the way his face hung, as if his bulk had been sucked out of him suddenly leaving him sagging and empty. His hair was greying and the skin of his neck, continuing down under the blankets that covered him, was pocked with raw and seeping wounds, like clusters of tiny bite marks.

The man looked up at Orfos and smiled.

'You have come,' he said.

'You let it be known,' replied Orfos, 'that you would speak only with a member of the Adeptus Astartes. I am here.'

'I cannot... I can trust no one else,' said the man. 'I have seen what happened to Opis. Sometimes it seemed I alone was aware. We were infiltrated slowly, man by man it seemed.

Oh, that vengeance has fallen on us! I welcome it. I wish only that I could have done something to bring it about sooner.'

'I must first ask,' said Orfos, 'who you are.'

The man held out a clenched fist. His trembling fingers opened to reveal a badge, such as might be pinned to the lapel of an adept's uniform to denote his rank. It was in the shape of a skull over a quill. 'My name is Lhossen,' he said.

'You are an adept of the Administratum,' said Orfos.

'I was, once. But no longer. I was… heh… I was rather lax in the upholding of my vows to the Imperium.'

'What did you do?'

'I stole rather a lot of money. Or rather, I tried to. I was found out, stripped of my adept status and marooned here, to await the return of the tithing mission and the imposition of my punishment. But the tithing mission did not come. You did, and with you, all the fires of the Emperor's fury. I still serve the Imperium, Space Marine. I am not a good man, but I am dying. My lungs are scarred with acid from the shells of your artillery. And in my final moments I will serve my Emperor.'

Orfos knelt by the dying once-adept. 'Then tell me what you know.'

'There is a legend of these people,' said Lhossen. 'Of the King of Crows.'

'I have heard of it,' said Orfos. 'It is a folk tale of Opis, one that Imperial intelligence thought might be used in propaganda against us.'

'Yes, it is true. The kindly robber, the master trickster, the fox! But it is true. I kept my ears open, Space Marine, all the time I was in exile here. The folklore of this world is more than folklore. The King of Crows is real, and he is here. I have heard tell that traitors among the refugees here are moving him through the camp to safety.'

'This King of Crows – is he a moral threat?'

'I believe so. Perhaps some demagogue native to Opis. Perhaps just a name adopted by one of the heretics in Khezal. But the name buys him loyalty from the malcontented among the citizens. He merely speaks it, and they seek to aid him. He is here, in the camp. It is death to speak of it to an outsider, but death has me already and I do not care.' Lhossen sat up, grimacing with the pain of it. 'Do you hear? I do not care! The King of Crows can take me, I have already given my soul to my Emperor!'

'Where is he?' said Orfos.

'Somewhere near. He cannot move in the open. Whatever he is, he must…'

Orfos held up a hand to silence Lhossen.

The sound he had heard, hidden among the chatter and construction of the camp, was the cocking of a weapon.

Orfos drew his own bolt pistol, unsheathing his combat knife with his left hand.

Bullets shredded the curtain of rags, and the air was filled with superheated lead. Lhossen was thrown against the back wall of the hab-block, body torn open, bored through with explosive fire.

Impacts shuddered Orfos's greaves and breastplate. A Scout's armour did not have the resilience of a full suit of power armour, but it held.

The gloom would have hindered anyone else, but Orfos's enhanced eyes could make out the figures advancing on him. They looked like any other refugees, save for the rags they wore around their faces and the autoguns and stub pistols they held. Six of them had made it into the hab-block, the citizens inside too terrified to even move to stop them.

In the first second or so, Orfos shot two of them: one in the head, the other through the upper chest. Explosive bolter shots against the unarmoured targets left an appalling mess of blood and shattered bone against the walls and ceiling. The others scattered, save for one who charged at Orfos, stub pistol blazing in his hand. Orfos trusted in his battlegear, felt a round impact against the chestplate of his armour, and rammed the combat knife into the man's abdomen. He felt the resistance as the blade met the spine.

Orfos dropped the body on the ground. The enemy were thrown back for the moment. He glanced back – Lhossen was dead, no doubt about that. Orfos left his curse unvoiced.

Orfos ran to the door of the hab-block, backing up against the doorframe. A body at his feet could have been any of the citizens here, any of the hundreds of thousands fleeing Khezal, or even of the millions on this planet. But this particular citizen had decided to give his life to the powers that ruled Khezal, in the hope of keeping the secrets of the King of Crows from the Imperial Fists.

People were running in every direction. Some were screaming. Orfos made out the face scarves of the attackers on a few and he snapped shots at them, uncertain if he hit them. The Chimera's engine was starting and Scout Geryius was manipulating the vehicle's mounted heavy stubber into position.

'Vengeance upon you!' yelled Geryius, and opened up with the heavy stubber. The hammering of the weapon drowned out the sound of panic and one of the shanties disintegrated, taking the gunman inside with it. Geryius panned the weapon around, shredding an alleyway between the shanties where two of the enemy had fled.

Orfos recognised the silhouette of a shoulder-mounted rocket launcher on the roof of a hab-block opposite. A rocket spiralled down before he could react, missing the Chimera by a metre or so and ripping a great explosion of dust and debris out of the mass of makeshift housing. Orfos sighted through the dust and shot the enemy down before he could reload. The body fell, and Orfos could see it wore the coveralls of a foundry worker, the same as thousands of the refugees in the Emperor's Embrace.

Geryius fired another burst into the people wandering dazed from the explosion. Some had guns in their hands and their faces covered. Some did not.

'Cease fire!' yelled Orfos. 'Geryius, cease fire!' He sprinted from the doorway and vaulted up into the Chimera's passenger compartment.

'See?' said the driver. 'They'd all have our bloody heads if they could! All of 'em!'

'Get us out of here,' said Orfos.

Gunfire pinged against the vehicle, sporadic and ill-directed. Orfos looked over the edge of the top hatch to see the wounded crawling away with limbs blown off; the dead with torsos or heads ruined. Some were the enemy, without doubt. Some were not. Some, he couldn't tell.

He could hear the panic and the anger spreading. Like a shockwave, like a virulent disease, it was rippling out through the Emperor's Embrace. The dead here would become martyrs in the minds of everyone who believed the Imperium were here to destroy and enslave. The guns in the hands of the enemy would become proof to the Imperial forces that the Emperor's Embrace was infested with heretics.

And the King of Crows?

Orfos would keep that to himself.

K-Day +4 Days
*Subjugation of traitor activity in the Emperor's Embrace refugee
camp*

Orfos watched from the hab-block rooftop at the train of
plague victims shambling through the winding, cramped
streets. They waded through makeshift open sewers and
piles of trash, past stacks of bodies and burning piles of
refuse.

The refugees made the signs of some native superstition
as they passed, calling to be protected against the disease
carried by the procession of the damned. The damned
themselves were shrouded in grave vestments taken from
the few refugees to have been given a proper burial, stained
with corpse liquor, their feet bound with rags and their faces
covered in hoods with nothing but torn eyeholes for features. About twenty of them were making their way through
the camp, picking up new members as they went, seeking
somewhere out of the way and uninhabited to die.

The disease rotted the insides, leaving organs a foul decaying mush.

And it left the lungs a heaving, pulpy mass full of writhing worms.

And it shrivelled the brain. And caused the spine to heat up and burn out through the victim's back. It drove them mad, too, and catatonic, all at once.

The disease itself had been the clue. Everyone knew what it did, but everyone knew something different. Each man and woman ascribed to the disease whatever fate they themselves feared most. If they feared going mad, that was how the plague killed. If they were religious, it was a moral disease that took hold through impure thoughts and killed by mimicking the wounds of saints. If they had family and friends, then the disease spread like a fire between close-knit groups.

There was no one truth, no one consistency. That was what had suggested to Orfos there was no disease. Or rather, there was no plague. There were plenty of diseases brought about by inadequate water supply and cramped living conditions, but those were all the same. They could be described and even treated, by medicae officers accompanied by units of Imperial Guard who watched the camp's population through the sights of a lasgun. But the plague was different. The plague was a fiction.

Orfos rolled to the edge of the hab-block roof, keeping his cameleoline cloak wrapped around him. He could see now the path the plague victim procession was taking – towards the north-western corner of the camp, in a winding path that kept them away from the guard towers manned by Imperial

Guard snipers, and through the concentrations of the most hostile refugees. The belief that the plague was a deliberate Imperial creation was widespread and the procession was viewed as a display of martyrdom by those refugees who hated the Imperium, a fact which did more than anything to keep Imperial scrutiny away from these shambling, doomed figures.

Orfos knew that he could not be completely invisible. He hid when he could, and when he could not, he went by night and let his silhouette stand out against the night sky. The people believed that an Imperial killer was stalking through them, eliminating those who spoke out against the Imperium. Orfos was certain he had been assumed the perpetrator of countless deaths and murders in the camp already. It was a legend that suited him. As long as he kept a distance between himself and the procession, the fiction was useful because it meant no one would approach him. People fled into their houses and murmured prayers of protection, and would not interfere.

If the plague was an invention, why had it been invented? Were these two dozen people, who were now trudging through pools of fuel-tainted mud, making their miserable journey to maintain the illusion that the Imperium had infected them? No. Some of them were genuine victims of disease who had joined the procession as it went, but Orfos had kept a count and noted that those who joined soon disappeared, vanishing in the shadows of the darkest streets, and the same core of plague victims continued. For such a deadly disease, the Emperor's Embrace plague did not seem to have killed those who had been walking with it for two days. The

Ben Counter

plague story was supposed to keep people away, to ensure safe passage through the camp, and to provide an excuse to shield the walkers' faces.

Orfos would have been willing to wager that the masks did not hide plague scars or hollow, dying eyes. This was how the traitors were moving themselves out of the camp, westwards towards the escape into the mountains that bounded the Battle Plains. No one stopped them, no one got close. Those who joined them suffered unquestioned deaths. The disguise was perfect. This was how the King of Crows was making his way to freedom.

The jungle of the Dvolian Coil, like a great sickle of emerald reaching out into a glittering ocean, shone beneath the *Sanctifier* so brightly it might have been painted. Four hundred kilometres south and an entire ocean away from Khezal, the second front for the battle of Opis was opening up far above the ground, between the wispy clouds and the bright green canopies of the jungle. The Dvolian Coil itself, a long curved peninsula notched with coves and inlets between sheer chasms of granite cliffs, had been the centre of an empire ruled by the Dvolian Navarchs. Once they had vied with Khezal for domination of the planet. The Coil and the city that served it, the metropolis of Rekaba, were home to ancient martial traditions that had never died even when the Dvolian Empire fell. For centuries the Navarchs, now absorbed into the structure of the Aristeia, had maintained their fleets and splendid armies as they had always done. Now the silken-sailed warships and grand parades were mostly for show, but that Naval prowess had developed into a mastery of flight and aerial warfare that the Aristeia had encouraged.

The fruits of that obsession, first with the sea and now with the sky, streaked up from a hidden airfield beneath the canopy, lighting up the warning runes in the *Sanctifier*'s cockpit.

'Heathen forces, eleven o'clock below us, five kilometres,' said Kebriones, scanning rapidly through the various tactical readouts in front of him. 'Approaching fast. Mach point four.'

'I see them,' said Gorgythion calmly.

Five bogies he counted in an instant, and then they were out of view, hurtling past below the *Sanctifier*. Gorgythion gauged their speed and manoeuvrability as he turned the gunship to get on their tails.

They were small. Fast. Probably much more aerobatic, at least at high speeds, than the gunship. In the brief glimpse he had they looked like single-seater fighters, probably dedicated interceptors with a loadout of cannon and air-to-air missiles.

'Dangerous in swarms,' he said.

'Does five count as a swarm?' asked Kebriones, barely registering the conversation as he ran through the many tactical views developing on his pict-screens.

'Not quite,' replied Gorgythion.

The enemy were still in formation, arcing upwards and turning as they did so, showing the shining purple and white of their upper hull designs. There was little need, evidently, to camouflage the fighters on the ground when they had the cover of the jungle canopy. Instead they proudly wore the colours of their squadron or of the noble house that paid for them, just as the *Sanctifier* wore the heraldry of the Imperial Fists.

'Apex on my mark,' said Kebriones.

Gorgythion aimed the *Sanctifier* down, as if to dive low and skim along the canopy. He wanted the enemy to think he was running. He wanted them to be grinning behind their oxygen masks, wagering one another who would win the ensuing chase.

'Mark,' said Kebriones.

At that moment, the enemy reached the apex of their climb and aimed down, diving towards the *Sanctifier*. Eager to get their name on the kill, they launched their missiles almost as one, as soon as the gunship was in their sights. Lock-ons barely registered before the missile launch warnings blared all over the cockpit. Gorgythion focused on a retinal rune and silenced them.

'Primus away,' he said, and flicked an arming and release switch.

One of the fragmentation bombs with which the *Sanctifier* was loaded dropped out of the weapons bay. Its fuse was short, far too short for safety. But the first lesson Gorgythion had learned in battle was that one does not win a dogfight by being safe.

The bomb exploded in the tree canopy. A great fountain of shredded wood shrapnel burst up in a dark hemisphere just behind the gunship. Suddenly overwhelmed with potential targets, the missiles streaked into the debris cloud and exploded, sharp blue-white bursts of radiation and flame impacting just above the jungle.

In the chaos and heat, the enemy fighters would be blinded. Masked by the smoke and heat radiation, the *Sanctifier* turned rather more quickly than a fighter could, its slow speed suddenly a virtue.

By the time the fighters passed overhead, Gorgythion's thumb was ready on the firing stud.

'Feast, *Sanctifier*!' he yelled as the fighters roared past the gunship. They could not see the gunship, but the gunship's machine-spirit, ancient and cunning, could see them.

The *Sanctifier* growled with hunger. Gorgythion had to rein it in for a second more, until his vision was full of the blue-white exhaust of the fighters rocketing past.

Gorgythion ordered the launch, and the belly of the *Sanctifier* blazed with fire. Five missiles burst out of their housings and arrowed upwards, the archeotech of the gunship's cogitator calculating millions of angles and velocities per second. The interlocking contrails of each missile created a burning spiral in the sky, caging the rearmost fighter even as the first missile ripped up through the rear edge of its right wing and blew it apart.

Explosions stuttered overhead. Three of the fighters were destroyed in the air, creating an expanding caul of burning debris. A fourth missile sheared a chunk out of its target's tail and the fighter fell away, flipping to one side and tumbling towards the canopy. It plunged through the mantle of leaves and a split second later, a column of fire and black smoke punched back up into the air.

The fifth missile missed. The *Sanctifier* howled in frustration and its engines leapt. Gorgythion wrestled the yoke back and kept the gunship on the fighter's tail as it looped back up and away to escape.

'Do we have the speed?' said Kebriones.

'His engine's flaring,' replied Gorgythion. 'He sucked in too much debris.'

The fighter's exhaust was sputtering, yellow shooting through the blue flame. The pilot was climbing and dropping to keep up airspeed. The *Sanctifier* followed in a straight line, keeping pace with the faster fighter.

'Rend, *Sanctifier*! Bring out your talons!' Gorgythion switched to the nose-mounted assault cannon and the swinging reticule lit up red on the viewscreen. Gorgythion fired and sprays of silver lashed out towards the enemy.

The enemy pilot was good. He kept the fighter moving in all planes, and only a few shots found their mark. A shower of burning metallic countermeasures sprayed out from the fighter's weapons bay, the viewscreen shuddering with static as they deflected the mundane sensors of the *Sanctifier*. But the gunship's archeotech included sensors that could see through anything the enemy might throw. The coughing of the engines, as Gorgythion forced them to maximum, sounded like a deep, mocking laughter.

Another burst of cannon fire kicked a spatter of black specks from the rear of the fighter. It was already hurt. It would not take much more to destroy it.

Below, the jungle clung to hills and valleys, creating a landscape that rose and fell like the waves of a green ocean. Spurs of rock broke the canopy, curved and gnarled like old fingers, arranged in clutches to form great stone cages. The fighter ducked through one and the *Sanctifier* whipped to one side to avoid it, buying the enemy pilot a half-second of distance over its pursuer.

Another cannon burst. This one missed, blowing the top knuckle off a stone finger.

One more shot. One more good burst and the enemy would fall.

A lash of blue-white energy whipped up from beneath the jungle canopy. It cut through the fighter, so rapidly it was gone before Gorgythion's eye could properly register what had happened. The fighter did not explode – it fell apart, bisected at an angle through the centre of its fuselage, spilling components as the two parts fell as dead weight into the canopy below.

'What was that?' said Gorgythion.

'No bogies in range,' replied Kebriones. 'It's blinded the sensors. The output was massive. It's an energy weapon.'

'Damnation, there isn't anything like that on this planet!' said Gorgythion, wrenching the *Sanctifier* around to avoid the area where the fighter had gone down. 'Must be on the ground,' said Kebriones.

Gorgythion could see the black tear in the jungle where the weapon had discharged. The trees were burning.

Ahead, columns of crackling blue energy punched up into the sky, pulses of electricity shuddering through the canopy. Half a dozen of them were suddenly burning ahead of the *Sanctifier*.

'They're everywhere,' said Kebriones. 'Behind us, too. We've flown into the middle of it.'

'Whatever it is,' said Gorgythion.

He slalomed the *Sanctifier* between the pillars of energy. With the sensors still blinded he had to do it all by eye. The runes on the viewscreen were blinking in and out and the instrument readings were spinning haywire. Crackles of power were playing across the surfaces of the cockpit, jumping between the cables overhead. One of the pict-screens in front of Kebriones cracked, spilling sparks over the Imperial Fist.

They were almost out. A few hundred metres further and the energy field ended, giving way to an expanse of jungle and beyond that, the ocean.

The *Sanctifier* bucked wildly. Air was suddenly shrieking around the cockpit. Gorgythion glanced back and in that fraction of a second noted that the cockpit door had blown out to reveal a huge section at the gunship's rear torn away. Through the back of the *Sanctifier* he could see the vivid blue of the sky and the green of the jungle hurtling by.

Gorgythion tested the controls. He still had command, just, though they were sluggish and feeble.

'I'm bringing us down!' he shouted over the howl of the wind.

This time Gorgythion saw the lash of energy coiling up towards him. It sliced just to one side of the gunship and he saw the *Sanctifier's* left wing ripped off, tumbling away from the craft. The gunship fell to one side as if rolling off a cliff and the canopy was rushing up towards Gorgythion's face.

He braced himself. The only thought he had as he fell was

that this was the only Shadowhawk in service, and if it was not recovered from the jungle floor, there would never be any more.

The *Sanctifier* hit the canopy. The last thing Gorgythion saw was a branch spearing through the viewscreen, impaling Kebriones through the throat and exiting through the back of his head.

Then the world spun around him and blackness fell, then Gorgythion felt nothing.

Lysander kicked his way through another wall of dry mud and human bones, and in the gloom his enhanced sight picked out walls of skulls staring back at him.

'I like this not,' said Brother Stentor.

'You like nothing,' replied Brother Beros. It was Beros who had taken up the flamer of the fallen Brother Apollonios, and he held the weapon in front of him now, the flame flickering at its tip. Apollonios's name was inscribed in the weapon's casing. Beros's lightning claw was clamped to the backpack of his armour. 'The enemy must fight us toe to toe down here. We see him dying! We smell him burning! What is there not to like?'

The catacombs beneath Rekaba were cramped and noisome. They would be close enough for normal soldiers, but the Imperial Fists barely fit crouched over into the corridors lined with burial niches. Miniature chapels at the junctions were decorated with domes of skulls and pillars of femurs, and underfoot the earth gave way into even older graves with bones that disappeared into dust under their armoured feet. Lysander's fire-team made as good speed as they could through the labyrinth, readings from Sergeant Kirav's auspex scanner keeping them closing in on their destination.

'They watch,' said Stentor. 'They seek to surround us.'

'If they attack us from behind we will just turn around,' said Beros. 'Let them come to us. I challenge them to try their hand. Slaves of the Dark Gods! Here is meat for you! Just lever us open and take it!'

'Stay focused, brethren!' snapped Kirav, his face lit pale green as he read from the auspex. 'We are the First! We are Imperial Fists!'

'How close are we?' said Lysander.

'Five hundred metres,' said Kirav.

'Ucalegon?' voxed Lysander. He was greeted only with static over the vox-channel. 'Curse these catacombs,' he said. 'Something is blocking the vox-traffic.'

'There!' hissed Stentor, peering down a side passage too narrow for a man to move along without turning sideways.

'Your imagination is your biggest enemy,' said Beros. 'We have troubles enough down here without–'

Stentor's bolter opened up, filling the close confines with strobing light and noise. Spindly shapes squirmed away down the passage, slick, silvery flesh illuminated in the gunfire.

'Watch the rear!' yelled Kirav. Stentor kept firing, churning up the walls of the passage. Clumps of dirt and shattered bone showered down. Brother Mortz crouched and turned, watching the passageway behind the Imperial Fists with his storm bolter levelled.

Lysander saw the creature flit out of view. Stentor's eyes were good. It would not do to let the thing get away.

Lysander raised his shield in front of him and charged towards the wall, gauging the angle of the thing's movement. He powered forward into the wall and through it, the compacted earth giving way in front of him. He burst into the space beyond and kept running, the massive weight of his Terminator armour careering through the labyrinth walls.

He burst into an open space. The floor was stone and an altar stood in the centre of it, with the image of a sun carved into its lid. On the altar squatted the enemy and Lysander saw that it might only generously be described as human.

Its torso was grossly elongated, resembling the body of a thick, muscular snake. Its skin was like that of a fish, scaled and silver. Its long arms and legs had too many joints and its feet had spindly fingers in place of toes. Its face was long and its features almost vestigial, with twin slits for a nose and narrow, sunken eyes.

Its mouth opened. Lysander glimpsed a bundle of bony spines in place of a tongue. Its eyes flared green and gills down the sides of its sinuous torso fluttered open.

Lysander held up his shield and dropped to one knee as the thing spat a hail of bone at him. The shards were propelled with such force they punched through, their points studding the inside of the shield. Lysander powered off his back leg and slammed into the creature, pinning it to the altar with his shield.

The creature writhed and hissed. Lysander could see nothing human remaining in its face. Whoever it had once been, he was long gone. Lysander raised the Fist of Dorn over his head and brought it straight down into the thing's face. Its skull was crushed flat and after a second it stopped thrashing about beneath him.

More of them were slithering around, just visible crawling rapidly along the ceilings and walls. Passageways radiated off from the altar room and the enemy seemed to be closing in, forming a noose around it and tightening.

Beros leapt into the room, vaulting over the altar and letting his flamer spit a tremendous gout of flame down one corridor. The skeletons in their niches were blasted to ash and Lysander could just see the creatures writhing there, stripped to their mutated skeletons by the intensity of the heat.

In the ruination behind Lysander, the rough tunnel formed by his charge, Brother Stentor wrestled with another. The thing had its body coiled around him. Stentor stunned it with a strike from the butt of his bolter, then drew his combat knife and slit a long wet wound along its belly. The thing thrashed as its organs spilled out into the dirt. As he rolled back to his feet Brother Mortz moved towards him, walking backwards, storm bolter spitting out bursts of fire.

They were everywhere. They crawled from the walls and ceiling. Scaly hands reached up from beneath the flagstones of the floor.

'Close in and bring the rage, my brethren!' yelled Lysander.

In his Terminator armour he was like a walking fortification, a lynchpin of the battlefield around which his fire-team gathered as if he were a tower to be defended. Mutants slithered towards them from every angle and were shot down by bolter fire, their long bodies split open and entrails spilled everywhere. Those that weathered the storm were slashed into bloody ribbons by lightning claw and combat knife, or slammed into the ground by the Fist of Dorn.

For a moment, they relented. Either their numbers were expended or they were regrouping to attack anew.

'Which damnable thing summoned these vermin?' spat Beros. 'Every abomination on this planet spawns its own breed of lackey.'

'We are close,' said Stentor, 'for it to break its followers against us.'

'Or it is stupid,' added Beros.

He was met with a deep rumbling, shuddering the whole catacomb. Clods of earth and old bones fell from the walls. Lysander crouched down instinctively, waiting for the next attack to strike home.

Darkness swarmed towards him. With the sound of a crashing wave it rushed through the corridors, and battered against Lysander's shield in a wall of pure black.

It was ink. A sea of ink, pouring through the catacombs.

'It knows we are here!' yelled Lysander. 'Now is the time to close! Forward, brethren! Forward!'

Lysander forced himself onwards through the surging tide. The ink was already waist-deep to a Space Marine. 'Up!' shouted Stentor over the rushing tide. 'We have to go up!'

Lysander realised Stentor was right. The ink was rising too fast. A Space Marine in full armour could fight underwater, but even his enhanced senses could not see enough to fight beneath the surface here. Lysander slammed his shield up into the ceiling and earth showered down over him, the skulls and femurs of disturbed burials clattering against his shoulder guards.

He had opened up a higher level of the catacombs, one that had perhaps not been disturbed since it had been filled with bodies and sealed. Lysander could see the walls encrusted with bone above him. He hauled himself up through the hole and scrambled into the upper level, reaching down to haul a battle-brother up after him.

The ink was still rising. A great torrent of it was emptying into the catacombs and soon it would breach this level, too. The fire-team made it out of the lower level and Lysander led them on, shouldering through what walls stood in his way, the bones of generations of Opis's dead crunching to dust under his feet.

Ahead was a wall, solid this time, part of a massive foundation sunk deep into the earth of Rekaba.

'Make ready to breach!' ordered Lysander. As the Imperial Fists stacked up alongside him, he saw their armour was smeared black from foot to shoulder.

Lysander swung the Fist of Dorn into the wall. The power field discharged with a sound like a lightning bolt and the stone blocks of the wall crumbled. The stagnant, ancient air of the catacombs was replaced by the stench of something rotting, like the desiccated heart of something vast and dead.

Ahead was the Sealed Wing of the Temple of the Muses, Rekaba's most secret and well-guarded place. Here were the family records of the Aristeia, their bloodlines and their secrets. Everyone who claimed membership of the Aristeia had to find proof here, among the sub-lines and usurpers who had turned the questions of inheritance and legitimacy into a labyrinth. A whole caste of Rekaba's citizens were trained to research the families of the Aristeia, to answer the hundreds of claims and counter-claims made every year.

Most of that caste's members were impaled, flayed and bloody, on glistening chains strung along the ceiling of the cavernous Sealed Wing. Their skins had been fashioned into banners upon which were carved red runes that squirmed and migrated, tumbling through one another to form an infinite variety of obscene curses in the tongues of the warp.

The bookcases that ran from floor to ceiling were half empty, their contents heaped up across the floor. Thousands upon thousands of books had been thrown down, and those that remained on the shelves were changed. They shuddered and growled, covers pulsing like cocoons full of some insect young, and blood ran down the shelves.

The books lying open at Lysander's feet were blank. Their words had been bled away to feed the great pool in the centre of the Sealed Wing, in which squatted the foulest thing he had yet seen on Opis.

The pool was full of ink, drained from the enormous totality of knowledge kept in the Temple of the Muses. Half-submerged in it was the creature that Imperial intelligence had tentatively identified as Skarkrave, sometimes known as the Black Sun, sometimes the Drinker of Thoughts. Skarkrave resembled nothing so much as a vast, half-developed foetus from the womb of some enormous, roughly humanoid alien. Its swollen cranium pulsed with dark veins loaded with stolen knowledge, and its wide, flat eyes were solid pools of bluish energy. The rest of its face seemed barely sketched onto its skull and its bent, feeble torso and vestigial arms suggested that what made it terrible was not any physical prowess, but whatever was contained within that misshapen skull.

Skarkrave the Black Sun was a sciovore – an eater of knowledge. The ink in which it bathed carried the information stolen from the Temple of the Muses, and it was absorbing every word, every secret, of the Aristeia.

The servants of Skarkrave, the serpentine mutants who had attacked the Imperial Fists in the catacombs, writhed through the ink or the remains of shredded books that formed drifts of stained pages at the edges of the Sealed Wing. They raised a hissing, shrieking din at the sight of Lysander striding through the broken wall, and swarmed over the massive body of Skarkrave yelping warnings into its half-formed ears.

Skarkrave's watery eyes turned towards Lysander. Lysander could feel the weight of its psychic interrogation as it sought a way into his mind. It felt like a great dark hand was crushing his consciousness, but his soul did not give. There were few minds in the galaxy that could break a spirit like Lysander's.

'Onwards!' shouted Lysander. 'These will all taste the wrath of Dorn!'

Lysander charged. He trusted in his battle-brothers to

take care of Skarkrave's attendants. He had to kill the moral threat before its psychic powers overwhelmed them. Speed and shock were his weapons here. He could not falter or pause, for the little information the Imperial forces had on Skarkrave emphasised the sheer scale of his mental abilities.

Lysander vaulted a heap of gutted books and batted aside the mutant who reared up at him with a swipe of his shield.

'You are Lysander,' said Skarkrave, the deep, crystal-clear voice resonating around the inside of his skull.

'Out of my mind!' yelled Lysander in response. Another few steps, closer, and he could see one of Skarkrave's spindly hands raised.

'Would that I could tell you, Captain Lysander, of why I am here.'

Skarkrave's eyes flared. Bloodstained spiked chains erupted from the floor in front of Lysander, aimed to impale and entangle. Lysander dropped to one knee and rolled, snapping the chains under his shield. He leapt over another, even as a gout of fire from Beros's flamer rippled over a handful of mutants scrambling out of the black pool towards him.

'I care not!' shouted Lysander. 'I care only that you die!'

'Would that I could give you their names, Lysander, so you might peel them open page by page, and tear their secrets from them,' continued Skarkrave. His voice was calm and unmoved, even as bolter fire exploded around him.

Lysander was in Skarkrave's shadow now. The floor beneath him split open into a great fanged mouth. Lysander leapt, hitting chest-first into the lip opposite, feet kicking out over nothing. The mouth ground shut and Lysander scrambled out of it, rolling away from the teeth as they gnashed closed underneath him.

'But I am bound, Imperial Fist! Ancient pacts were called upon and under them I only serve. My silence is compelled under pain of annihilation.'

'And silence is all you will know,' shouted Lysander. 'When I throw you back to the warp!'

'So many have promised,' said Skarkrave. 'Not yet have they delivered.'

Tentacles, black and rubbery, extruded themselves from the inky pool in front of Lysander. The First Captain ripped through them with a swing of his hammer. One wrapped around his leg and he kicked free, tearing the tentacle off at the root. It sprayed ink as it thrashed around and Lysander planted a foot on the edge of the pool, ready to leap.

'Such secrets I have,' said Skarkrave. 'I pray to my gods that I could tell you.'

'I said, begone from my mind!' Lysander leapt at Skarkrave. He covered the distance across the pool and thudded into Skarkrave's enormous body. The monster's rubbery flesh gave under his fingers as he tore handholds to climb up onto its shoulders.

Around the Sealed Wing, the Imperial Fists were butchering the mutants who attended on Skarkrave. Stentor slammed the head of one into a bookshelf, splintering its skull. Mortz's storm bolter cut down another two as they slithered along the walls. They had bought Lysander this chance. They had rewarded his trust. Now he had to repay it, for they trusted him in turn to finish this.

Lysander raised the Fist of Dorn.

'You want to know,' said Skarkrave. 'I can tell you. Spare me. Free me. All your questions will be answered.'

Lysander's answer came in the form of the Fist of Dorn arcing downwards, power field blazing blue-white as it fell. The hammer crunched into Skarkrave's skull and the power field blew its head apart.

Lysander fell back in the shower of bone and brain. Skarkrave's death cry was a long and terrible scream, a thousand voices pouring out of its fractured mind as all the secrets it had devoured poured out of it in a great gale of information. The whole Sealed Wing shook, the scholars' bodies falling from the walls, books raining down.

Lysander hit the floor. Skarkrave's body swayed above him, fountaining gore from its caved-in skull. It toppled to one side and the silence that fell was the signal that it was dead.

Lysander got to his feet and shook his head to throw off the worst of the gore. A few bolter shots sounded as Brother Stentor shot down the last of the mutants, the last resistance dying as it thrashed out its death throes.

'I heard it,' said Sergeant Kirav. 'It spoke of secrets. What did it mean?'

'Heed not its lies,' said Lysander. He switched to the vox. 'Ucalegon! Do you hear me, brother?'

<<I hear, captain!>> came Ucalegon's voice, distorted but recognisable over the vox. <<Resistance was heavy, but it falters.>>

'Skarkrave is destroyed,' said Lysander. 'Meet us at the Muses' Altar.'

<<It shall be so, captain.>>

Lysander led the fire-team through the wreckage of the Sealed Wing. Already Skarkrave's body was collapsing, as if decaying at an accelerated pace. Through an archway, flanked with statues of Aristeia scholar-lords, the rest of the Temple of the Muses opened up. It was strewn with the detritus of battle, dozens of bodies lying heaped up behind the makeshift barricades of overturned tables and the piles of smouldering books they had defended. Among them Lysander recognised the grey-and-black camouflage fatigues of the Subiacan penal legions. The enemy here were not so dramatically mutated as those in the Sealed Wing – they resembled the militia reported all over Khezal, a mix of household troops and compelled citizens armed with anything they could find in the armouries of the Aristeia.

Knots of surviving Subiacans stood, heads bowed, as they heard the prayers of the preachers who had accompanied them to battle. The prayers included the code-phrases that controlled the combat drug injectors implanted in each trooper's throat, and now the Temple of the Muses was won the injectors were flooding them with sedatives to rein in their instincts to kill.

The temple was mostly given over to museum and library wings, where the Aristeia stored their knowledge and the artefacts of their history. But it was also a place of worship, built on the site where offerings were left to the deities of Opis's past. Those remembered in the current incarnation of the temple were gods and goddesses of creation, art, heredity and nobility, and their images looked down from the stained glass that flanked the three walls of the altar chapel that nested in one corner of the temple. It had been defended by two ranks of Subiacans, relatively well-disciplined penal soldiers who had mown down the dozens of militia whose bodies littered the approach to the chapel. Even with their drug injectors keeping them calm, there was no doubting the fear, and a little anger, in their eyes as they saw the Imperial Fists walking through the devastation into the chapel.

'Champion of the Emperor,' said Lysander as he saw Ucalegon approaching the chapel. Squad Ctesiphon was with him, a unit from the Second Company who had been given the task by Lysander of supporting the Imperial assaults on Rekaba. Lysander's own fire-team went among them, and the Imperial Fists congratulated one another that the enemy in the Temple of the Muses was broken and that Skarkrave was dead.

'It is good it was us who broke this place,' said Ucalegon. 'The Guard will soon fortify it and turn it into their forward base in this area. We might not have had the opportunity to recover any evidence then.'

'Then let us do so now,' said Lysander.

'Many men died here,' said Ucalegon. 'We would have fought over it sooner or later, but it was our word that saw it assaulted when its defenders were still at full strength. This Serrick woman's information had better be worth it.'

'If it is not,' said Lysander, 'she will never leave Opis. I think she knows that.'

The altar at the back of the chapel was a stone block carved with the symbols of the various arts – quills, actors' masks, draughtsman's tools and paintbrushes. Lysander knelt before it and examined the lid, on which the Aristeia had been accustomed to leave offerings of gold and artworks before war had come to Opis.

'Captain,' said Ucalegon. 'Could there be secrets on this world to uncover that are not to anyone's benefit?'

'Quite possibly,' said Lysander. 'Many secrets bring only suffering. But that does not mean the truth should go on being hidden. The truth is its own justification, is it not?'

Lysander levered the top off the altar. The stone slab came away, revealing the hollowed-out interior of the altar, in which was a small decorated box. Lysander picked up the box – it seemed tiny and delicate in his armoured hand.

'This is it,' he said. 'This is what Serrick hid here before she was caught. This is proof.'

Lysander carefully opened the box. Inside was a single bullet.

Lysander held the bullet up close to his eye.

'What is it?' asked Ucalegon.

'I shall have to ask Serrick for confirmation,' said Lysander, 'but I suspect it is the bullet that killed Inquisitor Kekrops.'

<<Captain!>> came a voice over the vox. <<Ctesiphon here. The Guard snipers are reporting a large enemy concentration moving along the canals to our north. They wish to make a proper fight of this place, it seems.>>

'What reinforcement have we en route?' replied Lysander. He put the bullet back in the box and pocketed it in one of the ammo pouches on the waist of his armour.

<<Five thousand Deucalians,>> came the reply. <<On their

way from the Basilica Prime. And the landing zone is established in the parade ground east of here, so the Navy should give us support from the air.>>

'Then we will hold,' said Lysander. He closed the vox and turned to face the two squads of Imperial Fists at the chapel entrance. 'Brothers! Hear your commander. We have struck a blow and the enemy is reeling. They are angry, and in their rage they will lash out at us for revenge. But we have with us the guns of the Imperial Fists, and the blade of the Emperor's own champion! Then let the enemy come! We will bleed Rekaba white, and when the traitors around us can fight no more, we will hunt down their leaders and do to them what we did to Skarkrave. Prepare defences! Break down your zones of fire! This place will withstand as if its foundations were laid by Dorn himself!'

Sergeants Ctesiphon and Kirav began organising the Imperial Fists, sending the battle-brothers in twos and threes to cover the approaches to the temple. The Subiacan preachers began their order-sermons and the cogs of battle began to turn again. The killing was not yet done.

'What is happening on this world?' asked Ucalegon. 'Truly, Lysander? What is happening?'

'Set these questions aside, Ucalegon, and let Dorn's ways of battle replace them. When the killing lets up, then we will find the answers.'

Already Lysander could hear the chanting from the canals, thousands of voices raised in celebration of the dark powers who had infiltrated their world. He could hear the engines of the vehicles the Deucalians were driving, too, and the distant screams of fighter-bomber engines overhead.

Another battle. One of a hundred opening up on Opis. Behind it all lay a pattern, maddening and elusive, that might stop the fighting or make it a hundred times worse. That would all have to wait until the Temple of the Muses was quiet again.

'Every day,' said the first soldier, 'there are more. When will they stop?'

The first soldier took the feet of the next corpse, and the second took the arms. Together they heaved the body into the pit. It was a natural ravine, shaded by the jungle canopy so the darkness inside almost hid the heap of bodies that had already built up at the bottom. The insects, fat and bloated on blood and decaying meat, hung in a cloud over the hole. Both soldiers wore full hazardous environment suits, decorated with the heraldry of House Krix of Rekaba, to protect from the stench and infections carried by the insects. The first soldier was taller, with a long face and red hair visible through the suit's faceplate. The second was darker and powerfully built, with meaty arms and hands that made light work of stocking the ravine with fresh dead.

'There are only so many people in Rekaba,' said the second soldier. 'They'll stop.'

'When?'

'When they run out, or when people learn.'

There were still a good thirty bodies heaped up beneath the trees. They had been dumped there that morning, as evidenced by the vehicle tracks still glistening in the jungle mud. They were traitors to the Aristeia. They were as varied as the living who now fought the invaders in the streets of Rekaba.

'Could be worse, I suppose,' said the first soldier. 'Could be back in the city. Saints know what we might be turned into then.' The two stooped and picked up another body. This one was a woman.

'How old do you think she is?' said the first soldier, looking at the relatively unblemished face. It was just possible to put aside the glassy eyes and thick bloodstain on the front of her dress, and imagine what she once looked like.

'Does it matter?' said the second, and hauled the body into the ravine by himself. He stood, arms out. 'What does any of that matter? What do you think is happening on this planet?'

'That's the problem!' retorted the first soldier. 'No one knows! You have seen what they're turning us into back in the city. Do you know what they're saying about the people in charge? It's not the Aristeia any more. They're sorcerers and mutants! We don't know who we're fighting for. No one does.'

'We fight because we fight,' said the other soldier. 'That's the way it has always been. Every man has his place on Opis. Some fight, some work, some rule. We fight. We were born into it. When you question that, it all falls apart. That was why these people were executed. If it gets out of control it's nothing but chaos.'

'And those people who have been turned into something else? I saw them fighting at Daggerfall Park. They didn't even know their own names. They were walking bombs, psychic bombs. What if that was us? Would you have been born for that, too?'

'You think the Imperium is any different? Once we stop fighting they'll seal off the cities and virus bomb us. That's how they deal with anyone who doesn't kneel to the Throne.'

The first soldier pointed at the second, the work of dumping the bodies forgotten for the moment. 'Maybe it would be better to die like that than live like those things in the city.'

'Really?' The second soldier drew his autopistol from its holster. 'You can die right now if it's all the same to you. Just stand at the edge and I won't even have to bother throwing you in.' He took aim at his fellow soldier's chest.

The second soldier froze. The noise behind him had been barely enough to register, but it was enough. He looked slowly around.

The figure in the jungle had been trying to conceal itself, but it was far too big to be completely hidden. The sound had come from branches breaking as it crept forwards, again too big to be silent.

Its armour was gold, streaked with mud, and it must have been two metres high even half-crouched in the foliage. In the shadows, a face stained with mud stared out, eyes narrowed.

The second soldier aimed at the figure in the jungle. In the time it took him to bring the weapon to bear the armoured man had lunged from his hiding place and dived onto the soldier, tackling him to the ground and pinning him down in the mud. A massive armoured hand grabbed the back of the suit's hood and ripped it open. His second hand grabbed the soldier by the face and snapped his head around. The sound of his spine coming apart was a sharp crack, like a distant gunshot.

The first soldier fumbled with his own autopistol. The catch on the holster was pinned closed, to keep the gun slipping out as he worked.

'Don't,' said the armoured man.

The soldier got the gun out.

The armoured man took a combat knife from his waist. In anyone else's hand it would have been as long as a short sword. With a smooth motion he drew and threw it, and the blade punched through the soldier's sternum. The soldier took a couple of steps back, gun still in his hand, and fell backwards as his brain caught up with the fact that he was dead.

Brother Gorgythion waited in the sudden silence for more men to emerge from the jungle. But they didn't. He stood up, dropping the body of the soldier whose neck he had just broken. He looked down at the heap of bodies they had been disposing of. From their conversation, he guessed that the dead had been executed by the forces of the Aristeia – in the eyes of whatever ruled Opis through the Aristeia, they were traitors and deserters. They had bullet wounds in the backs of their heads.

Gorgythion took the autopistols from the dead soldiers and rifled through their pockets for extra ammunition. His own weapons had been lost when the *Sanctifier* crashed. Gorgythion himself had been forced to crawl from the wreckage, the cockpit crumpled around him and the fuel igniting as he struggled out. He had left Kebriones in the wreckage, and his body had burned. At least he had been dead before that. Kebriones's gene-seed was lost, however, the organ that regulated his many augmentations and the symbol of the Chapter's connection with their primarch, and it would be greatly lamented that it had not been returned for implanting into a new Space Marine.

Through the jungle canopy were just visible the towers of Rekaba. Gorgythion had only seen the city before from the air – its pale stone and red-tiled roofs leapt out from the jungle surrounding it, and the glittering ocean on which it sat. It was a place of antiquity and history, one of the historical power bases of Opis, and no doubt it was being torn apart by the Imperial invasion at that very moment. Gorgythion knew that Lysander had a force of Imperial Fists in there, somewhere, and that he had to get to them.

On one of Gorgythion's greaves was inscribed a crude map he had scratched, showing the location of the installation whose defences had shot down the *Sanctifier*. The Imperium didn't know it was there. Neither, judging by the destruction of the Aristeia fighter plane, did the natives of Opis. And someone was most determined to keep its location secret.

The jungle was darkening as the sun was dipping below green-covered hills. The noise of the jungle changed at night as the nocturnal creatures came out. Gorgythion had seen prowling lizard-like creatures that were rather larger than a man and could climb the trees, and aerial hunters that looked like bundles of stinging tentacles trailing from a series of delicate sails. The soldiers here had left a previous day's work unfinished because they had been afraid to spend the night out here.

Gorgythion pulled the combat knife from the corpse of the soldier.

'You don't know,' he said to the body as the blade came free. 'You're as blind as the rest of us. You are traitors and you must be fought. We will not relent. But we will also discover what turned you into this, before more are turned from the light.'

No reply came from the dead soldier's mouth, which lolled open as Gorgythion let the body flop back down into the mud. Then Gorgythion turned to the outline of Rekaba, silhouetted in the silver-gold light of the dusk, and began the rest of his journey to rejoin his brothers.

The temperate plains had given way to the cold of the mountains. The air had dropped off quickly in oxygen levels and temperature as the squad had ascended into an intermediate layer of the atmosphere, for the richest air clung tightly to Opis's surface as if afraid it would dissipate into space. A Space Marine's lungs could cope easily enough, and his hyper-oxygenated blood was more than up to the task of keeping altitude sickness at bay. The cold did not bother him, either, for those same systems kept his extremities safe from numbness or frostbite.

But there was something still inhospitable about those ridges of reddish-black stone, the peaks and valleys like a great stony scab covering a wound in the planet's surface. It was less easy for Scout-Sergeant Orfos to put his finger on just why it was such an unfriendly landscape in which to hunt, but its menace was still there.

The King of Crows must have been desperate indeed to flee through here. Orfos had followed a trail that consisted mostly of the dead – members of the plague procession who had broken limbs in falls or succumbed to the conditions, and been left to die. They had no sign of any plague upon them. Indeed, many had the manicured nails and fine teeth of the Aristeia. A few even had jewellery they could not bear to part with. Orfos had been right. Someone powerful and dangerous had escaped Imperial forces via the Emperor's Embrace refugee camp, and the Aristeia were helping him do it.

At that moment Orfos lay on the reverse edge of a ridge that formed part of the downward slope of the last mountain his squad had negotiated. The mountain fell away below into a deep valley in which the ice had not thawed from that winter – perhaps it had never thawed down there, where the sun could not quite reach. He scanned for movement, letting the superior peripheral vision of a Space Marine cover the whole valley.

'Anything?' Orfos asked.

The surface of the rock beside Orfos shifted, revealing the face of Scout Enriaan where it had been hidden by the cameleoline cloak lain over him. Enriaan wore a magnocular visor, which let him focus on specific areas as Orfos scanned the whole valley. 'There's another body down there,' he said. 'Robed, like the procession. Decent boots, though.'

'They are shedding members more quickly,' said Orfos. 'How many is your count?'

'They have lost twelve,' replied Enriaan. 'They have nine left.'

<<My kind of fight,>> came Geryius's voice over the squad's vox-link. Instinctively, Orfos looked across the valley to a bank of loose flinty shards clinging to the opposite side, where he knew Geryius was concealed. <<We can let the enemy kill themselves.>>

'My kind of fight is the one where we take the enemy alive before anything can do for them,' replied Orfos. 'I want the King of Crows, brothers, and I do not mean as a trophy to take back to the *Wings of Dorn*.'

A long, low sound raked across the mountain peaks, changing pitch as it approached. A flight of two Imperial Navy fighters ripped across the sky overhead, leaving white contrails against the vivid cold sky.

'If Tchepikov thinks the enemy are using these mountain passes, they'll bomb them,' said Orfos. 'We might never find the King.'

<<If there's a King of Crows to find,>> said Geryius.

'You believe there isn't?' said Orfos.

<<I believe,>> replied Geryius, <<we should not be surprised if we are just trailing a band of refugees fleeing the camp.>>

'You certainly gave them enough to flee from, brother,' said Orfos.

'Refugees with electoos that cost more than a commoner is worth,' said Enriaan. 'And xenos-hide hiking boots.' If he intended any humour or sarcasm, it did not touch the inflection of his words.

<<We're clear to the front,>> voxed Vonretz from down the valley. He, too, was invisible to the naked eye, concealed

among the boulders deposited along the valley bed by glaciers an age ago.

'Move up,' said Orfos. 'No silhouettes. Enriaan, watch behind us.'

Orfos kept his cloak wrapped tight, its brown and grey colours shifting to mimic the pattern of the stone around him. Enriaan snapped his visor up and shouldered his sniper rifle, walking carefully backwards to keep watch to the rear. The squad moved down the valley, Orfos keeping them moving quickly. Even though they moved as quietly as they could Orfos winced at the sound of stones falling down the valley sides as they walked. He saw Vonretz up ahead, moving between the fallen boulders, keeping ahead of them.

Orfos felt the blast a moment before he heard it, and his muscle memory was already throwing him down to the slope beneath without thinking. The side of the valley just ahead erupted into a great reaching claw of darkness, the concussion slamming against him. Orfos tumbled, deaf and blind, sharp rocks lashing at him as he tumbled down the slope.

He fought the ringing in his ears. A deep rumble reached through the shock and Orfos knew the side of the valley was coming down. The soldier's instinct, both sleep-taught and hammered into him on the battlefield, took over and he was running. Rocks fell on a tide of shattered scree that flowed like liquid down the valley. Orfos was scrambling away from the collapse, and more by instinct than choice he grabbed a handful of Enriaan's cloak and dragged the Scout behind him.

The collapse was knee-deep when it was spent. A thick

plume of smoke and dust rolled over it, and the valley darkened as if the sun had gone down.

'Report!' shouted Orfos into the vox. 'Report!'

'I am unhurt,' said Enriaan beside him.

<<And I, sergeant,>> voxed Geryius.

'Privar!' voxed Orfos. 'Vonretz!'

The shape of Scout Privar emerged from the swirling darkness, clutching his left arm. 'A broken humerus, sergeant,' he said. 'Nothing more.' Orfos saw Privar was dark grey from head to toe with dust and grime from the explosion.

'It's an ambush,' said Orfos. 'Be ready, brothers! Eyes everywhere! Vonretz, report, brother!'

Geryius half slid down the intact slope and ran to where Vonretz had been, which was now deep in pulverised rock.

Orfos drew his bolt pistol and scanned the valley ridges. 'How in the hells did they get around us?' he growled. 'They knew we were here. All the way, they knew.'

The first gunshot fell among them before the dust had cleared enough for a decent aim. A bullet pinged among the rocks, followed a second later by the report from high up.

'I am on it,' said Enriaan, rolling onto his front with his rifle in front of him.

Orfos ran up the slope towards the source of the shot, keeping low, using the folds and breaks in the rock for cover. He wiped a hand over his eyes to get the worst of the grime out. He half spotted movement on the ridge above, and the corresponding shot from Enriaan's rifle. He could not tell if his fellow Scout had hit anything.

Geryius was still below, digging with his hands in the loose stone. He couldn't see Privar among the falling masses of dirt.

Orfos could see more clearly now. Nothing above him. The top of the ridge was a short sprint away. He put his head down and ran. The doctrines of the Space Marines taught that a battle-brother was safer the closer he was to the enemy, where his greater strength, his training, his force of will, counted for the most. A Space Marine was not trained to be a speck in anyone else's gunsight.

Orfos reached the ridge. He dropped to his belly. The ridge looked across to a great tumult of upheaval, where thousands of years ago pressures in the planet's crust had formed jagged spikes that stuck up in every direction, a pathless mass of mountain which looked like it never ended.

Right in front of him, from the reverse slope of the ridge, lurched a human form swathed in plague-stained rags. Orfos sized it up in the split second it took for it to reach him. Its head and upper torso were horribly swollen, forming a single neckless lump giving it an awful, top-heavy outline. Asymmetrical eyes rolled through tears in the green-black rags. In one clawed hand, wrapped in sodden greyish flesh like that of a drowned man, was the long-barrelled autogun he had used to snipe at the Scout squad.

Orfos blew a fist-sized hole in the mutant at point-blank range with his bolt pistol. The exit wound, rather larger, was a fountain of greyish flesh erupting from the mutant's back.

The mutant's upper torso split open like the egg sac of a giant spider. Segmented limbs unfolded in a shower of colourless, lumpy gore that spattered down over Orfos.

Each limb ended in a blade. Not a talon, but a blade, a knife or a piece of hammered metal, forced between the split end of each limb and tied closed like a primitive's spear.

Orfos ducked as the mutant slashed at him. His combat knife sliced over his head and took off a limb. The limb thrashed and sprayed blood like a water hose. Orfos dived into the mutant, tackling it to the ground, forcing his weight down onto it. It reached up at him, one blade carving a long line of pain across his face and another punching into the flesh of his upper arm.

Orfos had the bolt pistol barrel up under what remained of the mutant's ribs. He blew another two holes in it, even as an eye rolled up to stare at him from the innards crowding its sundered chest.

'Whatever you are,' snarled Orfos, forcing his knife up out of the mutant's grip, 'I am the last thing you see.'

He rammed the knife down into the mass of organs. There had to be something in there it could not do without. He tore the blade out again and plunged again and again, and each time a fibrous wreck of tissue and bone was thrown out.

The mutant stopped moving, save for a few hindbrain spasms that kept its limbs twitching. 'Brothers!' Orfos gasped into the vox. 'Eyes about us! There will be more.'

He kicked himself free of the mutant's wrecked body. He looked down into the smoke-choked valley. Enriaan and Privar were emerging from the smoke and running up the slope. Geryius was behind them, covered in grime and smoke dust.

'Vonretz?' voxed Orfos.

'We should have razed the camp!' yelled Geryius. 'We

should have killed the whole damn lot of them! I'd have lined them up myself!'

'Brother, focus!' ordered Orfos. 'We are beset by enemies!'

'Enemies we could have killed days ago! What cost would a camp full of scum have been, to kill the traitors among them?' He pointed up at the two Naval fighter-bombers just visible over the opposite ridge as they made a return pass. 'One payload from a bomber and these filth would have burned in the mud!'

'You forget why we are here!' snapped Orfos. 'Even in the claws of wickedness, we fight for the humanity that bore us!'

Orfos's eyes did not leave the pair of fighter-bombers. Something about their path caught his attention and would not let go.

One spiralled off path. It fell, caught in a flat spin, dropping out of view as sparks showered from the control surfaces of its wings.

The other kept on course, ignoring the loss of its twin. A few seconds later and the sound of the first fighter's crash reached Orfos's ears, a rumbling, shattering boom in the distance.

'Scatter!' yelled Orfos. 'Scatter! Strike incoming!'

The fighter-bombers were compromised. One of the pilots had survived the attempt to take his craft over – perhaps, of the pair of pilot and co-pilot, only one was a traitor and in their struggle they had thrown the fighter-bomber into a spin from which it could not recover. The other had been taken over cleanly. The many scenarios that flashed through Orfos's head all ended in one fighter lost and one compromised, its mission to wipe out the Scouts tracking the pilot's fellow traitors through the mountains.

Orfos leapt over the crest of the ridge, leaving the mutant's torn corpse where it lay, and slid down the scree slope on one hip. Enriaan and Privar were not far behind. Privar slipped and fell, rolling end over end and yelling as his broken arm was forced further out of shape.

Orfos was on his feet and running. A cleft in the rock ahead formed the entrance to a pitch-black cave. It was impossible to tell how far in it went, or whether a Space Marine Scout could force his body all the way in at all, but it was the only shelter anywhere near.

He looked back. Geryius was silhouetted at the top of the ridge as the fighter boomed over, dangerously low, fast and straight as an arrow. A shower of black specks fell from it into the valley.

Cluster munitions. A hundred bomblets detonated at once. The valley exploded in flame. Geryius was lit up and thrown off his feet, hurled off the ridge down the slope. The valley shook and a wave of darkness was vomited up into the air. Orfos dived into the cave, the other two Scouts close behind him. Rogue bomblets were falling everywhere, sharp cracks bursting somewhere overhead, each followed by a shaking like an earthquake. The sound of the mountains themselves complaining, a terrible creaking and cracking from far below, shuddered the ground.

Orfos could see Enriaan and Privar in the entrance behind him, Geryius scrambling down the slope, as debris rained down as thick as a blizzard. Beside Privar, tucked up against the opening in the rock, was a body. It was human, wrapped in the same robes the King of Crows and his cohorts had worn since they escaped from the Emperor's Embrace. The feet were bloody and torn, wrapped only in red-soaked bandages. A single bullet wound glinted in the back of the head.

'There,' said Orfos, over the pattering of stone on stone from outside. 'A straggler. He was slowing them down. They executed him, and the blood is not dry yet. They went this way.'

Geryius made it into the cave. His face was streaming with blood from the wounds to his scalp caused by the falling shards of stone.

'He's gone,' said Geryius. 'The sons of dogs. Vonretz is gone. I couldn't find him.'

'Focus, brother, and avenge him,' said Orfos. 'We cannot pause to pay our respects now. We move. With me.'

The caves spiralled into the mountain, cramped, wet and pitch-black. Chill wind howled through them as if through the pipes of a flute. Orfos moved as fast as he could, shouldering through confines almost too cramped for a hunched-over human let alone a Space Marine.

Vonretz was dead. Nothing could change that now. But the mission could still succeed. The King of Crows could still be brought in, alive, and the truth about the war on Opis could be wrestled from him. Orfos told himself this as he stepped knee-deep in freezing water, an underground stream rushing through the heart of the mountain.

Light strobed. Gunfire hammered out, echoing against the walls of the many-chambered cavern that opened up above the Scout squad. Orfos half glimpsed ragged figures with autoguns aimed down at him and opened fire, shooting down one with a burst of bolt pistol fire. Another was lost in the shadows.

The Scouts splashed past him. 'You take one brother, you must take us all!' yelled Geryius, and rattled off half a magazine at the shelves of dripping rock.

A grenade splashed into the water. Orfos dived against one wall and stone showered against him, opening up cuts on his face and hands. But it was nothing that would slow him down.

A mutant lurched from the water, its form skeletal and its face a skull wrapped in dripping muscle, its hands talons. Orfos picked it up, folded it backwards, felt its spine come apart and rammed it down into the stone floor. Its skull crunched and it fell still.

A chainblade whirled. In the darkness Orfos could gauge its location, arrowing towards Enriaan, but Enriaan turned the blade aside with the body of his sniper rifle and threw a crunching elbow into the ribs of the attacker. Orfos barely glimpsed scaled skin and bony spines as Enriaan slid a combat knife up into the mutant's chest and carved it open from navel to neck.

Privar was backed up against one wall, peering into the shadows overhead, looking for targets.

'Onwards!' yelled Orfos. 'They want us trapped down here! Onwards, and bring the fight to them!'

Gunfire spattered down. Impacts cracked off the back of Orfos's Scout armour as he sought a way out. Ahead, groping almost blindly, he found a cleft through which the stream was rushing. Chest-deep now, he followed it into utter darkness. Even a Space Marine's eyes could not see. Geryius was still firing, and Orfos could tell it was at random.

'Geryius, follow!' shouted Orfos. 'Enriaan, bring him! Bring him!'

Geryius swore and fought as Enriaan almost dragged him into the darkness. The sound of the rushing water was louder here, and Orfos fancied that more than one stream converged in the freezing waters that swirled up to his shoulders.

Light glimmered ahead, catching the foaming water. Orfos could see sky through a crack in the rock.

The mutants had been posted there to slow the Scouts down, in case the traitors on the fighter-bombers failed to kill them. They were protecting something. That something was the King of Crows, Orfos knew it. He had to push on, he had to pursue. He knew that he was close. The desperation in the enemy's tactics was obvious now. They were throwing their lives away to buy time for the King to escape. But there was not enough time to escape an Imperial Fist when he had an enemy's scent.

Orfos lost his footing on the slippery rock. He tumbled out into the light on a rushing tide. He rolled onto his front and saw that the underground river emerged onto a rocky ledge overlooking an endless expanse of mountains, as if the land itself had been torn up by a giant hand. The water spilled, fast and shallow, over the ledge into a waterfall that plunged out of view.

One of the ragged plague victims was waiting for the

Scouts. Orfos's hand was quicker. His bolt pistol was up and he just had time to recognise the fatigues, webbing and body armour of an elite Aristeia household trooper before he put two bolt-rounds into the soldier's chest. The soldier took a couple of steps back and fell over the edge, off the ledge and out of sight.

Orfos glanced left and right. He saw movement to the left, where the remainder of the plague procession was hurrying out of sight. Orfos ran after them, splashing through the rushing water and fighting to stay on his feet.

He backed up against an outcrop of rock and checked his bolt pistol's load. He had two shells left in the magazine. He took out a new magazine to swap it in.

Before he could reload, a shadow fell over him. It was a horror in tattered skin, wings spreading. Tentacles hung from its chest and abdomen, snaring around Orfos's face and neck as it glided over him.

Orfos was on his back in the water before he could think; head bound, unable to breathe. His pistol was out of his hand as he grabbed at the tentacles wrapping around his face. He turned over, feeling them bunch up and entwine, and with all the strength he had he tore them free.

He heard a scream. The freezing water was suddenly warm for a moment as blood poured out of the thing's torn chest. Orfos was up out of the water, gasped down a desperate breath, and saw the mutant rearing up over him. Its wings were stretched across bony spines spreading from behind its shoulders, its skin was a slimy grey-black and its face was split in two by a vertical mouth. It had three eyes, the one in the centre of its forehead a red sphere without a pupil. Its chest and stomach were a ruined mess, the stumps of its snaring tentacles oozing gore. Bony blades speared out from its elbows, dark with long-dried blood.

Orfos leapt on it, knocking it back with his weight. He grabbed one wing and wrenched it, feeling the spines break and the membrane of skin tearing.

Then he dropped to one knee, grabbed a wrist and ankle, and lifted the winged mutant out of the water. He spun and let go, hurling the thing off the edge of the waterfall.

Its good wing tried to flap, to keep it aloft, but it could do nothing but spin as it fell over the waterfall. Orfos could hear it shrieking, like a bird of prey with a victim in sight, the sound falling away as it fell.

Orfos was aware of Geryius and Enriaan struggling onto the ledge through the freezing torrent. But Orfos was too close now. He couldn't pause, not when the King of Crows had thrown so much into stopping him here.

Orfos jumped over the rock and saw, on a narrow path winding off down the mountainside, the King of Crows.

Orfos had not known what he would see when he came face to face with the King of Crows. He could not stop various images pressing their way into his imagination – a towering being with a crown of black feathers, a man without a face or a form, a regal man enrobed and dripping with gold. But he had forced them all out and left his mind open, so he would not be led astray by a preconception about what the King of Crows actually was.

Even so, it was no surprise at all to be looking into the face of Lord Speaker Kallistan vel Sephronaas.

Orfos had last seen that meaty, finely-bred face on the pict-broadcast vel Sephronaas had sent to the Imperial forces. Now he was without his periwig or the robes of a Lord Speaker of the Aristeia, and wore the drab fatigues of a household soldier, but it was unmistakably the same man. He even had the translator with him, the mousy scrap of a woman crouching behind him like a whipped dog. Even on the run, forced to scrape and crawl like a rat through the Emperor's Embrace camp, vel Sephronaas had not been willing to give up the one luxury, his translator, that marked him out as living in a different world to the masses of Opis.

Vel Sephronaas, the King of Crows, froze as he realised he was face to face with Orfos. Vel Sephronaas was a large man but Orfos was far, far taller. And though he did not have his bolt pistol with him, the combat knife that Orfos drew was more than enough to slice the Lord Speaker of the Aristeia clean in two.

'You need not die,' said Orfos. 'You need not even suffer. Give yourself to the Imperial Fists. It is over.'

Impossibly, vel Sephronaas smiled. 'You really know nothing, do you?' he said. He used Low Gothic instead of the Aristeia's own language. 'What does suffering mean to me? What does death mean, when I have seen what I have seen?

Orfos took a step closer. 'Lord Speaker. It is over.'

'It was over before you got here,' came the reply. 'When you walk into the hell they have prepared, it will be over for you, as well.'

'Who are they?' said Orfos. 'Who rules Opis? If not the

King of Crows, who has done this to your world?'

Vel Sephronaas laughed, and Orfos knew it was a cover for something. Vel Sephronaas was drawing a weapon from the webbing of his fatigues. Orfos recognised the shape of a plasma pistol before it was out, and had weighed up the distance between him and vel Sephronaas. A Space Marine with a combat blade could lunge and kill, creating a long lethal distance, but vel Sephronaas was a step or two too far away. Orfos would be shot before he struck home.

Orfos jumped back, rolling over the rock behind which he had taken cover a few moments before. The first plasma shot boiled away half the rock and Orfos was forced back by the wave of superheated air.

He hit the water. There was gunfire all around. Orfos realised that Privar and Geryius were swapping gunfire with troopers on the other side of the ledge. Enriaan was wrestling with something down in the foam.

Vel Sephronaas was aiming at Orfos, the plasma pistol in his hand glowing as its power coil recharged.

Orfos plunged his hand into the water. It closed on the butt of his bolt pistol.

It had two shots left. Orfos only needed one.

Orfos aimed and fired, and blew the upper half of vel Sephronaas's head off.

Orfos turned and saw Enriaan slitting the throat of the trooper he was wrestling with. Another was stumbling back, chest blown open by Privar's pistol. Geryius had the last of them in a headlock and Orfos could hear the wrenching snap as he broke the soldier's neck.

The only sound was the rushing of the waterfall and the wind through the mountains.

Vel Sephronaas's body was still upright. Everything above the upper jaw was gone.

'That's the King of Crows?' said Geryius.

'It was,' said Orfos, approaching the body carefully. There was nothing to say vel Sephronaas wasn't a mutant himself, one who kept his brain somewhere other than his skull.

A prickling on the back of his neck was all the warning Orfos had, and it wasn't nearly enough.

The shot whistled past him. The pain hit a moment before he heard the report of the shot from far behind him, echoing around the mountains.

The pain was a hammer against his senses. He reeled and almost fell back. He raised his hand to steady himself against the half-melted rock, but no hand came up.

Orfos's right arm had been blown off at the elbow. Splinters of bone stuck out of the gory mess of the stump.

The shot had gone through Geryius first. It had punched through the Scout's midriff, blowing a wide red hole in his stomach. Geryius fell back against Privar, who caught him and dragged him into the shelter of the cave entrance.

Orfos was on his knees now. His stomachs were turning with the shock and he couldn't breathe. He had just enough wits left to follow the path of the bullet, and on a distant mountaintop he saw the pattern of the rock shifting as someone moved out of a sniping position. Orfos could just make out a masked face and a long sniping rifle, the shooter's form disguised by the way its bodysuit mimicked the rock around it like cameleoline.

Orfos's vision was whiting out and he could not move.

'Here, brother,' said Enriaan, putting Orfos's remaining arm over his shoulder, and helping him towards cover. 'You will live. We are victorious.'

As Orfos passed out, the last thing he saw was the pure, cold sky as it spun above him.

K-Day +11 Days
Operation Catullus

The night brought the real attack. Those that broke against the Temple of the Muses during the evening hours were probing the defences, looking for ways in. The horde that seethed through the dry canals around the temple seemed heedless of their own survival, but they were not led by fools. The men shot down by Subiacan lasguns and Imperial Fists bolters were sacrificed, and they now served to mark out the deadliest crossfires with the piles of their bodies.

The 91st Deucalian Lancers, infantry heavily supported with tanks and mobile artillery, reached the temple doors as the enemy were massing. Captain Lysander, who had learned siegecraft from the writings of Rogal Dorn himself, had the Imperial Guardsmen bristling the roof and windows of the temple with lasguns and the artillery lifted to the upper floors with chains hauled by gangs of Subiacan penal troopers.

Tanks rumbled through the ground floor, setting up as gun emplacements amid the rubble of the earlier battle.

The 1179th Ground Support Wing of the Imperial Navy dropped cluster bombs into the canals and raked what enemy they saw with autocannon fire, but the enemy were well sheltered among the storm drains and bridges of the Wiseman's Quarter. Castellan bombs scattered hundreds of mines across the murky sediment along the canal beds, and the stragglers and poorly sheltered died in their dozens to the explosive rain – but the enemy endured.

The Imperial Guard still spoke of the enemy as 'the Aristeia', the forces loyal to the ruling caste of Opis. But it was obvious even to many of the troopers on the ground that the Aristeia had not ruled Opis at least from the beginning of the Imperial invasion. More likely, the planet's moral threats had been pulling the strings since before Lord Inquisitor Kekrops had arrived to hunt them down. Every soldier seemed to have sighted a formless monster, or a witch wreathed in lightning, from the windows of the temple. Daemons were said to be dancing among the enemy, and Guardsmen swapped their certainties that witch covens were piling pyres of bodies high and gates into the warp were being opened in shrines to dark gods beneath Rekaba.

The tide of fanatics broke cover after night fell. The guns of the Imperial Fists cut them down in such numbers that the next waves were wading through swamps of blood and torn bodies. The Deucalian tanks hammered explosive fire into the enemy.

Lysander ordered the Subiacan preachers to send in the

penal legion troopers. A flood of combat drugs flowed into the veins of the Subiacans, and their entire strength swarmed out into the canals. They met the enemy in a brutal melee, a murderous crush with no way forward or back.

The Subiacans were the inmates of a prison world, and had been condemned for their crimes to fight and die for the Emperor. This was a fitting end for them, both a brutal punishment and a redemptive fate, and they bought back a few glimmers of the Emperor's grace in death that they had forsaken in life. Captain Lysander, the Deucalians said, would do the same to every Guardsman on the planet if that was what it took. They crouched at their firing positions, watching the appalling bloodletting below, and thanked the Emperor that it was not their time yet.

The Imperial Navy craft shrieked over the canals and dropped enough incendiaries to turn the dry waterways into rivers of fire. Thousands of enemy militia and Subiacans died. By the time the fire died down, the remaining waves of enemy had little to do except rush through the ashes and get shot down by Deucalian lasgun fire.

The enemy withdrew. Some of them were too crazed to retreat, and wandered the scorched battlefield being picked off by Imperial Guard marksmen on the temple roof. A few strange sights were revealed in those moments – glowing-eyed, hovering creatures, witches or daemons shrouded in darkness, gathering the remains of their army and ushering them into the drains and sewers under Rekaba. Several Guardsmen swore they had seen a winged creature surrounded by a halo of silver lights overflying the battlefield, as if calmly taking a tally of the dead. Four gun crews were found dead on the upper floors, their eyes and hands later to be discovered heaped up at the foot of a gargoyle on the roof as if in offering. But the enemy were defeated at the Temple of the Muses.

The Imperial Guard knew better than to celebrate.

A dozen battles of the same scale and severity took place across Rekaba that night. Twelve city blocks in the Orphan's Ward collapsed into the natural caves and underground rivers beneath the city, delivering almost the entire Manikrave Hussars regiment into the hands of an enemy horde with pallid white flesh and blank, blind skin where their eyes should have been. A Naval landing field, hastily built among the playing fields of Rekaba's university, was overrun by an enemy regiment who marched and fought in perfect formation and were led by a towering warrior in molten steel armour. For every victory in Rekaba, the Imperial forces suffered a catastrophic defeat. Rekaba was no more willing to give itself up than Khezal, and Operation Catullus was following Operation Requiem in becoming a grinding cycle of murder.

In the Temple of the Muses, two thousand Guardsmen from the Luthermak Deathworlders regiment arrived to reinforce the Deucalians. Together they patched up their wounded, carried off their dead, and tried to keep their thoughts from turning to what the next night would hold.

Gorgythion found Lysander in the Grand Reading Room, the lavish domed auditorium where Opis's greatest scholars had once held court. Now the Imperial Fists were using it as their command post, with vox-net boosters bringing in information from the Space Marines elsewhere on Opis.

Lysander looked up from a parchment map of Rekaba that had been found among the temple's library stacks. 'Gorgythion!' he said. 'I thought you lost.'

'Lost no longer,' replied Gorgythion, 'now I am among brothers.'

Lysander looked Gorgythion up and down. 'Where is your weapon?'

'She lies in flames, in the jungle,' replied Gorgythion. 'The last of her kind, and now there will never be another. But you speak of my boltgun, captain? That lies there too, along with the body of my battle-brother, Kebriones.'

'He will be mourned,' said Lysander. 'As will the *Sanctifier*.'

'And how goes the battle here?'

Lysander glanced through the archway leading into the main floors of the temple, where Deucalian Guardsmen were hauling artillery pieces into place and handing out power packs for their lasguns. 'The enemy will try again tonight. And again, and again, until the defenders break. The Temple of the Muses will hold if the enemy numbers run out, but without any such end in sight it is the duty of these soldiers to bleed the besieging force of as many men as they can.'

'Then Rekaba will become a quagmire,' said Gorgythion, 'when we came to Opis to take its cities in days.'

'You speak most freely, brother,' said Lysander. 'As if you do not trust that victory will belong to the Emperor on Opis. Do you have some greater insight, which I and the Imperial commanders do not?'

Gorgythion held up a hand. 'Forgive me. I have seen my

brother dead, my mission failed and my steed fallen. I forget myself. But I do have intelligence that others do not. In the jungle, some way from Rekaba, lies an installation surrounded by defences well beyond the capability of Opis. It was these defences, an energy weapon, that brought down the *Sanctifier*.'

'And what is this installation?' said Lysander.

'Something that someone wishes to protect against intrusion,' said Gorgythion. 'It destroyed my craft and those of the Aristeia alike. Someone who is neither a part of the Imperial force nor of Opis's rulers places great value on something in that jungle.'

'I see,' said Lysander. 'This must be thought on. Yours is not the only such evidence we have come across. For now, brother, join Sergeant Kirav and find a weapon. We will need every gun tonight.'

'Captain, sir!' came a voice from the archway. A Deucalian, with a badly wounded right arm heavily bandaged, stood there, evidently despatched as a messenger.

'Speak,' said Lysander.

The Guardsman looked terrified to be in the same room as a Space Marine. 'The enemy are sighted. They are moving through the buildings adjoining, at every level!'

'Another test,' said Lysander. 'They know how we will react to an assault in the open. Now they fight room to room. Gorgythion, find Kirav. He should be at roof level. Go!'

The Temple of the Muses was suddenly wound up for war. The Deucalians were at their firing positions, leading one another in prayers for deliverance from the enemy or calling on the Emperor to guide their guns. Many of them ignored

Lysander as he walked among them, wrapped up in their thoughts and fears of the coming action. Already the sounds of war, a constant dim thunder from elsewhere in the city, were growing closer. Squad Ctesiphon was stationed on the lower level, and the Deucalians there offered thanks to the Emperor that they would fight in the presence of the Adeptus Astartes.

'Ctesiphon,' ordered Lysander, 'man the lower floors. Form up for volley fire. Fall back to the fountain room if you are surrounded.'

'Understood, Captain,' said Ctesiphon. His tactical squad, ten bolters strong, was the best line of defence the Imperial forces in Rekaba had.

Lysander ascended a spiralling marble staircase that led to the temple's upper floors. They had escaped assault in the earlier battle. That would not be true for long. The enemy was acting in the way that all besieging forces with superior numbers would act – using their great numbers to test the defences, seek weaknesses at every level with repeated attacks, even if just to drain the ammunition and will to fight of the defenders.

The upper floors held museum and gallery rooms. A few of the portraits had been torn down or stolen, a few display cases of royal jewels and regalia smashed open and looted, but most remained. What looter had anywhere to take them?

Kirav's squad were up here, among the rafters of the temple, along with the spotters for the Deucalian artillery and a few Imperial Guard snipers.

Brother Stentor was leading the pre-battle rites. Each of

the squad had his bolter laid on the floor in front of him, gleaming from the wargear rituals that kept them in the best working order. Each man's armour had been cleaned of the inky filth of the morning's battle – even the white trim of their golden power armour shone, to denote their status as veterans of the First Company. Stentor's words were Rogal Dorn's, taken from one of the many volumes of battle speeches he had left to the Librarium of the Chapter. Every battle-brother knew them by heart, but when they were spoken before battle, they all heard them as if for the first time.

'There is no enemy,' said Dorn, his words relayed through the ages by Brother Stentor. 'The foe on the battlefield is merely the manifestation of that which we must overcome. He is doubt, and fear, and despair. Every battle is fought within. Conquer the battlefield that lies inside you, and the enemy disappears like the illusion he is.'

'Amen,' said the battle-brothers of the squad, their heads bowed.

'Captain,' said Kirav, looking up. 'What are your orders?'

'Hold the rooftop,' said Lysander. 'I will be with you.'

'Then we shall do as Dorn did on Terra!' said Brother Beros. 'We will cast the enemy from the battlements!'

Through the rips in the roof, Lysander could see the skyline of Rekaba picked out in the dying light. The parade ground nearby was burning, with Imperial Navy fighter-bombers on fire beside the improvised landing strip. Guardsmen were already swapping stories about the daemons conjured there, leaping monsters who bled flaming blood and hung their captives from gibbets of twisted thorns. The Butchers' Vale, where thousands of tiny workshops and forges cramped over one another along mazes of narrow streets, was a dark, seething mass obscured by the smoke from dozens of fires. There the enemy were sheltering almost impervious to Imperial artillery, and several thousand Gathalamorian Guardsmen were manning the barricades to keep a cordon around the whole district. The Stadium of the Amethyst burned, a lake of fire from which incandescent winged shapes flitted up towards the sky. The spiralling dome of the Tower of Rats was half-collapsed, covered by a seething caul of mobile darkness. The city of Rekaba was devolving into a hundred battles, each one a grinding drain of manpower.

This was not a battle that could be won, because the enemy did not want to win. The battle was an end in itself. The enemy objective in both Khezal and Rekaba was simply to fight. They were not trying to expel the Imperial forces, just draw them in and keep them battling over every street and building. Lysander had seen enough sieges, and learned enough from the volumes of battle-lore Rogal Dorn and countless Imperial Fists heroes had penned, to see that.

And even though the enemy wanted him to fight, he would have to oblige them. For across the rooftops adjoining the Temple of the Muses were leaping a host of mutants, their bodies long and loping, whooping and shrieking as they bounded from gargoyle to chimney stack. They stuttered through the air, their unstable forms skipping across reality in impossible trajectories. They carried two-handed swords and axes looted from some Aristeia household's armoury, and they were followed by bright trails of blood and sparks. Their skin was stretched haphazardly over altered skeletons, and tiny wriggling creatures swarmed from their ribcages.

Lysander swung himself up onto the roof. He could hear the orders of Sergeant Kirav and the cocking of bolters. He took the Fist of Dorn in both hands, ready to drop into a guard or lunge into a strike.

The enemy closed.

The farce would have one more scene before the Imperial Fists could strike out and find the truth. If Lysander had to lose himself in battle for a little longer, then that was what he would do.

The mutants shrieked. The closest had a contorted, elongated parody of a face, cackling imps spilling from its grinning jaws.

Lysander swung the Fist of Dorn into it, and took comfort in the breaking of its bones.

Deiphobus read their thoughts this time not by tearing them from the prisoners' minds, but by letting them come to him. The lower level of the *Merciless*'s brig lacked the psychic defences of the cell where Filthammer had been kept, and the inmates were captured militia and mutants without psychic abilities. Nevertheless the first sight of them illustrated how dangerous they were. One vomited a constant stream of biting insects, which were now captured and drawn off by the drain installed in his cell. Another had oozed through his bars when first imprisoned, and was now sealed in a transparent cylinder with no opening through which his malleable form could escape. Perhaps the most striking had brightly patterned skin like that of a venomous lizard, which was appropriate given that his blood was highly poisonous, flammable and rather radioactive. He was welded into a voidsuit normally used for operations in a vacuum.

Two dozen militia were imprisoned on this brig floor. Most of them had crept to the back of their cells when they had seen Deiphobus. A few had pushed against the bars of their cells and hurled insults and threats at him.

Deiphobus sat in the centre of the brig corridor, on the steel floor. He bowed his head and allowed the first doors of his mind to open. For this exercise he constructed in his mind a fortress, with Imperial Fists standing on the battlements and a great black gate. The walls were hundreds of metres high and impossible to scale, and the foundations plunged down further than anyone could dig. The gate was the only way in.

The minds of the prisoners were outside the fortress. Deiphobus controlled which ones he let in and which he forced to remain outside. He imagined them lined up outside the gate and himself as a castellan on the battlements, looking down on them and judging them.

None of them was completely human. Even those who looked outwardly normal had deformed, discoloured minds. Some he instantly turned away, for they were roiling, mindless bundles of anger and fear, and they would tell him nothing. They thrashed about in protest, so Deiphobus threw cages of black iron around them and sank them into the ground. They were banished from his mind, and would find no way in.

Others stood proud and fearless. Deiphobus discarded them, too. They did not fear him. Fear was one of the greatest weapons a Space Marine could wield. Whole worlds had surrendered when they saw the strike cruisers of the Space Marines hovering in orbit. The fearless ones were irretrievably insane and would try to confound Deiphobus with lies. They were useless to him, too, at least until their souls were broken.

The rest, the desperate and miserable, the terrified and the crushed, he let in. The black gate swung open just wide enough for them. In the gunsights of his mental guardians the captives filed in, heads bowed.

Manacles constrained them. The walls closed in and held them fast. The floor dropped away and they were held, suspended, as Deiphobus walked among them. The image he created for himself was a fusion of man and machine, a tall, muscular creature with limbs altered to incorporate every tool of interrogation that could be imagined and many that could not. He glided on a dozen segmented legs beneath a skirt of skin. His eyes were huge and multi-lensed, so he would miss nothing. As he bent over the captives, he could see their fear.

On one level, the fear was a particular configuration of brainwaves, picked up and interpreted by Deiphobus's psychic talent. On the level he envisioned, it was blood that ran from their eyes, a physical manifestation of a mental injury.

'Tell me everything,' said Deiphobus to the first captive. Then he went to each of them in turn, bending over them so they could see all the surgical tools he carried and the infinite depth of his eyes.

'Tell me everything.'

And they did.

One of the greatest challenges facing the interrogator was that once a subject gave up the defence of his mind, the information then had to be sorted. The great majority of it was useless. He glimpsed snatches of childhoods on Opis, and from this it was enough to confirm that the peasants and the Aristeia had such markedly different experiences it was like reading the minds of two different species. The peasants were steeped in the idea of inferiority, that there was something wrong with them from the moment they were born and that the Aristeia were their betters in every possible way. The Aristeia, meanwhile, were harried by a desperate corruption, a sort of social panic in which they maintained their status by ever more wanton expenditure and acts of oppression. They turned themselves into miserable, obsessed people, islands eternally disconnected, ripe for turning to a dark cause. Perfect chattels for those who could control them.

It was remarkable that Opis had taken so long to become prey to the Dark Gods' champions. Deiphobus wondered if moral threats had always held Opis in their grip, and that Kekrops had simply been the first to notice.

But no. The moral threats were new. He could taste that in their minds. He had a feeling of a previous age, not so long ago, still grim and devoid of happiness, but one now fondly remembered like a golden-hued youth. Darkness had come to Opis. Each captive had the same concept of time.

Five years. He could be no more accurate than that, given the ragged state of the prisoners' minds. Five years ago, something had come to Opis and in its wake followed moral threats from off-world. There had been dark things on Opis before, pleasure-cults and rebels who sought supernatural aid, but nothing like this. Opis was invaded and silently, without mercy or pause, a power structure had embedded itself in Opis's society above the level of the Aristeia. The Aristeia still ruled, but the planet's new lords permitted the Aristeia to exist.

Then the Imperium had arrived. The mutations began. The new lords were seen in the open. Deiphobus recognised in the prisoners' memories the moral threats Tchepikov's staff had held briefings on. A glowing, winged woman, reported during the assault supported by the *Sanctifier*. A thing like an enormous spider with a human face, which was recalled holding thunderous, hypnotic sermons somewhere in Khezal. Even Filthammer, glimpsed holding a great sacrificial rite on the eve of the first Imperial assaults.

Deiphobus let his mind withdraw. The captives fell away, back into their own bodies. The brig corridor swam back into view.

Why were they here? What was on Opis that they wanted?

And who? Who had brought them?

Booted footsteps caught Deiphobus's attention. He was on his feet as the brig's heavy blast door slid open.

'Librarian,' said Commander Tchepikov, who walked in flanked by a pair of intelligence officers. He wore his full uniform, and Deiphobus wondered if he was ever out of it. 'The battle in Rekaba continues.'

'So I understand,' said Deiphobus. 'I have seen the dispatches for the day. The enemy will not relinquish, that much is proven.'

'And the Imperial Fists have abandoned their post,' said Tchepikov. It was stated as more of a fact than a rebuke.

Deiphobus folded his arms and looked down at the commander. At his full height he dwarfed Tchepikov. He was probably more massive than Tchepikov and the two officers put together. But Tchepikov did not back down. 'The implications of your words,' Deiphobus said, 'are most grave.'

'Facts, Librarian,' continued Tchepikov. 'Nothing more. The Temple of the Muses held during the night, and in the morning the Imperial Fists left. It is now defended only by the Imperial Guard.'

'Who are being reinforced as we speak,' replied Deiphobus.

'That is not my point, Librarian, as you well know. The plan for the invasion of Rekaba was drawn up in the belief that the Imperial Fists would be a part of it. Now, they are not. When my best soldiers abandon me, they become worse than no soldiers at all.'

'Your soldiers?' Deiphobus took a step closer to Tchepikov. 'We are not your soldiers. We belong to the Emperor, and to the legacy of Rogal Dorn. We hold our own counsel and then fight our own battles. Our commander is Captain Lysander, not Tchepikov. You knew when you requested our aid that the Imperial Fists are an independent force, a sovereign and autonomous Chapter who owe loyalty to the Imperium but obedience to no one.'

'And where are your battle-brothers, Imperial Fist?'

'We will hold our own counsel on that, too.'

Tchepikov had not risen to his rank by losing his composure when crossed. 'Come with me,' he said. 'Unless you have urgent business among these vermin.'

Deiphobus followed Tchepikov as the commander walked out of the brig. He was trusted by Lysander to act as a link between the Imperial Fists and the rest of the strike force, and the insult of being given such a blunt order by Tchepikov could be ignored for now. Tchepikov led him up to the command deck, where only a couple of officers now sat at the huge conference table poring over reports from the field.

'Here,' said Tchepikov. With a gesture he activated the holo-servitor which scrabbled along the ceiling. Its metallic torso split open and the lenses of the holo-projector lit up, casting a strategic map of Opis over the table.

'The Khezal and Rekaba fronts,' said Tchepikov. 'Operations Requiem and Catullus. Already my reserves are committed maintaining the cordons and policing the refugee camps. And arriving in orbit within the next seventy-two hours, reinforcements to be deployed immediately.' The map shifted, showing new lines of attack around the continent of plains and river deltas to the north of Khezal, leading up into tundras and then to icy wastes towards the pole.

'The third front,' said Tchepikov. 'The population not contained in the cities is being bled out of their towns and villages, northwards. We don't know where. The Aristeia are welding them into new armies. Millions of them, Librarian. It will take everything I have to pen them in and keep them from gathering into a force that could besiege Khezal and sweep us off this planet. And you, your Chapter, are off fighting your own war. Do you understand why I must have every soldier on this planet fighting as I deploy them? If any front collapses, we are lost. Any battle could turn the tide of the war, and the Imperial Fists can turn the tide of any battle.'

'Do you think we are ignorant of this, commander?' said Deiphobus. 'We arrived here willing to follow your orders because the enemy was clear. The killers of Inquisitor Kekrops had to be rooted out and punished, and Opis's government torn out and replaced. But this war is no longer so simple. We do not know who the enemy truly is. We do not know what he wants or who we can trust. Answering those questions will do as much for victory on Opis as a million Imperial Guardsmen.'

Tchepikov looked at the strategic map again. The deployment of well over half a million Imperial Guardsmen was allocated to the third front, with the same again in Khezal and Rekaba. Thousands of tanks and artillery pieces were scheduled to drop in from orbit in vast landings in the trackless terrain of the northern continent. 'I know I cannot command you,' said Tchepikov. 'But I can appeal to your honour.'

'Our honour is satisfied only in victory,' said Deiphobus. 'And we will pursue it in the way Captain Lysander sees fit. There is nothing further to discuss.'

'Then leave my ship,' said Tchepikov. 'It will damage morale if it becomes known that the Space Marines and the Imperial commander are not of the same mind. I will not allow that rot to set in. Join your battle-brothers and report back to me when you are willing to fight my war.'

Deiphobus left Tchepikov in the gloom of the command deck, absorbed in the potential battles marked out on the holographic map, the nameless plains and gulleys which would soon be the graves of thousands of men.

K-Day +13 Days
Independent Adeptus Astartes operations

Scout-Sergeant Orfos's arm had not been fully accepted by his body. The muscles and bones of his upper arm had still to bond fully with the new bionic. His forearm and hand were now fashioned of dull metal, articulated with servos and cabling. The feedback was buzzing and metallic, an alien feeling that he wondered if he would ever get used to, and phantom pains flashed through nerves that were no longer there.

His arm hurt now, as he crept ahead of the main force, knife in his bionic hand as he scanned for booby traps. A Scout learned rapidly about trip-wires and pits, training his enhanced vision to pick out subtle anomalies that might indicate a grenade rigged in the undergrowth or a deadfall trap almost invisible through the foliage above.

The jungle was dark. Beams of sunlight reached through

the many layers of the canopy, but they were few. Sound was everywhere, the endless chirping and humming of insects, the almost-human shrieks of hunting birds and the howls of predators. The wind picked up and the trees overhead sighed among each other with a sound like the ocean. Among the movement of the wind and of the creatures that flitted just out of sight, Orfos strained to pick out a threat.

Enriaan and Privar were spaced out, almost too far to see, advancing at the same pace. Vonretz was dead, buried up in the mountains, and Geryius was at Sigismund Point, missing a good chunk of his spine and several organs. He would probably live, but he might never fight.

A structure loomed from the trees up ahead. 'Halt,' voxed Orfos quietly. He could just see Enriaan through the trees, crouching to scan the terrain ahead through the scope of his sniper rifle.

The structure was a tower, rising almost as high as the canopy, and draped with hanging vines and moss. It was metallic, segmented like a column, with ribbed cabling running down one side. Cylindrical structures were half-buried in the ground around it.

'There's a structure up ahead,' voxed Orfos. 'I think we're here.'

<<Get closer,>> came the reply from Lysander. <<Verify it's safe to move up. And remember, brother, something here brought down the *Sanctifier*.>>

Orfos moved closer. Beside the tower was the charred wreck of a fighter craft – not the *Sanctifier* but one of the Aristeia's own Naval fliers. It had been sliced in two, and the two chunks had slammed into the jungle floor. A shaft of sunlight still fell through the hole in the canopy the fighter had torn as it crashed.

'It's an energy weapon,' said Orfos. His eyes followed the power lines from the buried generators up the tower to the array of projector vanes at the top. 'An air interdiction system. It's a Standard Template Construct pattern. It's advanced, but I still recognise it.'

<<Then it's Imperial,>> voxed Lysander.

'Originally, maybe.' Orfos stepped over the tangle of thick roots underfoot. The dirt gave way and he stopped before his foot sank into it.

He scuffed the surface away. A skull looked back at him, jumbled together with ribs and limb bones from many more bodies.

'Got a mass grave here,' said Orfos.

<<Here too,>> voxed Enriaan. Orfos could see Privar through the jungle. The Scout's arm was braced as his broken bone healed. 'Lasgun wounds to the back of the skull.'

A creature with a feline shape and scaled hide slunk out from behind the tower. Its lean musculature undulated under its reptilian skin, and four amber eyes focused on Orfos. Its tail curled up over its back and it crouched down, shoulders meeting over its head, bunched up ready to strike.

Orfos didn't move. Sleep-taught instincts weighed up the predator's combat capabilities. It had six limbs, the back pair powerful for both leaping and raking prey on the ground. The teeth were long and slender, for latching onto an adversary's neck and severing the spine. Its place at the top of the food chain had honed it into a sleek and effective killer.

The creature darted out of Orfos's sight, gone with barely a rustle of the leaves.

Orfos hadn't moved. Something else had spooked it.

Orfos whirled around. A section of the jungle floor powered up – it was the roof of a concealed bunker, forced up to the surface by hydraulics. Revealed was a compartment in which was crouched a mass of muscle and machinery. Orfos identified quad autoguns unfolding.

'Servitors,' voxed Orfos. He didn't have time to elaborate before the servitor's armoured cranium turned to him, lenses whirring.

Orfos vaulted a bank of entangled roots and dropped to the ground on the other side. Gunfire opened up and slammed into the roots. Splinters burst everywhere.

He glanced at the servitor through the roots. It was built for toughness and not mobility, with wide shoulders and short, heavy legs, the head unit set low in the chest. Orfos rolled out from behind cover and ran, head down, past the arc of fire as the autoguns hammered shots just past him.

Orfos grabbed the upper edge of the servitor's shoulder guard, swinging himself up onto its back. He blasted into the thick spinal column with his bolt pistol, and black hydraulic fluid sprayed. The servitor bucked like an animal, Orfos losing his footing and barely hanging on. He rammed the tip of his knife blade between the ruptured plates of its back and twisted. Sparks fountained over him. The servitor threw its body forwards and Orfos was catapulted over its head, tearing off a handful of armour as he fell.

He rolled as he landed, up onto one knee. The four guns were trained on him. The servitor's skull was exposed, red and raw, the armour-plating pulled away. Some echo of a face was there, the face of the condemned man or woman who had been converted into this machine, their brain programmed with its orders, their nervous system hooked up to its weapons.

The head snapped back, brains sprayed across the armoured shoulders. The servitor sank back onto its haunches, weapons drooping.

Behind Orfos was Enriaan, on his knees, focusing through the scope of his sniper rifle. The shot he had fired had blown the back of the servitor's skull out, and he fired a second, shattering what remained. The remnants of the servitor's head hung by a bundle of cables. A targeter lens fell out into the dirt.

'Good kill,' said Orfos.

<<There's another one here,>> voxed Privar. Orfos could see another bunker near Privar's position, which had similarly burst up from the ground. 'It failed to activate. I think the biological components have putrefied.'

'Captain, we're clear here,' voxed Orfos. 'Someone has gone to great pains to keep intruders out.'

<<Good,>> replied Lysander. <<Then we are in the right place.>>

A hundred metres ahead was another perimeter, this time of trip-wires and motion sensors. Orfos could see them from here, picked out by his training as if they had been lit up against the jungle gloom. Beyond them, arched over by trees so as to be invisible from above, was a rockcrete structure sealed with a heavy steel door.

'Looks like a way in,' voxed Orfos. 'It's underground.'

<<Understood,>> came Lysander's vox in reply. <<Take us in, Scouts.>>

The air carried death on it.

Not just the smell of decay. That was there, too, and was as familiar to a Space Marine as sweat or the smoke from a bolter impact. It was the sterility of the heavily scrubbed air, the way footsteps on the floor grilles had no echo. Life had been torn away, and a stillness remained.

Lysander had led the way in. Once a path in was secured, the Scouts had done their job. A captain among the Space Marines had a clear duty to lead from the front.

He had torn the blast doors open with a swipe of the Fist of Dorn. He had kicked his way through the walls of the decontamination chamber he found beyond, and had been the first to walk into the immense chamber the Rekaban jungles had kept hidden until now.

An enormous shaft sank hundreds of metres straight down. A series of elevators, like suspended cages, gave access to the floors below leading off from the shaft. The darkness below did not quite conceal the grinders at the base of the shaft, units used to shred whatever was thrown down there. Whatever happened here, it sometimes produced results that had to be destroyed in a hurry.

Squad Ctesiphon and Assault Squad Septuron spread out behind Lysander to secure the upper floors. Librarian

Deiphobus was next in. His armour, painted mostly blue to denote his membership of the Chapter Librarium, lacked the grime and battle scars of the other Imperial Fists, his time on Opis being spent liaising with Commander Tchepikov and his intelligence staff.

'I think we are going to need you here,' said Lysander.

'Death is everywhere,' said Deiphobus. 'It's thick. I can feel it pushing me back. It doesn't want me here.'

'The perimeter looks firm,' came Orfos's voice from the entrance, where his Scouts remained to watch for threats from outside. Kirav and his fire-team stuck close to Lysander as he followed Ctesiphon into a sprawl of laboratories strewn with benches and equipment.

Tissue samples still lay on microscope slides. The contents of test tubes and flasks had dried up, leaving rings of sediment. This was just one lab – half a dozen more made up the upper floor.

'Someone left here fast,' said Lysander. 'Their work undone. Was it of their own accord?'

'It was not,' replied Deiphobus. The Librarian picked up a skull, thoroughly cleaned and lacking its lower jaw, and turned it over in his hand. The cranium was scored across with marks, as if being used as a guide for some surgical procedure.

<<This floor is clear,>> voxed Sergeant Ctesiphon. <<We're heading down.>>

Lysander opened the door of a large booth in one lab, hooked up to a generator and surrounded by a ring of crystals mounted on a metal halo. Inside was a seat, moulded to accept a human form, with restraints on the ankles, wrists and neck. Several sizes of callipers hung on one wall, for measuring skull dimensions. On another wall were cabinets containing hundreds of glass slides in which were preserved slices of brain. A guard post still had a brace of autoguns racked under a desk.

'Were they keeping intruders out, or the scientists in?' said Sergeant Kirav.

Ctesiphon was holding position one floor down, where a single large room looked onto the abyss of the central shaft. The walls were lined with transparent cylinders. All but three were empty.

In the remaining three were human bodies, suspended in viscous clear fluid. They were naked, and the flesh had become sodden and peeled away from the bones in scraps. Electrodes still clung to the remains of the scalps. Ribs and organs were visible through the rents in the skin.

'These are sleep-teaching units,' said Lysander. It was lost on none of the Imperial Fists that Space Marines were educated in similar units, filling their heads with principles of the *Codex Astartes* and battle-philosophy as they were converted from aspirants.

'Open it,' said Deiphobus. Sergeant Ctesiphon found a wheel lock on the base of one unit and hauled it open. The bottom of the cylinder swung open, dumping a foul sludge of flesh and organ onto the floor.

'Cranial surgery,' said Lysander, pointing towards the marks on the partially-fleshed skull. 'The body Orfos brought in from the Battle Plains had the same scars.'

Deiphobus knelt by the body. He placed a hand on its skull,

just as he had done to Janeak Filthammer.

'The dead,' he said, 'are always more difficult. The last thing he saw was... an orderly. A medicae's smock. Bionic eyes. These units are all full. He flicked a switch and then all goes dark. Then this man died.'

'Not much to go on,' said Lysander. 'What else can you see, brother?'

Somewhere back in Deiphobus's mind was a wall with a door set into it. The door was of solid steel with a lock that could not be picked or broken. Only Deiphobus himself could open it. Behind the door was the part of him that dealt with death. There was so much death around a Space Marine that this place had to be sealed off, partly by years of hypno-training and mental exercises, and partly by Deiphobus's raw mental strength – to keep it from being overwhelmed.

The door opened.

The dead man's memories flooded through. Like his body, they were decayed and fragmented. His brain had turned to mush and Deiphobus imagined himself standing knee-deep in it, scraps of sensations floating past in the gory soup.

A recurring dream, something that surfaced again and again, was of drowning. Falling into a dark, cold abyss, and struggling for breath, then oblivion. Every time this man had slept, this was what he had seen.

Another was of pain. Not in waves or great episodes of agony, but constant, a prickling, a direct stimulation of the nerves in what Deiphobus recognised as treatment to improve reactions as well as gauge resistance to pain. Deiphobus had gone through it himself early in the stages of his transformation into a Space Marine, though those memories seemed to belong to a different man now.

And then there was…

Nothing.

Deiphobus sifted through the torn memories. There was just darkness. Endless tracts of darkness where a childhood should have been. Or an adolescence, or a career as the soldier this man clearly had been. All gone. Stripped out, painted over with nothing.

Deiphobus reversed the flow of memories. They seeped back past the death barrier. He crammed them into the space beyond and shut the door.

'We have found the source of the off-world troops,' said Deiphobus. 'They're mind-wiped. Sleep-taught elites. They were programmed here.'

'By whom?' said Lysander.

'That was scrubbed away,' replied Deiphobus. 'If this man ever knew in the first place.'

Sergeant Septuron emerged from an archway leading into a side passage. Septuron was an assault veteran and looked it, his armour carefully painted with dozens of kill-markings, and trophies of fangs and jawbones hanging from the length of his chainsword. 'The rest of this floor is barracks and training rooms,' he said. 'Nothing to kill.' He sounded slightly disappointed.

'Any more bodies?' asked Lysander.

'Not yet. But it goes down.'

'Then so do we.'

'Who do you think built this?' said Deiphobus. 'Who trained these men?'

'I have my own opinions on that,' said Lysander. 'But I do not place any value in opinions. When it becomes a fact, then I shall act upon it. Septuron, what is on the lower levels?'

'I know not, captain. But something down there is still drawing power.'

Lysander led the way out of the chamber, leaving the sorry remains of the dead soldier spreading on the floor. Septuron and Deiphobus followed, training careful eyes on the shadows that clung everywhere. The light down here was dim, afforded only by a few glow-globes. The facility was powered down, running on minimum. The barracks rooms were devoid of decoration, of the signs that human beings had lived there, save for the inscriptions carved into the black walls.

IN OBEDIENCE, read one.

IN IGNORANCE, read another. Each footlocker contained a single standard Imperial prayer book and nothing else.

Below, the air was colder. The narrow metal staircase spiralled down to the level of the grinder. The floor here was open to the machine's gnarled teeth. To Lysander's eye, the grinding cylinders looked configured to shred flesh and crunch bone, but he could not be sure. They were clean – even the oil had been stripped away, and patches of the metal were faintly pitted as if by acid.

A hatch in the floor was sealed by a wheel lock. Lysander knelt to open it.

'Wait,' said Deiphobus.

Lysander looked up at him.

'This chamber is shielded,' said the Librarian. 'But the sensations beyond are leaking out. Just enough to be sure.'

'Of what?'

'A moral threat.'

'This world has enough of those,' said Lysander. 'We will destroy one more. Ctesiphon! Septuron! At the ready!'

Septuron's squad drew their chainblades. The chamber hummed with the whirring of the blades' teeth. Squad Ctesiphon descended the stairs and lined up, bolters ready to cut down anything that got past Lysander's hammer and Septuron's blades.

Lysander hauled the wheel round. The hatch swung open.

The stench was appalling. The death above had been one thing. The death from below was a distillation of rot, a breath from hell. The dim light touched wet ridges of foulness.

The chamber beneath the grinder was coated, walls and floor, in rotting gore. Some of it had dried to stringy, spongy masses of shredded flesh. Some was still oozing as if shed only moments before. The stench rolled up in thick, filthy waves.

Lysander stared into the mass for a moment.

'Deiphobus?' he asked.

'I can go on, captain,' came the reply. 'It is… painful, but I can go on.'

Lysander swung down into the chamber. Bones crunched under his feet. He could see skulls, pelvises, ribs, femurs, half buried in the sludge.

'How many legends are buried here?' he said. 'Tales of people gone missing from Opis's cities. Snatched away by monsters or ghosts. How many ended up in this place?'

In the middle of the chamber was a standing stone. Moss still clung to it, as if it had only just been ripped out of some forgotten forest. Chiselled into its surface were runes that would not be focused on. Lysander's eyes slid off them, as if they were afraid of what would happen if he read them.

Sergeant Septuron was next down. He could not keep the disgust off his face.

'What were they doing down here?' he said.

'Sacrifices,' said Lysander.

'It's a beacon,' said Deiphobus from above. 'It is calling out. Screaming. When this place was opened up and active… Throne alive, it is deafening to me even now. It must have reached out…'

'Light years,' said Lysander.

The chamber shuddered. The gory filth squirmed like a mass of vermin. Septuron almost lost his footing as the floor shifted.

With a cry of torn metal the walls parted. Lysander had the sense of space and depth beyond. From below and all around came the sound of stone against metal. The grinding cylinders overhead shuddered and scraps of flesh fell from between their teeth, where the cleaning above had missed them.

'Hold on!' yelled Septuron. The floor gave way beneath the two Space Marines. Lysander grabbed a beam that pierced the wall as the chamber deformed, his legs suddenly kicking out over a great drop that fell away into darkness.

The standing stone was the capstone of an enormous obelisk. The shaft to contain it speared down far below the facility. Rings of walkways were even now falling away with the shaking of the chamber.

One wall fell in, revealing the stone wall of the shaft. Septuron went with it, falling into the blackness.

Lightning crackled down there, illuminating Septuron as he slammed into one of the walkways. It held, just. Multicoloured fire swirled around the base of the obelisk, and Lysander could see the carvings that covered it, geometric patterns that broke into biological swirls and back again.

Lysander could see shapes in the fire. They leapt and shrieked.

Daemons. The predators of the warp, animalistic, always hungry. Unclean and damned.

Lysander let go and fell, plummeting towards the daemons swarming up at Septuron.

He hit one of the walkways hard. It parted under him but arrested his fall. He fell past Septuron and into the midst of the daemons.

They were something like wolves, something like lizards, something like shapes conjured by the mind's eye from the random flickering of a flame. Their fur writhed like nests of worms. Their eyes rolled in pits along their necks, and their faces were nothing but a lopsided, circular maw, ringed with teeth like a deep-sea predator.

Lysander swatted one against the wall – the stone wall, he saw now, carved with thousands of asymmetrical faces. He pivoted on his front foot and swept the Fist of Dorn around him, feeling the shock of impacts run up his arm. The space let one daemon in – Lysander stamped down on its neck and felt vertebrae shattering.

Septuron vaulted down and landed next to him. His chain-blade screamed as he plunged it down through the back of one daemon. He blasted holes in the torso of another with his bolt pistol – Lysander followed up and crushed its head into the floor with a downwards swing of his hammer.

'In the name of the Emperor most high! In the name of Rogal Dorn! All the hate you have drunk from my people, all the suffering you have wrought, I now repay!'

Lysander didn't have to look up to know that Deiphobus had jumped down into the pit after him. Lines of white light scribbled across the floor, and the daemons' flesh burned where the light touched them. The geometric wards taught to Deiphobus in the Chapter Librarium flared bright, and the daemons were thrown back.

'I banish thee!' yelled Deiphobus. He jumped down from the walkway above and landed beside Lysander. 'To the warp! To oblivion! I banish thee!'

'And that gate through which you may not return,' yelled Lysander, 'is manned by this Imperial Fist!'

The daemons were shrieking and burning. Lysander waded into them, hacking left and right with the Fist of Dorn, feeling the hammer slamming the daemons aside at the apex of each pendular swing.

Against one wall churned a mass of liquid rock, like bubbling mud, with the shapes of more daemons pushing against it from the other side. A clawed forelimb reached out of the wall, like the hand of a drowning man from the surface of quicksand.

Lysander rammed his shoulder against the wall, driving the

daemon back out of reality. Deiphobus was at his side, tracing glowing symbols in the air that scorched against the portal in the wall. Daemons writhed, trapped in the solidifying mass.

The gnashing maw of a daemon pushed through the wall. Lysander slammed his storm shield into it, and Deiphobus traced the final syllable of the banishment rite. The portal solidified, encasing the daemon in stone, and the screams from the other side died away.

Lysander stepped back, drawing in deep breaths. 'Is there any place on this planet that is not rotten?' he said.

'If there is, Opis has hidden it well,' said Deiphobus. Lysander saw the Librarian's face was pallid and waxy, running with sweat. A Space Marine very rarely looked weak, but the effort of the banishment had taken most of what Deiphobus had.

'Speak, brother,' said Lysander, 'if you wish.'

Deiphobus shook his head. 'We go on. There are answers here. I will not take a backwards step.'

'Good. We are with you.'

'And I with you, captain.'

'Who do you think this was?' said Septuron from the other side of the shaft. Against the wall hung the upper half of a man, bisected at the waist, and fixed to the rock with rivets through his elbows, wrists and collarbones. Into his chest was carved an intricate mass of runes and symbols.

The other Imperial Fists were climbing down what remained of the ladders and walkways. They passed the whole length of the obelisk. The blood that ran down it had pooled in the incised runes and picked out its own language in rust-red.

Lysander walked up to Septuron and the sorry, withered half-corpse on the wall. 'Can you read this?' he said to Deiphobus.

Deiphobus peered at the incisions on the man's chest. 'I wish that I could not,' he said. 'But yes. It makes itself legible to the third eye, the sight within a psyker.'

'And?'

'It is a contract.' Deiphobus swallowed and ran a finger along the dried-out skin, following the lines of script. 'Made by… the name cannot be read. It is probably a ritual name, used to conceal the author's true name. That means the author was present when this pact was made. It says that under pain of the very worst of the warp, the very foulest depredations of the Dark Gods, the… the Six-Fingered One? Also named Karnikhal. This Karnikhal is bound by the threat of such punishments to serve the author in return for his existence being spared. The power to create this bond was through conquest. Karnikhal's life was spared, and so that life belonged to the author.' Deiphobus took a step back. 'Karnikhal Six-Finger was at Khezal,' he said. 'He was one of the moral threats that attacked on K-Day.'

'And he was summoned here,' said Lysander. 'And bound into service by whoever built this obelisk.'

'Filthammer arrived under his own power,' said Deiphobus, 'but he was afraid of someone, maybe someone he was forced to serve.'

'I would wager,' said Lysander, 'that there was once a soul hanging here with a contract binding Filthammer into service, too.'

'There's another way out here,' said Sergeant Kirav. He had made it to the bottom of the shaft along with his fire-team, and was examining a sealed door set into the wall.

'Open it,' said Lysander. 'Be ready to fight.'

Kirav kicked the door open. The door sheared off its hinges and boomed as it landed flat on the other side.

There was no other sound, save the hum of power cabling.

Beyond was a medical facility. Three autosurgeons were fixed to the ceiling, their scalpel-tipped limbs folded up and indicator runes dark. Several autopsy slabs were fixed to one wall, and in the dimness Lysander could make out cabinets of medical implements and monitoring equipment.

In the middle of the room was a cabinet surrounded by thick ribbed piping, from which issued a freezing haze that clung to the floor. The cabinet was the size and shape of a coffin with a glass lid, but it was frosted over. Lysander walked up to it, trying to see what was inside.

He wiped a gauntlet across the lid. The frost was cleared. A skull stared back at him.

Not a real, human skull. A mask shaped like a skull, with intricate targeting lenses in the eye sockets and an armoured collar around the neck giving way to black synskin with hexagonal armoured scales.

Kirav stood just behind Lysander. 'What is it?' he asked.

'Eversor,' said Lysander. 'It's an Eversor.'

'An Assassin?' said Kirav.

'Have you ever fought alongside an agent of the Officio Assassinorum?' said Lysander.

'I have not.'

'It is like death itself is on your side. Like the enemy's shadow has come alive and turned on him. I have never seen such death as that dealt out by an Imperial Assassin. That is what lies here, my brothers. Death incarnate, harnessed as a weapon of the Imperium.'

Deiphobus had entered the chamber, and held a hand over the coffin. He shook his head, as if greeted only by silence. 'What is one doing in this place?' he said.

'It's in storage,' said Kirav. 'This is an Officio Assassinorum facility. They must have built this place.'

'And the obelisk?' countered Deiphobus. 'Did they build that, too?'

Lysander stood back from the Assassin's coffin. 'They have done more than that on Opis,' he said. 'Here.' He took from his belt the fragment of metal that he had recovered from the Temple of the Muses, the item stored there by Acolyte Serrick. 'This is the bullet that killed Inquisitor Kekrops. I last saw its kind being loaded into an Exitus longrifle, the weapon of a Vindicare Assassin. It is a Shield-Breaker round, doubtless employed in case Kekrops was protected by a personal energy shield. Only the Vindicare Assassin has access to such rare technology.

'The Officio Assassinorum started this war when one of their agents shot down Kekrops. This war, the moral threats that infest Opis, the Officio Assassinorum is at the heart of it all. Serrick's bullet placed the suspicion in my heart, but it was not enough. This place… this place is enough.'

'Could they have Assassins operating on Opis now?' asked Deiphobus.

'At least one,' said Lysander. 'This bullet matches the fragments pulled out of Scout Geryius and Sergeant Orfos's arm. It was probably fired by the same Vindicare who killed Kekrops.'

'And to think,' said Deiphobus. 'We came here to find answers. I do not hear the answer to anything. What does it benefit the Assassinorum to have a war on Opis? What could be worth the heresy of trafficking with daemons?' He looked down at the Eversor's skull-mask. 'We must open this.'

Kirav held up a hand. 'That would be…'

Lysander hefted the Fist of Dorn and smashed the coffin's lid. Freezing vapour poured out and rolled across the floor. 'If it stirs,' said Lysander, 'we must kill it before it can strike. The Assassinorum designed the Eversor as a spree-killer. It will attack without pause until it is destroyed.'

Deiphobus held his hand over the Eversor's mask. With the frosted glass gone the Assassin's breathing was just perceptible, greatly slowed down.

'Anything?' asked Lysander.

Deiphobus's face creased in concentration. 'He's been… emptied out,' he said. 'Everything has been replaced with rage. I've never felt anything so pure.' Deiphobus's eyes opened. 'There's a name.'

'Who?' said Lysander.

Deiphobus looked at the captain. 'Legienstrasse,' he said.

K-Day +15 Days
Operation Starfall

A prophet, a hermit who had lived for the better part of a century in the wooded hills a thousand kilometres north-west of Khezal, emerged from his cave as morning broke.

Streams of people were making their way across the trackless wilderness, through this bleak landscape where the temperate belt across the middle of the continent met the chill arctic climate and gave way to coniferous forests, then tundra, then snowy wastes. They had travelled from the towns and cities that owed their ancient allegiances to Khezal. They knew that the Imperium was killing everything in Khezal and in Rekaba across the sea. They knew they would be next, so they had gathered everything they could carry and left their homes.

In ages past, their peoples had fled to hidden settlements in the north, nomadic towns that could move on horseback as the seasons and enemy attacks required. So they made their way there now, in their hundreds of thousands, then their millions, in ragged caravans trudging into regions where winter never lost its grip.

The hermit found one such caravan. Three hundred men, women and children, trundling along in the few vehicles that still had fuel, with the stronger ones on foot.

'My brothers and my sisters!' he cried. 'My sons and my daughters! It pains me so to see such misery on your faces! Ah, it was to escape such sorrow that I made this cave my home. Come, I have food and water, and the warmth of my fire. Enough for all of you. From the grief on your faces, I see you have already lost many loved ones. You need lose no more. Come, share in what little I have.'

The prophet was happy to see them file into his cave, gratitude in their eyes. They had not seen a friendly face since they had abandoned their homes, and they had known nothing but misery since then. What made the prophet particularly happy was that a serpent had come to him two years before, a mighty crimson snake with scales that shone, and which sang in a beautiful voice about the gods who dwelt beyond the veil.

The snake was always hungry, and the prophet clapped and wept with joy as he heard the sound of it feeding. The screams mingled with the sound of its jaws as it crunched through bone, and it made the most wonderful music.

Finally the snake emerged.

'You have done well,' it said. 'When I was brought to this world, I feared I would perish. Now I am strong. Now I can fulfil the purpose to which I am bound. War is coming, and I must fight.'

Finally the Warp Serpent, as its worshippers had once called it, ate the prophet who had cared for it, and slithered its way across the wastes towards the coming battle.

The concentric stone rings of Lhuur stood as the only memorial to a civilisation that was long dead when the Age of Imperium began, the foundations of a metropolis that had presumably thrived when the climate of the continent's north was more hospitable. Now drifts of snow gathered among the stones, all but burying the outer rings where the paupers and foreigners had lived, and crowning the taller walls of the inner palace district.

Lhuur provided rare shelter from the snows and chill winds. The western coast had few large settlements and those that existed were now empty, drained of their population by the decrees of the Aristeia that had given dire warnings of the Imperium's impending attacks on that region. A colony of more than a thousand such evacuees had made it to Lhuur, setting up tents and makeshift dormitories among the low walls that remained of those ancient homes.

The leader of the evacuees was an old man, a scholar of leadership and heredity who had been educated at one of the universities of Khezal. He accompanied the sturdy younger men and women who explored the interior of Lhuur, seeking better shelter, perhaps somewhere underground that could be used in the event of a blizzard.

When they returned, only the leader remained. On his face was a brand with eight points, and three fingers had been severed from his left hand. He was singing as he walked through the snows, a dirge that rose and fell as he sang about beautiful creatures that roosted in a chamber of crystal, of a city in the sky carved from ivory, of silver towers standing against an endless black ocean.

The people heard the song. Through its tune and its words, the creature that had laired in Lhuur made its way into their minds. It had abandoned its body a long time ago, finding a physical form a tiresome liability, and existed only as thoughts. It had been worshipped once by a cult of intellectuals and artists who sacrificed what they created to it. Now these ragged, desperate men and women would have to do. It divided itself into a thousand fragments, each with a hunger equal to the whole. Those people, huddled screaming in Lhuur as their minds disintegrated, felt their flesh burning as eight-pointed scars rose on their skin. Black tears ran from their eyes. They shuddered and thrashed, bones cracking under the strain.

Then they walked off into the snows. They were hungry. The creature who had laired in Lhuur had not drunk of any souls for almost five years, since it had been torn from its native steppes of the warp and plunged into Opis. Some of their memories were delicious – terror, love, abandonment, betrayal, joy. But they were never enough. They still hungered, and many lost souls were wandering those wastes, eager to band up with other survivors of the walk north. And so a thousand Walkers of Lhuur spread out, all eager to propagate the seeds of the creature they carried inside them.

The Aristeia had their hunting lodges and hideaways. Some of them had even made it from Khezal or Rekaba, or all the way from Makoshaam, in defiance of the Imperial attempts to round them up, and were now lying low in those secret places. But none of them now maintained the pretence that they had any real authority over the millions of people filtering up from the southern regions and the coasts. That honour belonged to the recent visitors, the usurpers.

They were everywhere. They had laired here, in the seemingly lifeless regions of the continent, knowing all along that they would have millions of refugees to use. They were witches and the daemon-possessed, sorcerers and arch-mutants. The Aristeia hated them, those who still had their own minds, not because they were heretics and daemons but because they were new. They had no thousand-year family tree to look back on. They had no history of conquest and superiority to justify their power. But no one dared voice their hatred. Fully one-third of the Aristeia had disappeared in the five years since the invasion had begun. Another third were not themselves – brainwashed, possessed, or mad. The remainder stayed silent and cowered where they could. The ones who had made it out of the cities told themselves they were lucky, but they did not believe it.

The armies of the north were gathering whether the Aristeia wanted it or not. A mighty mountain range, the Thornholds, broke down into valleys and ranges of foothills in which hundreds of thousands could hide. Legends told of how the Thornholds held up the sky, or how they were the petrified remains of a race of giants who built Opis. Now their shadows concealed the champions of Chaos as they stood, surrounded by haloes of crackling power, drawing towards them the vast hordes who had headed here seeking survival and freedom.

'Seek liberation in blood!' cried the Warp Serpent, crimson jaws and golden teeth snapping as it spoke. 'Sweep down and put the invaders to the sword! Only in death can the Imperial yoke be cast off!'

'We are one,' said a thousand Walkers. 'We are you, and so you are one. In unity we shall triumph. The Imperium believe they face a million individuals, to be lined up and murdered one at a time. But they face one being, one mighty, infinitely powerful warrior, and they will be crushed.'

'To arms!' bellowed Karnikhal Six-Finger, surrounded by a veil of mist as his molten armour met the freezing air. 'To war! In malice bathe your hearts! In rage cleanse your souls! In war alone, honour your gods!'

At the same moment, well south of the Thornholds, Operation Starfall was in effect. A line of Imperial Guard, from the Kar Dunaish Obsidian Legion on the extreme left to the 90th Algol Siegebreakers anchoring the right, was strung across a region of broken river deltas and coniferous forests where the temperate region met the tundra. The open areas, flood plains between river tributaries and rocky near-deserts, were overlooked by the Basilisks and Griffons of the Lord Governor's Artillery and the flight paths of the Navy's Starfall Flight Group. Hundreds of thousands of men were committed, almost as many again as in Khezal and Rekaba, and the majority of the strike force's vehicles and aircraft.

Operation Starfall could not fail. Khezal might hold out. Rekaba might refuse to break. Either eventuality could be dealt with in the long term, even if both cities had to be bombed into dust. But if the battle here was lost, the whole strike force could be driven off the planet by an army sweeping south.

Tchepikov appointed the Lord Colonel of the Obsidian Legion, Ladislaus Kudelbrecht, as the commander of Operation Starfall. Kudelbrecht had earned his stripes in the crushing of the prison world rebellion on Dorrholtz, and was said to be a man who engendered greater fear in his troops than the enemy. His first act was to set up gibbets all along the front line, standing proud of the trenches and gun emplacements, where field punishments could be enacted in the full view of as many Guardsmen as possible. Starfall would not fail while Kudelbrecht still had living men to throw into the fight.

Regimental battle-scribes began naming potential battles in anticipation. Many features of the region didn't even have names, and received them then only so the Guard regiments stationed there might have a name to embroider on their standards. Skistalmein Hills. The Blutwald, Greenfire and Lower Manse forests. The River Expiatus.

Recon fighters made flyovers and brought back news of vast, ragged columns openly led by moral threats. Half a million men were making their way through the passes of the Thornhold foothills. Two hundred thousand were following the rivers that flowed southwards from the mountains, and met the strongpoints in the Guard line head on.

Imperial preachers set up chapels among the trenchworks. There was not one single Guardsman or Naval airman who did not kneel and hear a sermon. Kudelbrecht himself took confession, and needed four straight hours before he was ready to be ritually scourged. There were no atheists in Operation Starfall.

The first sighting shells from the Imperial artillery fell. They landed some way short of the main column, some way to the right of the Imperial centre, on an enemy force assumed by all to be led by the Traitor Marine known as Karnikhal Six-Fingers. The second shot was a bolt of crimson lightning that fell from an ice-clear sky, incinerating more than forty men of the 90th Algol Siegebreakers.

The hundred battles of Operation Starfall had begun.

K-Day +15 Days
Operation Requiem

Tchepikov was accustomed to keeping abreast of everything that happened in his war. Some commanders delegated such tasks, trusting senior officers under them to filter through the bedlam and bring them only what really mattered. Not Tchepikov, not now, when any one of three fronts might seal victory or collapse at any moment. He knelt at that moment in prayer, a selection of Imperial prayer books laid out in front of the prayer cushion. In the velvet dark of the prayer dome the Emperor felt close, as if His hand hovered over Tchepikov, His eyes watching from whatever plane of existence He now ruled.

A hundred pict-screens carried images from the war for Opis. Some were juddering images transmitted from pict-stealers on tanks or fighter craft. On one screen the ocean churned, waves lashing at the ruined defences of Khezal's harbour. On another the Rekaban jungle jerked past, as seen by an intelligence observer embedded in Imperial forces trying to crush the guerilla fighters mounting raids from the jungle around the city. Grainy monochrome images from an artillery spotter showed the opening salvoes of Operation Starfall dropping Castellan missiles loaded with mine clusters across an expanse of barren plain.

The cogitators of the *Merciless* transmitted any audio which met the criteria of importance and urgency.

<<Bring the right flank in!>> shouted an officer, relaying his orders through a vox-operator's rig. <<Form up along the street! Give 'em a crossfire!>> In the background was gunfire and shrieking, as his force closed in around a concentration of crazed enemy militia in the ruins of a palatial Aristeia courthouse in Khezal.

<<They're gone! They're all gone! We're... we're holding here. The Deucalians are gone, they've collapsed. We're cut off...>> The voice was of a junior officer who had found himself in command of a pioneer unit building barricades and strongpoints in the wake of a Deucalian advance through the streets of Rekaba. That advance had halted and the foremost units had gone, vanished into a labyrinth of pitfalls and open sewers infested with mutants. That assault, then, had failed, and it would be only luck that saw more than a handful make it back to Imperial-held territory. But it was only one of dozens of probing attacks. Some would succeed, some would fail.

<<This is the troop transport *Fulminatus Tertius*, reporting the safe arrival in orbit of the 8th and 12th Arkhanos Demi-Cavalry.>> More reinforcements, part of the steady tide of

men and armour on which the battles for Opis relied.

More voices. More good and bad news. More death, defeat and triumph. Tchepikov absorbed it all, seeking the overall truth of Opis's war that would help him sift out the truth from the platitudes when his intelligence officers briefed him on the day's events.

The screens flickered. One by one they went dark. The audio feeds distorted, then died.

Tchepikov knelt up, looking around him.

'What has happened?' he demanded. 'Where are my comms?'

The door to the prayer dome boomed open. Unwelcome light flooded in, silhouetting a shape far larger than a man.

'Damn it, Deiphobus!' barked Tchepikov. 'I told you to get off my ship. Have the Imperial Fists come back to the fold? Has Lysander accepted my command?'

Deiphobus walked into the dome. In one hand he was dragging the sagging form of a Naval soldier, part of the intelligence support battalion who provided the security on board the *Merciless*. The Librarian dropped the man, who curled up and moaned. 'The Space Marines have not abandoned ten thousand years of independence at your request, commander,' he said. 'And as for staying off this ship, if you want to keep an Imperial Fist away you should step up your security. To their credit, I almost broke a sweat disarming them.'

'Have you not antagonised this command enough?' retorted Tchepikov. 'I have a war to run. I cannot spare the attention to answer these insults.'

Deiphobus took two long strides to where Tchepikov stood, and before the Imperial commander could move Deiphobus's gauntlet was around his neck. 'Insults?' said Deiphobus in a low, dangerous tone. 'I speak of death. Guns raised against my brother Imperial Fists. Mind-wiped troops, under the orders of the Officio Assassinorum. Speak, Tchepikov. Tell me all you know.'

Tchepikov did not back down. His capacity to do so had been killed off some time ago, as he ascended the ranks of the Imperial Guard. If fear flickered in his eyes, he forced it back down a split second later. 'I need explain nothing,' said Tchepikov. 'I do not answer to the Imperial Fists. I do not respond to those who threaten and defy me. Go back to your own war, Deiphobus. You have made it clear you will not fight in mine, and I have no reason to assist in yours.'

'I said talk!' yelled Deiphobus. He threw Tchepikov to the floor. 'Do you think this a game? My battle-brothers have died at Imperial hands! The Assassinorum has men and agents on this planet, and they see fit to take the lives of Imperial Fists to fulfil their mission! You are the lord of the Imperial forces on Opis. You cannot pretend you know nothing of the Assassinorum's aims here. We have seen the facility in the Rekaban jungle. We know how Kekrops died. Lest you become an enemy of the Imperial Fists, Tchepikov, tell me everything.'

'I am the Lord Commander of this world!' yelled Tchepikov, picking himself up from the floor, one hand holding his throat. 'I answer to none but the God-Emperor Himself!'

A pistol was in Tchepikov's hand. Deiphobus saw it was an inferno pistol, a miniaturised melta-weapon of ancient design, its barrel inlaid with golden scrollwork and its handle encased in pearl. It was a duellist's weapon, rare and valuable, with which a nobleman could cut through the armour that a dishonourable opponent might wear.

It could cut through power armour.

Deiphobus leapt on Tchepikov and batted the commander's gun hand away with his own. The pistol fired, a fat, deep-red bolt of power punching through the prayer dome's wall. Deiphobus lifted Tchepikov off the floor, snapped his wrist with a twist of his hand, and threw the commander into the bank of pict-screens.

Screens shattered. Sparks burst around Tchepikov as he tumbled to the ground.

The clattering of boots on the deck caught Deiphobus's attention. Naval troopers were gathering at the door, lasguns in hand.

'Fire!' shouted Deiphobus. 'Try to shoot me down, I beg of you! I yearn to kill an honest foe!'

None of the troopers pulled the trigger. The barrels of their lasguns lowered, and they seemed to shrink as Deiphobus stared them down.

'For the last time,' said Deiphobus, turning to Tchepikov. 'Speak.'

Tchepikov struggled into a seated position. His hand hung awkwardly, wrist wrenched at an unnatural angle, and the colour had drained from him. He, too, looked like he had shrunk, now swamped by his uniform coat. Tiny cuts on his face from the shattered pict-screens were starting to bleed.

'They will kill me,' he gasped.

'I'll kill you!' shouted Deiphobus, drawing his bolt pistol.

Tchepikov held up his good hand. 'I know. I know you will,

Imperial Fist. But… but they told me they would have free run of Opis, and that I would not stand in their way. It was not a request. And I knew that I would be killed and replaced if I defied them. I will do my duty here on Opis. I will see this war through to the end. I cannot do that if they have me assassinated.'

'Who?' demanded Deiphobus. 'Give me a name.'

'I know no names!' said Tchepikov. 'The Assassinorum. That much I know. Sightings of agents and Assassinorum troops on Opis were to be suppressed. Any support they requested, they would receive. This came to me through the highest encrypted channels, no names, no specifics, but the implications were clear.'

'That is not enough. Give me more. Something we can use. Something we can act on. The Imperial Fists are no less relentless than the Assassinorum, Tchepikov, and even they cannot match us in our anger.'

Tchepikov swallowed. The commander was gone – in his place was a normal man, as capable of fear as anyone else. 'Scarfinal Island,' he said. 'I had to keep it clear for spacecraft landings. I know nothing more. Not who is there, not what they are doing. That is all I know. The Emperor's eyes upon me, that is all I know. I swear it.'

Deiphobus holstered his gun. 'You said you have a duty to do on Opis,' he said. 'You are right. For this reason I will let you live. Whether Lysander agrees with my decision depends much on what we find at Scarfinal Island.' He turned back to the troops at the door. 'We are both servants of the same Emperor,' he said to them. 'Stand aside.'

'Do as he says,' said Tchepikov. 'Stand down, men. Shoulder your weapons.'

The troops stood aside and Deiphobus left the prayer dome.

'You would do well,' he said as he walked away, 'to offer another prayer. This time, pray that I do not have to return.'

Three hundred troops stood to attention, as they always did for ten hours per day, unmoving, unthinking.

General Seven walked up and down the ranks. He inspected the troops once every two hours for signs of physical degradation, equipment disrepair or the various physiological ailments that tended to hamper the effectiveness of a mind-wiped soldier. Nervous systems were particularly at risk. Repeated mind scourging and reprogramming shortened the life of nerve clusters and certain areas of the brain. Malcoordination and tics were particularly dangerous signs.

There were no anomalies that cycle.

'Seven here,' said the general in response to the vox-chirp in his ear.

A series of code chirrups sounded.

'I acknowledge. Time query.'

The response suggested a time span of between two and four hours.

'Thy will be done,' said General Seven. Like his men, General Seven lacked a name or discrete personality, but was capable of much more autonomy of thought than the majority of the troopers. He had to be trusted with leading them as well as fighting, and for that reason had many more of his original faculties intact.

'Landing detail!' he ordered. 'Clear the landing pad and stow the defence cannon! Docking clamps and refuelling made ready! Hundred-man protocol detail, full dress. To your duties!'

The men of the Officio Assassinorum broke up into work teams to prepare the landing pad, a circle of rockcrete studded with docking clamps and maintenance access hatches. Scarfinal Island protected the pad well, being the relic of a volcanic eruption that had left high, deadly basalt cliffs and peaks surrounding a large central depression. Overhead clouds of seabirds wheeled and screeched as they flitted back and forth between the ocean feeding grounds and the nesting caves among the cliffs. There were few other sounds, for the troopers did not speak unless it was strictly necessary.

They had once been judged by the Temples of the Officio Assassinorum, these men. Some were death cultists picked from the many deviant churches of the Emperor. Others were the hereditary offerings of famous bloodlines, who were bound to hand over their most martially able offspring to the agents of the Imperium. A few had even been psychopaths chosen from Imperial prisons, whose skills and temperaments made them ripe for training.

But they had all failed. The great majority always failed – some were killed during their training, others were deemed too dangerous to live. Those that were intact were scrubbed clean of their memories and placed in the blank uniforms, devoid of name or rank, of the Officio Assassinorum's own army.

The *Damnatio Memoriae* descended from the overcast sky, parting the clouds and the ocean spray, driving away the flocks of seabirds. It was a plain black craft of an ungainly shape, with an asymmetrical, blocky nose and great flaring engines. It was small by the standards of war-craft, easily able to fit onto the island's small landing pad, but it was ancient even by the standards of the finest Imperial spaceships and hence was faster and more reliable that almost any other craft in the service of the Emperor. It had to be, for it had ferried its passengers across a good expanse of the Imperium in less than a week. A pilgrim craft or battleship might have made the same journey in a year.

The ship landed in a sweep of hot exhaust. The engines powered down and the docking clamps slammed shut around its landing gear.

The honour guard of troopers, in their black-and-purple dress uniforms, filed up to flank the disembarkation ramp as it descended. Lector Gydwyllien, in a black greatcoat with the iron skull badge of the Officio's lower orders, hurried from the island's command building to greet the half-dozen figures who descended.

Two were scribes, partly augmetic individuals accompanied

by trundling lectern-servitors, whole libraries of history and execution lore filed away in the datamedia concealed in their skulls. Two were bodyguards in gilded power armour forged to resemble ancient plate, carrying power greatswords and shields bearing the heraldry of a coiled snake and a rose. One was a medicae officer, in plain black with serpentine mechadendrites fixed to both shoulders.

The final figure wore a long ball-gown of deep-maroon velvet trimmed with ermine, long white gloves and a heavy mechanical collar which did nothing to dull the elegance and beauty she carried with her. Her skin was the colour of polished hardwood and her face could not have been more perfect if it had been sculpted. A thin rapier hung at her waist and she walked with a cane, although she had no signs of infirmity.

'Lady Syncella,' said the Lector, kneeling at the foot of the ramp. 'The honour is more than any of my station could deserve.'

'And yet this honour is brought about by failure,' said Syncella. Her voice had a flat, mechanical quality, as if she were speaking the words of someone else. 'As grave a failure as can befall the Temples of the Death.'

'All who transgress shall be punished,' said Lector Gydwyllien.

'All who transgress,' echoed Lady Syncella, 'shall be punished.' They were the same words inscribed above the bridge of the *Damnatio Memoriae*, and into the memories of those Assassinorum troops who still had the capacity to remember for themselves. They were the first lesson an agent of the Temples ever learned. 'I will speak with Agent Skult.'

'Agent Skult is in the field,' said Gydwyllien. 'I shall have a summons transmitted–'

'No,' said Syncella. 'I will go to him. The *Damnatio Memoriae* can take me to him faster than he can get to the island. Where is he?'

'In the Blood Eyrie,' replied Gydwyllien.

'Has he reported any sightings?'

'None since Mountain 1194.'

'Then time becomes more pertinent still. I shall require a hundred and fifty men, fully armed with heavy and squad weapons. See to it.'

Gydwyllien bowed his head. 'It will be done within the hour.'

Lady Syncella laid a delicate hand on the Lector's brow. 'The Emperor's own will out,' she said. 'The stain will be washed away. Shadows will fall over the Temples again.'

'I pray,' said Lector Gydwyllien. 'Every hour, I pray anew.'

'You will not be permitted to remember.'

'Then I will pray for my mind to be scoured clean.'

Lady Syncella shook her head and smiled. It was a convincing facsimile, an expression of comforting sorrow. Like so much else, it had been sleep-taught to her, her facial features stimulated until the muscle memory had built up and she could pick this particular configuration from a list she kept filed away in her mind.

'No, Lector,' she said. 'That will not be enough.'

'Then my next prayer,' said Gydwyllien, 'shall be for death.'

'Rejoice then that its hour is known,' said Syncella. 'I must leave you now, and maintain silence. I will speak to you again soon, when our work is done.'

Lady Syncella glanced at her attendants. The mind-impulse unit built into her hindbrain sent a signal to them to accompany her back on board the *Damnatio Memoriae*.

Gydwyllien turned back to the troops who stood silently ranked up.

General Seven walked to the front of the troops and turned smartly. 'Squad armaments and make ready to depart!' he barked. 'At the double!

The troops marched off towards the barracks and storerooms. Already other soldiers were hauling refuelling lines and adjusting the control surfaces of the *Damnatio Memoriae's* stunted wings for prolonged atmospheric flight.

Gydwyllien wiped away the tear that had gathered in his eye. True beauty always made him weep, and there was nothing as beautiful as the purity of death.

'There,' said Gorgythion. His face was bathed in the green of the sensor display, projected across the viewing port in front of him. 'Exhaust wash leaving the island, staying low. They're not going back into orbit. We were too late.'

'Are you certain?' said Sergeant Kirav, watching through the door to the passenger compartment. 'That's past sensor range.'

'A Thunderhawk does not have the sensors of the *Sanctifier*,' said Gorgythion. 'But they can tell much to someone who knows how to read them.'

The blotches of grainy light, building up a picture of the telltale energy signatures around the Thunderhawk, meant nothing to the eye of a man like Kirav. But Gorgythion was the best pilot in the Imperial Fists.

'Follow them,' said Kirav. 'Stay low.'

The gunship prowled at wave height, salt spray lashing at the viewport. Red warning runes winked across the controls and Gorgythion ignored them. Scarfinal Island, a crown of black basalt lashed by the roughening waves, flashed by to one side. On the other side was the coastline north of Khezal, its towns and cities now empty of souls, all of whom had fled north to join the growing catastrophe there. Within a few moments Scarfinal Island was out of view. The Thunderhawk, which bore the name of the *Gilded Pyre*, whistled into the open ocean, guided only by the faintest traces left by the passage of a ship that was several minutes ahead of it.

'Slow and ungainly,' said Gorgythion, seemingly to himself. 'Half the bird the *Sanctifier* was. But I'll show you what you are. I'll teach you.'

Kirav turned back to the Imperial Fists assembled in the *Gilded Pyre*. 'We're following them.'

'Who?' asked Captain Lysander. In the grav-restraints around him were strapped the Imperial Fists of Squad Kirav, Scout Squad Orfos and Squad Septuron, along with Brother Ucalegon.

'We don't know,' said Kirav.

'Whoever it is,' said Lysander, 'these twenty battle-brothers and this single gunship will have to be enough to take them on.'

'And we will prevail,' said Ucalegon. The obsidian sword was strapped into the restraint beside him, its blade glinting in the weak compartment light. 'As Rogal Dorn prevailed on the *Vengeful Spirit*. As we have always done.'

'I see her,' came Gorgythion's voice from the cockpit. 'She's fast. A spaceship configured for atmospheric flight.'

'Can you keep up?' said Kirav.

'I shall teach this machine how,' replied Gorgythion. 'I have not had a single enemy in my sights that has ever escaped. The *Gilded Pyre* wants to fall behind. She wants to give up. But one such as I has never flown her, and I will teach her what she can really do.'

'Then the occasion lends itself to prayer,' said Lysander. 'Lead us, Brother Ucalegon.'

The Blood Eyrie was named after the rust-red stones of a cluster of peaks which crowned a clutch of mountains in the very heart of the range. In this same mountain range, many kilometres away, Squad Orfos had lost two brothers, one dead and one wounded. One of Opis's least-known civilisations, absent entirely from the history of the Aristeia and its conquered enemies, had once performed the impossible feat of surviving up here in the ice-cold sky. The Eyrie was a series of great caverns, open to the air, and cut through the red peaks. Some peaks were completely hollowed out, open like bell towers to the elements, their peaks a lattice of stone ribs. Stone bridges between the peaks seemed as thin and delicate as the strands of a spider's web.

Eagles and spindly, winged humans were carved everywhere. Their long, mournful faces looked out across the expanse of mountains which from here looked endless. Once thousands of people had lived in wooden buildings built into the structure of the Eyrie, but now they had decayed away leaving only the skeleton of a city higher than the clouds.

For the first time in the better part of three thousand years, the wind was not the only sound. The drone of engines changed pitch as the black slab of the *Damnatio Memoriae* swept down between the peaks of the Blood Eyrie. It slowed and hovered, the cannon in its nose playing across the skeletons of the city.

It descended as if to land in one of the peaks, where the stone ribs were spaced widely enough for it to set down. Then its descent halted and it jerked upwards, like a bird startled into flight. Burning silver flares sprayed from its back, exploding in showers of sparks.

Its sensors had spotted the second craft, one which wove its way through the mountains. It was all but a shadow in the valleys of the mountain range, but now, between the soaring peaks of the Blood Eyrie, it had been forced to emerge into the open.

It was a Thunderhawk gunship of the Imperial Fists.

The guns of the *Damnatio Memoriae* erupted. Explosive fire hammered into the mountainside behind the gunship, throwing down cascades of rock.

But the gunship did not flee. It was outgunned by the huge-calibre guns of the far larger spacefaring ship. Its own weapons were not designed to penetrate the hide of the *Damnatio Memoriae*. But nevertheless, it turned towards the larger ship, and its own weapons blazed in reply.

* * *

'Rise up, *Gilded Pyre*!' shouted Gorgythion. 'Rise and be counted! The spirit of the *Sanctifier* burns in you!'

The Thunderhawk spun and dropped a hundred metres, sprays of fire from the enemy ship shrieking over it.

'How did they see us?' yelled Kirav from the passenger compartment.

'Their eyes are keen!' replied Gorgythion. 'But we are here to fight! In the air or on the ground, we are here to kill!'

'Beros! Stentor!' ordered Lysander. 'Get on the heavy bolters!'

Beros and Stentor hauled open two side hatches, and the freezing mountain air swirled in. Two heavy bolters swung out on either side of the Thunderhawk.

Beros sighted the black shape of the enemy ship swinging past his sights. His heavy bolter slammed out chains of fire, bursting against the enemy's hull. The enemy ship was small for a spacegoing vessel, but it was still easily four or five times the Thunderhawk's size and the impacts seemed barely to dent its plain black livery.

'My guns are the faculties of my mind,' said Gorgythion. His hands played over the gunship's controls as if without any effort on his part, his piloting instincts so finely honed they were a reflex action that left his mind free. 'My bullets are the thoughts of my revenge. My sword is my honour. My armour is the certainty that I will prevail. Thus spake Rogal Dorn.'

One of the carved peaks loomed between the Thunderhawk and the enemy ship.

'I turn faster than you,' said Gorgythion. 'Dread lumbering

beast. Compared to me, you have the guns of a battleship. But you turn like one, too.'

The Thunderhawk's nose cannons fired – not into the enemy ship, but into the spurs of stone that encompassed the abandoned city of the eyrie.

Brother Stentor saw what his pilot was doing. He swung his heavy bolter to fire parallel to the gunship's nose, almost leaning out of the gun port. The heavy bolter jumped in his hands and explosive shells tore through the spur directly ahead, shattering it until it was cut right through.

The *Damnatio Memoriae* turned its nose up, it engines gunning to push it clear of the Eyrie, but it was half a second too late.

One of the bony spurs fell and sliced off the ship's stubby left wing. The engine at the root of the wing exploded, throwing shards of spinning metal in every direction. The ship dropped to its wounded side, pivoting as it fell, and crunched into the mountain peak. It brought more stonework down with it, and fragments of ancient carvings rained down.

The *Damnatio Memoriae* came to rest a few metres from the edge of the peak. Burning fuel poured from the wound in its side, spreading into a lake of fire that fell over the mountainside in a waterfall of flame.

Hatches swung open. Black-armoured soldiers jumped out, running from the fire and forming up for cover among the rubble. More than a hundred of them fled the wreck. Among them was the dark, flitting shape of Lady Syncella, skittering across the hull like a black spider.

The Thunderhawk gunship was not finished. The smoke

pouring from the ruptured engine was thrown aside into twisting columns as the Thunderhawk swept low over the wreck, ready to bring the battle to the ground.

Orfos jumped from the opening rear ramp of the *Gilded Pyre*. Squad Septuron jumped beside him, Assault-Sergeant Septuron himself almost head-first with his chainsword in hand.

Orfos threw out his right hand instinctively as the mountaintop rushed up at him. The bionic responded and he took the impact of his landing on his new iron palm.

He took in his situation in a second. The enemy troops were sheltering ahead of him, in the cover of the fallen rubble. Orfos was in the open. He knew how long it would take for the enemy to get him in their sights and to open fire. He knew what would happen to him if he was caught by the full force of their fire. The rules and probabilities of battle rushed through his mind, placed there by sleep-teaching sessions and the study of Rogal Dorn's war-parables.

Orfos put his head down and ran. Las-fire was already hissing through the air around him. He dropped down and skidded into the cover of the enemy ship's fallen wing, a burning black slab that had embedded itself in the stone of some ancient mountaintop street.

'Brothers!' he called into his squad's vox-channel. 'On me! Be swift, and give not a moment to breathe!'

Enriaan was firing as he ran. Shots from his rifle cracked among the las-fire. Scout Privar leapt up onto the severed wing, slamming back-first against a control surface that was jammed sticking straight up.

Orfos risked a look past the edge of the wing. The enemy were the same visored troops his squad had faced when they took down the convoy outside Khezal on K-Day. Among them moved one who was faster than a man, who skittered between the fallen stone as fast as a striking snake. It was a woman, wearing a ball-gown of all things, but one artfully slit to give her full freedom of movement. Bolter fire stitched around her and she flipped over it even as one of the troopers beside her was blasted open. She had a metal collar around her neck and a knife in her hand that glowed golden yellow.

Squad Septuron were landing around Orfos. 'Onward! Onward! Speed and death!' yelled Assault-Sergeant Septuron. The cold mountain light glinted on the medals and trophies hung from his blade as he held it high like an army's standard. His squad ran forward in his wake, charging through the opening las-shots to close with the enemy.

Orfos broke cover and ran behind them. Already Septuron's blade was blooded, thrust through the stomach of a trooper who had leapt forwards to meet him. The other Imperial Fists were among the enemy in a second, swinging their own blades left and right, carving limbs from bodies.

The enemy were not running. Orfos shot one down with his bolt pistol, blowing his leg off at the hip. The head of another snapped back, hit between the eyes, and Orfos did not have to turn to know that Scout Enriaan had fired the shot.

In the bedlam, the impact of the Imperial Fists was winning. As resolute as the enemy were, and as numerous, Squad Septuron had hit them too hard. Blood was spattered across the stones and suddenly the fallen masonry was not cover at all, but a cruel labyrinth which forced the enemy to fight in ones and twos against Space Marines who could fight them at a range too close for their lasguns to be brought to bear.

Somewhere in Orfos's mind, he registered movement overhead. It was something familiar, something he had seen before and which had embedded itself in his mind as a warning.

He looked up. Among the still-intact stonework of the Blood Eyrie a shape crouched, nothing more than a shadow upon a shadow, the same colour as the dark stone and barely distinguishable. But it was a human shape.

'You!' yelled Orfos. 'I see you!'

The enemy sniper, the same who had taken Orfos's hand and left Scout Geryius critically wounded, the same who had killed Lord Inquisitor Kekrops and brought war to Opis, knew he had been spotted. He jumped down from his perch and vanished among the scattered wreckage that had spilled from the crashed ship's ruined engine.

Orfos ran again, leaping over a fallen chunk of stone. Squad Septuron had their battle, the close-quarters murder for which they had been trained by their Chapter. Orfos had his. He ignored the las-fire and death all around him, and ran straight for the man who had taken his hand.

'An Assassin does not stand and fight,' said Ucalegon. 'An Assassin flees the battle, to return and bring death when the guns are silent.'

'The words of Roboute Guilliman,' said Lady Syncella. 'In the *Codex Astartes*.'

Lady Syncella had made it halfway across the stone bridge

when the Emperor's Champion had leapt from the Thunder-hawk and landed on the bridge ahead of her. The stone had splintered under his weight, but had held, just barely. Now his armoured bulk formed a complete barrier across the bridge.

'You know of the Codex,' said Ucalegon.

'One never knows when a Space Marine might be one's next target,' replied Lady Syncella. 'I must be familiar with the battle-lore of anyone I might have to kill.'

Their words covered up the process of weighing up one another's strengths and weaknesses. Both knew it.

Lady Syncella was an extraordinary sight. Ucalegon had never faced anything like her. Compared even to the mind-wiped Assassinorum troops, she was slight in form – tall, but seemingly without muscle. Compared to a Space Marine, she was hardly there at all. Her dress was as unlike a soldier's uni-form as could be imagined. Her skin was flawless. Only the ugly, thick iron collar around her neck, and the power knife in her hand, spoiled the effect. But for them, she could have been hosting a ball for the elites of the Imperium's noble houses.

Ucalegon took a two-handed grip on the obsidian sword, aiming its tip at the woman's throat. 'The Officio Assas-sinorum brought war to Opis,' he said. 'A war in which battle-brothers of mine have lost their lives. Their blood is on your hands. You have manipulated my Chapter into fighting your battles. Our honour is befouled. Either crime would be enough to compel me to exact satisfaction. Of both are you guilty, Assassin.'

'I marvel, Imperial Fist, that the Imperium's finest soldiers can be so damnably blind.' The woman switched to a reverse grip on her power knife. 'Is that all you see? Crimes against your Chapter? Mine is the Imperium to save. We are here on Opis for the good of mankind.'

'Then you will not be swerved by words,' said Ucalegon. 'Only deeds remain.'

'Only deeds,' said the woman. 'Well put.'

Lady Syncella moved so fast it seemed that slices of time fell out as she moved, jolting her from point to point with no visible movement in between. She handsprang over Ucalegon, landing behind him before he had powered the obsidian blade forward in a thrust. Ucalegon swivelled on his front foot, bringing the sword around in a wide arc, but Lady Syncella flipped over the blade.

The power knife in her hand was aimed at Ucalegon's heart. It flickered forwards quicker than Ucalegon could react. Its power field spat blue sparks as the blade punched through the ceramite of Ucalegon's breastplate and the inner armour of his fused ribcage.

It speared through his heart. He could feel it, feel the spasms of pain running down his limbs as his heart was sliced in two. He fell, coldness flooding through his body.

Syncella stepped over him, heading for the adjacent mountaintop of the Blood Eyrie.

Ucalegon's gauntlet closed on her ankle. Syncella was thrown forwards onto her face.

'We have two hearts,' said Ucalegon. 'You forget your prey.'

The second blade was in Syncella's hand as quickly as a magic trick. Without a word she stabbed it down through

Ucalegon's hand, transfixing it to the stone. It was a normal blade, without a power field, and it lodged in the stone.

'I left you a heart intact so the Imperium would not be robbed of such a warrior,' she said. 'I take it a man of honour would not stoop to scorn such a gift?'

'Harpy!' spat Ucalegon, and tore his hand free. He jumped to his feet, regaining his grip on the obsidian blade. 'I will take your heart for mine. And you will not fare as well without it.'

'I tire of this!' snapped Syncella. With a mental impulse she unfastened the clamps holding the collar around her neck.

The wave of cold, agonising hatred hit Ucalegon as hard as a gunshot. He fell back onto one knee. He had never felt anything like it before. Perhaps it was something like being plunged into ice-cold water, but the chill ran right through him, as if every cell of his body was immersed. And it had an emotion, as well. It was pure scorn, the emotion of someone who despised him made real, congealing into reality and encasing him from head to toe.

His internal organs felt frozen solid. He had barely enough control over his body to keep himself from toppling off the edge of the narrow bridge. This was not pain – a Space Marine knew pain well enough to understand it when it came, set it aside and keep fighting. This was something else. A violation of mind and body, an invisible hand that closed around his soul and crushed.

'I gift you your life again,' said the woman, giving Ucalegon a final backwards glance. 'Take care you do not owe me too much.'

Then she flitted the rest of the way across the bridge,

disappearing among the spurs of the mountaintop, leaving Ucalegon gasping for breath.

Lysander stepped out just as Syncella passed, and could not keep the feeling of satisfaction from his mind as he felt her slam into his storm shield.

The woman did not fall. She rolled as she fell, coming up in a low, dangerous crouch, power knife in hand, her lips drawn back in a look of feline rage.

Lysander bit down on the ice rising in him, keeping it from filling up his veins.

'I faced an Untouchable on Fortis Magna,' he said. He teeth were clenched with the effort. 'It was an abomination. It was an affront to the very soul. The closest I ever came to giving in to fear. But I overcame. I killed him. And now your favourite trick has failed.'

Syncella growled and stalked to one side, circling Lysander. The waves of anti-emotion coming off her faltered a little, a ripple running through them, as she refocused on a new enemy.

'We are alone on this mountaintop,' said Lysander. 'Your men are assailed by my battle-brothers and soon they will die.'

'I am nothing,' she said. 'Even now my best agent takes your brothers in his sights…'

'I saw you fleeing your ship!' retorted Lysander. 'I knew you were the one. You cannot hide the trappings of an Assassin. Not many of my brothers have witnessed the ways of the Culexus Temple, but I have.'

'And now you are going to kill me,' said Syncella, 'because that is what you do. You are no more sophisticated a weapon than the mindless souls who do my bidding. At least they do not claim to be anything more.'

She darted forwards as fast as a bullet. Lysander jumped forwards to meet her and deflected the power knife off his shield. He swept the Fist of Dorn around to trip her up but she spun in the air as she leapt over it, landing behind him.

'Unless,' she said, 'you want answers.'

'It is not a case of wanting anything,' said Lysander. 'I will have them.'

Syncella leapt backwards and powered off the stone spur behind her, diving at Lysander from above. Lysander held his shield up but Syncella had read the movement before he made it. She hit the ground just in front of him, knife flicking up towards his abdomen.

Lysander had read her, too. He did not have the room to bring the Fist of Dorn to bear, so he cracked the back of his fist into the side of her head.

Syncella sprawled away across the stone. Lysander stepped after her and brought the Fist of Dorn down towards her. She rolled to one side as the hammer's head fell and smashed a crater into the mountaintop. Splinters of stone fell.

'How long since someone laid a hand on you?' said Lysander. 'What are you? A Grand Master of the Assassinorum? How long since you faced someone who could defeat you?'

Syncella touched a hand to her face. She was bleeding.

'It seems that every day, I face a foe who can beat me,' said

Lysander. 'One who can hurt me. But not one of them has done for me yet. That is why I call myself a soldier, and not an Assassin.'

'I am Lady Syncella of the Culexus! And I thank you, Captain Lysander. I have not felt a hostile hand on me for three hundred years. I had forgotten what it really was to fight.'

'Then tell me why you brought war to Opis,' said Lysander. 'Or I will teach you what it means to lose.'

'Stop killing my men, Lysander, and perhaps I will be minded to talk.'

For a moment the two faced one another, every muscle wound up ready to pounce.

Then Lysander switched to the all-squads vox. 'Cease fire, brothers! Cease fire! Put up your swords!'

Scout-Sergeant Orfos dived at the Assassin, his combat knife in one hand and bolt pistol in another, forcing his eyes to focus on the barely visible shadow that was his opponent.

He hit the Assassin shoulder-first. But his opponent was ready, wrapping an arm around Orfos's waist and throwing him over his body to slam back-first onto the rock.

The Assassin's camouflage flickered and Orfos saw him properly for the first time. He was dressed in a complete covering of black synskin, ribbed and panelled to protect the vital organs. The synskin covered his scalp, and his face was concealed by a mask with an opaque eyepiece and breathing grille. His sniper rifle was as long as he was tall, with a pistol in a holster as a backup. Orfos recognised the technology of the synskin from the Assassinorum facility, but had no time to register anything else before the Assassin's pistol was in his hand.

Orfos knocked the gun aside with his knife. The Assassin kicked Orfos's own bolt pistol out of his hand. Orfos kicked up into the Assassin's midriff but the Assassin was suddenly not there.

He had moved faster than anything Orfos had fought before. The cold against the back of his skull was surely the barrel of the Assassin's pistol, and he had a split second to live.

'Cease fire, brothers!' came Lysander's voice over the vox. 'Cease fire!'

The pistol did not fire. Orfos did not die.

'I have been given my orders,' said the Assassin. 'And so have you.' His voice was utterly calm, as if synthesised. He was not even out of breath.

'Holster your gun,' said Orfos.

'I have not been given that order,' replied the Assassin.

In the corner of his eye, Orfos could see the Assassinorum soldiers, their lasguns lowered, standing motionless. Their dead lay around their feet. The only sound from the battle was now the whirring of Squad Septuron's chainblades.

'You killed Kekrops,' said Orfos.

The Assassin did not reply.

'You shot my brother Scout and me.'

'You were in my way.'

Orfos thought back to the mountainside where he had last encountered the Assassin. The face of Lord Speaker vel Sephronaas before Orfos had blown the traitor's head off. The feel of hot steel slicing through his arm, Geryius's blood spraying across his back.

Suddenly, he began to understand.

'You seeded Opis with moral threats,' said Lysander. 'And killed Kekrops when he came here to investigate them. Why?'

'Why else does an Assassin do anything?' said Lady Syncella.

Neither had moved. Each was still ready to kill the other.

'You have a target on Opis.'

'Of course we do,' said Syncella. 'Would the Assassinorum have come here at all, have sacrificed so much for this war, if there was no target?'

'Who is it?'

'Someone whose existence is prejudicial to the continued survival of the human race,' replied Lady Syncella. 'The worst kind of foe that exists.'

'The same could be said of every target the Assassinorum hunts down,' replied Lysander. 'I would imagine those exact words are used in the Senatorum Imperialis when debating the Assassinorum's use. What makes this different?'

'It is enough that we know,' replied Syncella.

'Then the honour of my Chapter is not satisfied!' snapped Lysander. 'The duty of the Imperial Guard is to fight and die without ever asking why. But I am a Space Marine! I am the chosen of the Emperor! I will not see the blood of my brethren shed in the darkness! When we risk our lives, we do it on our terms, not yours!'

'Honour?' said Syncella, her voice heavy with scorn. 'You are better than that! Are you not Captain Lysander, for whom no sacrifice is too great? We know what you will do for victory. We know how many have died, and much worse, at your behest, for victory.'

Lysander took a half-step forward. With the tension crackling between them, it was as threatening a gesture as the cocking of a gun. 'You will watch your words,' he said.

'Why?' said Syncella. 'Because of honour?' She shook her head. 'The common soldier must believe that he is fighting for good against evil. Perhaps even a Space Marine must believe this. But you and I, Lysander, know the war we fight is not a matter of right or wrong. It is a clash between two different flavours of amorality. One path has us survive. One, the path of disorder, Chaos and the predatory xenos, has us die out. Neither is right or wrong. You know this, Lysander, he for whom no sacrifice is too great for victory, as well as I. As well as anyone.'

Lysander fought for an answer, but he could find none.

She was right. It was not about right or wrong. Lysander had done things that any right-minded man would call evil, because that was the only way to secure victory.

'But this is Opis,' he said finally. 'This is war. Millions will die.'

'You can do better than that,' said Lady Syncella, and even to Lysander his words had sounded hollow. 'Do not fight us,' continued Syncella. 'We are both on the side of survival, and nothing else matters. Not right or wrong, not honour, nothing. You who would do anything for victory must also let us conduct this war as we will. For victory.'

'You summoned the daemons of the warp!' retorted

Lysander. 'You made pacts with sorcerers and witches!'

'We broke them!' snapped Syncella. The remark had hit a nerve. 'We tracked them down and shattered their will. We bound them into our service. And when we are done, they will be summoned into our presence and executed. We will have done more to eliminate such threats to the Imperium than any servant of the Emperor could claim, and in doing so, will have destroyed a far greater threat. Do not pretend that great men, saviours of the Imperium, have not stepped over that line, too.'

Lysander took a long breath. 'What is your target?' he asked.

'I cannot ask you to burden yourself with that knowledge,' said Syncella. 'Fight as you have done. Or leave Opis to us. It makes little difference. Do not fight us, and your duty here is done.'

'If there is an enemy of the Imperium here, if it is as serious as you claim, then my duty is to kill it.'

'Do not follow us, Imperial Fist. I will not allow myself to be brought to battle again as here. And there must be no more blood shed between allies. Agreed?'

'What is your target?' repeated Lysander.

'I will not tell you,' said Syncella. 'And mine is one mind from which your Librarian Deiphobus will be tearing no secrets. Serve on, Captain Lysander, as we shall.'

Syncella turned her back on Lysander and walked away, towards the narrow stone bridge that led to the crash site.

On the bridge were two more figures. One was Scout-Sergeant Orfos. The other was an Assassin going by his synskin suit, and a follower of the Vindicare Temple going by the sniper rifle he carried, an elaborate weapon with a large suppressor and a scope with a multiple lens selector. Lysander could tell its high craftsmanship even from the other side of the bridge.

Orfos was running. The Assassin was pursuing him, with his pistol sidearm in his hand, ready to shoot.

Syncella seemed prepared for the Assassin, but not for Orfos.

'It's the translator,' said Orfos. 'The Assassinorum's target. It's vel Sephronaas's translator. He was shooting at her but Geryius and I got in the way.'

'Skult?' demanded Syncella of the Assassin.

'Say the word, mistress,' replied the Vindicare.

'It is too late now,' said Syncella.

'The translator?' said Lysander. Lysander had an image in his mind of perhaps the least threatening opponent he could imagine. The skinny, miserable woman who crouched at the Lord Speaker's side and translated the language of the Aristeia into the Low Gothic used by its commoners. She had barely made any impression on his memory at all.

'She could twist the Lord Speaker's words into anything,' continued Orfos. 'She was controlling the Aristeia through him. That's who was being moved through the refugee camp. Not vel Sephronaas. His translator. She's the target. She's the reason we're here.' Orfos took another few steps forwards and stopped, having walked into the area of the psychic anomaly generated by Syncella.

'Syncella?' demanded Lysander. 'Is this so?'

Syncella looked at him. There was no expression on her face now. Her previous interactions had been feigned, the nuances of facial movement and vocal inflection the result of sleep-taught routines. Now there was no need to keep up a pretence. She clamped the collar back shut around her neck, and the unnatural, hateful waves stopped breaking against Lysander's mind. 'It is so,' she said.

'Is her name Legienstrasse?'

'It matters not what its name is.'

'It does,' said Lysander. 'Because if you are hunting Legienstrasse, there is something we know that you do not.'

'Oh?' said Syncella.

'The champions of Chaos on this world are afraid of her. We have looked inside their minds. They obey her. She has taken control of the same weapons you deployed to bring about this war. That means when you face her, you face them. You need not just one bullet, Syncella. You need enough to kill a whole planet's worth of moral threats. You do not have them. We have.'

'Then you will fight alongside us, Captain Lysander?' said Syncella.

'Not as an ally. As an enemy of your enemy. Not for honour. For victory. For survival. But you must tell us everything, Lady Syncella. As unaccustomed as you are to it, there must be no more secrets.'

Lady Syncella held up a hand. 'Or?'

'Or the Imperial Fists continue to fight. We will not give up on Opis. We will not allow its people to be condemned by the servants of Chaos. And we will not forget who brought those servants here.'

'Then it is settled,' said Syncella. 'Though all parties no doubt dislike it. The Imperial Fists and the Officio Assassinorum will fight together to acquire and kill the target Legienstrasse.'

'Then what must we do first?' asked Lysander.

'First,' said Syncella, 'we must tell you what Legienstrasse is.'

Many stories described the birth of the Officio Assassinorum. All of them were lies.

Some were perpetuated longer than others, and that made them as close to the truth as was possible when discussing the Assassinorum. The truth was buried so deep, recorded in so many writings later obliterated and memories later withered away, that the truth might as well never have existed.

The days of the Horus Heresy were so dark that their shadows would stain the next ten thousand years. The Emperor and the commander of his armies, the Warmaster Horus, fought a civil war to determine the future of the Imperium and of the human race.

It was in this war, and in the upheavals that followed it that the Imperium, as it currently existed, was founded. The Adeptus Terra took over the government of the human race in the name of the critically wounded God-Emperor. His church arose to enforce its piety. The Imperial Guard and Navy, and the Chapters of the Adeptus Astartes, were reorganised to defend it. And somewhere in the darkness, the Officio Assassinorum was born.

Killers were selected by the Emperor. Six murderers without peer, each so skilled at a particular form of death that their skill was akin to worship. When the Heresy ended, with Horus dead and the Emperor crippled, they vowed to pass on their skills to the next generations who would do murder in the Emperor's name.

Or, the Emperor's Church, the newly-founded Adeptus Ministorum, sought to reconcile the savagery of the Emperor's many deviant cults with the word of the Imperial creed. These cultists offered up their murdered victims as sacrifices to the Emperor. Instead of purging them, the Ministorum brought them into the fold, focusing their bloodlust on the skills needed to hunt down the Emperor's foes and building six mighty Temples to house and train them. Eventually the six Temples broke from the Adeptus Ministorum, and vanished into the deepest shadows of the Imperium.

Or, of all the most deadly killers deployed by the Ruinous Powers under Horus's leadership, a handful were captured during the Heresy and its aftermath instead of being killed. The fledgling government of the Imperium offered to indulge their wildest excesses of bloodshed, in return for teaching their skills to the Imperium's own killers and founding the six Temples.

None was true, but none was truly a lie, for the truth itself did not exist any more.

Ten thousand years passed.

The Imperial Assassins honed their craft to such an extent that one man or woman could do what might take an army to do by conventional warfare. Even the High Lords of Terra, whose permission was required by Imperial law before an Assassin could be deployed, did not know where the Assassin Temples were located or even if there were physical temples at all. The very finest archeotech was made available for the

Temples' Grand Masters to arm and armour their agents.

A well-placed bullet or blade ended thousands upon thousands of lives. Governors who sought to secede from the Imperium. The commanders of Traitor Legions or alien armies. The admirals of pirate fleets. Apostate cardinals who preached words abhorrent to the Imperial creed. Heretechs whose innovations and tech-abominations threatened to destabilise the Adeptus Mechanicus. Whole Imperial armies and fleets were spared when a war was ended before it began, with a key enemy general or spiritual leader executed by the agents of the Assassinorum. There was never any shortage of deserving throats to slit, never any lack of certain misery and death to be averted by a bullet through the correct brain.

'The Callidus,' said Lady Syncella. 'Who kills through deceit and disguise. She can take on any form, even mimic the pheromones of certain noisome aliens, and thereby get close enough to the target to place a knife through whatever vital organ is the most vulnerable.'

The back of the *Gilded Pyre* was not as luxurious as the inside of the *Damnatio Memoriae* to which she was accustomed, but she showed no discomfort strapped in to the grav-restraints. The Imperial Fists had two Thunderhawks on Opis and the second, the *Peril Swift*, had been recalled from Rekaba to support the transporting of Lysander's strike force from the Blood Eyrie. The *Gilded Pyre* was currently for the use of Lysander and Lady Syncella, with Agent Skult taking a seat in the passenger compartment's corner. He said nothing, and Lysander had still not seen the face under his stealth mask.

'The Second Temple is the Eversor. The berserker. A weapon to be pointed at the enemy and unleashed. Even in death, his body chemistry will cause a biological meltdown destroying whatever has slain it. When the target is known for martial superiority and an insistence on fighting its assailants in person, it is to the Eversor's way of death we turn.'

'I know,' said Lysander, 'of the Eversor.'

'Then yours is great fortune, Lysander. For many the existence of the Eversor is the last thing they ever learn. Third is the Venenum Temple. Masters of poisons. Theirs is the mantra that every enemy has a weakness. Even the alien and the daemon are not immune. Xenos-tailored toxins can be synthesised in such small doses that only Venenum can be trusted with their use, lest the last drops be wasted. Psychic poisons, such as those gathered from the Emperor's own tears at the foot of the Golden Throne, might lay low the daemon. Again, only the Venenum can be given the task of delivering it. Fourth is the Vindicare.'

'The sniper,' said Lysander. 'I witnessed one on the battlefield. Agent Skult is not the first I have encountered.'

'Quite so,' said Syncella. 'Masters of death from a distance. A perfect mission is one in which the target is slain without anyone ever knowing from whence the bullet came.'

'Like the assassination of Inquisitor Kekrops?'

'That was, as you suggest, a perfectly executed mission.'

'The killing of Legienstrasse,' said Lysander, 'was not?'

The Vindicare, Agent Skult, spoke for the first time. 'I had calculated for the effect of one Space Marine's body impeding my shot,' he said. 'I was not prepared for the bullet to pass through two bodies. Yet this is unforgivable. The failure was a sin, and shall be repented of when the target is dead.'

'Fifth is the Culexus Temple,' continued Syncella, 'into which I was inducted. A hunter of psykers. Any witch or sorcerer draws his power from the warp, where that power boils and blazes without containment. Every human mind has its echo in the warp. But the mind of a Culexus is a negative presence, a psychic void, like a black hole, and where we walk no psyker's art can prevail.'

'Your collar renders you almost normal, then?'

'It does. As a Grand Master of the Culexus Temple I sometimes must attend to diplomatic duties among the other Adeptae. It would not be prudent to deploy the Culexus's weapon on such occasions. The Sixth Temple is the Vanus. His purpose is to erase not just the physical being, but the memory, the existence of the target as a social construct, eliminating all who know the target and erasing all data pertaining to him.'

'And what could the target be,' said Lysander, 'that three Assassins are despatched to kill her?'

'What else?' said Syncella. 'Another Assassin.'

The Aristeia had not always been noted for their mercy.

Opis's rulers were adept at absorbing their enemies into their own ranks, founding new bloodlines from surrendered kings and welcoming their princes and councillors into their parliaments. In this way, as much as on the battlefield, was Opis conquered. But sometimes, the Aristeia of Khezal had been angered too greatly to show such compassion.

The city of Krae had resisted the Aristeia for thousands of years. Ancient pacts ensured its independence, and it ruled its own hinterland by the sea with what, on Opis, passed for peace. The Aristeia swapped ambassadors with Krae, which became a city of poets and scholars, or artists and intellectuals. Every member of the Aristeia had hung paintings by one of Krae's masters on his wall, or had a book written by one of the city's literary elite in his library.

But the Aristeia, in silence, was jealous. Krae was beautiful. Krae was rich. Commoners dreamed of living there. The city's artists were patronised by the planet's most powerful. For hundreds of years the desire was voiced, first as a whisper, in the counting-houses and salons of Khezal. Bring Krae into the fold. Conquer it, by arms or by politics, and take that cultural wealth for ourselves.

One hundred years before Inquisitor Kekrops landed on Opis, the Aristeia sent an envoy to the Panopticon of Krae, carrying with him a declaration that Krae belonged to the Aristeia and always had done. A signatory to some ancient pact of independence had been revealed, through careful perusal of the records in the Temple of Muses, to be of an unqualified bloodline. Krae would allow the Aristeia to take over its government and continue as it had done, with only minimal impact on the everyday lives of its people.

Krae knew the Aristeia were jealous. The city's greatest minds had gathered once every few decades to discuss what would be done when the moment came. Some had created elaborate plans for war machines and hidden death-traps surrounding the city. Others wanted to mobilise the citizenry, train and arm them so they could be turned into an army at a moment's notice. But none of these plans played to the strengths of Krae. They were not warriors. Mechanical war machines could only do so much without fighting men. The peasants could not hold out against the Aristeia's armies for long.

So they attacked with ideas.

The envoy was sent back with a reply that Krae did not recognise the legitimacy of the Aristeia's authority. Writings flooded out of Krae describing the many philosophical reasons why the Aristeia could not legitimately rule the planet. Works on the nature of power, of the right and wrongs of government, of the possibility for a planet's common citizens to rule themselves, emerged to catch the imagination of academics and commoners worldwide.

The Aristeia were furious. It would have been one thing for Krae's soldiers to face the Aristeia on the battlefield. Dead commoners were of little concern, and the Aristeia's sons always needed new wars in which to earn their commendations and glorify their bloodlines. But this was an assault on the very fabric of the Aristeia, on the concept of power itself.

Krae could not be brought into the fold. Its people could not be trusted to embrace the Aristeia as their betters and their rulers. Its elite would plot just as they had done, to find a new path of independence. Krae had to die.

Khezal threw everything it had at Krae. It was no longer interested in bringing the city's military to battle, and forcing the city to surrender. The city itself was the target.

The intellectuals of the universities and galleries were herded out into the street and their brains dashed out against the cobbles. The people were forced at bayonet point from their homes. Works of art were defaced and the libraries burned.

When it was done, Krae was empty save for the bodies. The Aristeia forbade anyone to settle there again. The city was left for the forest to swallow, and over the decades the trees broke through its streets and broke apart the foundations of its opera houses and museums. It had stood like this, abandoned and decaying, for a century, when Operation Starfall began two hundred kilometres to the west of the abandoned city.

Karnikhal Six-Finger wrenched his blade from the body of another Imperial Guardsman.

The dirt under his feet was sodden with blood. Blood dripped from the leaves of the trees around him, like a red rain.

It was the blood of his own soldiers, who in their madness had hammered sections of jagged black metal armour to their bodies. It was the blood of his enemies, Guardsmen in desert camouflage ill-suited to their sudden deployment in the coniferous forests towards the eastern edge of the Starfall Line. Karnikhal did not care whose blood it was, for his god did not care, either.

'Bathe deep!' he yelled. 'It will wash away your weakness! Drink deep! It is strength!'

His soldiers ran through the trees. He saw two or three cut down by las-fire. The enemy, shocked by the force of his charge, were scattered but still fighting, trying to organise themselves into firing lines.

An Imperial officer, wearing a long black greatcoat with a

peaked cap, stood in front of him. Karnikhal's height was so great that he looked down on the man as the officer yelled out the words of a prayer and ran straight at him.

The officer had a power sword, a fine weapon with an elaborate basket hilt and a blade that was a sliver of silver light. Karnikhal sidestepped the first thrust and sliced his chainsword through the back of the officer's leg. The chainteeth, already clotted with a dozen enemies' worth of gore, carved through the man's leg at mid-thigh. The officer sprawled into the wet dirt and Karnikhal picked him up by the neck. The power sword had dropped from the officer's hands, the blade hissing where it touched the mud.

Karnikhal looked into the officer's face. Already the blood had drained from it. It was whitening as he watched.

A memory surfaced from the bubbling red ocean of Karnikhal's mind. Half-recalled, fragmented by the centuries. A face like this. But not exactly – it was the face of another Space Marine, as Karnikhal himself had once been.

'Side with us!' the face cried. Karnikhal could not put a name to it, for he had obliterated that information from his memory. 'With us! Angron is mad and Horus desires power. My brother, do not…'

Karnikhal's hand was around the Space Marine's throat in his memory, just as it was around the Imperial officer's now. And both hands now closed, crunching through bone and cartilage. Both faces contorted in death, both pairs of eyes rolled up and went dull.

Karnikhal threw the memory out of his mind, at the same time slamming the officer's body against a tree trunk.

It was good. There was blood. The smouldering armour he wore smoked where blood had sprayed across it, filling the forest with the stench of burning men. His head pounded with signals from his cranial implants, which dispensed the painkillers that dulled the agony of the molten armour with every life he took.

He strode through the forest, lashing left and right with his sword. Men fled before him as if he were a natural disaster darkening the horizon in front of them. Some stood to fight, and those who tried were gifted a dismemberment with his chainblade, or were grappled and held against Karnikhal's molten armour so they burst into flames and were released, screaming and dying, to run at random among their fellow soldiers.

Karnikhal's own soldiers followed in his wake, leaping on the enemy fallen and tearing them apart. They used the metal blades with which each man had replaced his left hand and forearm. They painted themselves in blood, then moved on to find the next kill.

The painkillers flooded through Karnikhal. His full strength unfolded and he knocked half a dozen men away from him with a great sweep of his blade. Severed heads and limbs rained down. Karnikhal roared with the sheer exhilaration, with the great tide of adrenaline pumping through his hearts.

A shadow passed overhead. Karnikhal looked up to see the iridescent scaled belly of the Warp Serpent coiling overhead.

Hate rose in Karnikhal. It was barely caged. But it could not break out. Pacts had been made.

'You! Poxy worm!' bellowed Karnikhal. 'Do you come to

steal my kill? The blood shed here is mine! The skulls I take belong to the throne of Khorne!'

The Warp Serpent's sinuous body unravelled until its enormous head looked down at Karnikhal. 'Stay your hand, Six-Fingered One,' said the serpent, its forked tongue flickering between its lips. Two of its eyes focused on Karnikhal, the other two observing the battle around him. 'I have no designs on your pretty pile of bodies. I bring word.'

'Word? What use is talk when there are warm hearts to be stopped?'

'From her.'

'From Legienstrasse?'

'From Legienstrasse.'

Karnikhal felt the cold, bloodless bindings around him, invisible but impossible to ignore. They surrounded his soul. They were the work of cowards, of sorcerers, and they wrapped around him and forced him to do their will. He could forget them when the blood was flowing and the skulls were falling. But not now. Not when her name was invoked.

'What is her bidding?' growled Karnikhal.

'To Krae,' said the Warp Serpent. 'The city lost to Opis's history.'

'Abandon this fight?' replied Karnikhal. 'What is at Krae that can equal the bloodshed of this battle?'

'She cares not for blood,' replied the Warp Serpent. 'But I have no doubt there will be a great deal of death. And she demands it, Six-Finger.'

'What has she demanded of you?'

'To serve as her messenger, for I am the swiftest creature on

Opis. To gather a force of champions at Krae. She seeks a victory there that will decide Opis's fate.'

'Its fate is decided!' roared Karnikhal. 'It will drown in blood! I shall reap an ocean of it, and drown a million captives there in honour of Khorne!'

'Your words,' said the Warp Serpent drily, 'mean less than these worthless souls you kill so gleefully. You will obey. You have no more choice than I. I will see you next at Krae, Six-Finger.'

The Warp Serpent slid off into the sky, rippling through the columns of smoke rising from the battlefield.

Karnikhal looked down at the ruined bodies around him. His armour was starting to sear, lines of pain forming along his arms and legs to mirror the streams of molten metal that always ran down his armour's plates. He drove his chainblade into a moaning Guardsman who was trying to gather his entrails back into his abdomen – the blade sawed through his chest and the recognition of his death caused his implants to dull the growing pain just a little.

'There had better be death,' said Karnikhal Six-Finger. 'There had better be blood.'

'You lost control of one of your own,' said Lysander. It was an accusation. The Thunderhawk pitched slightly as it made a course change, heading back from the mountain range to Khezal and Sigismund Point.

'Do not pretend that no Space Marine has ever left the fold, Lysander!' replied Lady Syncella. 'How many of our targets have been renegade Space Marines?'

'But that is what happened,' pressed Lysander. 'You lost an agent. Legienstrasse is an Assassin gone rogue.'

Lady Syncella raised an eyebrow. 'That is one way of putting it,' she said.

'Captain!' said Gorgythion from the cockpit. 'Tchepikov is signalling us.'

'Tchepikov?' Lysander did not try to hide his annoyance. 'What in the hells does he want of us?'

'Operation Starfall is reporting major troop movements towards Krae.'

'Krae's abandoned,' said Lysander. 'The intelligence briefing stated no one has lived there for a hundred years.'

'It was abandoned overnight,' replied Gorgythion. 'Most of the city is intact. It's got a spaceport. Thought it might be–'

'She's there!' interjected Lady Syncella. 'Our operation here was to flush her out into the open. To force her to flee Opis, and then strike at her when she made to escape! The spaceport of an abandoned city is too obvious a choice for her, but she is desperate. We almost killed her once and she is afraid. That is where we will find her, Captain Lysander.'

'How many men have died to drive this rogue Assassin out of cover?' said Lysander.

'Too many to let them die in vain,' said Lady Syncella. 'Our combined force is enough to take her down.'

'And our combined force will do just that,' said Lysander. 'This absolves the Assassinorum of nothing, Syncella. But we will fight alongside you for as long as it takes to kill her.'

'Good. We must make speed to Krae. Legienstrasse may be desperate but she will have a plan in place. There will be allies with her and they will grow in number with every hour.'

The Thunderhawk pitched again as Gorgythion turned it onto its new heading. The coast hurtled past below, lashed with the white-capped waves of a coming storm.

'It will be rough flying,' said Gorgythion.

'Not as rough as the landing,' replied Lysander. 'Syncella, if we are to kill Legienstrasse, we must know how. No more secrets. Which Temple trained her? What can be done?'

'That is a complicated question,' said Syncella, and Lysander could not read from her expression if she meant any humour. 'I believe the telling of one of the Assassinorum's most closely-held secrets must now be allowed. Let me explain to you, captain, just what Legienstrasse is.'

When Tchepikov reached the command deck, the medical servitor was still trundling behind him. Its fingers were divided into several dexterous manipulators, each as fine as a centipede's leg, which were working on knitting the broken bone of his arm closed. A skin of medical gel covered the open incision, the muscle visible as the white bone was carefully rebuilt layer by layer. Intravenous lines hooked Tchepikov's veins to the bottles and pumps set into the servitor's torso. His greatcoat hung off his shoulder and he put his officer's cap on as he approached the comms helm.

The Naval intelligence officer manning the helm saluted Tchepikov. Tchepikov could not return the salute, and the officer looked uncertain for a moment.

'You said the code had been received.'

'Yes, commander,' said the officer. Her eyes flickered to his damaged arm, then back to his face. 'Encryption vermilion. Marked priority.' She handed Tchepikov the data-slate on which the message had been transcribed.

'Krae?' he said. 'Bloody Krae? There's nothing there! I have thousands of men dying on the Starfall front and now I am to divert them to defend a pile of stones!'

'Sir, I...'

Tchepikov didn't notice the officer had spoken. 'Do you see?' he yelled, waving the data-slate in the air. 'It's not enough that I am defied to my face, on my very ship! The lords above us want my soldiers to dance and die to their tune!'

Most of the officers on the command deck kept their heads bowed, eyes fixed on the pict-screens or stacks of reports in front of them.

'But that is all we do,' said Tchepikov. 'Someone else plays, and we dance.' He swept aside an armful of papers from the conference table, revealing the heavily annotated map of Operation Starfall's front. Reports of battles and casualties were coming in from points all along the line. The enemy was fighting here for its own sake – not to capture ground or defend a position, but to bring the Imperial army to battle and force it to fight for survival when it could be helping to bulldoze the resistance in Khezal and Rekaba.

'Despatch to the 90th Algol Siegebreakers, Colonel Messk. Disengage and redeploy to Krae. Fully motorise for speed. Take vehicles and armour from other regiments if needs be.' He looked around at the comms officer. 'Tell Messk that he is to let my right flank collapse and bring the whole line down, because that is how the dance goes.'

'Commander,' said the officer, and her fingers tapped on the console as she transmitted the orders in rapid war-code.

Tchepikov pushed the medical servitor away as it rolled after him. He pulled its delicate fingers away from his arm. The medical gel came away with this and he flexed his fingers, teeth gritted, as he let the blood flow.

Krae was a good choice for an escape.

It was abandoned. No one officially lived there, and those that did so unofficially numbered no more than a few hundred outcasts and scavengers picking over the well-plundered ruins left behind by Krae's evacuation. Much of the city had fallen into ruin, but the forest had left the great expanse of the city's spaceport mostly intact. The spaceport was inland from the rest of the city, a series of great rockcrete circles punctuated with control towers, maintenance hangars and refuelling stations. All the automated functions had long ceased but it could still be used to launch or land a spacecraft, albeit one which needed a more competent crew than the average.

All one needed was the spaceship.

Fifty minutes after Commander Tchepikov had given his order, contact with the *Raging Sky* was lost.

Legienstrasse was a creature who planned ahead. Not just for one eventuality, but many, so the groundwork was laid for several potential plans to deal with all the likely turns of fate. With every move, several redundant plots were left unfinished, their preparations unused. They were not wasted.

Their existence had helped make success a certainty. They had played their part.

The King of Crows had been adapted from Opis's folklore, as had several other useful legends and customs. Masquerading as the King of Crows had turned out to be the most expedient method of escaping Khezal, but it had not got Legienstrasse all the way to the northern part of the continent where preparations had been made to depart Opis quietly and invisibly. Instead, Legienstrasse had activated a fallback plan. It was almost as good as the previous several options, with the only drawback being that it could not be accomplished entirely beyond the notice of the Imperial forces that had come to Opis to find Legienstrasse.

The *Raging Sky* had been compromised some decades before Inquisitor Kekrops had begun the crusade that led him to Opis. It was an armoured troop carrier, one of several in the sector battlefleet that, due to the need to transport men and materiel quickly to an embattled planet such as Opis, would certainly be used by Imperial forces if they attacked the planet. Because of this the *Raging Sky*, and a number of other ships, were seeded with cultists who believed that they were doing the bidding of the Emperor who had been reborn in the form of an infant girl. This cult had been created by Legienstrasse and a sect of useful psykers, native to Opis, that she had gathered to help her in her exile. Visions were transmitted into the minds of trainee crewmen who were then placed on the *Raging Sky* to let their cult grow and recruit further, always with frequent visions sent by Legienstrasse to ensure they emphasised the need for secrecy and loyalty above all else.

On some ships, the cult (which was known by various names, including the Children of the Later God and the Eternal Stair) was purged by the commissars of the sector fleet. On others the cult died away, its members poached by other cults which had developed among the battlefleet's crews independent of Legienstrasse's influence. But Legienstrasse knew that on some ships it would survive, and on the *Raging Sky*, it did.

To Legienstrasse, it was a message sent through arcane channels to the psykers now fighting alongside the forces opposing Operation Starfall. To the brothers and sisters of the Thirteen Pillars, as the cult named itself on the *Raging Sky*, it was the apocalypse.

They had waited for years for the day to come when the voice of the infant Goddess-Emperor spoke to them more directly than ever before, and told them to undertake their sacred mission. They had known since the cult's foundation that their task would see them taking over the ship and landing it in the spaceport at Krae, there to witness the apotheosis of the Goddess-Emperor as she arose and took her place on the throne of mankind.

The Master of the Watch, a mere initiate of the cult but the one who held the highest shipboard rank, was given the task of beginning the great work. He drew his dress laspistol on the bridge and shot the ship's captain in the back of the head. His second target was the ship's commissar, who he shot several times in the chest, fatally, before the security battalion troops on the bridge finally reacted and martyred the Master of the Watch in a hail of shotgun blasts.

This was the catalyst for the rest of the great work. The mess was sealed off with two hundred and fifty crew inside, and the whole deck was decompressed to hard vacuum. The most difficult task was to take the engines, where the tough engine-gangs had resisted infiltration by the cult. The devotees of the Thirteen Pillars broke open the armoury, shot down the gangers who tried to rush them and offered the rest the option of serving the cult or dying.

The bridge held out for an hour before las-cutters were hauled up from the engine decks and used to cut through the ceiling. The short and bloody gun battle left twice as many cultists as officers dead, but it did not matter how many were made martyrs as long as the great work was completed.

The Goddess-Emperor smiled on them as the Thirteen Pillars, named after the commandments that Legienstrasse's psykers had implanted in them, took over the controls of the *Raging Sky* and aimed it towards the cloudy surface of Opis.

'There's the ship,' said Scout-Sergeant Orfos, pointing at the glimmer among the dark-grey clouds.

Lysander followed the Scout's gaze. From the top of the apartment block he had an excellent view of Krae. The northern quadrant of the city was a patchwork of exposed rockcrete and tumbledown buildings, broken up by banks of dense coniferous forest. Mossy gulleys criss-crossed the ruins, marking where the city's grid of canals and sunken roadways had run. Here and there were hints of the city's past – an equestrian statue crowning a half-fallen dome, a series of pillars that once held up a long-vanished glass roof, a great stone book that had once dominated the entrance to a vast gallery and now lay half-buried in greenery. A few of the landmarks were still visible – the Illuminated Gate, with its marble blocks cracked and its intricately painted scenes peeling and defaced. A trio of grand towers, the Three Princesses, once centres of philosophy and now lopsided death-traps due to collapse at any moment. The huge artificial waterfall, the Descent of Dreams, reduced by time to a dry stone shelf hung with straggling vines.

Above the city, Lysander followed the path of the ship towards the grey circles of the spaceport. 'Our quarry does not disappoint,' he said. 'The timing will be close. What of Imperial forces?'

'Enriaan reports armour making all haste along the city's north-western outskirts,' said Orfos. 'They'll get to the spaceport before we do.'

'And the enemy?'

'Not yet. Most likely they're already there.'

Gorgythion on board the *Gilded Pyre* had detected the presence of surface-to-air sensors as soon as the Imperial Fists and Assassins had breached the perimeter of Krae. With the whole strike force loaded onto just two Thunderhawks, Lysander could not risk continuing to fly in case Krae's air defences had been activated by Legienstrasse's allies. The Imperial Fists would make the rest of the way on foot, about nine kilometres of urban ruin. Lysander had Squad Kirav, Septuron's assault squad and Ctesiphon's tactical squad, Orfos and his Scouts, Librarian Deiphobus and Champion Ucalegon. That was the whole Imperial Fists force on Opis, save for the two Thunderhawks, the *Gilded Pyre* and *Peril Swift* now grounded at the city's outskirts, and Vindicator Squadron Sthenelus which was still embattled deep in Khezal.

Orfos offered Lysander a pair of magnoculars. Lysander took them and peered through them in the direction of the spaceport. No sign of enemies, but lights burned among the buildings clustered around the landing pads. He scanned along the city's outskirts and picked up the cloud of dust kicked up by the engines and tracks of the Imperial Guard speeding towards the battle.

'If we are wrong,' said Lysander, 'if this is a ruse, we might never find her.'

'We are not wrong,' said Lady Syncella. Lysander turned to see her standing behind him on the rooftop, her dress fluttering in the wind. It was cold, and the dress was rather tattered after the Blood Eyrie, but she had not changed it.

'You sound certain,' said Lysander.

'We have calculated every action that Legienstrasse might take,' said Syncella. 'This is one of them. She was foiled in her attempt to escape as the King of Crows, and she has not failed to get what she wants for many decades. It is an unfamiliar feeling for her. She is desperate. She has called off her longer-term plans and used one that will get her off this planet quickly.'

'When we reach the spaceport,' said Lysander, 'I need to know that you and Agent Skult will fight as our allies. Not as a third party. As our allies under my orders. Can you promise me that, Lady Syncella?'

'When it comes to open warfare, Lysander, I have no complaints about deferring to a First Captain of the Adeptus

Astartes. I request that you allow me to take the kill.'

Lysander smiled without humour. 'Of course. The Assassin must have her kill. Even if Legienstrasse was dead, it is a dishonour not to take her head with your own hand.'

'We do not concern ourselves with honour as obsessively as a Space Marine, captain,' replied Syncella, equally humourless. 'I request the chance to kill Legienstrasse because it is likely Skult and myself are the only ones capable of doing it. You do not know her capabilities in battle. You have not been witness to her proving in combat or the details of her creation.'

'Ah, yes.' Lysander handed the magnoculars back to Orfos and faced Syncella across the rooftop. The evening was drawing in close and the sun broke through a gap in the clouds on the horizon, and the shadows turned long. 'You never finished telling me what Legienstrasse can do.'

'Or what she is,' said Syncella. 'I have spoken to you of the six Assassin Temples. Six forms of retribution primed to fall on the Emperor's enemies. So much is known by many among the Imperium's Adeptae. But there was once another Temple. A seventh retribution.'

'A seventh Temple?' said Orfos. 'What happened to it?'

'These are words that will not be repeated,' said Syncella. 'Your Imperial Fists may know of them, as it may be crucial in the battle ahead. But they will go no further. This I ask of you, as you have asked much of me.'

'We can keep a secret,' said Lysander, not a little grudgingly.

'Each Temple is dedicated to a particular form of death that can be visited upon a particular type of enemy,' said Syncella.

'A Callidus is employed when an enemy is well protected and inaccessible. A psychic target is typically eliminated by a Culexus Assassin such as myself. A Vindicare is used when only a kill from a distance is possible, and so on. The Maerorus Temple was created to deal with a target which, while being a single entity conceptually, is spread over a number of individuals. A rebel parliament, for example. A cult or similar deviant organisation. Families, a number of targets connected by a bloodline, were considered likely targets and hence the Maerorus was given the capacity to track particular gene signatures.'

'How did the Maerorus kill?' asked Lysander.

'By the hand,' replied Syncella. 'The number of potential sub-targets was such that technology could not be relied upon. A gun can run out of bullets. A knife can break. Poison can run dry. Only unarmed killing would do. The Maerorus's modus operandi was to enter into a target-rich area, typically a meeting or gathering, and kill every sub-target present as quickly as possible, without recourse to weaponry or fallible technology.'

'So,' said Orfos, 'she's designed to kill everyone in the room.'

'Quite so.'

'You know,' said Orfos, turning to Lysander, 'that's not light years away from what we're trained to do.'

'The difference being,' replied Syncella, 'that given enough resistance, you could be stopped.'

'What happened to the Maerorus Temple?' asked Lysander.

Syncella's expression did not change. 'That information is not relevant to Legienstrasse's destruction.'

'Then how does she do it?' said Lysander, impatience in his voice. 'How is she able to kill so many, so quickly, with nothing but her hands?'

Lady Syncella began to explain, and Lysander understood for the first time just why so much had to be sacrificed for the chance to kill Legienstrasse.

The army was made in its master's image. His armour of burning iron was echoed in the steel plates riveted and nailed to their flesh. They carried swords in imitation of his, and all the guns they could lay their hands on because he would kill from afar or up close as the whim took him.

And they wore skulls. Necklaces of them, jawbones, skulls impaled on spikes welded to their armour.

They filed their teeth to points. They cut off their noses to give them the appearance of a living skull. Some wore helmets without faces, so there was no emotion, no pity in them.

They charged across the open space of Landing Pad Three, and Karnikhal Six-Finger led them.

The Imperial Guardsmen of the 90th Algol Siegebreakers faced them. They were behind the shelter of the western terminal building, a series of half-fallen buildings and hangars where tens of thousands of Kraeites had once teemed, arriving or leaving their city. Its ornamental indoor gardens were overgrown and turned wild, and the businesses and pleasure parlours were now choked labyrinths of wild growth and collapse. The Siegebreakers had thrown together debris and sandbags to make barricades plugging the gaps in the cover.

The Siegebreakers were heavy infantry specialising in

destroying and storming fortifications. The Guardsmen, numbering more than four thousand, had left their heavy weapons behind on the Starfall Line in the hurry to reach Krae. They strapped on their blastshield suits, bulky cocoons of layered flakweave and steel, and the regimental priests walked up and down the line offering blessings and taking final confessions. The regiment's banner was unfurled – it was a shroud that had once wrapped the body of Saint Levissa, Algol's patron saint and martyr to the green-skinned xenos. The officers lined up and knelt before it, the bloody imprint of their saint's face looking down sternly on them as if to warn them to do their duty.

The howling and yelling of the enemy brought them to their firing positions. Thousands of ironclad foes were rushing at them. And Karnikhal Six-Finger himself was there. That could be the only identity of the monster, three metres tall, surrounded by a wreath of smoke and steam, the glow of molten steel outlining a huge and brutal shape. Blood sprayed endlessly from the whirring teeth of his chainblade.

'Though none may yet live to speak of us,' said Colonel Messk, 'yet we will not go forgotten. For the Emperor sees all. For every hero of the Imperium who loses his life to the unending war, He weeps a single tear. Though the pain of battle's fires and death be dreadful to us, yet there can be no fear, for I have faith in all of you. You will do Algol proud. You will win this victory, or you will be tears in the Emperor's eye. There is no dishonour in either fate. It is a privilege to have lived among you, sons of Algol. To die among you will be a greater honour still. Fight well, check your targets, conserve your las-packs and give thanks to the Emperor who watches.'

The first gunfire crackled from the enemy, ill-aimed ranging shots. Some fell on the expanse of cracked rockcrete in front of the terminal buildings. Others pinged against the ruins of control towers. The Siegebreakers held firm, for they had been raised on discipline. Some Guardsmen were savage berserkers recruited from feral worlds. Others were stealthy killers without mercy or morals who would scatter and skulk to fight tomorrow. But the Algol Siegebreakers were proud and well drilled, and they died standing up, front to the enemy, braced to fire and in formation.

Drops of blood spattered onto the flakweave suits of the Guardsmen. They fell thicker, pattering down like rain. A rain of blood that gathered in the cracks of the fallen walls and pooled underfoot. The smell of it, like burning metal, filled the air. Men shook it from their visors. Sharpshooters wiped it off the scopes of their lasguns.

There were omens. Flashes and strange shapes in the sky. Some men heard, in the battlefield sermons of the preachers, strange words or phrases inserted, praises to a god of blood or a promise of an appalling sacrifice.

The mouth of Saint Levissa opened up into a silent scream, as tears of blood ran down her.

The sharpshooters opened fire at extreme range. Hissing lasshots left dripping red welts in steel armour-plates. A couple of the enemy fell, a helmetless warrior shot through one eye, another caught in a gap between the plates fixed to his abdomen. Shots hit Karnikhal Six-Finger, lost in the glow of his molten armour without doing any harm at all.

'Fix bayonets!' yelled Messk, drawing his own dress sword. The order was relayed up and down the line. A hot wind blew in and lashed the falling blood drops against the Guardsmen. A Guardsman injured in the previous battles on the Starfall Line, detailed to carry ammo supplies from the rear, threw a violent fit and was held down by a regimental medic as he started coughing up foam. The priests continued to pray, their words lost in the whistling of the blood-laden wind and the cries of anger and madness from the approaching enemy.

Fire from the horde thunked into sandbags and fallen masonry. The Guardsmen sighted down their lasguns, each picking out a target through the red veil of rain.

Karnikhal himself loped ahead of his army, more eager than any of them to get into the fray. His armour had once been that of a Space Marine, thousands of years ago when he marched among the Legions. Now it was deformed, the shoulder guards wrought into wide mouths full of churning fire, the helm welded so tightly to his face that it took on his own features, creasing and warping with his emotions, molten light bleeding from the eyes and mouth. He left burning footprints on the rockcrete.

In a few short moments, he was looming huge in the eyes of every Algol Guardsman. And then, faster than anything so big should be able to move, he was within a lunge of the barricades.

Las-fire opened up, a great glittering fusillade of it that shredded the air. But the energy of the las-bolts just fed the fires of Karnikhal's armour. He glowed bright, as if made of fire, as he vaulted the barricades and fell among the Guardsmen.

'Let the stains of their blood never fade!' bellowed Karnikhal as he crushed two men beneath him, lanced another through the gut with his sword and sprayed bolter fire in all directions. A priest ran towards him, his power fist, intricately inlaid with prayers, glowing blue with its power field. Before the priest could swing the cumbersome fist, Karnikhal had grabbed him around the throat with his free hand and hauled him up off his feet. The fires of Karnikhal's gauntlet set light to the priest's robes and he yelled wordlessly, perhaps a prayer, perhaps just pain, as flames licked around his face. Karnikhal fired the bolter mounted on the back of his forearm and blew the priest's head apart, the shower of brains and bone added to the blood rain that swirled around Karnikhal in a red tornado.

Karnikhal's soldiers were dying in the hundreds, bodies clattering to the ground. Those behind them clambered over the bodies into more volleys of fire, and were cut down in turn.

'Kill! Die! Bleed and suffer!' Karnikhal threw another soldier aside and brought his chainblade down into the shoulder of an officer, carving down through the man's body until the blade sawed out through his hip. 'Khorne cares not from whom the blood flows! The Blood God cares not from whose neck the skull is taken!'

'Fall back!' yelled Colonel Messk. 'To the second line! Fall back and keep up the fire! Sons of Algol, draw them on, draw them on!'

Karnikhal's men had reached the line now. They were laying about them with their swords, knocking aside bayonets and hacking at the flak armour of the Guardsmen. The Siegebreakers broke from behind their cover and ran towards the barricades and rubble further back in the terminal building, trying to keep formation even as more enemies rushed at them and the terrible figure of Karnikhal Six-Finger carved a gory path through the centre of their line.

Long ago, Colonel Messk had sworn to his men that he would never send them into a battle he would not be willing to fight in himself. And so, because he had been raised to keep his word, he drew his sidearm, tightened his grip on his dress sword, and ran towards the thickest of the bloodshed, to seek his death fighting Karnikhal Six-Finger.

It was Enriaan who saw the Warp Serpent, blue-pink fire coiling over the spaceport, surrounded by flashing lightning.

'We are late,' said Lysander, receiving the vox-message from the Scouts up ahead. 'Brethren! The enemy is sighted! Make all speed!'

Lysander led the strike force through the tangle of ruined tenements and basilica that marked the southern boundary of the spaceport. Headless statues stood ready to topple everywhere, for this was a region inhabited by artists and poets who had erected monuments to the rich patrons of Krae's elite. Some buildings were completely fallen, with a dozen storeys pancaked into crushed strata of marble and rockcrete, while others stood all but intact with blind windows looking onto gutted interiors. The going was rough, with drifts of rubble everywhere, but the Imperial Fists made good time across it as they passed through shattered lower floors and canyons of stone walls.

The Scouts ran up ahead, occasionally visible as flashes of

golden armour amid the gloom. They weren't trying to stay hidden now, for speed was more important than surprise.

<<The winds change,>> voxed Librarian Deiphobus. <<The realm invisible, it recoils. Something foul approaches.>>

'Make ready!' ordered Lysander. 'Septuron, be ready to intercept!'

A ruined building to Lysander's right was pierced by a bolt of red light. It was the Warp Serpent, diving down from overhead, flying straight as an arrow at Lysander.

Lysander rolled to one side and the Warp Serpent hurtled past, air screaming with it. Lysander got a glimpse of its scales, alight with fire, pink flames trailing from vents down its sides. Its head was huge and fanged, like a dragon's with barbels hanging from its jaws and rippling in its wake.

The other Imperial Fists dived out of its way. Ctesiphon's squad, bringing up the formation's rear, had the time to fire a bolter volley at it, and explosions stuttered across the cracked walls of the tenement block up ahead as the serpent flew by.

The Warp Serpent curved up into the sky, just visible between the buildings as it coiled back on itself to fly down at the Imperial Fists again. Bolts of blue and pink fire rained down from it, slamming into the rubble in multicoloured explosions. The Imperial Fists scattered into what overhead cover they could find. One of Septuron's squad was thrown off his feet by a blast, and Lysander could not see if he was wounded or not.

Ucalegon did not run. The Emperor's Champion ran up a slope of rubble and jumped up onto a plinth that had once held a statue, now reduced to a pair of broken marble legs.

'Warp-spawned thing!' yelled Ucalegon. 'Here is meat for you! Here is a head to take back to your god! Just descend and take it!'

Lysander could not have stopped Ucalegon if he had wanted to. The role of the Emperor's Champion was to seek out the highest-ranking enemy or the most dangerous, and challenge him to single combat. It was a role passed down from the days of Rogal Dorn, when Dorn himself had refused to back down from any taunt or calling-out in battle. The Emperor's Champion was a psychological weapon, for his obsidian blade could lay low an enemy leader and send the rest of the enemy army reeling with shock and dismay. Even a First Captain of the Imperial Fists could not call off the Emperor's Champion when his challenge had been set. No Emperor's Champion had ever backed down once he had called out an enemy. Many had died duelling with a foe, but none had ever run from a fight.

The Warp Serpent heard, and its great head turned down towards the lone Space Marine standing in the middle of the valley of ruins. Perhaps it recognised a challenge and, like Ucalegon himself, could not refuse it. Perhaps it just took advantage of a lone target in the open.

The Warp Serpent arrowed down towards Ucalegon, trailing fire. Ucalegon reversed his grip on the obsidian sword and dived to one side as the Warp Serpent shrieked towards him. The point of the blade scored into its flesh as it passed, biting deeper until it had ripped a straight gash along the whole length of the serpent's body.

Burning entrails spilled out, a curtain of incandescent gore.

The Warp Serpent howled, an appalling sound that shuddered what remained of the glass from the windows of the surrounding buildings. Ucalegon was caught in the torrent and stumbled from his perch, shaking the cloak of burning daemon's flesh from his armour.

'Whelps! Blinded children!' The Warp Serpent's voice crackled down as lightning flashed from its wound. 'You will burn in your ignorance! If you knew of the warp, of my gods, you would cut your own throats to join me!'

Sergeant Ctesiphon didn't have to give the order. His squad stepped out from cover, took aim and hammered out a great sheet of bolter fire into the air. Squad Kirav joined in, storm bolter fire chattering up into the Warp Serpent. Explosive shells burst around the daemon. It shook drops of burning power from its head, and they fell like miniature comets.

Agent Skult knelt and took aim with his longrifle. He fired a single shot that punched up through the Warp Serpent's jaw and out through the top of its head in a black flash.

A void bullet, Lysander recognised. A bullet that imploded inside a biological target, leaving a great gory cavity.

The Warp Serpent howled and almost tied itself in a knot as it changed direction and rattled off between the buildings.

Lysander reached Ucalegon, who was pulling a length of smouldering intestine from one shoulder. 'It is wounded, Brother Ucalegon,' he said. 'But it will return.'

'Then I will finish the job,' said Ucalegon.

'Press on, brothers!' cried Lysander. 'The enemy has our scent! We must reach him before he reaches us!'

Through the lower floors of the building ahead, the expanse

of the nearest landing pad began. Trees and undergrowth had broken through in patches and lifted sections of the rockcrete surface. The spaceship was making its final approach to land, held up on columns of burning exhaust as it descended.

'She's here,' said Lady Syncella, who was running through the ruins alongside Lysander. 'Remember that.'

Lysander could see crimson flashes of las-fire around the terminal building to the west. Something there was burning, and corpses lay heaped around makeshift barricades blocking doors and windows.

'It is too late for them, captain,' said Syncella. 'Their struggle is a distraction. Legienstrasse will be going to meet the ship.'

Her words were met with the shriek of falling artillery. Lysander glimpsed the shells curving over the landing pad towards him leaving trails of smoke.

<<Incoming!>> voxed Scout-Sergeant Orfos. <<Ordnance strike! Scatter!>>

Lysander ducked behind a support pillar as the first shells hammered into the ground. The shockwave hit him, throwing a tide of debris through the building. A black wave of dust swept over him and everything turned dark.

More explosions hit, and Lysander was just a passenger, holding on to the pillar to keep from being thrown to the bucking ground.

His ears rang. He couldn't see. He stumbled forwards, knowing that he had to get out of the building.

Then sound returned to him, and he could hear the building groaning as it shifted. It was a tenement block with perhaps twelve floors above his head. Other Imperial Fists were yelling, a couple crying out in pain.

The dust parted before Lysander. He had made it onto the landing pad, now a swathe of pulverised debris. The Imperial Fists were running alongside him as the building came down behind them. Lysander glanced back to see the lower floors come crashing down, the floors above them following, spraying out another wave of dust. For the second time in moments everything went dark.

'Onward! Onward!' yelled Lysander, not sure if anyone could hear him over the roar of crushing stone. 'Bring blade and fist, sons of Dorn! Bring fire and vengeance! Onward!'

Through the mist, through the still-falling debris, Lysander could see the enemy force approaching. It was a whole regiment of the Aristeia household guard, walking in formation across the landing pad. Above them, already the air was warped with heat haze from the landing jets of the spaceship. Lysander could see the banners the troops held high, embroidered with the coats of arms of the Aristeia houses they served, the bright colours and gold brocade of their uniforms. Behind them trundled a pair of self-propelled artillery pieces, their crews reloading them even as Lysander watched.

And in the middle of their formation, incongruous and appalling, squatted the thing that had taken over their minds. Its shape was roughly equivalent to an enormous spider, though it had far too many legs, and chitinous armour covered its bulbous abdomen. Its face was something like a distorted mask representing a human, its mouth an obscene leer. Fleshy pinkish feelers writhed around its face, and Lysander could hear the thick honey of its voice as it urged its thralls to keep marching forwards.

Lysander recognised its description as one of the many moral threats reported on Opis, a witch-thing that had led whole regiments of Guard into battlefield traps. Already it was the subject of legend and rumour among the Guardsmen, an icon of Opis's corruption. They said that if you saw it, you had at the most an hour to live – or that its abdomen was swollen with the bodies of still-living Guard captives, or that it could scuttle through walls and liquefy a man's flesh with its song. Every man ascribed to it whatever he feared most, so to one it was a cannibal, to another a ghost, to another a creature that could force the dark secrets right out of his mind. It didn't have a name, because to the Guardsmen on Opis, it didn't need one.

Lysander ran out of the clinging dust. 'Moral threat, my brothers! Guard your souls! Onwards, Imperial Fists!'

The other Imperial Fists were running alongside him. There was no time to stop and redeploy, to weigh up all the tactical options. That way was death. The Imperial Fists had to get toe to toe with the enemy, now, before their artillery and guns could decide the battle.

Assault-Sergeant Septuron, probably the fastest man among the Imperial Fists, overtook Lysander, holding up his chainblade like the Aristeia troopers were holding up their household standards. The spider rose up on its hind legs, exposing the drooling fringe of feelers that ran along its underside, and its voice became a high wail that scratched against Lysander's mind.

One of the artillery pieces fired. It well overshot its target, the dull explosion bursting somewhere in the wreckage behind Lysander.

Septuron was a hundred metres from the enemy. Still the Aristeia troopers were in parade-ground formation, their neat ranks marching in step. An officer at the front drew a sword with a brilliant golden blade. Another standard unfurled, the one with a map of the whole of Opis, a standard representing the planet itself and the entire Aristeia.

Septuron dived into the front rank. His squad followed. Chainblades screamed.

The shadow of the descending ship passed over Lysander. He landed heavily on his front leg, let it bend under him, and powered himself forwards.

Gunfire hammered all around him. It stuttered off his shield and the armour of his legs and shoulder. Then there were bodies crunching under his shield, arms and legs reaching around it. He swept the Fist of Dorn into the enemy mass and bodies flew, broken apart or half crushed by the impact.

The sound was like the roaring of the ocean. The enemy surged forward in a great murderous crowd. Lysander was submerged in them, bodies around and above him, gun butts and combat blades stabbing at him from every direction. Lysander hauled his shield over his head, pushing one soldier away and pistoning the Fist of Dorn into the men in front.

He forced some breathing room. Somewhere behind him was a terrible chorus of bolter fire. Lysander turned his head enough to see dozens of men running into the volley fire of Squad Ctesiphon. Already tens of bodies were piling up, more dead slumping onto the heap of the fallen. Troops were surging around them to get to the side and rear of Squad Ctesiphon but they were swamped by a great burst of flame and Lysander saw Squad Kirav fending them off. The power field of a lightning claw flashed as Beros leapt into the enemy.

Lysander looked to the front. The spider was clambering over the soldiers around it. Purple lightning crackled about it and lanced out into the mass of fighting men almost at random, blasting showers of torn men and limbs into the air.

They didn't matter. The Imperial Fists mattered. The spider would be perfectly happy for every one of its soldiers to die, if that meant the Imperial Fists were stopped.

Lysander kicked out and felt bodies under his foot. He forced himself up over them, elevated on a heap of bodies. 'Ucalegon!' he yelled, head barely above the ocean of fighting bodies. 'Emperor's Champion!'

'Here, my captain!' came the reply. Ucalegon looked like he was fighting in a crater of torn flesh, as he hacked left and right with his obsidian sword.

'Follow, brother!' shouted Lysander. He let himself sink back down into the mass of the enemy and drove forwards, slamming the Aristeia troops down to the ground or knocking them out of the way with the Fist of Dorn. Sometimes it was like forging through a pit full of rubble, at other moments he opened up enough space around him to see the inhuman, hollow-eyed faces of the troops. Their minds were no longer their own. They were puppets, their minds scraped clean of any soul, their bodies owned by the will of the spider.

Lysander heard the sound of a blade through muscle and bone. He knew that Ucalegon was somewhere behind him, following the gory wake that Lysander left. Ucalegon could not make his own way through the enemy army, but Lysander, with the weight of his Terminator armour and the force he brought to bear with his shield and hammer, certainly could.

Bones cracked. Bodies fell under Lysander's feet and were ground to paste beneath them. Faces loomed through the mass, jaws lolling, eyes empty. Lysander tore through an Aristeia standard, its silks soaked already in blood.

The press of bodies was denser around the spider. Men were heaping themselves up in front of Lysander to form a barrier around their master. Lysander could just glimpse, through the crush, the towering segmented legs reaching above him, studded with black bristles.

And he saw Ucalegon, clambering over the Aristeia troops, obsidian blade in one hand as he made right for the spider.

'Will you stand when the Warmaster would not?' yelled Ucalegon. 'Will you face the hand of Rogal Dorn?'

The spider turned its great face towards the Emperor's Champion. 'What is this?' it said in its treacly dark voice. 'Is it a new toy? Is it a bauble to hang upon my carapace? A pet to be coddled and tormented? Yes, yes it is all these things, but it doesn't know it yet.'

The thing's words were woven with sorcery. No doubt the men of the Aristeia had fallen to it, their minds bent to the service of the spider. Lysander felt it pulling at his own mind. But Ucalegon would not be swayed. His resistance to such witchcraft, as thoroughly demonstrated under testing from the Chapter Librarians, was one of the reasons he had been given the mantle of Emperor's Champion.

Lysander yelled and hauled the tide of men off him, shoving them back with his shield. He could now hear clearly, as if he had surfaced from underwater, the crackle of bolter fire behind him, the howl of chainblades and the shouting of orders as the Imperial Fists dismembered the waves of household troops storming them.

Scarlet lightning burst down from the sky. It hit Ucalegon in one shoulder, earthing through him and the bodies beneath him. The stench of charred meat, instead of blood and torn bowels, now filled the air.

Ucalegon convulsed, still on his feet. He planted the obsidian blade in the mass of bodies to steady himself. The lightning flashed again but this time Ucalegon strode forward, through the pain, ascending the mountain of the dead and dying to come level with the spider's face.

Ucalegon's armour smouldered, flickers of power grounding off it. He was reflected in the spider's eyes as he drew back the obsidian blade.

'In the name of Holy Terra I challenge!' shouted Ucalegon. 'Take up arms, for the Emperor's Justice falls on you!'

The spider lurched forwards. Its face split open to animal dimensions, revealing a huge, drooling mouth with thousands of needle-like teeth. It was easily big enough to swallow Ucalegon whole and take a bite out of the mound of bodies on which he stood.

Ucalegon did not step back. He lunged forwards, driving the obsidian sword up into the spider's top palate.

The blade sheared into its upper jaw and one of its eyes burst as the point forced its way up through the socket. The lower jaw slackened and Ucalegon planted a foot against its bank of teeth to wrench the sword free.

He struck again before the spider could recover. This time the sword went in through its remaining eye. Ucalegon twisted the blade and pulled it out, bringing a great fountain of shredded brain and purple-black gore with it.

Blinded and maddened, the spider reared up, almost throwing Ucalegon aside. But Ucalegon held onto the sword which was still lodged in the spider's skull and grabbed the edge of a chitin plate, pulling himself up onto the spider's head, then straddling its midsection and pulling himself up onto its abdomen.

The spider howled and bucked. The seductiveness in its voice was gone. Its control was gone, too. The Aristeia troops were left mindless, suddenly without purpose. They screamed and gibbered like animals as they fought to get out of the crushing mass around Lysander. Elsewhere they were suddenly fleeing in every direction, dropping their guns and running. Lysander kicked himself free of them and saw Ucalegon shearing off two of the spider's legs with a sweep of his sword. The spider sank down to one side like a listing ship.

'Septuron!' ordered Lysander over the vox. 'Take it apart!'

Squad Septuron ran through the collapsing Aristeia formation and set about the spider with their chainblades. Its midsection was rapidly denuded of legs, leaving it an immobile, mewling lump that bucked and writhed as it tried to throw off the Space Marines around it.

A chainblade sheared into its neck and more blood flowed than Lysander thought could be contained within even so huge a creature. Ucalegon levered an armour-plate away from it and hacked at the organs inside. The sinewy connections between its head and midsection came apart and its head was off, features still churning as the head rolled away.

'Syncella! Skult! Where are you?' voxed Lysander. There was no reply.

Beneath the shadow of the spacecraft, which had paused in its descent, Lysander saw Lady Syncella. The downwash of the spaceship's jets rendered the scene blurry and veiled in smoke, but the face of the skinny, ragged blonde woman in front of Syncella was the same as the translator from vel Sephronaas's transmission.

It was Legienstrasse.

She did not look like someone who could kill anyone, let alone an Imperial Assassin. She still wore the drab translator's uniform, reduced to grubby rags by her flight across the mountains.

Syncella's collar split in two and the halves clattered to the rockcrete. Lysander felt the cold, hateful aura that was released from her. If he had been forced to describe it he could have done no better than to say it was like having his soul plunged into ice – but that was barely adequate as a description. What Syncella truly was, Lysander couldn't put into words.

Syncella's power knives were in her hands. She crouched low, a predator about to pounce. Legienstrasse was down on one knee, hands spread on the ground, in the attitude of a sprinter on the start line.

But she was not about to break into a run. Lysander saw now that the spider's blood, mixed in with the blood of the dead Aristeia troops, had run across the landing pad and was spreading around the feet of the two Assassins.

The skin of Legienstrasse's forearms rippled as she drew the blood up into her, through the tiny mouths opening up on her hands. Beneath her rags, ridges of bone and muscle shifted.

Lysander had learned from Syncella what Legienstrasse was, and he understood now why she had ordered the spider and the other moral threats to bring what forces they could to the spaceport of Krae. She needed bodies. She needed blood. Above all, she needed their biomass.

Syncella leapt at Legienstrasse. Legienstrasse flitted to one side, almost too fast for Lysander to follow. She lashed out with a whip of knotted gore, twisted into a weapon that slithered from the palm of her hand by a physiology created in some forbidden Mechanicus lab millennia ago. Each of her legs split in two and she dodged on four lower limbs now, their muscle and bone exposed. And still she changed, as rapidly as it was possible to think of the next mutation.

Syncella lunged. Legienstrasse's other arm fanned out into a shield of bony spurs and leathery membrane, catching the power knife and twisting it point-down into the rockcrete. The whip lashed around Syncella's neck and flung her aside, sending her sprawling across the ground. It was the first time Lysander had seen the Grand Master of the Culexus Temple without grace, reduced to a mere ill-coordinated human.

Legienstrasse's mutations withdrew, rendering her indistinguishable from a normal human woman again. Most disturbingly, her face had not changed throughout the opening exchanges. The whip slithered back into her hand.

When the Assassin of the Maerorus Temple killed, it was with the bare hand. Her Assassin's training could guarantee that the first target would fall. It was the subsequent targets that were the problem – alerted to the danger, probably armed and with the advantage of numbers, even an Assassin would be hard pressed to kill them all empty-handed. So the Maerorus Assassin made use of that first victim and turned him into a weapon she could use – her physiology broke the body down into its raw biomass and transformed it instantly into weapon mutations. She was a living weapon, fuelled by the bodies of the dead, so that with every target she killed she became stronger. The Officio Assassinorum had bargained for centuries to gain the leverage over certain Adeptus Mechanicus tech-heretics to have the necessary research performed on rare mutant strains and shapeshifting xenos. The Maerorus Temple itself had started out as a huge, forbidden experiment camp, where thousands of subjects were rendered down to create the genetic material required to make the first Maerorus Assassin.

Lysander was looking at that Assassin now, the first and last graduate of the Maerorus Temple, as she sprinted towards Lady Syncella on an array of centipede-like limbs that suddenly sprouted from a lengthening abdomen.

Lady Syncella's eyes turned black and a bolt of nothingness shot from her. The concentrated essence of the Culexus, a shard of utter void, was enough to blast clean the soul of any normal target. To a psyker, it was utter oblivion, the annihilation of the spirit, a casting into an anti-realm that a psyker feared worse than death. To anyone else it was an instant cessation of existence. Focused by the Animus Speculum, a psyniscience device built into Syncella's skull, it was the ultimate expression of their killing art.

Lysander's soul recoiled. The whole world seemed skewed sideways, somehow infinitely but indescribably wrong.

Legienstrasse did not miss a step. She skittered under the blast and rose up to slam into Syncella. Her torso split open into four clawed limbs, grabbing Syncella and yanking her up into the air. Arteries pulsed under her skin as they drew up the blood from the fallen Aristeia, and within her chest Lysander could see three great hearts, each larger than a man's head, thudding wildly as they forced it all into her new extremities.

Syncella writhed and struggled. Her power knives darted in and out, shearing off limbs as new ones grew in their place. She had not reached the rank of Grand Master without being one of the most efficient killing machines the Imperium could call upon. A bony spike lanced at her head – she twisted to one side, caught it in the crook of her elbow and snapped it off. She wrenched another limb out of its socket and, as it released its grip on her, she grabbed a handful of Legienstrasse's ratty blonde hair and drew back her fist to ram her knife into her enemy's throat.

Blood-red whips lashed around Syncella's wrist and held it firm. For a moment the two were locked together, face to face. Legienstrasse's expression had still not changed.

Legienstrasse raised a human-looking hand. It split apart, fingers fanning out, forming a shield that covered one side of her face.

A bullet smacked into it and detonated, leaving the hand a smoking ruin.

Legienstrasse glanced sideways, just once, at Agent Skult. The Vindicare had timed his shot perfectly, and any other target would have been felled by a direct headshot. Skult was crouching away from the battle, nestled between the steel blocks of a rusting docking clamp, where he had taken up position to wait for his shot. Now he had taken it, and the chance was gone.

Any other target would have died, but not a fellow Assassin. Legienstrasse knew how a Vindicare fought. She knew the shot was coming. She knew when, and how, and the opportunity for a surprise kill-shot was gone.

Lysander was forging through the bodies and the fleeing Aristeia troops to close with Legienstrasse. Where Syncella could not succeed on her own, perhaps she and an Imperial Fist could. Bolter fire was kicking into the rockcrete around Legienstrasse even as she turned to hold up Syncella between her and the Vindicare, an impromptu shield that protected her vital organs as Skult fired shot after shot into her rapidly growing collection of limbs and appendages. Moment by moment Legienstrasse grew, a dizzying mass of pulsing flesh, here with petals like a flower, there with pincers like a predatory insect.

And in the heart of it her face, unchanged, still the same woman Lysander had seen on vel Sephronaas's broadcast. If there had been nothing human about her, it would have been better. She would have been an enemy on a par with the alien or the daemon, utterly inhuman and easy to hate. But that human core was more disturbing than anything the rest of her became. Perhaps that was another weapon she carried with her – the fact that whoever faced her saw something of themselves in that innocent feminine face, nestled in a tangled mass of horror.

Legienstrasse plunged a limb into the ground and it rippled along the blood-soaked landing pad, exploding beneath Lysander in a spray of glistening red tentacles. They wrapped around Lysander and dragged him back, and suddenly every step forwards took an enormous force of will. Lysander tore one arm free and swung the Fist of Dorn around him, but the blunt hammer did little against the tentacles – they bent under the force and snapped around the hammer, too, so suddenly it felt like it weighed too much for Lysander to lift.

Lysander roared in frustration. The bolter fire from his battle-brothers was doing almost nothing, for every chunk of flesh they blasted out of Legienstrasse was replaced as gore welled up in the wound and solidified.

Sergeant Septuron sprinted through the chaos towards Legienstrasse. Tentacles sprouted to grab him but he slashed through them with his chainsword as he ran. One of Legienstrasse's clawed limbs reached down for him but he dropped and rolled under it, bringing his blade up as he passed under to slice through it at a joint. It thudded to the ground behind him as he came back up to his feet.

'Whatever in the hells you are,' cried Septuron, 'you will be it no longer! This is the blade that ends you, Assassin!'

Legienstrasse's answer was a blade of bone that speared out from the centre of her torso, from between the pulsing mass of her multiple hearts. It impaled Septuron through the stomach and split the backpack of his armour in two as it exited through his back. Sparks showered out of the armour's ruptured power unit. Septuron was still alive as Legienstrasse lifted him up off the ground.

'Brother!' yelled Lysander, and the most awful feeling of all was the helplessness of being almost unable to move while a fellow Imperial Fist was dying in front of him.

Two new, slimmer limbs grabbed Septuron by the arms. The bone blade twisted, forcing Septuron's torso wide open, and for a second Lysander could see Legienstrasse's face through the hole torn in the assault sergeant. Then the blade withdrew and Septuron dropped to the ground, by now dead.

The thought of Septuron's muscle and bone being absorbed for Legienstrasse's use was what spurred Lysander on, tentacles snapping at him as he took another few tortuous steps towards the Assassin.

Legienstrasse looked at Syncella now, as if she had momentarily forgotten about the Grand Master. Syncella was twisting in her grasp, her own unnatural strength fighting against the alien muscle that wrapped every part of Legienstrasse's mutating skeleton. Legienstrasse forced Syncella towards her chest, where her organs throbbed inside an open torso.

Syncella twisted one arm free. A knife punched into one of Legienstrasse's hearts and blood sprayed out, flowing from the Assassin's chest as if from a fountain. Then the teeth slid from the edges of her open ribcage, forming a huge set of vertically hinged jaws that closed shut on Lady Syncella.

Syncella's legs kicked as the teeth gouged into her waist. She was strong and she lived a few seconds longer than anyone had a right to, bracing her arms against the side of the maw to hold it wide. Bones snapped and her arms gave way, and the jaws clamped shut on her.

Lady Syncella's lower half flopped to the blood-soaked ground, still kicking.

Legienstrasse turned now to Lysander, and new limbs, great bladed arms like those of a huge fleshy mantis, grew from her shoulders.

'Keep her here!' ordered Lysander into the vox. 'If we can't kill her, keep her on Opis!'

Agent Skult's next two shots were aimed upwards, towards the spacecraft still hovering overhead. Twin explosions bloomed against the rearward engines, and a plume of burning fuel poured out, plunging like a waterfall of flame to the landing pad a hundred metres away. The ship suddenly drifted to one side, secondary explosions bursting around the jet holding one side of it aloft.

Legienstrasse looked up and saw the spacecraft, her way off this planet, was mortally wounded. Skult's turbo-penetrator shots had punched through a fuel tank or coolant line and one of the landing jets was shaking itself apart in bursts of promethium flame.

Legienstrasse broke and ran. Her weapons were withdrawn and suddenly long limbs, like those of a gazelle, were propelling her westwards towards the embattled terminal building. The tentacles slid into the pools of blood and Lysander was free. He ran after Legienstrasse, shouldering aside the dazed Aristeia troops too exhausted or confused to flee. He could hear the whining, then the screaming, of the spaceship's engines as its remaining thruster failed to cope with the strain and sent the ship into a rapidly spinning descent. Gunfire crackled as Lysander reached earshot of the terminal, and he was aware of other Imperial Fists following him as he ran. His Terminator armour was not ideally suited to a foot pursuit, but once he had built up momentum he could keep pace with the other Imperial Fists as Legienstrasse leapt a burning barricade and vanished into the terminal building.

Lysander smashed through the barricade, kicking away sheets of steel reinforcement. Inside, gunfire hammered in every direction, filling the air with blurry chains of fire that rattled between the high girders. Sparks showered down as bullets and las-bolts burst against the corroded bronze-plated walls, and smoke hung heavy; a pall of greyish vapour that caught at Lysander's throat. He felt his lungs contracting even as he registered the bodies heaped up around him, draped lifeless over fallen bronze pillars in the deflated, unnatural attitudes of death. Imperial Guardsmen and steel-plated heretics lay mixed up with one another, their blood mingling in gory mounds of torn flesh.

Lysander charged through friend and foe. Guardsmen huddling behind a fallen slab of wall were thrown aside as he stormed through them. A sweep of his shield knocked two heretics aside. The Guardsmen they were bearing down on had to scramble out of the way to avoid Lysander's boots crunching down at them.

Legienstrasse was ahead, just visible through the bedlam. Men were flung aside by her long legs as she loped past. Lasfire streaked around her. Lysander followed in her wake, just keeping pace as she ducked under a sunken section of the roof that bowed down in a spray of torn girders. She vaulted the remains of an interior wall – Lysander dropped a shoulder and barged through it, throwing bricks and mortar outwards like an exploding grenade.

The battle was not his. The men of the Algol Siegebreakers would have to fight and die without Lysander's aid. Lysander glimpsed a huge armoured figure and recognised with a lurch that it was a Space Marine – not a fellow soldier of the Emperor but one of the Traitor Legions, his power armour smouldering with inner fire, gnarled and smoking like the outcrops of a living volcano. In one hand the Traitor Marine held up an Imperial Guard officer, a colonel, by the throat. Flames were already licking around the officer's throat. Under the Traitor Marine's feet was a regimental standard, the face of the saint embroidered on it stained with blood and filth.

Any other time, the obscenity of a Traitor Marine would be met with Lysander's every attention. Any other time. But not this time. The enemy was Legienstrasse. She had to die. Even the matter of honour that a Traitor Marine represented was relegated to second place to the only victory that mattered on Opis.

The hand around the officer's throat had six fingers. Lysander knew he was looking at Karnikhal, champion of the Blood God Khorne, who had marched alongside Angron the Cursed in the black days of the Horus Heresy.

A section of the roof collapsed up ahead, showering twisted metal and masonry down in Lysander's path. He dropped down and halted to keep from being buried.

'We will return!' yelled Lysander at the Traitor Marine. 'We will find you, and all will be repaid!'

In reply, Karnikhal Six-Finger snapped the colonel's neck and dropped his body into the dust. He stamped on the man's torso, grinding his bones and organs into the defaced standard.

Legienstrasse had stopped too, on the other side of the fallen roof section. Her legs were fusing together into sturdy supports banded around with muscle and her forelimbs were now great shovel-like wedges of bone. Her expression did not change as she rammed them into the ground ahead of her, tearing up the floor and revealing a deep hole beneath her.

Lysander scrambled over the rubble. Men from both sides were trapped under him, still yelling. As he watched, Legienstrasse opened a hole just big enough for her swollen form and forced her way down, into the hole and out of sight.

Lysander reached the edge of the hole. Wetness shone beneath him in the red flashes of las-fire. He jumped down and landed hip-deep in rushing water.

No, not water. Fuel. Legienstrasse had found one of the fuel lines that ran under the spaceport. The stench of it was so great an unaugmented man could not have breathed at all.

Lysander could hear Legienstrasse splashing and slithering up ahead. He glimpsed fish-like, scaled masses writhing away into the darkness. He ran after her, forcing his way against the flow.

Legienstrasse left bony spikes in her wake, embedded in the side of the pipe. Lysander kicked them aside and knocked them away with his hammer. A web of stringy membrane clung to him but he ripped it aside and wrenched the worst of it out of his eyes.

He was closing on her. A muscular tail was powering her forwards but she had absorbed so much biomass that she was scraping along the sides of the pipe. She was shedding bony spurs and lashes of muscle, edged with teeth, that slashed at Lysander as he ran, but they did not slow him down. His Terminator armour, and the armament of shield and hammer, meant he was a soldier built to charge on and not slow down no matter what was thrown at him.

Fire sparked behind him. Lysander caught it in the corner of his eye and risked a glance behind him.

Karnikhal Six-Finger was leaning down through the hole, illuminating the section of pipe with the molten fires of his armour. He reached down and a six-fingered hand shone in the darkness, liquid ceramite dripping from a slash in its palm.

The molten metal hit the torrent of fuel.

Lysander saw the flames as if in slow motion. Liquid fire billowed up towards him, the fuel torrent vaporising into a flash of boiling flame. Lysander threw his shield up in front of him as the impact hit it and the shield slammed into him with the force of a battering ram.

He heard the biological screech of Legienstrasse ahead of him. But he saw nothing. Instead of the fire, there was darkness.

Then the scream was the ringing of the bedlam in his ears, and by the time he slammed into the crumbling rockcrete of the fuel pipe, he was able to feel nothing at all.

K-Day +17 Days
Operation Requiem

The rituals of Khezal had, more than two weeks after the first Imperial Guard troops went in, become rooted in the minds of the men.

One never went into any underground structure, even a half-collapsed cellar or sunken maintenance shed, alone. Ever. Enough had been devoured by fist-sized fleshy spiders, or had shot themselves for no reason, or simply vanished, after descending alone.

Each day, before sunrise, almost every soldier who was able wrote a request to the Emperor on whatever he had to hand – a page torn from a field manual, a shard of metal shrapnel – and buried it in the rubble dust that choked Khezal's streets. It was a tradition of one of the Guard regiments that had caught on. Most of them simply asked to see the next sunrise. Some begged for one confirmed kill that day, so that when the writer's own death came he would have at least balanced it against the stolen life of an enemy. A few asked for a hated officer to fall in battle before he fed any more of his men into the choked killing alleys and lightless underground warrens.

A few drops of water were allowed to fall on the ground before drinking, no matter how scarce clean water might be, because the earth of Opis would drink your blood if you did not slake its thirst.

Boots were blessed every morning, because if you lost your boots, you were sure to die that day.

Sergeant Sthenelus of the Imperial Fists was watching one of those rituals now, being enacted among the Imperial Guardsmen sheltering in foxholes and waist-deep trenches dug into the southern end of the Garden of Astriina the Comely. This pleasure garden stretched for whole city blocks on each edge, and before the battle had been a sculpted landscape in miniature, with summer houses and follies on ornamental lakes separated by stands of trees. False temple ruins had stood on low hills, to be enjoyed by the Aristeia and wealthy craftsmen who lived in the exclusive housing blocks overlooking the Garden.

Now it was a grotesque scar, an open wound where torn earth replaced shattered buildings, where the remnants of the place's forced beauty served only to make it all even uglier. The firing lanes across the Garden were all but impossible to avoid so the Guardsmen who held its southern third dug themselves into the ground, crawling on their bellies to keep out of the sights of snipers who occupied the shattered habitation blocks overlooking the northern reaches. They were

Deucalians, a mixture of the 120th and 309th, with a few squads from the 122nd Storm Troopers. A few thousand men crouched in ones and twos as grey dawn broke through the pall of smoke and rubble dust that turned the sky the colour of stone.

The ritual was the confession. Only a couple of priests remained so men too wounded to fight, but still able to move, had taken up the spiritual slack. They went from trench to fox-hole, hearing the sins of the day and night before. Everyone had something to confess. If you didn't the Emperor would forget about you, and His grace would not save you from a sniper's bullet or booby trap.

'I lived when my friends did not.'

'I killed a man, but I do not know if it was a friend or an enemy.'

'I let my lasgun run dry, and did not realise until the firing had stopped.'

'I was too afraid to move, and lay here all through the night.'

There were no punishments demanded by the makeshift confessors. If there was a punishment due, the Garden of Astriina the Comely would surely be generous in handing it out.

Sthenelus watched this through the vision blocks mounted around the hatch of his Vindicator siege tank. His three-strong squadron was sheltered as much as was possible in a series of artillery craters that had scoured one corner of the Garden. His tank was the *Beast of Mardon*, and the battle-brothers of his squadron manned the *Granitefang* and the *Bonecracker* nearby.

<<Trajack here,>> came a voice over the squadron vox.

'The time is close, lieutenant,' replied Sthenelus. 'Glory does not wait for us. She drives us on.'

<<Though I do not share your enthusiasm, sergeant,>> said Lieutenant Trajack, <<we are close. The rearward squads are getting into position. The word will be given as soon as we hear they are ready.>> Sthenelus had not yet seen Trajack face to face but the storm trooper officer was the de facto commander in the Garden.

'I can feel the teeth of my tanks,' said Sthenelus. 'They grind in frustration. The longer I hold them back the wilder they will be. They will yearn to charge forward, and their shots will be ill-aimed.'

<<As long as my men can see them,>> said Trajack. <<That will do as much damage to the enemy as your guns. I fear many of these men will not advance unless they see the Imperial Fists alongside them.>>

'Your fear is your failing,' replied Sthenelus. 'If your men see it, they too will be afraid. But if you show no fear, they will forget, in the chaos of battle, what fear is.'

Voices chattered over the vox. Acknowledgement messages flashed in rapid regimental code.

Through the vision blocks, Sthenelus could see a tattered standard being unrolled. It was carried by a man who had lost one hand and most of his other arm, and who now served by carrying the standard in the crook of his remaining elbow. It was the standard of the 309th Deucalian Lancers, and carried the emblem of a warhorse in full gallop with a dozen battle honours named underneath.

<<We're set! This is the general advance! All units, this is the general advance!>> Trajack's voice over the vox was swamped by the battle-cries rising up and down the Imperial Guard line, as every unit yelled its own oath to the saints of the Imperium and the Emperor on high.

'Onwards!' ordered Sthenelus. The *Beast of Mardon* ground forwards on its tracks, riding up over the sodden sandbags that had corralled it against sniper fire. The Vindicator's driver, Brother Morsk, was almost hidden by the huge breech of the tank's siege cannon and Techmarine Daedelon, the squadron's engineer, was crushed into the rear of the tank in a space between the cannon's huge shells. Morsk swung the tank around so it showed its front dozer blade to the direction of the enemy.

The Imperial Guard jumped from cover and advanced. Few of them ran. Officers held swords high and led the way, walking out across the chewed-up mud and shattered tree stumps. A pair of Sentinel scout walkers strode towards one flank, surrounded by the incongruous jungle world camouflage of the storm troopers.

Sniper fire took the first toll. Men's heads snapped back and they fell, left where they lay by the advance. Others were cut down and wounded but not killed, and their cries mixed with the battle-oaths.

Sthenelus's squadron was some way behind the front rank of men, and he saw through the vision blocks as the gunfire took ones and twos, then handfuls. A preacher continued to shout the words of the Emperor's scribes even though the men around him had all been cut down and few ears could hear him. A Deucalian Guardsman was shot through the abdomen and slumped against a dry fountain, alongside bodies that had lain there for days.

The enemy were concealed among the hard cover around the north of the Garden. The snipers were huddled among false ruins and summer houses, or concealed on the banks of ornamental lakes. Others – no one could be sure of their numbers – occupied the buildings that stood, some almost completely intact, along the northern edge, or held the streets that terminated at the Garden's boundaries.

Sthenelus thought he could see movement up ahead, almost hidden by the drifting smoke and kicks of mud and blood from sniper shots. He hauled open the hatch above his head and the damp, smoky air of the battlefield filled the *Beast of Mardon.*

Snipers were cowering around the statue of Astriina the Comely, just beyond a torn-up section of low hillside studded with falsely aged fallen pillars and archways. They wore cowls with gas masks over their heads, cables from the masks hooked up to gas bottles strapped to their backs. They carried hunting rifles, perhaps looted from the armouries of Aristeia nobles. Even as Sthenelus watched, they were lining up shots among the advancing Imperial Guards.

Astriina's statue had showed her as an imperious, beautiful woman swathed in furs and jewels. Now she was so pocked with bullet scars she looked like her skin was sloughing off her.

'Firing! Brace for recoil!' shouted Sthenelus. He fulfilled three roles on the *Beast* – squadron commander, tank commander and gunner. He slammed a fist against a control stud beside him and a shell was rammed into the gun's breech. The barrel of the gun was a short, wide mouth protruding beyond the dozer blade. Auto-senses built into Sthenelus's armour projected the likely firing trajectory onto his retina, but in case those failed the simple iron sights mounted on the commander's hatch told the same story. The firing line intersected with the shape of Astriina the Comely and Sthenelus yanked on the firing lever.

The cannon bellowed. Sthenelus could just see the dark streak of the shell carried on its long line of burning propellant. It slammed into the base of the statue and the snipers disappeared in a cloud of torn earth. The report followed a moment later, a deep boom rumbling through the earth. Astriina toppled sideways, disappearing in the smoke and debris.

Through the darkness, the enemy were charging.

<<They're here!>> came Trajack's voice over the vox. <<Why didn't they wait? They're counter-attacking!>> Trajack switched to the vox-channel linking all the Imperial Guard units. <<All units, fix bayonets and assault! Charge, Guardsmen! Charge!>>

The enemy soldiers were emerging from the gloom of the Vindicator's shot. There seemed to be hundreds of them, appearing suddenly in the Garden's northern expanses as if they had been waiting for the Imperial Guard to cross a line. They were hooded and masked, surrounded by a pall of green-grey smoke that bled from the gas bottles and breathing masks they wore.

<<The enemy is eager for death,>> came a vox from Brother Kallistar, commander of the *Granitefang*.

'Too eager,' said Sthenelus. 'They are vermin, but they are cunning. They had hard cover and they abandon it just as we walk into the teeth of their guns.'

'Is it another sacrifice?' asked Techmarine Daedelon. 'As the *Sanctifier* witnessed?'

'They do not yet kill their own,' said Sthenelus. 'So I think not. Squadron, support the advance! Fire at will!'

The Vindicators hurled booming artillery shells into the host of enemy troops. Whatever they had once been, the enemy had long since ceased to suffer the doubts and fears of human beings. Explosions threw clouds of torn bodies into the air, but they still advanced. Las-fire shredded their front ranks, but they did not run. They seemed more intent on a suicidal advance than the Imperial Guard had been a few moments before.

The *Beast of Mardon* bucked as it fired, roaring plumes of flame across the battlefield. Among the detonations, las-fire streaked back and forth between the Imperial Guard and the enemy, and the battlefield was a mad cauldron that even a Space Marine's experience could make no sense of.

It was without reason or purpose, as if this bedlam were its own reward.

It was chaos.

The ground shuddered and split open. A hundred Guardsmen fell in as the fissure ripped across the Gardens, a vast torrent of torn earth swept into the black gash underfoot. Everything tilted sideways as the entire Garden of Astriina the

Comely sank several metres. Nearby buildings collapsed and the banks of dust rolled in like dense thunderclouds. Suddenly Sthenelus could barely see anything beyond the dozer blade of his tank.

'Back! Back!' he ordered. 'Turn us around! They are beneath us!'

Morsk wrenched the controls around and the *Beast's* tracks spun in opposite directions, slewing the tank around even as the ground tilted underneath it. Sthenelus could see the *Bonecracker* sliding with the masses of earth pouring into the fissure that was reaching closer with every moment. Guardsmen were running in every direction, yelling for their squadmates or just sprinting away from the worst of the insanity. A Sentinel walker limped past, one of its legs almost too badly twisted to support it.

'Trajack!' called Sthenelus into the vox. The only reply was static, shot through with gunfire and screaming.

The *Beast of Mardon* was losing its fight against gravity. The tracks were spinning through loose earth. Sthenelus pulled the hatch closed over him and crouched down beside the breech of the siege cannon.

'If they wish to fight their battle beneath the earth,' shouted Sthenelus over the tearing of the fissure, 'then we shall fight that battle and win it! For we will march into hell, if the enemy but halts there and faces our guns!'

The ground dropped out from under the *Beast of Mardon*. For a moment it was weightless as it lurched. Then the sides boomed as debris hammered against it and it finally landed with an awful crunch.

Sthenelus was rattled against the sides of the tank, drummed into the breech and the side of the hull. His head swam and the tank seemed to scream, its engine still grinding its tracks against the loose debris beneath it.

Morsk got himself upright and cut the engine.

'Report!' said Sthenelus.

'I am unhurt,' said Daedelon. 'The machine-spirit is anguished.'

Sthenelus looked through the vision blocks but he could not see anything but a coating of grime. He opened the hatch and earth showered in.

The forces of Khezal had indeed decided to fight this battle beneath the ground, for they had built hell under the Garden.

Naked, writhing bodies, knitted together into an appalling tangled mess, formed a landscape that stretched off into the darkness. The sky of raw stone overhead was hung with tree roots reaching down from the Garden, the faintest light glistening on the expanses of skin from the tears in the ground.

The sound of their breathing was like a whistling wind, rising and falling, and the smell was an awful mixture of sweat, blood and ordure. Guardsmen, some living, some dead, lay among the bodies, the conscious trying to disentangle themselves from the limbs that suddenly surrounded them. Sthenelus could see men and women in there; all skin hues and sizes, scrawny arms wrapped around pallid guts, and no sign of the ground beneath the mass.

'My sword,' said Sthenelus.

Morsk pulled Sthenelus's chainsword from its scabbard near his feet and passed it up to the sergeant.

'They have built a vision of the warp beneath Khezal,' said Sthenelus. 'They have made a hell from the wretched of this world. So give thanks! For Dorn taught us to fight in hell!'

Guardsmen were crying out as they sank into the smothering mass. Others had been wounded in the battle or the fall, and wailed like animals. They reached for the *Beast of Mardon*, as if swimming against the current, but the blind, grasping hands held them back.

'Brothers, do you hear me?' voxed Sthenelus.

<<*Granitefang* here,>> came the reply from Brother Kallistar. <<We have thrown a track and cannot move. Brother Vellion is hurt, but not badly. I see the *Bonecracker*. They have come down on their roof. I cannot raise them on the vox.>>

A long, low trumpeting sound echoed across the underground landscape. The gloom would have been impenetrable to a normal man's vision and Sthenelus could only just make out the movement in the distance. Picking their way across the layer of living bodies were monstrous forms, three or four of them, towering almost to the earthen ceiling on long stilt-like limbs. The fleshy bags of their bodies supported drooping heads with long proposces that poked and groped among the bodies, occasionally snatching one up, perhaps out of curiosity, perhaps to feed. The lowing sound was emanating from these enormous creatures, and around their spindly legs scampered smaller things, indistinct structures of flesh.

'Do you have a visual on that?' voxed Sthenelus.

<<Aye, sergeant,>> replied Kallistar.

'Can you fire upon them?'

<<Not unless they come closer, into our line of fire. Throne knows what they are.>>

'The works of the enemy,' said Sthenelus. 'By such works shall we know them. Morsk! Take us into firing range! Forwards and right twenty!'

The *Beast of Mardon* crunched through the bodies around it, tracks slurping through the sucking murk of churned bodies. Blood spattered up against Sthenelus. The *Beast*'s targeting still worked and the vectors lined up, lighting the outline of the closest beast as they came into range.

Sthenelus let another shell slam into the breech. The beast seemed to recognise the sound, its head turning towards the Vindicator. Sthenelus could see the eyes dotted on its head, scattered asymmetrically around its trunk.

It was made of bodies. They had lost much of their definition, as if melted or partly dissolved, but torsos and limbs were still just visible among the wrinkles of its sagging body.

'Recall, my brothers, the parable of Rodrigar,' said Sthenelus. 'Though he fought from within a Predator tank, he carried with him always his chainsword, and always gave it the greatest honours when it came to his weapon-rites.'

Sthenelus fired, and the Vindicator's cannon roared. The corresponding blast bloomed in the middle of the beast's torso and its legs buckled, as it let out a terrible bleak trumpeting. Torn flesh poured down.

Purplish fire tore from the massive wound, spraying down into the massed bodies. An unnatural light, in colours that could not properly be comprehended by a human eye, bled in every direction and reality seemed to twist, twitching in response to the sudden burst of energy.

'And his battle-brothers mocked him,' continued Sthenelus. 'Brother Rodrigar, they cried, why place such trust in a blade when the might of the war machine protects you?'

The remains of the beast's torso split open. Instead of a ragged hole, the space was filled with swirling purple flame, boiling and flashing with power. More fire vomited out in a waterfall, carrying half-formed bodies, indistinct and quivering.

<<They're warp portals!>> said Kallistar over the vox. <<Living doors to the warp! They're breeding them down here!>>

'But Rodrigar,' said Sthenelus, his train of thought unbroken, 'listened not. He polished the teeth of his chainblade and communed with the machine-spirit of its motor. And came the time his Predator tank joined battle against the liars that men call eldar.'

The half-formed things uncoiled and struggled to the surface of the human mass. They were misshapen and asymmetrical, crowned with malformed horns. Their skin tore and bulged and their lopsided faces were twisted with the agony of their sudden birth.

'Daemons,' hissed Brother Morsk. 'Throne above us, hells below, daemons spill forth from the immaterium.'

'Recall, Morsk, the parable,' said Sthenelus, 'and act accordingly.'

The *Beast of Mardon* lurched forwards, bodies crunching. It rode up over knots of bodies and down again, as the eyes of the other warp gate beasts turned to fix on it. Blood and gore were sprayed up the sides of the tank and Sthenelus wiped blood from the eyepieces of his helmet.

'Then,' continued Sthenelus, 'the xenos crippled Rodrigar's Predator with an alien weapon of deceitful design. The war machine was laid low, its mighty tracks torn, its engine weeping clouds of oily smoke. The alien sought to breach the war machine and defile its machine-spirit. But face to face they came with Brother Rodrigar!'

The *Beast of Mardon* crunched closer to the warp gate. Liquid fire was now lapping at its front armour, carrying on it a tide of charred and disintegrating bodies as well as half-formed daemons. The mewling daemon-things were raking at the tank with their claws, trying to grab a handhold and drag themselves onto it. Sthenelus fired again and the blast from the cannon shredded the daemons clustering in front of the tank. The shell detonated at knee height to the beast and it fell, the torn warp gate plunging into the sea of burning bodies.

'And Rodrigar despaired not! For he had honoured his humble blade with the same fervour as the war machine, and it served him now! For while the war machine was lame and weakened, the blade did not falter!'

Sthenelus leaned out of the hatch and speared one daemon through the neck with his own sword, the chainteeth shredding the glowing daemon's flesh. They were translucent, their organs visible squirming under their transparent skin, and they howled as they reached blindly for the tank.

The tank pitched up against a tightly packed mass of bodies. It lurched down again, and Sthenelus was face to face with the fallen beast. Its glassy black eyes rolled to stare at him. The massive wound in its side looked out onto a boiling starscape, a window into another realm. It sought to drag Sthenelus's eye to stare into it, but it was a fragment of the warp and to become lost in it was to invite madness. The weak-willed would walk dumbly into it. The stronger might still have their minds haunted by what they saw in there – glimpses of the future or the past, carefully poised lies wrought to drive them mad or turn them on their own. Sthenelus focused on the gate beast instead, even as its trunk split open to reveal rows of tooth-like barbs reaching up into a wet, slurping gullet.

'With every thrust, a head!' cried Sthenelus. He hacked left and right at the daemons trying to clamber up to him. He cut through a hand, bisected a skull. The daemons had barely enough cohesion to maintain a physical form and they fell apart under his blade, or were ground beneath the tank's tracks. Another metre closer and Sthenelus was within striking range of the beast. 'With every slash, a life lain down before the Emperor's wrath! And when his brothers came to reclaim the shattered war machine, Rodrigar had heaped up around it a host of the alien dead!'

Sthenelus leapt onto the top of the hull and rammed the chainblade down into the warp gate beast's head. It punched in through one eye and emerged from the orifice formed by its split trunk, blood spraying from the whirring teeth. He twisted it back and forth, wrenching deeper into the gristle and brain. The thing's eyes rolled back and bulged, oozing pale gore as the brain matter behind them was pulped.

The whole beast spasmed. Flashes, like lightning, burst from the warp portal, and like breaking glass cracks of power crazed across the portal surface.

Sthenelus tore the blade free.

'Thus ends the parable of Rodrigar.'

'We're bogged down,' said Morsk. 'Any deeper and we won't get out.'

'Take us back, brother! Reverse, all speed! We have struck what blows we can. The Chapter must know of the enemy's works here.'

The *Beast of Mardon* forced its way backwards through the tide of burning bodies. More daemons clawed at it, their bodies being forced up into the track housings and shredded.

Like a sea monster breaching the surface, the warp gate beast erupted back out of the burning mass. It bellowed, spraying gore from its ruined head, power pouring uncontrolled from the open wound in the warp in its side. It loomed up on torn and broken legs, high above the *Beast of Mardon*, dedicating its last moments to crashing down on the tank and crushing Sthenelus who was only halfway back into the commander's hatch.

The roar of a siege cannon broke through the howling of the daemons. The shell slammed into the face of the beast and blew it back, shattering it into a rain of shredded meat and bone.

Sthenelus threw himself flat on the tank's hull as gore spattered down over him. He wiped the back of his gauntlet across his faceplate to reveal the *Bonecracker* behind him, riding up over the knotted bodies. Its siege cannon smouldered from the shot it had just fired, the shot that had blasted the stricken warp gate beast into bloody chunks.

Brother Kallistar clung to the tank's upper hull and Brother

Dyess, commander of the *Bonecracker*, stood in the commander's hatch shooting down the clambering daemons with his bolt pistol.

'Brothers!' cried Sthenelus into the vox. 'The *Bonecracker* yet lives!'

'These daemons you set free!' came Dyess's reply. He had to shout, for his tank's comms no longer worked. 'They did us the honour of turning us right side up! And my brothers from the *Granitefang* begged a ride!'

'My thanks will have to wait until we are free of this place,' said Sthenelus. 'Take us back, drivers, find us a way up and away! Lysander must learn of this!'

The two Vindicators made better headway now through the bodies as the daemons writhed, blind and ill-coordinated with the shock of the warp gate's implosion. The beasts were lowing and stampeding at random in the distance, the fires of the warp dying down.

The warp gate glimmered out, its last energies bleeding into the grazing-place of the warp gate beasts. In those last moments narrowed eyes stared from the other side, hungry daemons denied their feast.

But they were content to wait a little longer. They would not stay hungry for long.

Lysander threw open the doors of the Apothecary's bay.

Sigismund Point greeted him, the Imperial Fists base on the Battle Plains, with the smudgy grey mountains in the distance to the west and the pall of smoke over Khezal to the north-east. Labour servitors were taking delivery of crates of ammunition and supplies from an Imperial transport vehicle at the gates. Sergeant Kirav was conducting bolter drills with his fire-team, which now included some of the battle-brothers from Septuron's squad. The Thunderhawks *Peril Swift* and *Gilded Pyre* were parked at the far end of the camp being refuelled under the eye of Brother Gorgythion.

Kirav saw Lysander emerging from the bay and left the fire-team running through sprint and target stance drills.

'Captain!' said Kirav. 'It is good that you are well. We did not think to see you on your feet this day.'

Lysander looked down at himself. He was without his Terminator armour, and wore simple fatigues. The back of one hand was pink and puckered – a makeshift skin graft, to repair his burns. By the tightness of his torso and face, similar grafts covered a good percentage of his body. They stung, but that was good. The nerves worked. It was better than having no feeling at all.

'At first, we thought you dead,' said Kirav.

'They thought the Emperor dead when he lay struck down by Horus,' said Lysander. 'Dorn knew better.'

'And so we went into the fuel lines and brought you back,' said Kirav. 'Death will have a damned time getting to Lysander, we said. We might yet reach him first.'

'And Legienstrasse?'

'Fled,' said Kirav. 'She left plenty of herself behind in the fire, but we think she got away with all her crucial parts.'

'Karnikhal knew she would survive,' said Lysander. 'He set the fire.'

'We did not find him, either.'

Lysander pushed his chest out and stretched. His new skin complained. Some muscle had also been replaced with hasty nerve-fibre bundle implants between his ribs and the tops of his thighs. 'We kept her on Opis, and we drove her away. Legienstrasse will be more desperate now. She will take ever greater risks. We might not have won the laurels of a victory, but we did not fail.'

'None of us,' said Kirav, 'have suggested that we did.'

'That is not what I see in this place,' said Lysander. 'Not what I feel. I know the spirits of my battle-brothers, sergeant. I know their minds. Perhaps none have voiced the belief that our brothers are falling in a war which achieved little, but that belief lurks in them. What were our losses at Krae?'

'Assault-Sergeant Septuron,' said Kirav. 'Brothers Tisiphorn, Kreuz and Euskelos from his squad. Skaen from Squad Ctesiphon. Lady Syncella fell, as well.'

'I saw her die,' said Lysander.

'Few of us miss her,' said Kirav. 'That sentiment, at least, has been voiced. That they died fighting a war she created, to hunt down the Assassinorum's mistake… It has angered them.'

'And I,' said Lysander. 'But my anger cannot decide how I lead my fellow Imperial Fists. Sometimes it is a weapon, to be deployed in the pursuit of victory. But sometimes, it leads us astray, and I must swallow that holy rage that so many Space Marines pursue to their own destruction. That is what it means to command. I must make decisions my brothers cannot, such as to follow Syncella against Legienstrasse. Sometimes those decisions cost us the lives of those we call brothers. I know well the anger that will engender in the hearts of those same brothers, but I must command them nonetheless.'

'I understand, commander.'

'No, Kirav. You do not. Where is my battlegear?'

Kirav pointed at the Thunderhawks. 'Still on board the *Gilded Pyre*, captain. That was how we brought you back here.'

'And the Fist of Dorn?'

'Recovered alongside you.'

'That is good. It is a relic of the Chapter. An Imperial Fist might well lay his life down to bring it back. I give thanks that such was not required.'

'Captain!' said Sergeant Ctesiphon, emerging from the bunker used for housing prisoners – where Lysander had spoken with Serrick before. 'Praise to the primarch that you wake. There is something you must see.'

'Have you activated it?' said Kirav. 'I had assumed it was protected by machine-cipher.'

'Not so,' replied Ctesiphon. 'Or if it was, such safeguards were deactivated with her death.'

'What do you speak of?' said Lysander.

'It is best that we show you,' said Ctesiphon. 'It is inside.'

Inside the bunker, one of the cells stood open. An operating table from the Apothecary's suite had been set up in the cell. On the table lay several chunks of scorched flesh, still smelling of cooked meat and fuel.

'Lady Syncella,' explained Ctesiphon. 'This is all of her upper half we recovered. Whatever organ Legienstrasse was using to digest her, she abandoned it in her flight. The Chapter serfs recovered something from her remains.' Ctesiphon picked up a small metallic device, no longer than a man's finger. 'This,' he said. 'It was buried in her spine. Possibly there were other such devices, but they have been lost. It's a datavault.'

Ctesiphon turned to the back of the cell block, where a holomat servitor lay curled up against the wall. It was a simple, rugged device, used for displaying tactical maps and important communications. Its biological components were hidden somewhere in a base that supported a long projector arm, now retracted.

Ctesiphon plugged the datavault into a socket on the holomat. The servitor's arm unfolded, reaching up to the ceiling and projecting down a cone of flickering greenish light.

The image picked out in three dimensions was grainy, but clear enough to show that it was a soaring vault, a mighty temple of shadows and granite. Freezing mist coiled in the air as a procession of adepts, their hoods and robes not quite enough to hide their ungainly bionics, tramped towards an altar surrounded by braziers belching incense smoke.

Someone sang, a low voice in a mournful dirge, like something from a primitive funeral rite. Each adept carried a body part – a hand, a thigh, a section of ribcage – contained in transparent cylinders filled with fluid.

On a balcony overlooking the great temple chamber stood a lone figure in polished black armour, as bulky as full plate from a feudal world, but which moved with every breath as fluidly as water. The armour's helmet was a skull, and on one hand the figure wore a gauntlet with blades for fingers.

'Eversor,' said Lysander. 'A Grand Master, perhaps. And that is a suit of Shadowplate armour. Its like has not been replicated for a thousand years and the last suits were lost when the forge world Lumias Vex fell. This recording is old. A thousand years or more.'

The adepts took the body parts from their containers and began to assemble them on the altar. The adepts had long given up their humanity. Their limbs were wrapped with ribbed bundles of artificial muscle and their grainy grey skin was stretched over long, equine skulls that grinned as they went about their work. Servo-arms tipped with syringes injected each part as it was laid on the altar and gradually a naked human form took shape. It could have been male or female – it was like a doll or a mannequin, without any features that might give it an identity. The head held the only distinguishing features, for the nose was long and straight, the eyes small, the mouth a thin severe line.

The eyes opened. They were black. A hand shot out and grabbed an adept round its neck. The fist closed and the neck snapped, the adept's head lolling to one side.

The figure sat up and sank its teeth into the adept's throat, tearing out a greyish mass of muscle. It gulped it down and suddenly another limb was unfolding from its back, a lashing spiny tentacle that wrapped around another adept's torso and whipped it up into the air, slamming it down against the altar.

Tendrils shot from the body's mouth and pulled the skull of a third adept apart. Brain matter spilled out. Three had died in as many seconds. The other adepts fell over one another in a panic, robes and hoods pulled aside to reveal the biomechanics of their bodies.

'Enough!' yelled the Eversor. Instantly great billows of white gas sprayed from hidden vents in the floor and frost suddenly covered everything. The adepts fell, their artificial muscle freezing, and the naked figure was hidden in the white mist.

The image shuddered and was lost in static.

It shifted, this time showing a fighter deck on a spacecraft. Huge blast doors sealed off the deck from the vacuum. The viewer, presumably a servitor recording proceedings, stood aside and an airlock door was slammed shut. The viewer continued to watch as several dozen figures ran for the airlock door. The first to reach it wore the rust-red uniform of the Adeptus Mechanicus. Through the porthole in the airlock Lysander could see it was a woman, one arm replaced with a bulky servo-lifter, her shaved cranium plated with circuitry.

'If I must die,' she cried, her voice muffled through the door, 'then let me know! I must know! Knowledge is why I am, it means more than life! Give me this, at least, before I die!'

Warning lights flashed around the blast doors behind the tech-priest. Others, some tech-priests, some menials in simple labourers' uniforms, were rushing in every direction, looking for a way out.

'Tell me!' the tech-priest cried. 'The samples! The first templates! They were xenos, weren't they? Tell me! Before I die, tell me!'

A black-gloved hand slammed down on a control stud. The blast doors boomed open and sudden silence flooded the fighter deck. The tech-priest was yanked backwards as the air rushed out and her body was lost in the blackness of the void revealed beyond the blast doors. If she had time to scream, the sound was lost in the vacuum.

'How did Syncella find all this?' said Kirav.

'Throne knows what cunning a Grand Master of the Assassinorum must possess,' said Lysander. 'Perhaps it was her mission alone to find Legienstrasse, and she pieced together the evidence herself. And she left it to make sure that someone would complete the task if she failed.'

The next image was one of confusion. Light strobed and distant klaxons sounded. It could have been a scene from a spacecraft or a space station, or some industrial facility. Skulls grinned from the false pillars lining the walls and the faltering light fell on fresh bloodstains on the metal plating of the floor.

Troops were running in every direction. They resembled the mind-wiped soldiers the Imperial Fists had encountered on Opis, but their armour revealed their bare arms, which were covered in scrollwork electoos, and each man sported a bionic eye linked by a bundle of cables to his hellgun.

'Move!' someone was yelling. 'It's behind us! It got around us! Keep moving!'

'How could it get behind us?' someone else cried.

The image shuddered and became almost unreadable. Whoever was filming it was running through corridors and labs, at every turn blinded by warning lights or plunged into darkness as power failed.

Bodies lay torn and broken. Troops tried to force open bulkhead doors that were sealed tight.

'Emperor preserve,' someone panted, their voice shaking. 'Emperor preserve. *Salve nos, O Imperator.*'

A soldier screamed. He stumbled back, clutching at his face. A mass of pulsing, bloody flesh clung to him, devouring him even as the trooper fell to his knees. His scream choked off into a gurgling rattle. Las-fire pulsed and the trooper's body vanished in a spray of blood and fire.

'More of them!' came a voice. Everything was motion and noise now, yelling, las-fire, boots on metal and panicked screams.

For a moment the viewer paused at an intersection of corridors. Fleshy masses, about knee-high, were oozing across the walls and floor. Mewling, fanged mouths opened up as they dragged themselves along. With a spasm of muscle one leapt, shooting past the viewer. The viewer spun and saw another trooper fall back, the pinkish mass latched onto his chest. Las-fire streaked into him, punching through his body. He fell, lifeless, the thing that had attacked him now a blackened, quivering lump.

The image focused on the face of one trooper. His helmet was off and aside from his bionic eye he looked too human – covered in grime and spattered blood, and afraid. 'They budded off her,' he said. 'Record that. You hear that? When they cart our bodies back to the Temple, tell them that. They… they hatched. Dozens of them. And every one of us they kill, they grow. Understand? Got that? Is that what you wanted to know? Is that why you sent us in here?'

Confusion again. Screaming and howling, not all of it human. The trooper who had just spoken running away from the viewer, shooting as he did so. The viewer was on the ground, looking down the corridor as more of the fleshy young crawled towards him. And behind them, through a tear in the wall, walked a thing with many limbs folded up around its oversized torso, multiple hoofed feet carrying it forwards. The most appalling thing about it was not its alien form, or even the way its young were writhing in translucent sacs hanging in the hollow formed by its extended ribcage. It was the unmistakably human face, the woman's face, looking completely calm as it lumbered towards the fallen soldier who was recording all this.

The young leapt at him. The image cut out.

Static filled the holo-image for a few seconds. Then the image went blank and the holomat's projector arm folded back up.

'So,' said Lysander. 'She breeds.'

'That is why the Assassinorum wants Legienstrasse dead?' said Kirav. 'Because she can create more?'

'The Maerorus Temple is based around a cycle,' said Lysander. 'As Syncella explained it, Legienstrasse was created to kill whole groups of targets. When one is dead, its biomass can be used to create new weapons to kill more. And so on, each kill making the Maerorus a more effective killer. A cycle that goes on until every target is dead. It seems the Assassinorum neglected to make sure the cycle ended there. One Maerorus they could contain and bring back to the fold, especially once there is no more biomass available. But a dozen more like her, that can harvest their own biomass? That can spread and breed themselves? Worlds could be lost. Sectors. If Legienstrasse breeds, she will become more than a killing machine. She will become a plague, an intelligent plague that kills because it wants to.'

'No wonder they wanted her dead,' said Kirav.

'And no wonder they failed,' replied Lysander. 'They should have exterminated her. These recordings were ancient, they knew long ago how dangerous one such Assassin could be. But they kept her alive. They lost control of her the moment they decided to let her live. Everything that followed was inevitable. Fate had written this story's end a thousand years ago.' Lysander looked at Kirav. 'Have we news from Tchepikov?'

'But little,' said Kirav. 'Just what is distributed to the other commanders. Starfall is a catastrophe. The right flank fell and the Imperial army is fighting to keep from being encircled. Fighting is back and forth over Rekaba and Khezal. There is talk of a fourth front to surround Makoshaam and cut off the other moral threats Tchepikov is certain must be there.'

'The war spreads and continues,' said Lysander. 'As it always will. And it will not end until there is no Opis to fight over. That was what the Assassinorum put in place, to give them the best chance of catching Legienstrasse.'

Lysander's vox chirped. The sound was mostly static.

<<Sthenelus here!>> came the voice over the vox, and Lysander recognised the voice of the squadron commander who had accompanied the Imperial thrust into Khezal on K-Day. <<Commander, can you hear me?>>

'Barely,' said Lysander, hurrying out of the cell bunker in the hope of a better signal.

<<I am using a Guard vox-caster,>> said Sthenelus. <<Communications are a shambles. Commander, we have found the works of the enemy beneath Khezal! Warp gates! Living beasts bred to be wrought into portals to the empyrean! We destroyed one, but there are others.>>

'Where are you?'

<<In the Amphitheatre of Carcarellon,>> said Sthenelus. <<We joined Imperial forces falling back but the enemy is counter-attacking and we…>>

Sthenelus's voice broke up into waves of white noise.

'Sergeant! Squadron commander, come in! We have lost you! Come in!'

<<We're… Captain, we are holding here and assisting with the defence.>> Sthenelus's voice was barely audible, and, along with the interference, gunfire and explosions rumbled in the background. <<But if the enemy's warp gates are opened there will be no city left to hold.>>

'Sthenelus, stay fighting and have faith,' said Lysander. 'You are a beacon to the Guardsmen around you. They will not fall while you stand. Do you understand, brother?'

There was no reply. The vox was a howl of static and feedback. Lysander listened for another few seconds, then cut the link. 'Keep monitoring that channel,' he said to Ctesiphon. 'Kirav, make your fire-team ready. Are the brothers of Septuron's squad reassigned?'

'They are, captain, and they have made their oaths of retribution to me.'

'Good. Have Gorgythion make the Thunderhawks ready for flight. We must go to Khezal.'

'That is where we began,' said Ctesiphon, with a faint air of humour. 'We took the long way around to go back.'

'Khezal is where our brothers need help,' said Lysander. 'And if she really is as desperate as we hope, it is where we will find Legienstrasse, too.'

K-Day +18 Days
Operation Requiem

The *Raging Sky*, and the cult placed among its crew, represented one of several dozen contingencies put in place by Legienstrasse. There were many other choices.

She had been trained to adapt to her situation. More than any Temple Assassin, a Maerorus had to be prepared to work with whatever was to hand, for it was assumed that she would enter the target zone unarmed, with only her altered physiology to give her the edge over her first kill. Whatever might surround her would have to be her weapon. Thus to Legienstrasse, Opis itself – its society, its Aristeia and its cities teeming with commoners – were weapons.

Before war had come to Opis, as the subjugated servants of Chaos seeded the planet at the behest of the Officio Assassinorum, one of those weapons had already been put into action in the foulness and filth of Khezal's underbelly. Below the commoners, below the debt-prisoners and the madmen, seethed society's lowest stratum that no right-thinking citizen of Opis would have the poor taste to mention. They writhed through the remnants of the city's siege-filled past, in the burned shells of buildings now buried beneath the grand works of the Aristeia. They were human, but they were not, for when one emerged into the light its worm-like pallid skin and milky eyes were things of horror.

These were the crouched rats, who crawled on their bellies through the buried sections of Khezal, which had been slums and charnel grounds before they had been bombed or burned and crushed beneath the Aristeia's new city. Perhaps the crouched rats had always been there – perhaps they found themselves there after fleeing into the underworld or sinking so low they could not even scrape a sleeping place in a doorway or alley. No one acknowledged they existed, so no one cared.

Legienstrasse descended into their world, where the crouched rats gnawed on their dead for food. She read their marks, cut into the skin of corpses or burned into the walls of collapsed buildings, and learned their territories and pathways. When she saw them, she did not flee in terror or try to kill them. Eventually, they stopped fleeing from her and let her observe them, even as they clawed one another to death over breeding rights and left body parts to make boundaries.

Then she spoke to them. She had learned their language, a handful of growls and yelps that covered all the subjects needed for their short existence.

She said that they were human. That they were just as

human as anyone who walked the distant streets of Khezal, who resided in the spires and palaces which they did not, at first, believe could exist. This city was as much theirs as anyone's. This city deserved to have done to it, what it had done to the crouched rats.

Many did not believe her. Many thought she was a god. It did not matter what they thought. Already they had served their purpose, and been primed to fall just how Legienstrasse needed when the time came.

'Power,' said the priest, 'pours forth from the barrel of a lasgun. Power oozes from the wounds inflicted on a traitor's body. And the fount of this power is the Throne of Terra! All power, all authority, all command and all obedience radiate from the undying soul of the Emperor on high!'

The mortars, fired from the tangle of ruined tenement blocks outside, were slow that evening. The sermon had been long overdue. Attacks by enemy militia on the ground floor entrances had been solid for three days and the spiritual health of the regiment had suffered as a result. The Hektaon Lowlanders, placed in Khezal to act as combat engineers, had been pressed into service instead as infantry holding the pyramid of the Chalcedony Throne. The many levels of this necropolis were crammed with tombs and sarcophagi, the burial places of several prominent Aristeia bloodlines who had competed to see the most lavish paintings and sculptures, the most fawning epic poetry, and the most sinisterly lifelike deathmasks plastered all over the resting places of their ancestors. Each floor was a tight warren bounded by the faces of the dead and painted friezes depicting lavish processions of servants and kneeling commoners. Death was everywhere.

The upper floors were forbidden. Something terrible had been found up there, and had been burned – some soldiers said the Imperial Fists, the Space Marines, had killed it.

It was not a place conducive to spiritual health. The Lowlanders kneeling to hear Father Mortulas's sermon needed his words like they needed clean water and ammunition.

Mortulas was not a fighting man, but he wore a laspistol in a holster on one side of his webbing and a knife sheathed at the other. If it came to it, he would let blood and shed it with the men whose souls he tended. If the Emperor demanded it, if the Chalcedony Throne forced it, he would fight. He looked down at the faces of the men who listened. Two thousand men were gathered there in a lower floor, which bore the least prestige for the buried and had been used for storage before its stashes of supplies and weaponry had been looted early in the fight for Khezal. From his makeshift pulpit on a low tomb of some lesser functionary, Mortulas could see every face. There was not one he did not recognise.

'This war, like all wars, is about power,' Mortulas said. 'Power belongs to the Emperor. While He slumbers on the Golden Throne, it belongs to Terra. On Opis, the enemies of Terra seek to take the power. They wish to rule themselves. They call it freedom.' Mortulas spat the word as if it were a curse. 'But it is the usurpation of the Emperor's rule. If the Emperor does not have power over Opis, then it is no longer an Imperial world. A human world. It is an enemy world, for the Emperor decreed that all humanity, all the galaxy, must bow to His power. That is all the justification a soldier of the Imperium needs to fight. For the power that must be the Emperor's alone.'

Mortulas looked closer at the faces lined up in front of him. Troopers and officers knelt alike. The eyes of most were closed, many looking at the floor. A few wept. Several were marred by fresh wounds and bandages.

'We have lost friends,' said Mortulas. 'We might call their loss a sacrifice, but none of them looked for their deaths. None of them laid down and let the enemy take them. They fought to survive and were cut down in battle. So is this truly a sacrifice, when it was not looked for? Their sacrifice is not their death, but the acceptance of the galaxy they must live in as a soldier. When we win a battle, it is not we who win the glory, for that glory is the due of the Emperor. It is not we who are happy, for we have lost our own. Even in victory, we are laid low. No, you soldiers, and those who have fallen, accept that sorrow and pain will befall them. Death and injury is a part of that, but no man escapes even a great victory unwounded. That is the sacrifice the fallen have made, and that you have all made. That was your choice. The reward for that choice is the Emperor's grace, a gift that can only manifest to the faithful. It is not a payment, like coin to the sellsword. It is not a promise, like a line in a contract. The very act of sacrifice brings that grace upon you. Not everyone can make that decision. You, you brave and you few, can make it.'

Explosions sounded nearby, the familiar crack of mortar rounds fired from the depths of the Cemetery district. Mortulas waited for the volley to finish, and for the sound of falling

debris to die down as it pattered against the side of the Chalcedony Throne's pyramid.

'In battle, our worlds shrink,' continued Mortulas. 'We can
conceive of nothing beyond our foxhole or our firing loop.
We comprehend no one but ourselves and the friends immediately around us. But even then, in the concentrated world
of war, we must not forget that this power, for which we fight,
is the domain of the Emperor, and that none dwell in that
domain without hope. Above all, even in death and the dark,
there is hope.'

Explosions rattled again, closer this time, shaking dust from
the ancient walls. Mortulas had to steady himself to keep his
feet. A couple of the Hektaon Lowlanders opened their eyes
and looked around nervously as the ground shuddered.

Then, another sound. Stone on stone, grinding, coming
from overhead.

The stone coffin under Mortulas's feet rocked, forcing the
paving slabs away around it. Mortulas jumped down as the
lid cracked. The other tombs on the lower level, mostly of
favoured servants and ill-favoured lesser relatives, were also
cracking open. The smell of ancient death, of mould and
decay, rolled out.

The Lowlanders jumped to their feet and fumbled to bring
their guns to bear. Officers shouted for calm and order, to
quell any panic.

'So,' said Mortulas. 'The enemy raise the dead. We had
known this would come to pass. We have waited for it. This
is the reckoning that was fated to us!' Mortulas drew his
laspistol. He was an unfit and ageing man, wearied by illness

and an arduous career, but he looked ready to fight.

Sarcophagi shattered. Guardsmen fell or ducked for cover.

What emerged was not the dead, not the mummified remains of past Aristeia, hung with gold and wielding the weapons buried with them. What emerged were the crouched rats. Their skin was pale and patchy, their frames shrunken with disease. They scurried like animals. Their eyes were screwed shut, for even in the weak light of the Chalcedony Throne they were blinded. It did not matter. They were born fighting blind.

'Heretics!' cried Mortulas. 'Put them to the sword! Put them to the flame!'

Dozens of the crouched rats poured out of shattered tombs and holes that suddenly opened up in the ground. And as soon as they emerged, they were cut down. Laspistol sidearms and combat knives did for the first few who emerged. By the time the next few made it out, many of the Guardsmen had their lasguns at the ready and the rats were picked off before they slithered all the way out of their hiding places.

There were a lot of them, and they did not seem afraid to die. These ragged people, as pale as worms, were apparently unarmed and determined to present themselves as targets to the Hektaon Lowlanders. Officers called for disciplined fire, and to keep out of each others' lines of sight. Another died, two las-shots through his torso. Another, one leg sheared at the thigh. Another, crawling with his abdomen split open, shot through with three tightly-placed shots from a sergeant's laspistol.

One lurched up when thought dead and grappled with a

Guardsman, trying to wrench the lasgun from his hands. It was thrown down and clubbed with the butts of his fellow soldiers' guns, its head caved in and its body twitching.

They saw a chunk of rock, glossy and black, implanted in the centre of its chest. None of them thought it might mean anything. Perhaps, when the influx of enemies was done and all were dead, they could examine the bodies and wonder why. But that would wait until the killing was over with.

One crouched rat did not die easily. He was much larger than the rest, his skin heavily scarred and his rope belt hung with human jawbones. He reared up as another shot caught him in the chest and punched right through. His lips drew back over bare teeth. His eyes opened, to show the sockets were hollow, the eyeballs scooped out leaving red-black pits. His tongue was forked, and it flickered from his mouth as he yelled wordlessly.

The chunk of rock in his chest glowed. Green light bled out, and arced into the floor like electricity. The crystals implanted in the other corpses did the same, and their power congealed above them, forming a layer of trapped light burning in the air.

'Fall back!' shouted Mortulas. 'This is witchcraft! Guard your souls!'

The leader of the crouched rats laughed, a horrible, raking sound from a torn throat. The skin of his chest blackened, his charred ribs showing through. More las-shots blew off an arm and ripped a chunk out of his shoulder. He did not die.

He was still alive when the disc of light tore open and madness bled through. A caged portal to another realm, a doorway to the warp, appeared as reality tore open.

The Guardsmen were in retreat, heading for the exits from the Chalcedony Throne's lower floors. Those nearest the portal were robbed of their senses, their eyes struck blind and their minds scoured clean. They dropped, minds wiped. Others went mad and turned their guns on their fellow soldiers or, if they still possessed some spark of awareness, on themselves.

Some fell to their knees and gave thanks that they had witnessed the realm of Chaos.

Most survived and ran, the regimental vox-operators already warning nearby units of a moral threat manifesting at the Chalcedony Throne.

The gate was short-lived, a makeshift work of sorcery that drained the life-force of the crouched rats in minutes. Those minutes were all it took for Karnikhal Six-Finger, World Eater and champion of Khorne, to stride through the doorway into the heart of Khezal. Alongside him, like pack hunters following their alpha, were a host of bloodletters, footsoldier daemons of Khorne, their muscular shapes dripping with scalding blood and their swords of black iron humming with the need to kill. Behind them was one of the warp gate beasts, the golems of corpses raised below the city, its legs folded under it as it forced its way through the gateway into the relatively cramped space of the Chalcedony Throne's lower floor.

The bloodletters set about executing the Guardsmen who survived in the chamber. It was sorry work, for the Guardsmen were driven mad or witless by their glimpse of the warp. The bloodletters' blades took every head, from Guardsman and crouched rat, and threw them into a bloody heap at

Karnikhal's feet as the gateway stuttered closed. The only light now was the molten glow of Karnikhal's armour and the fires in the daemons' eyes.

'Are you satisfied?' bellowed Karnikhal. 'Now I have swapped one master for another, the corpse-god's killers for you? Has your pet done well? You promised me sport. You promised me skulls. I shall take yours instead, if you cannot deliver!'

'Threats mean nothing, Six-Finger,' came a reply – a calm female voice. Karnikhal took a small mirror from an ammo pouch on his belt and held it up to the light bleeding from his armour. It reflected the face of the woman who he would be forced to call master for a few hours more. 'I care not for your god or for the honour of a World Eater. Your tally of skulls means nothing to me. I care only that you serve as you are bound. Kill me when you are released from my service, if it pleases you. It would be most educational to see you try. For now, do your part.'

'You stoke my rage, Legienstrasse!' replied Karnikhal. 'Those few who dared to do so now adorn my armour, and they live still, trapped in their skulls to witness the anger they provoked!'

'Play your part in the summoning of the tower,' said Legienstrasse. 'And be ready for my arrival.'

The Amphitheatre of Carcarellon was as much a monument to excess as it was a venue for the many sports and entertainments of Khezal. Seating for upwards of a hundred thousand citizens was enclosed in the soaring archways of the stadium, with the flag of every house of the Aristeia flying. Marble of hundreds of different colours made up the structure in an eye-watering clash only accentuated by the gilt and hanging silks of the most exclusive areas, where Aristeia nobles once lounged to be waited on and entertained.

The arena had, in the past, been adapted for everything from staged sea battles to lavish plays, and the weddings and assumption ceremonies of Khezal's most exalted Aristeia. Now it was a great circle of beaten earth transformed into a military camp where thousands of Imperial Guard were sheltering against the siege growing outside the stadium walls.

The golden colours of the two Imperial Fists Vindicator tanks stood out against the camouflage drab of the Plaudian and Deucalian vehicles. Imperial Guard Chimera APCs were parked where they had dropped off dozens of Guardsmen fleeing the advance of enemy forces. A couple of Basilisk self-propelled artillery pieces were having their guns calibrated to lob shells over the stadium walls into the streets outside. The most likely ways in were covered by Leman Russ battle tanks, dug in and surrounded by sandbags to serve as gun emplacements.

The Guardsmen in the stadium looked up as the whine of engines approached. A pair of golden gunships, like great mechanical eagles, swooped down low and circled as their pilots identified places to land. The *Gilded Pyre* and the *Peril Swift* came in to land among the camo netting and ammunition stores of the makeshift camp.

Lysander jumped down from the *Gilded Pyre*. He felt the reaction of the Guardsmen when they saw him – amazement and more than a little fear. The rest of the Imperial Fists strike force disembarked behind him.

Sergeant Sthenelus ran to meet them. 'Well met, my captain!' he said with a salute of a forearm clapped across his chest. 'The situation in Khezal grows more dire with every minute. The enemy is getting unprecedented numbers from somewhere. Major assaults are under way in all areas. They seek to drive us out of the city, captain! But they face the masters of the siege, the Imperial Fists, and we shall hold fast!'

'They seek,' said Lysander, 'to pin us in place until Legienstrasse can escape. Then as far as Opis's moral threats are concerned, this city and this planet can go to the hells, because they will have won. Gorgythion!'

'Captain?' said Gorgythion as he swung himself down from the cockpit of the *Gilded Pyre*.

'What is your opinion of the air defences we observed?'

'The enemy has not been lax in their work,' replied Gorgythion. 'Deeper into the city, flak guns and air defence lasers have been set up and adapted. We encountered little, but further in, it would be hazardous indeed to mount an air operation. I understand the Imperial Navy have already learned this to their cost.'

'We may have to take that risk,' said Lysander, 'if we need to move against Legienstrasse quickly.'

'You are certain she is in Khezal?' said Librarian Deiphobus, exiting the Thunderhawk behind Lysander.

'Nothing on Opis is certain,' said Lysander. 'But we must place ourselves where she is most likely to break cover, and she is most likely to do so in Khezal. This is where the enemy is making their move, as Sergeant Sthenelus has discovered. Legienstrasse was working with Opis's moral threats at Krae. If she is working with them here then–'

Lysander's words were cut off as a tremendous explosion shattered the upper levels on one side of the amphitheatre. Marble masonry rained down and Guardsmen fled the falling wreckage. A Leman Russ was buried by a great marble spur that shattered against it, hiding everything in a pall of dust.

'They're starting!' yelled an officer in the uniform of a lieutenant of the 4th Plaudis Shock Army. 'Man the fixed guns! Reserve men, draw to the centre!' The lieutenant turned to the Imperial Fists. 'My lord. Will you fight alongside us this day?'

'We will,' replied Lysander.

'My thanks. Lieutenant Fordrich, Fourth Plaudis.'

'Captain Lysander, Imperial Fists First.'

Fordrich looked young for an officer – quite possibly he had attained his rank through the opaque politics of the Imperium's officer class rather than battlefield experience. He went to the men under him who wore the uniforms of a dozen different Guard regiments. He was pointing at the Imperial Fists and Lysander saw the mix of awe and gratitude in their faces. When they fought alongside the Space Marines, an Imperial Guardsman felt like the Emperor Himself was beside them. It was one more weapon in a Space Marine's arsenal.

'Kirav!' ordered Lysander. 'Join the reserve. We will have need of you if the enemy break through. Ctesiphon, Orfos, I shall be at the walls with you. Ucalegon, be where the Emperor's blade is needed. Gorgythion, get the Thunderhawks in the air but bring them down rather than take fire. We will need them later. And Sthenelus?'

'Captain?'

'Have you calibrated for indirect fire?'

'We have, captain.'

'Then lend your might to the artillery. To battle, my brothers. Legienstrasse thinks she will slow us down here. But she merely hands us her allies to die.'

Near the damaged section of the stadium, great booming explosions rumbled and the whole building shuddered. An Aristeia banner fell and fluttered down from the upper reaches. Imperial Guardsmen were forming firing lines staggered across the arena floor.

The pink fire of her wings was what told them it was her. Like the rising dawn, the flame crested the summit of the wall and bathed the amphitheatre in rose-pink light.

The Plaudians recognised her feathers and the strips of skin waving from her scalp. Word had got out that she was Antiocha Wyraxx, once a witch and now a fusion of daemon and woman. Those who had seen her, and survived, were a combination of blessed and cursed. They had been among the few who had survived her appearance on K-Day, so they were lucky. But perhaps they had used up their luck on that day. Perhaps Wyraxx, the Phoenix of Khezal, would come looking for them.

She rose over the stadium, her long wings draping down over the uppermost spires. The artillery pieces threw explosive shells over the walls in the direction of the assault, and the din of battle mixed with the strange humming song of power that emanated from Wyraxx herself.

She raised a hand and cast down a bolt of pink fire. A burst of flame, billowing upwards like a blossoming flower, enveloped a handful of Guardsmen trying to bring a heavy bolter to bear on her. A second bolt of sorcery lanced through one of the dug-in tanks and the ammunition detonated, blasting shrapnel in every direction in a rattle of staccato explosions.

'Stay on the ground!' yelled Lysander to Gorgythion as he ran towards the wrecked wall.

'I must take flight!' shouted Gorgythion in response. 'I fought her once, I can do it again!'

'Stay on the ground, brother! That is an order!'

Lysander and Ctesiphon were running to the breach in the wall. Guardsmen were already clambering up the seating to get to the breach. Gunfire was sounding from there, raised voices and screams.

Wyraxx had been accompanied on K-Day by living biological weapons. The Guardsmen had all pulled on their gas masks. The Plaudians and Kirgallans among them said prayers of retribution over their guns.

The enemy broke through the breach in a tide of struggling flesh. They were almost naked, all but feral. They had once been citizens of Khezal. Perhaps a few of them had been Imperial Guard, captured, brutalised and changed by Wyraxx. Whatever they had been, they were now the enemy.

They fought with blades of bone that had grown from their hands. Bone fanned out through their torn bluish skin to form plates over their chests and shoulders. Their eyes were red, as if from burst blood vessels. Their tongues were bundles of tendrils, like sea anemones. And under their skin writhed translucent pods, squirming with life eager to get out.

'Hand of Dorn guide us! Fists of Dorn crush them!' Lysander led the charge with a war-cry, sprinting the hundred metres across the arena floor towards the breach. The Imperial Guard guns cut down a dozen of the enemy in the first few seconds, and spore-filled organs inside them burst, filling the air with an orange biological haze. The Imperial lasguns fell silent for a moment as officers yelled to fall back and take up second firing positions. Lysander charged right into the haze, and he felt the filters in his nose and throat contracting as they recognised airborne toxins.

The first horror loomed out at him. The man's face was split vertically, bony shards and white cilia poking through the wound. He drew back a bulbous fist, swollen and heavy with cysts primed to burst and deliver shards of biotoxin. Lysander hit the heretic so hard in the midriff with the Fist of Dorn that his deformed arm was torn off as his torso was smacked away across the arena. Lysander swung back and knocked the legs out from under a second heretic who charged at him – this one's forearms were mutated to twist together into a bony spear, like the ram of a ship, and blue crystals of congealed venom glistening along its cutting edge. Lysander swept the stricken mutant aside with a sweep of his shield.

Ucalegon ran past him, heading for the upper seating and higher ground. His duty as Emperor's Champion meant he had to go for the flying sorceress who was even now detonating the Plaudian tanks with bolts of pink fire.

A sniper shot blew the arm off another mutant beside Lysander. A second hit it in the jaw and sheared it off, and the mutant fell in a spray of corrupted purple-black blood. Lysander knew it was from Scout Enriaan, perched somewhere among the decorative marble surrounding the Aristeia section of the seating.

Toxin shards burst against Lysander's armour. One grazed his face and he felt the burning as the toxin dived into his blood and spread, leaping from cell receptor to receptor, breaking down everything it touched.

The flame rippled across his face, already tight and painful from the burns he received at Krae. It raced down his neck and into his chest, where his twin hearts hammered faster.

Then it receded, forced back into pockets and crushed by the immune system of a Space Marine, filtered out by his vat-grown organs, broken down into harmless components or expelled from his pores and his lungs.

Scythes of bone were flung at him, propelled by snapping bundles of muscles bunched around the chest and shoulders of one of the mutants. They hit his shield, and were shattered into dust by the suppression field around it. The mutants rushed him at once but Lysander crunched the Fist of Dorn into the pelvis of the first, crushed the second into the floor with his shield, and dodged around the bony axe-hand of the third to shatter its face with a headbutt.

Bolter fire was punching through the enemy at will. Squad Ctesiphon advanced steadily, half the brothers kneeling to fire volleys while the others moved up. In the breach ahead, a hundred more mutant heretics were forcing their way in, and half of them were dead to the explosive fire raking through them before they were inside the amphitheatre.

Lysander dived into them, and it was good. It was good to feel the enemy – an honest enemy, one he knew to be a foe of mankind to the death – crushed and broken beneath the Fist of Dorn. It was good to feel them break against his shield, and to see them mown down by the guns of his battle-brothers.

Another foe ran at him. They were desperate to die. Lysander ducked to one side and caught the enemy on his shield, flipping the mutant up over his head and dumping it face-down on the blood-slick ground behind him. He turned to drive the Fist of Dorn down through the mutant's skull.

'Captain, stop!' shouted Librarian Deiphobus, running through the carnage towards Lysander. 'A moment with him. Just a moment.'

Lysander paused and nodded at the Librarian. Deiphobus crouched down by the heretic. Lysander knelt behind Deiphobus, holding up his shield to ward off the worst of the bone and toxin shards raining down from the breach.

Deiphobus placed a hand against the heretic's skull. Lysander saw with distaste that larvae were squirming under the skin of the mutant's back, things like toothed worms that forced against the skin as if they knew they had only moments left to hatch out of that doomed body.

Deiphobus screwed his eyes shut and Lysander knew that in the Librarian's mind, compartmentalised and ordered by years of mental exercise, he was engaging the heretic's mind in a contest the heretic had no hope of winning.

'They're to keep us here,' said Deiphobus. 'That's it. It doesn't matter if they survive, or even if they kill us. They just have to keep us here.'

'As we thought,' said Lysander.

A screech from above caught Lysander's attention. Wyraxx was wheeling overhead, swooping over Ucalegon as the Emperor's Champion perched on a lone arching spur of marble that reached out over the arena seating.

Wyraxx lashed Ucalegon with fire. Ucalegon clung tight and weathered it, holding on even as the flame threatened to throw him down to the arena floor. The Phoenix of Khezal swept around for another pass, her trailing feathers coiling behind her.

Ucalegon leapt off the arch and landed on Wyraxx, grabbing a handful of the tendrils protruding from her scalp. Her face screwed up in pain and dismay. She lost altitude suddenly, the weight of an armoured Space Marine throwing her off course. Ucalegon twisted his hand, winding it deeper into her tendrils, and wrenched her head up. Wyraxx aimed upwards, lost speed and fell, spiralling down like a crippled jet as Ucalegon hung on.

'Kirav, help Ucalegon!' ordered Lysander into the vox. 'Clip the arch-heretic's wings!'

<<We will ground her for good,>> came Kirav's reply. Lysander could just see, through the biological haze surrounding the breach, the glint of golden armour as Kirav's veteran squad ran towards the multicoloured blaze of the Phoenix's crash site.

Deiphobus put a hand on Lysander's shoulder guard. 'There is a disturbance,' he said. 'An exhalation of the warp. Reality recoils. The whole city shakes with it.'

'From Wyraxx?' asked Lysander.

'No,' said Deiphobus. 'Look to the sky. Beyond the walls. Look to the sky.'

Lysander broke from the cover of his shield, carrying it before him as he ran forwards towards the breach. Bone spines thudded into his armour. He ignored them, just as he ignored the heretics who rushed at him. He knocked them aside or ran them over, trusting in Deiphobus and Squad Ctesiphon to deal with those who threatened him.

He reached the breach, a great crack in the amphitheatre's outer wall where heretics were still clambering through. Lysander knocked the head off one who leered out through the crack at him. Then he placed a foot on the torn masonry and pushed himself up. He climbed the crumbling stone, bolter shells cracking into the stone around him as Ctesiphon's bolters gave him cover. Las-fire was falling, too, as Imperial Guard in respirator masks advanced alongside Ctesiphon and raked the breach with volleys of fire.

Lysander cleared the blurry cloud of toxins and he could see into the district adjoining the amphitheatre. The street teemed with heretics, and among them were priests in purple robes, hung with bloody spiked chains, urging them on into the breach. The dead were being thrown back from the breach and torn apart, their blood smeared on the heretics yet to attack, like warpaint.

And in the centre of Khezal, blistered high above the skyline, was a new temple. It had grown like a bleeding tumour from the Cemetery district, a combination of volcanic outcrop and cathedral. It was a temple to gods whose names could not be spoken in real space, to the powers worshipped by the moral threats gathered on Opis. Sweeping buttresses reached up from torn rock, up through torrents of lava pouring from that fresh wound in the earth. They spread into balconies and eyries, asymmetrical battlements like blades and fangs of dark stone.

Staircases led to nowhere. Arched windows were blinded. Pillars held up nothing but air. Great thoroughfares emptied over the edges of its walls and supplicants poured out, tumbling onto the lower slopes of tortured rock or into the oozing torrents of lava. Like the men and women who had died to summon Wyraxx on K-Day, they were drawn from Khezal's citizens, their lives given to honour this new temple to Chaos.

The uppermost levels held the belfries, cages of stone hung with roosts of huge bronze bells. Daemons gathered there, leaping, spasming creatures with flesh that flowed and reformed, scampering like animals through the skeletal archways and pillars.

Lysander could hear the pealing of the bells from where he stood. They created terrible anti-harmonies that seemed loud and clashing enough to tear the sky apart. Multicoloured light bled through the clouds overhead. Lysander could just see the warp gate beasts Sthenelus had reported, crouched among the belfries, and he knew the purpose of that temple.

It was as he had guessed. It was a gate. A gateway to the warp – not to summon more hellish things to Opis, but to give one inhabitant the means to escape. The warp gate opening above the temple would lead to Throne knew where, as long as it was far away from Opis, far away from the Officio Assassinorum and from the Imperial Fists.

This was Legienstrasse's Plan C. Open a doorway into the warp and flee through it while Khezal devolved into a madness that swallowed anyone who might try to follow her.

'Brothers!' Lysander ordered. 'Concentrate on Wyraxx and let us not become swamped! We must break out and forge on soon. Even victory here will be failure. We must leave here. We must leave Khezal to its evils. The true enemy is almost beyond our reach!'

Ucalegon wrestled in the dust of the arena floor, and Wyraxx was strong. Far stronger than she looked. Her black eyes narrowed and her lips showed her pointed teeth, the sharp greenish tongue that flickered between them. The burning feathers of her wings were grasping at him and the flame burned him even through his armour as the ceramite plates heated up. Ucalegon still had his sword in his hand but it was pinned down on the floor by a bundle of feathers. Wyraxx got a hand underneath and Ucalegon felt the fire growing there – he rolled to one side and Wyraxx fired a bolt of flame that just missed him, scoring his breastplate as it shrieked up into the sky.

Ucalegon drove an elbow down into Wyraxx's ribs. The impact was crunching and she screamed, throwing her mouth grotesquely wide. From a distance she must have been achingly beautiful, a winged goddess. Up close, she was a horror.

Ucalegon pulled a fist back to punch down at her face. She spat a wave of fire at him and he fell back as it rushed around his head. Then she was on top of him, feathers around his neck.

Kirav's squad were running to Ucalegon's aid. Wyraxx flicked a hand at them, and two of them were thrown off their feet by a burst of flame. Kirav himself drove on through the fire and a second bolt caught him in the shoulder, spinning him around. Ucalegon lost sight of him as Wyraxx's wings curled around.

Ucalegon realised she was going to take off again, maybe power as far into the sky as she could before letting Ucalegon fall. He fought to wrench his sword-arm free and he felt feathers tearing out from her skin. Her eyes widened and she gasped in shock as Ucalegon's arm came free.

He slashed at the feathers around him. Feathers came apart in wisps of glowing tissue and Ucalegon fell to the ground, Wyraxx above him.

A ball of boiling pink fire grew between her eyes, aimed down at Ucalegon.

A gilded shape slammed into Wyraxx from behind. Ucalegon recognised Brother Gorgythion, still an unfamiliar sight outside the cockpit of a Thunderhawk. Wyraxx, caught by surprised, thudded back to the arena floor.

Ucalegon was on his feet and lunged. The obsidian blade slid between Wyraxx's ribs. He pulled it out and incandescent blood flowed. Wyraxx mouthed wordlessly, her eyes wide, dragging herself back across the bloodstained sand.

Gorgythion cracked the butt of his bolter into the side of Wyraxx's head.

'Remember,' he said.

He put a bolt-round through her temple and blew half her skull off.

She took a long time to die. The daemonic streaks in her substance refused to accept she was dead. Squad Kirav shot her down as she stumbled. Brother Stentor put two rounds into her abdomen and Mortz blasted one of her wings off with a rattle of storm bolter fire. It was Brother Beros who struck the last blow, impaling her chest with the blades of his lightning claw.

Ucalegon got to his feet as Antiocha Wyraxx breathed her last.

'Your kill,' he said to Gorgythion.

'Would that it was through a targeting rune,' said Gorgythion, 'from the cockpit of the *Sanctifier*.' He kicked over Wyraxx's body, as the last of her blood was draining out into the arena sand. 'But this will do, my brothers. This will do.'

The rumble of engines heralded the Vindicators of Squadron Sthenelus, riding over the bodies and the wreckage of the shattered Plaudian tanks. <<Behind me, my brethren,>> came Sthenelus's voice over the vox. <<Lysander orders us to break out. The steeds of my squadron will keep the heretics in the streets!>>

<<Gorgythion!>> voxed Lysander. <<We must reach the centre of Khezal. I fear only travel in the air will be fast enough. Can you do it?>>

Gorgythion looked down at the sorry corpse of Wyraxx. 'The enemy's greatest aerial threat will never fly again,' he said. 'I can do it.'

The bells were tolling, but the music was not there yet. Then daemons who had already bled through from the other realm were flitting around them on leathery wings, daubing the temple's stone in blood. Other creatures cowered behind pillars or in cracks between the great stones, asymmetrical eyes fixed on the shape of Legienstrasse as she walked up onto the temple's upper levels.

The stones were still warm, having been torn from the strata beneath Khezal's foundations. Bones and flesh were fused with them here and there, the dregs of the streets trapped there as the temple surged up through the city's buildings. It was a beautiful place, created by the pooled warp-knowledge of all the Chaos champions on Opis and reflected through the lens of its people, an echo of the magnificence in which the Aristeia had clothed themselves for thousands of years. Stained-glass windows had grown, like new scabs, across lopsided windows, depicting the swirling madness of the warp and the thousands of souls already cast there in the depravity taking over Opis. New stairways and rooms were growing, budding off from the temple like stone flowers. Beautiful.

Karnikhal Six-Fingers was waiting for her. Bloodletters crouched at his feet, panting like hunting dogs. He nodded his head very slightly at her approach, a gesture of supplication that was, for a warrior of Khorne, as humiliating as throwing himself prostrate at her feet.

Overhead, the Warp Serpent flew. The wound it had been dealt at Krae still bled, raining glowing blood over the hanging bells. A shadowy shape congealed in a dark corner, three eyes burning beneath its hood. It was the First Walker of Lhuur, drawn from the lines of the Starfall front where a thousand others made in its image still fought. A witch,

Dravin Stahl, stood ready. A spiked circle of black iron, woven into the tortured skin of his bare back, gave him a dark halo, echoed by the circular brands etched into his face and chest.

Another of those at the belfry was enormous, possibly an abhuman ogryn prior to his mutations. But his hulking, corpulent frame had absorbed several more individuals. Those with wit and intelligence had positions on his shoulders, their heads crowded around his. Others had been absorbed almost completely into his prodigious gut or biceps, their jaws slack and their eyes blank, criss-crossed by the heavy black tattooing on his torso. He was called the Penitent, though how or why he had acquired such a name was knowledge that had been lost in the chaos of Khezal, where he had risen to lead one of the many hordes of heretics thronging the city. Beside him was a horror in clockwork, a construction rather larger than a man with a body composed of cogs and armatures supporting a face that looked to have been scraped from the head of a giant doll, with rouged porcelain cheeks, wide eyes of emeralds and a leer that seemed to contain more threat than all the weaponry and fury of Karnikhal Six-Finger.

The many moral threats of Opis were there, all to attend upon Legienstrasse.

Karnikhal stepped forwards, wreathed in steam from his scalding armour. 'Legienstrasse,' he said. 'You have pulled the strings. We have danced. Now what?'

'I know you want me dead, Karnikhal,' replied Legienstrasse. There was no fear on her face – there was rarely anything at all. 'You swore once to kneel before no master but Angron of your Legion. That you obey me now burns inside you hotter than the armour you wear.'

'And yet you stand before me!' snarled Karnikhal.

'Because you have been bound in the name of powers greater than either of us to the service of the Officio Assassinorum. And I too am an Assassin. So according to the words of that contract, you may not harm me. But fear not, Brother Karnikhal. I have had my scribes reword that same contract. Now I alone am under its protection. Any other Assassin is yours to disembowel as you would.'

'And when will it end?' demanded Karnikhal. 'This abasement tears at me. When will it end? For how long must I serve?'

'Until I am off this rusting orb,' said Legienstrasse. 'When I am gone. When I am free, you will be free also.'

'If you lie,' said Karnikhal. 'If you betray us. If the contract does not burn. Then I will hunt you down, Legienstrasse. I will crack open your skull and make sport with your brain. I will bind you in iron until you think I am a god. I will…'

'Will you, Six-Fingered One?' said Legienstrasse. She walked up close to Karnikhal, closer than any sane person would dare. Legienstrasse was an athletic specimen now, tall and strongly built, but Karnikhal still towered over her. 'Then you will face not only me.'

Legienstrasse wore a fatigue suit, perhaps taken from a dead Imperial Guardsman in Khezal's streets. She unbuckled its front and pulled it down over her shoulders, turning to show the assembled threats of the belfry her bare back.

There hung, in translucent fluid-filled sacs, a dozen young.

They were roughly like curled, embryonic humans in shape, but their spines were disfigured with bony spurs and their distended skulls were home to too many eyes, each faceted like an insect's. Through the cloudy fluid could be seen the suggestions of mandibles and ridges of bone.

'I will give birth soon,' said Legienstrasse. 'I, who was created for death, will become a font of life. And each of my young will learn that Karnikhal Six-Finger once threatened the life of their mother. If you hunt Legienstrasse, World Eater, you will hunt an army of me. No doubt you are in the habit of making mortal enemies at every turn. This is a brood of enemies you do not wish to make.'

Even Karnikhal seemed disconcerted by Legienstrasse's young. Perhaps it was less their shape, and more the potential they represented. Karnikhal was among the few there who had witnessed first-hand what Legienstrasse really was. The idea of a host of them – a host who could birth their own versions, in a cycle that might never end, only grow – could number among a Chaos champion's most extravagant dreams of destruction.

'What news?' demanded Legienstrasse.

The witch Stahl took a limping step forwards, accompanied by the rattle of the brace fixed to his withered right leg. 'Two hours,' he said, 'and the bells can toll. The beasts will be up here and the rituals will be complete. The gate will open.'

The clockwork doll rattled and its face rotated, showing now a mask with a circle of holes punched through around its mouth, allowing sound to issue out. 'I have calculated your route,' it said, its synthesised voice that of an officious man perhaps originally programmed to give instruction. A punch card emerged from a slot in the front of its torso. 'Waystations in the warp will guide your way.'

'Where does it emerge?' said Legienstrasse.

'A long-forgotten world, once touched by the Imperium but now ignorant of it,' replied the clockwork doll. 'A small indigenous population of humans, some unintelligent xenos. A shrine was built thousands of years ago, when a prophet was visited by dreams from the warp. There I have sited the gate's far opening. It is a perfect world for a new god.'

'I like this not,' said Legienstrasse, turning away from Stahl and the doll. 'I am exposed here. Not one enemy on Opis will be ignorant of where I am.'

'Khezal is ours!' retorted Karnikhal. 'Every minute more of us arrive. There is no foe on Opis who can stand against Karnikhal. These other wretches will mop up what I leave behind. Is that not so, you showers of ordure? You who shrink from this Traitor Legionary even now?'

'Fear nothing,' came a whisper emanating from the collection of shadows that was the First Walker of Lhuur. 'If they walk upon your temple, they shall walk into shadow, and they will never find their way out.'

Stahl walked to the edge of the upper floor, where a drop led straight down to the torn streets of Khezal far below. He limped as he walked and blood spattered from the impalements on his back. 'They won't get that far,' he said. 'I have a hundred witches throwing beating hearts into the fire! A thousand supplicants begging the gods to tear their souls away so they can bleed their strength into us! The whole of Opis is joined in worship. A simple storm will be little effort.'

Stahl smiled, distorting the mutilations of his face. He held up both hands and the clouds overhead rushed towards a point directly above him. Lightning crashed in the boiling mass, and a deeper shadow grew over the temple. Wind whipped and rain lashed against the far side of the temple as the storm grew in a few seconds. Its winds wrapped around the temple as power wrapped around Stahl's hand.

The bloodletters snapped and growled at the sorcery. The daemons lurking in the dark were illuminated by the lightning, revealing toad-like hides and lolling spiny tongues.

'Shed blood!' cried Stahl. 'Give flesh! The eye of the warp is opening!'

It was the *Gilded Pyre* that took the lead, with the *Peril Swift* following in its wake.

They flew low. The proximity sensors sent a stream of warnings to the cockpits as both gunships weaved among the spires of Khezal. Brother Gorgythion threw his gunship through columns of smoke and under bridges connecting the spires, as anti-aircraft fire stuttered up from every district.

Gunfire punched through one wing. One of the main engines flared as pieces of the engine broke off, perforated by bursts of flak. The *Gilded Pyre* held its course, banking between chains of fire and swooping into the cover provided by the ragged valleys of half-ruined streets.

Up ahead was the storm. It surrounded the temple with a cage of lightning. The burning disc of the portal overhead was almost hidden by the walls of swirling clouds drawn down from the overcast sky. A haze of debris, captured by the vicious winds, seethed like a translucent dome over the temple.

The *Gilded Pyre* skimmed the rooftops as it made the final approach to the temple. Lightning danced everywhere, earthing through the ruins of buildings or right down into the streets, carving long charred furrows where it touched the ground.

A bolt licked out and caught the *Gilded Pyre* on the tip of one wing. The engine in that wing died and the gunship fell, flipping over with the sudden loss of thrust. The landing jets fired and somehow turned it upright, just as both engines guttered back into life and powered the gunship up from almost ground level.

'Damned sorcery!' yelled Gorgythion, wrestling with the controls of the Thunderhawk to keep it in the sky. The stricken engine had come back to life but was just barely holding on. Fuel was spraying from somewhere and the tank pressure was dropping. Every warning rune in the cockpit seemed lit up at once. 'If I don't set us down we're falling from the sky! I'll land us in the streets if I have to!'

'Then we'll never reach her!' shouted Lysander from the passenger compartment. Squad Kirav, Scout Squad Orfos and Librarian Deiphobus made up the rest of the *Gilded Pyre's* complement, all strapped into the grav-restraints as the Thunderhawk's wild flight rattled them around. 'Deiphobus, this is a sorcerous storm. What can you do?'

Deiphobus unbuckled his grav-restraints and pulled himself

close to the cockpit door. 'Brother Gorgythion, get me close and open the rear ramp!'

The Thunderhawk's ramp swung down and smoky, lightning-charged air howled in. Deiphobus grabbed a handhold on the ceiling and leaned out as far as he could, Khezal's dark sprawl hurtling past beneath him.

Gorgythion had the gunship circling the temple as close as he dared. Lightning crackled out at the ship like reaching hands, but came just short.

<<There!>> yelled Deiphobus, pointing to a bright shower of light at the edge of the temple's upper level. The Librarian's voice was barely audible even over the vox. <<That is Legienstrasse's pet witch! I can smell his corruption from here!>>

'What can you do?' shouted Lysander.

<<I'll tear out his secrets!>> replied Deiphobus.

The shape of the witch was just visible amid the light – a human form, floating just above the temple's flagstones, an iron hoop forming a corrupted halo behind him and lightning crackling off his spread fingertips.

Deiphobus focused on the shape. The Thunderhawk dissolved around him, and the witch's mind rolled out into a labyrinth. Deiphobus checked his grip and his footing, and then let go of his body completely, diving into the consciousness of the witch.

The witch's mind was an asylum, its cells and trepanning halls open to a sky the colour of dried blood. Each cell contained a memory, curled up and moaning, screaming, or clawing at the walls with bloody fingers. They looked, to Deiphobus's mind's eye, like variations on the same man – the witch himself – in various stages of disease or madness. Some were fastened to the walls with leather restraints. Some looked dead. Some were dead, their skeletons gnawed by fat, black rats. A few were laid on operating slabs, their skulls opened up and their brains being dissected by white-smocked doctors who looked just like them.

Deiphobus swooped low. He maintained the solidity of his mental form as the asylum rushed up to meet him. He felt it trying to force his shape to match that of the witch, so he could be herded into a cell and lobotomised there with all the other memories the witch had forsaken. But Deiphobus kept the shape of an Imperial Fist, and he made sure his golden armour shone to push back the shadows gathering around him.

'Witch!' yelled Deiphobus. 'Show yourself! I will tear the walls of this place down to find you! You will lose your mind to me before you die, if you defy me!'

The echo of Deiphobus's voice and the screams of the inmates were the only reply. Deiphobus snatched a patient's chart off a cell door and read the name 'Stahl' written on it. This enemy had a name, then – Dravin Stahl, reported active in Khezal shortly after K-Day.

'Stahl!' he shouted. 'At least die a man! Not a mindless thing, an animal, stripped of whatever human is left!'

Deiphobus let his form abandon its gravity and he flew through the asylum, rushing through doorways and gore-stained corridors, operating theatres and execution rooms where the skeletons of forcibly forgotten memories lay in electric chairs or curled up on the floor of gas chambers. Everywhere there was madness – curses scratched on the walls in languages no one had ever spoken, human figures with limbs and features jumbled and transposed, streamers of skin draped over broken torture racks of bone.

There was a pattern here, hidden in the bedlam. Deiphobus read the blood tracks smeared along the floors. They led to a single point in the labyrinth, hidden by switchbacks and dead ends. He let himself become shadowier still and punched through the walls, arrowing towards the asylum's heart.

And here he found the great hall, its floor tiled, its walls painted dark red in a futile measure to hide the blood. Fully half the volume of the enormous room was taken up with the heaps of corpses, thousands of dead Stahls piled up and decaying. White bones poked through banks of rotting flesh. The same face stared out in every stage of decay and mutilation. Blood and corpse liquor had dried, black and sticky like tar on the floor.

One was alive. Dressed in the stained white of a medicae, he was picking his way up the slope of corpses, sorting through the blackened organs and torn limbs, throwing them aside as they came up wanting. A pile of select parts had grown up on the floor, separate from the rest. They were the parts of memories that Stahl found useful – that were worth salvaging from this genocide of his own memories.

The collected parts were marked with brands – circular and spiked, derivations of the eight-pointed star with which the devotees of Chaos identified themselves to one another. The same brands covered the face of the living Stahl.

'There you are,' said Deiphobus, as he gave himself substance again and felt his weight settle on the floor beneath him.

Stahl looked around. His eyes were alive and aware. This was not some excised memory. This was the witch himself – a part of him, at least, whatever piece of the witch was dedicated to murdering the memories that reminded him of what it meant to be human.

'Get out,' snarled Stahl. 'You have no place here! My gods have made this place sacrosanct. It is theirs! Within this holy skull is nothing but sacred ground, which you profane!'

'Nothing lives here but blasphemy!' retorted Deiphobus. He drew his bolt pistol. 'You have forsaken the very human being you are. Your gods are liars and will abandon you. Your last chance is here. Repent, and die cleanly. Defy me, and those same gods will toy with your soul like predators with prey.'

'Repent? Repent of turning my back on the tyrant-corpse, the dead Emperor? On his kingdom of oppression and ignorance? I will die happy, Space Marine, if I die while your Emperor has no claim on me!'

'Then die happy,' said Deiphobus.

His first shot went wide, because in his own mind Stahl had all the powers of a witch beloved by the warp. He vanished and appeared a metre to the side, blinking out of the line of fire.

Stahl spat a few syllables of a forbidden tongue. The blood of Deiphobus's mental form boiled and ripped open the biceps of his left arm, the shock thrusting splinters of bone through his armour. Deiphobus fell back and crushed down the pain that threatened to flood from his instincts.

The floor rippled under him. Deiphobus hit the floor and realised the dead were moving at Stahl's request. The masses of rotting meat were reaching for him, fingers of blistered bone trying to grab his arms and legs and drag them into reach of a hundred gnashing jaws.

Behind Deiphobus was a door. A huge, iron-bound door, with scratches and old bloodstains that told him this was where the condemned memories were dragged in.

Deiphobus propelled himself towards the door. Another spell vaporised the blood in one of Deiphobus's legs and the armour burst, spraying a mist of blood everywhere. Deiphobus told himself he was not real, that this was just a part of his mind and that he had control. But he could not do so forever. Eventually, even the mind of a Space Marine psyker would become corroded until it was as vulnerable as a real body to Stahl's witchcraft.

Deiphobus pushed off with his remaining foot and slammed into the door. His remaining hand wrenched the bar away. The door boomed open.

Every cell door in the asylum slammed open at once.

'He is here!' yelled Deiphobus. 'The one who would forget you! The madman placed here by Chaos! He is here!'

From the depths of the asylum came a terrible howling. Every inmate who could move ran from his cell and towards the execution chamber. They streamed in a crowd towards the chamber doors and Deiphobus rolled out of the way as they burst in.

Stahl threw bolts of scalding blood at them. The frontmost

disappeared in bursts of boiling gore. Even those who were mangled and broken charged in, carried by others or dragging themselves on bloody fingers.

Stahl could not kill them all. They climbed up the corpse piles and leapt onto him. He was dragged down to the floor and the other memories piled onto him, tearing at him with hands and teeth.

'Gods of the warp!' Stahl screamed. 'Deliver me! Deliver me! You have all that I am! Deliver your slave!'

The gods did not answer.

Deiphobus let go the mental anchors holding him in the asylum, and the whole corrupted place rushed away from him as he was yanked back into his own mind.

Lysander grabbed Deiphobus's arm and hauled him into the back of the Thunderhawk. Below, the witch had slumped to the floor of the temple and the lightning cage had broken, now just random bolts of power lancing down in every direction.

'He is alive,' gasped Deiphobus over the vox. 'But he is broken. Not for long. The gods will make of him a puppet. We must land before then.'

'Gorgythion!' shouted Lysander to the cockpit. 'Take us in! Brace yourselves, my brethren! The battle is joined!'

Khezal pitched steeply to one side as the Thunderhawk turned – much as it had done when the Imperial Fists launched their first assault on the Chalcedony Throne. Now it was a tortured city, half-ruined and infested, that spun beneath them as the *Gilded Pyre* made its final approach.

The guns on the Thunderhawk opened up and blazed white tracer rounds down at the temple. Daemons scurried there, some of them muscular footsoldiers with blades of black iron, some of them skittering winged things. Some came apart in the hail of fire – some were pierced through then reformed, their unnatural daemon flesh refusing to bow to the rules of physics.

Gorgythion brought them in low. The *Gilded Pyre* touched down on the uppermost level, just beneath the soaring arches from which hung the huge bronze bells. Lysander jumped down first, followed by Deiphobus.

'Get the psyker!' shouted Lysander over the gale and the tolling of the bells, which were swinging back and forth in the wind. 'Deiphobus, Orfos, on him! Kirav, with me! We press on! We head down!'

The *Peril Swift* swung in overhead. It was in worse shape than the *Gilded Pyre*, one of its wings almost sheared off and one landing jet belching smoke. It skidded onto the top of the temple, spraying sparks from its belly. It crunched side-on into a pillar and Squad Ctesiphon were jumping out even before it came to a halt. Emperor's Champion Ucalegon followed.

'It's the Cacophonous Tower,' said Deiphobus, looking at the hellish architecture around him. 'It stands in the warp, tolling a song that opens holes in reality. Enough blood, enough souls pledged to the warp, and it can be summoned into the real world. When the bells finish their song, the door will open.'

'How long?' said Lysander.

'Not long.'

'Then we move. Ctesiphon, clear this floor! There are daemons all around, they must not get behind us! Then follow
and back us up!' He turned to Deiphobus. 'Emperor's wings
carry you, Librarian.'

'Dorn's hand guide you, captain.'

Kirav's squad, along with Ucalegon, gathered behind
Lysander as he ran across the top of the temple towards a
yawning archway. Steps led downwards. The howling from
below was more than the wind.

Lysander ran down the stone steps. They wound tightly
down into the Cacophonous Tower. The layers of stone
between him and the top levels did nothing to muffle the
sound of the bells and every footstep was met with another
peal of clashing notes.

The staircase opened up into a great hall where corpses were
hung like sides of meat in an abattoir. They were citizens of
Khezal, from every level of its society, their bodies hung from
iron hooks. They were alive, and they wept. Their tears formed
a waist-high lake into which Lysander ran.

'Legienstrasse!' he yelled. 'Assassin! We have found you!
You can run no more! Face me and show me what you truly
know of death!'

Through the hanging corpses came a great shape, taller than
even Lysander, glowing from within. Lysander recognised the
shape of Karnikhal Six-Finger, the World Eater, and around
him skulked a host of bloodletter daemons. They were the
legionaries of the Blood God, the swords of Khorne.

'I trusted the flame,' said Karnikhal, 'when I should have
trusted the blade. I let you burn when I should have stayed

to take your head. I will hang your skin as a banner above the throne of Khorne! I will plate your skull in bronze and mount it on my armour, and through its eyes you will watch your galaxy end!'

'Captain,' said Ucalegon, laying a hand on Lysander's shoulder. 'Go on. Find the Assassin and kill her. You cannot be held up here. Karnikhal must be mine.'

'The fates led you to him,' said Lysander. 'Cut out his heart, my brother.'

'It has been an honour.'

'And it shall be again, Ucalegon.'

Ucalegon nodded, hefted the obsidian blade, and ran towards Karnikhal. The daemons leapt towards him like attack dogs loosed from their chains. Karnikhal's own sword glowed dark red and molten ceramite dripped off him, kicking up a cloud of steam from the lake of tears. The cloud enveloped Ucalegon as he charged and he vanished from sight.

Howls and screams came from the daemons. Lysander could make out the sound of blades through flesh, but had no way of telling whose flesh or whose blade.

Scout Enriaan shot the witch Stahl through the spine. He fell to his knees, then was yanked up off the floor by spectral strings that wrapped around the metal halo implanted in his back. His legs dangled uselessly as he drifted out of Enriaan's line of sight behind a pillar.

Deiphobus ran through the sheets of rain that lashed down from the storm. Shadowy daemons leapt at him – Squad Ctesiphon shot them down as they charged. One dived down at his face from an archway overhead but Deiphobus raked a volley of shots from his bolter through it and it burst in a shower of black gore.

Stahl was up ahead. His head lolled on his neck as if he were not a man at all but a marionette, controlled by unseen hands. Deiphobus had blasted away much of Stahl's mind and now there was nothing left but the malevolence that Chaos had poured into him.

Deiphobus let his psychic force swell in him, focused through his mind's eye and unleashed like a white-hot needle right through Stahl. It was a crude attack, without any of the telepathic finesse he had trained so hard to acquire – it was the power over another's mind, used to batter and crush.

Stahl was thrown back and slammed into a pillar. The pillar fell, the stone drums scattering across the temple's roof. Stahl's response was a bolt of lightning that crashed down from above, stuttering glowing scars into the flagstones as it rippled towards Deiphobus. Deiphobus dived and rolled, and knew then that Stahl had so little mind left that a telepath couldn't do much more to harm him.

This time Deiphobus came up firing. Stahl put up a hand and glowing runes burst in the air in front of him as a mental shield deflected the bolter shots.

Deiphobus kept running. He drew his combat knife. Another bolt of lightning tore past him but Stahl – or whatever controlled him – was not expecting the Librarian to keep charging at him.

Deiphobus leapt at Stahl and slammed into him, shoulder-first.

Stahl grabbed the backpack of Deiphobus's armour. With strength born of the warp, he lifted up Deiphobus and threw him aside.

Deiphobus dropped his bolter and his hand closed around the corroded metal ring implanted in Stahl's back. He held on and Stahl tipped back and sank almost to the floor. Deiphobus planted a foot in the small of the witch's back, and pulled.

Skin and muscle tore. The halo came away, taking a good chunk of Stahl's back with it. Stahl flopped to the ground, those strings of light cut.

Deiphobus threw the steel hoop aside. Stahl looked at him with a face suddenly human, and he looked as if he were seeing the Imperial Fists Librarian for the first time.

The witch held up a hand as if begging Deiphobus not to hurt him. But Deiphobus spotted the spark of light in his other hand, as he gathered a shard of lightning there to hurl up at the Librarian.

Deiphobus kicked Stahl aside and stamped down on his spellcasting hand. The bones pulped and Stahl screeched, a very human sound. Deiphobus lifted the witch up by the scruff of his neck.

'I liked you better,' said Deiphobus, 'when you were a puppet.'

Deiphobus wrenched Stahl's head all the way around. He felt the witch's neck breaking. Stahl's body hung lifeless in his hands.

'The witch is dead,' voxed Deiphobus. He looked up – the light of the opening gate broke through the dissolving black clouds, and the wind had already dropped from the screaming gale of a few moments ago. 'The skies are clear, my brothers.'

Gunfire stuttered from across the rooftop, where Squads Ctesiphon and Orfos were fending off the daemons coalescing around them. Deiphobus paused only to throw the body of Stahl off the edge of the temple, and to watch it broken to pieces against the jagged balconies and buttresses it hit on the way down. Then the Librarian ran to join the fight.

The Cacophonous Tower devolved further into madness the lower Lysander descended. Squad Kirav, behind him, struggled to keep pace as they fended off the gangling spider-daemons that lurched at them, and shot down bat-winged creatures that swooped down from the rafters.

The tower was a single great instrument. A spiral staircase wound down, surrounded by ranks of pipes, their mouths wrought into grimacing daemons' heads, through which hot blasts of air howled from the molten levels that glowed far below. Every step Lysander took echoed like an orchestra of drums in the unnatural acoustics.

The lower floors, Lysander could see in the ruddy glow, were flooded with lava oozing up from the torn crust of Opis. Archways and columns sank into the bubbling fire. All the way down the floors were stacked haphazardly on top of each other, some of them seemingly ripped from another building altogether – a chunk of prison block, skeletons mouldering in manacles that hung in every cell. A stage from a theatre, bodies torn and mutilated into a tableau that resembled an orchard of bloody flesh with hearts hanging as its fruit. An operating theatre surrounded by glass jars containing deformed limbs and diseased organs, and things like over-sized embryos that were humanoid, but not human. At every turn there was something else, crushed into the dark stones of the Cacophonous Tower as if this structure of the warp had swallowed up other places of madness as it grew.

The tower burrowed at the surface of Lysander's mind. It felt as if a host of worms were underneath his scalp, inside his skull, chewing at his thoughts. He forced himself to keep his train of thought intact.

Legienstrasse.

He was here to kill Legienstrasse.

The spiral staircase shuddered. Blocks of it fell away, tumbling into the lava below. Squad Kirav scattered and grabbed any useful handhold as the staircase came apart underneath them. Brother Beros lost his footing and sprawled over the edge – Brother Stentor grabbed his arm and dragged him back to safety.

'My thanks, brother,' said Beros. 'This place knows we are here.'

'Then let us hope it can hear us, too,' said Stentor. 'Because we have come to tear out its heart. Let us hope it can feel fear, because we will throw it back to the warp in pieces.'

'Poetic,' said Beros. 'If words were bullets you would have won this war yesterday.'

Lysander reached the next level down. This was a library, floor-to-ceiling bookcases loaded with books bound in gold and held closed with silver clasps. The floor was an exquisite mosaic, depicting a thousand scholars kneeling before a burning sun at the centre of which was a great eye. Chandeliers of blue crystal hung from the ceiling. Stained-glass windows coloured everything a fractured rainbow of colours. Wherever the Cacophonous Tower had found this place, it had been a magnificently wealthy place of learning.

And it was corrupt. The eye was the eye of Horus, symbol of the great betrayer of mankind. The books were held closed to keep whatever evil they held inside them until needed. The windows were swirling galaxies and nebulae, an exaggeration of the night sky that represented the closest a human mind could get to imagining the sight of the warp.

A young blonde woman sat at a lectern in the centre of the room, a huge book laid out in front of her. Pinkish tendrils reached at her from the pages, but she did not look afraid.

'Legienstrasse!' said Lysander, walking into the library. He saw now that it was a complete floor wedged in between two strata of the tower, the grey daemon-touched stone breaking through the walls and ceiling like an infection.

Legienstrasse looked up. She wore grey-green Imperial Guard fatigues but even with the loose cut over her slender body, the deformities were clear. Her back was raised up in large blisters that pulsed and squirmed. She stood and closed the book.

'So,' she said. 'You have decided to fight. You agree with the Officio Assassinorum, and the war they started to find me.'

'The Assassinorum can rot,' retorted Lysander. 'I am here because you are an enemy of mankind.'

'I am a mistake the Assassinorum are using you to erase.'

Lysander took a dangerous few steps towards her. She did not move, even as Lysander drew back the Fist of Dorn and held up his shield.

'Then again,' continued Legienstrasse, 'you are Lysander. You are the man who will do anything for victory. The souls of your brothers. Deals with the warp. Anything to be on the winning side.'

Lysander roared and charged.

Legienstrasse had shed the biomass she had harvested at Khezal. Still, she moved faster than a Space Marine. She snapped out of range, leaping from the lectern and rolling to a halt by one of the great bookcases. Lysander's hammer shattered the lectern and threw the book to the floor, where it flapped wetly and squealed like a wounded creature.

'Do not presume to know my mind!' shouted Lysander. 'A mere man might give up on Opis and on your death. A Space Marine knows his duty.'

'Duty above all,' said Legienstrasse, stalking to the side as she and Lysander circled one another. 'Duty above honour. Duty above humanity. You would burn the galaxy to win. I seek only survival.'

'You will not find it here!'

Lysander ran at Legienstrasse again. This time he ducked to one side just as he hit, slamming into the bookcase and wrenching it down over Legienstrasse. The bookcase crashed down on her, tons of books sprawling across the mosaicked floor.

Legienstrasse tore her way out through the back of the bookcase, talons of bloody bone sprouting from her fingers.

Bolter shots thumped into her torso. Brother Mortz of Squad Kirav had reached the library level. Beros was just beside him, lightning claw activated.

Legienstrasse ran right at Beros. She dropped to the floor and skidded underneath the swipe of Beros's claw, the power field rippling centimetres over her head. Then she jumped to her feet in front of Mortz and punched her claws through his stomach.

Lysander ran after her. Mortz seemed to die in slow motion, every drop of blood arcing lazily through the air as Legienstrasse tore her claws out and took the contents of Mortz's abdomen with it. She tore the ceramite of his armour as easily as his skin.

Beros aimed a thrust of his claw at the back of Legienstrasse's head. Legienstrasse drew the biomass out of Mortz so quickly she was able to wrap a great globe of flesh around her fist and slam it into Beros as he ran at her. Beros was thrown against the wall and Legienstrasse turned to face Lysander.

Lysander barrelled into her at full tilt, shield raised in front of him. There was no room for finesse now, not against an enemy like Legienstrasse who was sprouting new weapons with every second.

Spikes slid from her heels and rooted her into the ground. Her new weight of muscle met Lysander's momentum and held him fast. The two wrestled, each trying to get the other off their feet. Legienstrasse's fatigues bulged and tore as new muscle wrapped around her arms and upper torso, and Lysander caught a glimpse of the young waiting to hatch from the egg sacs under her skin.

'Heretic!' yelled Beros. He ran at Legienstrasse, drawing back his claw to swipe at her.

The claw tore through her. Four deep slashes opened up in

Legienstrasse's swollen torso. But her organs reformed around the wounds, and Beros's momentum carried him right onto the spike of bone she thrust out of her elbow at him.

Beros was speared through the faceplate. He died just a couple of metres from Lysander, and Lysander could do nothing. If he had moved to save his brother, Legienstrasse would have dragged him down to the ground and probably disembowelled him as she had done Brother Mortz.

Lysander had a thousand oaths he wanted to spit at Legienstrasse in that moment. But there were no words. It was all he could do to match strength with Legienstrasse.

Beros slid to the ground. The bone spike had become a bony syringe that sucked out the blood and flesh from inside Beros's armour. Lysander felt the weight on him grow as Beros's biomass was added to Legienstrasse.

He could not hold her. New limbs were splitting off from her legs and lower torso to grab his legs and throw him to the ground. He dropped to one knee and ducked back, letting her surge forwards at him.

He slammed the shield into the side of her head. He brought the Fist of Dorn round to follow up with a blow to her ribcage, but she crashed down on him, smothering and crushing.

Lysander had his shield over him and used it to lever Legienstrasse off him. Already she was much bigger than him, new organs pulsing in a ribcage swollen too large for her skin to cover it, the spurs of bone wrapped with muscle that heaved as she drew in oxygen. A bone spike hammered down, shattering the mosaic by Lysander's head.

He had enough room to roll out from underneath her.

Insect-like legs were carrying her now, slashing down at him. He felt shots of pain as they cut through the ceramite of his leg and arm.

'Every brother I lose,' gasped Lysander, 'I will avenge ten times on you!'

'You wrap your sacrifices in lies of revenge,' said Legienstrasse. Her face was still human, surrounded by bulging masses of muscle, obscene by its very humanity. 'So desperate to deny what you are.'

A bladed whip-like limb snaked towards him. Lysander slammed the edge of his shield down onto it and severed it. It whipped uselessly around his feet.

It was a feint. Three more lashed at him and caught him around his hammer-arm and leg. Another caught him around his neck. Legienstrasse fought to reel Lysander in, but Lysander dropped down to a crouch, dug his feet in and would not budge.

Legienstrasse spun and whipped Lysander around, picking him up as she turned. The whip let go and Lysander was hurtling through the air, across the library and through the stained-glass window.

The grey labyrinth of Khezal whirled around him as he fell.

Ucalegon wrenched the blade out of the bloodletter's back. The daemon's boiling blood hissed as it seethed out into the salt lake of tears. Above, broken bodies swayed, hacked and torn by the flurry of blades beneath them.

Ucalegon's twin hearts hammered. His body was being pushed to its limit. The daemons were fast and strong, and they attacked relentlessly, heedless of anything but bloodshed.

The shadow that fell over him was of a Space Marine, like him, but not like him. Its armour was a fused nightmare, bullet and blade marks piled on top of one another until it resembled a mass of metallic scar tissue. It glowed from the inside, and light bled from the cracks around its joints and vents.

Vials of liquid were hooked up to the corroded helm, the faceplate melded with the face of the Space Marine inside so it cracked and distorted as he spoke.

'The last one of you I fought,' the Traitor Marine said, 'it was upon the battlements of Terra. I broke his back and watched him squirm at my feet. I threw him from the walls and he was torn apart by daemons. It was a good death. I would taste it again.'

'And the last time my kind fought you,' said Ucalegon, dipping his obsidian sword in the water to wash off the gore, 'we cast you from Terra and chased you into the warp. You have hidden from us for ten thousand years. My task is to remind you why.'

Karnikhal Six-Finger laughed as he lunged at Ucalegon. Karnikhal's weapon was a chainsword of ancient mark, its teeth bent and tarnished. It was alive and it was hungry.

Ucalegon caught the blade on his own, and sparks sprayed off the obsidian edge. The teeth chewed into Ucalegon's shoulder pad, throwing chunks of ceramite. Ucalegon kicked Karnikhal in the midriff and threw him off, and the two stumbled to keep their footing in the lake of tears.

'Hiding?' spat Karnikhal. 'I took a thousand skulls on Belian Minor. I martyred Saint Acelsius when I tore out her throat.

These bones around my neck are the fingers of Captain Kryos of the White Consuls, and they were all I left of him to take. I never hid from anything! I am a World Eater! I am death given form!'

He lunged again, and this time Ucalegon was ready. He ducked the blow, spun and drew his blade across the World Eater's midriff. The obsidian blade cut through the corroded ceramite. A spray of molten metal spurted from the wound and Karnikhal bellowed as he dropped to one knee.

'You are strong,' said Ucalegon. 'You are quick. But you are angry, too. You cannot control it. And you cannot wield a blade if you cannot even control yourself.'

Karnikhal turned and charged. His sword wasn't the weapon this time. He crashed shoulder-first into Ucalegon and slammed him into the wall of the chamber.

Bodies fell, shaken from their meathooks. Karnikhal grabbed Ucalegon around the throat and forced him down into the water.

'Control?' the World Eater snarled. 'Control is what cages you. Obedience makes you weak. Chaos makes me strong.'

Ucalegon planted a foot and pushed himself backwards. The wall behind him came apart under his weight and he rolled through into the chamber beyond, the waist-high tears flowing around him.

He was surrounded by towering columns of bone, thousands and thousands of skeletons, some forming the great shaft of the room he had fallen into, others piled up around him in bleached white drifts.

Ucalegon rolled up onto his feet. Karnikhal stalked through

the hole Ucalegon had left in the wall, crunching through the deep piles of bone.

'Did you make an oath to kill me, Imperial Fist?'

'I made an oath to kill you all.'

'An oath for my death! I collect them. I shall add yours to my own skull pile at the foot of Khorne's throne, each the head of a soul who swore to kill me first.'

Karnikhal's chainblade howled and snarled. It seemed ready to jump from his hand and feast.

Ucalegon used the second before Karnikhal got to him. He forced everything inside – his thoughts, his senses, the pounding of his hearts and the straining of his lungs. The Emperor's Champion was not just an expert swordsman. He could take all the battles he had fought, all the lives he had taken and all the brothers he had seen fall, and turn it all inside.

A single breath, and he was focused. The bone chamber was thrown into impossibly high relief. Karnikhal's armour was picked out in every detail. He moved slowly, as if recorded and played back in holo so Ucalegon could dissect his fighting style. Every one of Ucalegon's senses was enhanced to its maximum, and there was nothing in the world except for Ucalegon, his enemy, and his sword.

If he died, it did not matter. Because he would die fulfilling his duty to Rogal Dorn, to the Emperor. To the human race.

Karnikhal reached Ucalegon. He drove the point of the snarling chainsword towards Ucalegon's throat.

Ucalegon told himself it did not matter if he died, and brought the obsidian blade up to meet it.

* * *

Lysander shook the darkness out of his mind.

The wind and rain were lashing at him. He was outside the Cacophonous Tower.

He had come to rest on a balcony, seemingly torn from an Imperial church and absorbed by the predatory tower. It was from a balcony like this that a confessor might demand supplication from a crowd of the faithful, or a cardinal bless an army before it went to war. Now it jutted from the Cacophonous Tower like a half-pulled tooth.

Behind Lysander was a hole in the wall almost as wide as the balcony itself, looking onto a tangle of fallen columns that resembled the inside of a shattered ribcage. Gutted books and pages littered the floor – prayer books, defiled and discarded for their sacredness to bleed out into the stones. Black veins pulsed below the surface of the uneven flagstones as if the tower was alive, sustained by stolen holiness.

A huge shape shouldered its way past one of the pillars. It resembled an ogryn, one of the oversized humans the Imperial Guard used as shock troops or manual labourers. But this one was deformed by the shapes of faces and bodies straining against its skin, so the bulk of its corpulent form seemed composed of captives trapped inside it.

'The Penitent,' said Lysander, getting to his feet. He was battered and his fused ribcage felt cracked. His artificial skin was not holding up well and he felt the blood filling sections of his armour. But he could still fight. 'I heard tell of you from the Guardsmen in the field. They understated your foulness.'

The multi-legged shape of Legienstrasse dropped from the ceiling. She must have been waiting there, splayed across the ceiling like a spider in wait. The Penitent turned to look at her, bowing its great head.

Legienstrasse impaled the Penitent with a pair of limb-blades. She dragged the ogryn in close and her torso split open, dragging the Penitent inside. Teeth slid out from the gory edges of her body and sliced the Penitent into pieces, each chunk swallowed up into her body.

With more biomass, she grew. She was quadrupedal now, her lower limbs built to stampede and trample. Her torso now had four arms, two with clawed digits and two with blades, and her body had sheets of gristly armour that slid up to protect her head, leaving just enough room to see through.

'They should never have made you,' said Lysander. 'Better the Assassinorum's targets live than that mankind should be so perverted in you.'

'Do not speak to me of the desecration of humanity,' replied Legienstrasse. Her voice was that of a woman, unchanged by her altered form. 'You who have two hearts and three lungs. You who can eat the flesh of an enemy and know their thoughts. Of the two of us, Space Marine, I am the more human. I will bring new life into this galaxy. You will only destroy it.'

'We were both created to kill,' said Lysander. 'The difference is, you can only kill alone.'

The roar of engines heralded the *Gilded Pyre* as the Thunderhawk hovered down over the balcony. Through the viewshield, Brother Gorgythion was almost hidden behind the targeting runes converging.

Legienstrasse dived to one side. The heavy bolters mounted in the Thunderhawk's nose hammered a cannonade through the chamber, rattling over Lysander's head. Columns were severed and fell like cut trees. Explosive bolts blasted chunks out of the walls and ceiling.

Legienstrasse ran. One of her legs was blasted off, a hefty, meaty slab of a limb reduced to shattered bone and pulp. She leapt onto one wall and climbed faster than a man could run, the gunfire chasing her up onto the ceiling and between the dense pillars towards the back of the room.

Legienstrasse was out of sight. Lysander saw the Thunderhawk pivoting on its landing jets. Out of the side of the gunship, through a hatch where another heavy bolter was normally mounted, hung Agent Skult. The Vindicare was loading one of his specialist bullets into his Exitus longrifle, waiting for the Thunderhawk to get into position and for Legienstrasse to show herself.

'Hit her in the head,' voxed Lysander. 'It's the only part she can't change. Everything else she can do without.'

<<The head,>> came Skult's emotionless voice in reply, <<is always my first choice.>>

Legienstrasse dived down from the jumble of columns, all flying talons and fangs.

A round streaked into her. It blasted a chunk out of her chitinous collar, throwing fragments of shrapnel into her face. For the first time, the human part of her bled.

Legienstrasse ran right at Lysander, who rolled out of the way, just in time to realise she wasn't headed for him.

She raced towards the balcony and the Thunderhawk

gunship hovering above it. Blood ran down her cheek as she bared her teeth and leapt at the gunship.

Skult's second shot missed her face by a centimetre. It streaked down into her shoulder, blasting a gory tunnel through her body and detonating at the root of her back leg, blasting it off in a shower of blood and bone. Anything else would have died on the spot.

Legienstrasse crashed into the side of the Thunderhawk. Agent Skult disappeared in a flurry of bone and fang. The *Gilded Pyre* tipped to one side with the additional weight, and Gorgythion gunned the thruster on that side to compensate.

Legienstrasse ripped the wing off the Thunderhawk. Burning fuel sprayed. The thruster exploded and the Thunderhawk flipped over.

Lysander saw the gunship would spin over the balcony and into the chamber. He ran away from the tide of heat and noise rushing towards him. He felt the Thunderhawk crashing into the side of the opening, the crunching explosions as the rear fuel cells blew and its tail was sheared off. The hull followed in, spewing fire, and slammed into the floor.

The floor split and rose up, fractured as if by an earthquake. Lysander leapt for a pillar but it was falling too, uprooted by the force of the impact.

Fire was everywhere. It flowed around Lysander like water flooding in. And he was falling, sliding down the shattered section of the floor into the depths of the Cacophonous Tower. Everything was noise and the raging heat, battering against him, with ammunition cooking off in the blaze and peppering the stone with rogue shots.

He was Rogal Dorn on the battlements of Terra. He was Sigismund, diving into a galaxy full of xenos and heresy. He was Cortez on Rynn's World, both hearts all but exhausted, battling for days on a rampart of the dying and the dead. He was every Imperial Fist who should have given up but didn't know how, and in that moment went beyond death to fight on.

Lysander felt the heat all around him. Sinking into it. It was not burning fuel.

He was at the very root of the Cacophonous Tower, where the temple to Chaos met the living rock of Opis. Where the tormented architecture met the molten rock welling up through the shattered crust.

It was instinct, not any understanding of his surroundings, that forced Lysander to drag himself out of the sucking, burning mire. His hand found a ridge of stone and he hauled himself out of it, even as the ceramite of his greaves began to give way under the heat and pressure. He wiped the dirt and debris from his eyes.

The bubbling pit of lava was pierced by the pillars of the temple. Statues of intertwined bodies rose from the fire. The bones of daemons broke the surface here and there – the elongated fanged skull of a bloodletter, the twisted skeleton of a shapeshifting daemon forced into a single form in the moment of death.

The air was scalding to breathe. Lysander's throat and mouth were blistered with the heat. The haft of the Fist of Dorn protruded from the lava. His shield was nowhere to be seen. The wreck of the *Gilded Pyre* slid through the shattered ceiling, a burning mass of metal that crunched into a slab of stone that broke the lava's surface.

Legienstrasse, her form battered and bleeding from a hundred wounds, crawled down a fallen bridge of stone towards the relatively stable expanse of flooring where Lysander had landed. She was hurt. But even as Lysander watched her drag herself along, her legs reformed under her.

Lysander got to his feet. The stone under him tilted with his movement. The whole Cacophonous Tower seemed to be slowly sinking into the burning mire. Lysander jumped across to a chunk of shattered statue, a short leap away from what remained of the *Gilded Pyre*. He could see nothing of Agent Skult or Brother Gorgythion. Most of the passenger compartment was intact, albeit on fire.

'Lysander!' yelled Legienstrasse above the bubbling of the lava. 'Can you hear it?'

The bells were tolling. The sound mixed together into terrible echoing peals that reached down through the whole tower. A sound that echoed into the warp; that bridged the gap between two universes.

Lysander leaned across and jumped to the mass of fallen masonry on which the gunship had come to rest. He realised as he moved that one of his hips had probably become dislocated, shots of pain running up one side of his body. Breathing hurt. Shards of bone were loose somewhere in his chest.

In the burning mass above him was a cabinet of black metal, held in place with clamps that secured it to the side of the compartment.

Legienstrasse's upper limbs were growing by the second, bladed fingers unfolding and reaching across the lava for Lysander. The muscle and bone were charring in the heat. Legienstrasse's face didn't register any pain. There was just a look of determination, as if Lysander was one final thread to cut before she could clamber back up the tower and through the portal opening in the sky overhead.

A blade of bone speared through the back of Lysander's leg. He ripped his leg free, feeling the bone and muscle come apart inside. His armour was pumping him full of pain suppressants but they could not take it all away, and they would run out.

He dragged himself into the *Gilded Pyre*. The searing metal told him he could still feel at all. His nervous system was still working. He still had control, and he could still fight.

Another metre. The cabinet in the burning Thunderhawk was within reach. Lysander unbuckled the clamp restraints and the cabinet slid past him, clattering onto the stone.

Legienstrasse leapt up and slammed into one of the statues looming up from the lava. She was almost reformed now, her limbs shedding flakes of scorched muscle to reveal new wet growth underneath.

Lysander crawled out of the wreck and hauled the cabinet right side up. Freezing vapour was bleeding from its seals. He slammed a fist into the activation rune on its control panel.

The cabinet slid open. A cloud of vapour rushed out as the freezing air inside met the heat pulsing off the lava. From the vapour rose a figure, its face concealed by a skull-mask, wearing a synskin bodysuit. It wore a silver-bladed gauntlet on one hand and a rig fitted with combat drug dispensers around its shoulders.

The Eversor Assassin shrieked as it rose from the cryocabinet that had held it since the Assassinorum had built their facility in the Rekaban jungle. The sockets of its skull-mask fixed on Legienstrasse clambering overhead and the dispensers pumped its body full of combat drugs. Muscles and veins rippled under the synskin.

The Eversor surged from the cabinet and leapt up onto the statue that Legienstrasse was climbing. With supernatural agility he scrambled after Legienstrasse, drawing an elaborate pistol from a holster on his back.

It was Lysander's last gambit. The Eversor the Imperial Fists had discovered in the jungle facility, brought with them on the *Gilded Pyre* in the knowledge that the Assassin might land the killing blow if the Imperial Fists failed. Legienstrasse was the last target the Eversor had been given, and when an Eversor had a target, it sought it out and killed it to the exclusion of everything else.

Legienstrasse saw the Eversor as it took aim at her. If there was shock at seeing a fellow Assassin here, she did not let it slow her down. She brought up a chitinous shield as he fired a spray of silvery darts at her. Flesh blackened and fell away as neurotoxins flowed. Legienstrasse swept a scythe-like bony blade down at the Eversor – the Eversor leapt, kicked off a protrusion of stone and powered into Legienstrasse's central mass.

The two Assassins were evenly matched. They had trained in the same methods of death, before the same masters. They had butchered the same combat servitors and memorised the same treatises on murder. Every slash of the Eversor's gauntlet met a parry of a bony blade. Every lashing tendril from Legienstrasse was avoided or cut off.

Another movement caught Lysander's eye. Through the rippling heat haze, the huge smouldering shape of Karnikhal Six-Finger walked down the broken staircase. Over his shoulder was slung the body of Emperor's Champion Ucalegon.

'Brother!' shouted Lysander. 'Traitor! Blasphemy! You have killed my battle-brother!'

Ucalegon's helmet was split down the face, encrusted with dried blood. The wound carved down through one shoulder pad and out through his back.

'He fought like the warp was in him,' growled Karnikhal. 'But it was with me. My gods watch. My gods intervene. Yours sits dead on his throne, and does nothing.'

Lysander walked towards Karnikhal, for the moment letting the two Assassins fight. Karnikhal was smiling.

'I will join my Emperor at the end of time,' said Lysander, 'And at his side we will cleanse all that remains of filth like you from every level of reality. The warp will be scoured blank. Your gods will shrivel and die. You will watch, and you will know despair, to repay what you have done to my brother.'

Karnikhal laughed. He shrugged Ucalegon's body off his shoulder.

The hilt of Ucalegon's obsidian blade protruded from Karnikhal's chest. Karnikhal sank to one knee and Lysander saw the point of the blade protruded from Karnikhal's back.

'There is another life,' gasped Karnikhal. 'I will die a thousand times. I will find you. Every Imperial Fist. I will find you.'

On the statue above, the Eversor and the Maerorus wrestled, each matching every blow struck by the other. The Eversor's synskin was torn, and deep wounds were opened up across his ribcage. Severed limbs fell from Legienstrasse and withered as they sank into the lava.

A claw snickered out and sliced off the Eversor's gun hand. His pistol landed in the lava and disappeared. A second claw punched into the Eversor's stomach and tore out a welter of entrails.

Lysander ran to the dying form of Karnikhal. He tore the obsidian blade out of the Traitor Marine's body and drew it back, like a javelin.

The Eversor was dying, though he did not know it yet. He was all but disembowelled. Legienstrasse snared his claw hand and sliced off his arm with a bone scythe. The Eversor's blood spattered up against Legienstrasse's too-human face. Another blade speared through his throat, twisted, and tore out with another spray of blood.

Lysander had fought against agents of the Officio Assassinorum before. He knew what an Eversor Assassin was, and what it had been created to do. It was designed to kill, and nothing else, and even in death it did its duty.

Lysander hurled the blade. It speared through the air and punched into the dying Eversor's back. The blade passed right through and into Legienstrasse, lodging in the tough, fibrous matter she had grown to shield her torso and head.

The Eversor was pinned to Legienstrasse, as every dispenser on the Eversor's combat rig emptied into his veins. Legienstrasse knew what the Eversor could do, too, and she grew new limbs to try to force the Eversor off her and wrench out the obsidian blade. She pulled the blade halfway out when the Eversor put its head back and howled, forcing the last of the air from its shredded lungs.

Legienstrasse was a second too late. The volatile mix of chemicals in the Eversor's body reached the point where his veins and heart could not contain it. In a final act of spite, the Eversor Assassin exploded in a bio-meltdown of orange flame and venom.

Lysander dived to one side as the burning form of Legienstrasse slammed onto the slab of flooring. The stone immediately began to sink, the lava creeping further over its surface.

Legienstrasse was alive. Her chitinous armour had been blasted away, her attacking limbs reduced to charred and splintered bone. Her face had been spared the worst. The obsidian blade still protruded from her central mass, where burned organs pulsed and bled.

Lysander tore the blade from her. He reached over the lava and grabbed the haft of the Fist of Dorn, pulling it out of the molten rock. Its head glowed brightly with the heat but the exotic alloys of its construction had held intact. Its power field leapt back into life as it came free of the lava.

'You die, abomination,' said Lysander, 'not knowing what a blessing death is. You die not knowing what I do for you.'

For the first time, Legienstrasse's face showed fear. Her eyes opened wide and she screamed.

Lysander swung the obsidian blade at her. It sliced through her neck and cut her head clean off, and it tumbled through the air.

Red tendrils of nerve fibre and muscle lashed out from around her head, seeking out the bloody ruin of her neck.

Lysander swung the Fist of Dorn in his other hand. The hammer slammed into Legienstrasse's head. It was propelled across the chamber, smacking wetly into the side of the statue on which she and the Eversor had fought. Lysander watched as the head rolled down the statue, the same fear and shock on her face, until its skin blackened in the heat and her hair caught fire. A few seconds later and the head touched the surface of the lava. A few more and it was gone, turned to ash and swallowed up.

Lysander turned to the charred, broken hulk of Legienstrasse's body. Her young still squirmed in the sacs bundled inside her armoured torso. Lysander put a shoulder against the corpse and he pushed, and felt it tip over into the lava. It did not take long for the body to be wreathed in flames and disappear.

Lysander limped on his wounded leg to where Ucalegon's corpse lay beside that of Karnikhal. He picked up Ucalegon's body and threw it over his shoulder.

'Forgive me, brother, that you fell under my command,' said Lysander. 'By your own hand you are avenged. Your duty was done, my brother. Your duty was done.'

The shattered staircase led towards the upper levels of the Cacophonous Tower. Lysander could hear the gunfire from above, as the rest of the Imperial Fists strike force fended off the daemons native to the place.

As Lysander ascended from the pit of fire, the tolling bells quietened and fell silent.

K-Day +34 Days
Operation Requiem. Elimination of air defences prior
 to massed air assault on Khezal
Operation Catullus. Encirclement and destruction of
 enemy forces in Rekaba
Operation Starfall. Withdrawal from Starfall front
Operation Seismic. Reduction of enemy defences prior
 to invasion of Makoshaam

The trophy hall of the *Wings of Dorn* was not yet adorned with anything taken from Opis. Perhaps the head of Antiocha Wyraxx would find its way there, if it was ever released by Tchepikov's intelligence corps, or a segment of Karnikhal's armour. Those were decisions yet to be made. There were still fallen brothers to be honoured, their gene-seed extracted and their wargear reconsecrated for the recruits who would follow them into the Imperial Fists' ranks.

Serrick looked with curiosity at the head of an alien creature that hung on the wall, one of many trophies taken from defeated xenos. It hung among crystalline blades and strange firearms of polished stone. Its skull was elongated and plated with bony scales, and it had six eyepits arranged along its mandibled face.

'I saw these in the flesh,' she said. 'Clinging to our ship.

377

I had not thought the Imperium had encountered them before. Kekrops named it *Cryptoxenos ferrox tertiam*. We tried to get a sample to dissect but it was lost to the void.'

'We called them Glassfangs,' said Lysander. 'The inhabitants of a feral world polished their bones and read fortunes from the reflections. They were destroyed.'

Serrick looked around at Lysander. It was strange to see him out of his armour – he had removed it so he could be attended to in the ship's apothecarion. One leg was bandaged and braced. His face was still recovering, a new sheet of shiny artificial skin stretched across the side of his head. He wore the monastic robes of a Space Marine away from the battlefield. 'The aliens,' said Serrick, 'or the natives?'

'Both,' said Lysander. 'It was a world beyond hope.'

'And Opis?'

'The Imperial war machine will decide that,' said Lysander. 'There are still both moral threats and civilians down there. The Imperial Fists have no further part to play in the fate of either.'

'Have you decided,' said Serrick, 'what you will do with me?'

'I keep my word,' replied Lysander. 'An Inquisitorial fortress stands between us and our return to the *Phalanx*. You will be dropped off there. They need to hear what happened to Kekrops. And, Lady Serrick, I have one further task to request of you. It will cause you no risk and no great labour.'

Serrick considered this for a moment. 'I owe you my life, Captain Lysander. One more favour should not use up all my good will.'

'You are in a better position than us,' said Lysander, 'to deliver a message.'

'To whom?'

'To the Officio Assassinorum.'

Serrick raised an eyebrow. 'I see,' she said. 'That should not be beyond my capabilities. What do you want to say to our Assassinorum cousins?'

'That they have made a new enemy in the Imperial Fists,' said Lysander. 'I have heard it said by Space Marines of other Chapters that when the Adeptus Terra wills it, the Imperial Fists will act. That we are lapdogs of Earth. But the Officio Assassinorum have used us to wage a war of their making, against an enemy they created, to cover up the mistakes of their own past, and that is a wrong that cannot be forgotten. When next we cross paths, it will not be on friendly terms. And if the Assassinorum has more secrets like the Maerorus Temple, I shall see to it that they are rooted out. Such corruption cannot be permitted to exist at the heart of the Imperium. Tell them they can hide no longer, and that one day Lysander and the Imperial Fists will drag all their secrets out into the light.'

'Do you believe,' said Serrick, 'that the Imperial Fists do not yet have enough enemies, that you go out of your way to make another one?'

'It was the Assassinorum who shot down Kekrops,' said Lysander. 'Do not pretend to me that you do not have your own grudge against them, too.'

'Perhaps that is true,' said Serrick. 'I will keep my own motives to myself. But I will do as you ask. The Inquisition and the Assassinorum work often together and I have certain contacts. Your message will be delivered.'

'My thanks,' said Lysander. 'Now, I have the funeral rites of my brothers to oversee. Opis has claimed far too many lives.'

Lysander left Serrick inspecting the skulls and captured weapons of the trophy hall. He touched the pendant he now wore around his neck – the bullet that killed Inquisitor Kekrops.

Once, he had known no limit to the sacrifices that should be made in the pursuit of victory. Life and death, right and wrong, even honour – the very identity of a Space Marine – could be abandoned if that was what it took to secure victory.

But now he knew. The Assassinorum had showed him that. There was a limit. Though he had taken the head of Legien-strasse, too much had been paid by the Assassinorum to give him the chance.

Perhaps he had always been searching for the answer to the question of how far was too far when seeking victory. Now he had that answer.

He closed his eyes, felt the cold metal of the bullet in his hand, and prayed to Dorn and the Emperor that he would never have to approach that decision himself.

Outside the *Wings of Dorn*, the great orb of Opis turned, and a million Imperial Guard marched across it as its cities continued to burn.

ABOUT THE AUTHOR

Ben Counter is the author of the Soul Drinkers and
Grey Knights series, along with two Horus Heresy
novels, and is one of Black Library's most popular
Warhammer 40,000 authors. He has written RPG sup-
plements and comic books. He is a fanatical painter
of miniatures, a pursuit which has won him his most
prized possession: a prestigious Golden Demon award.
He lives in Portsmouth, England.

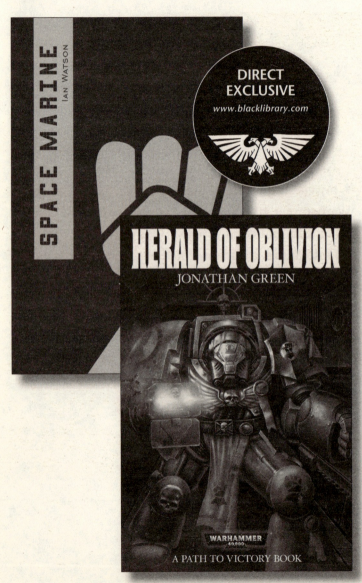

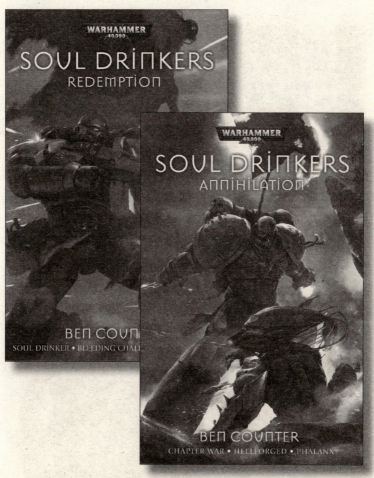

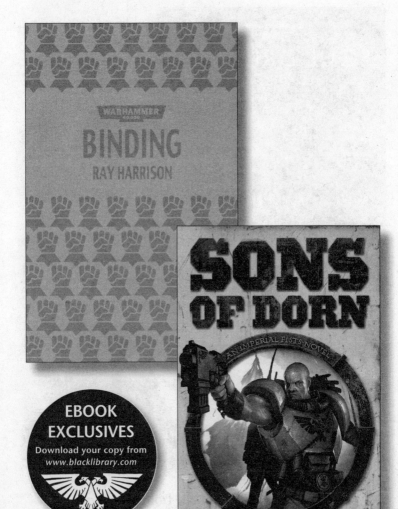